I0676123

Wicked War of Mine

Book Nine of the Overworld Chronicles

John Corwin

ISBN- 978-0-9850181-9-1

Printed in the U.S.A.

RAVEN
HOUSE

TIME FOR PAYBACK

Daelissa's attack on Queens Gate dealt Justin and the resistance a serious blow. The loss of his home and one of their strongest allies seems to mean certain defeat.

Justin isn't about to give up. He embarks on a mission to bring the houses of Daemos to his side and seeks help from Fjoeruss, Mr. Gray himself, even if the odds of success are slim.

As if the pressure isn't already high enough, Justin discovers something even more troubling. Daelissa is already in Seraphina. One silver lining remains: Justin might be able to end the war in one blow if his forces can disable the Grand Nexus before she returns with a Seraphim army.

If the good guys can't shut down the Grand Nexus in time, Daelissa will unleash a can of whoop-ass on Eden the likes of which has never been seen.

Connect with John Corwin online:
Facebook: http://www.facebook.com/johnhcorwinauthor
Website: http://johncorwin.net/
Twitter: http://twitter.com/#!/John_Corwin

Books by John Corwin:

Overworld Chronicles:
Sweet Blood of Mine
Dark Light of Mine
Fallen Angel of Mine
Dread Nemesis of Mine
Twisted Sister of Mine
Dearest Mother of Mine
Infernal Father of Mine
Sinister Seraphim of Mine
Wicked War of Mine
Coming Soon: Destructive Destiny of Mine

Stand Alone Novels:

No Darker Fate
The Next Thing I Knew
Outsourced
Seventh

To my wonderful support group:
Alana Rock
Karen Stansbury
Pat Owens

My amazing editors:
Annetta Ribken
Jennifer Wingard

My awesome cover artist:
Regina Wamba

Thanks so much for all your help and input!

Chapter 1

The clock on my phone struck midnight for a time zone halfway around the world from me. The Overworld New Year had just begun, and I had a wedding to stop.

Elyssa stepped inside the silver circle around the omniarch. "Justin, we're ready on your signal."

I glanced at the two Templar squads flanked by my mother, Alysea, and my sister, Ivy. Mom's blue eyes glowed as she looked at me. I almost felt sorry for my father's bride-to-be, Kassallandra. Then again, she'd betrayed us and summoned crawlers, scorps, and other demon spawn to help Daelissa.

Time for payback.

I raised an arm and lowered it. Portals flickered to life in the air between the columns of the two arches. Cold air and snowflakes drifted through the portal from the other side. Elyssa and I stepped through with a complement of Templars and into a thick drift of the white stuff. The boots of my Templar snow armor adjusted to the unsure footing and lengthened into short skis.

We stood atop a mountain in the Swiss Alps. Far below us and nestled between our slope and another, lights from a sprawling mansion glowed beneath a star-dusted sky. The way was steep with a scattering of rocks and boulders jutting from beneath the thick blanket of snow. The slope ended in a sheer drop. Even with my supernatural reflexes, it was enough to make me gulp. I had never been skiing, and this was a few levels above beginner. Unfortunately, the front entrance was heavily guarded and we had no pictures of the mansion interior to use with the omniarch.

Gotta do this the hard way.

Elyssa's gloved hand squeezed mine. "Just remember to hockey stop and you'll be fine."

"I never played hockey," I said. "I'm from Atlanta, not Toronto."

She touched a small tab of cloth near my armpit. "If you don't think you can land the jump at the drop-off, pull this and use the parachute."

I nodded. "Got it." I looked at the slope on the other side of the plateau and spotted the silhouettes of my mother and her squad. "Let's do this." I touched the communication pendant on the collar of my armor. "Go." Taking a deep breath, I stepped to the edge of the slope. My breath crystallized in the freezing air. A cold wind howled, blowing snow into my face. I touched the collar of the armor and it grew over my head, cutting off the cold.

A HUD—heads-up display—blinked on. A series of lines spread across the terrain in front of me, some of them dark red, and others a lighter shade of red. It highlighted the protruding rocks and gave me a recommended course to take. I adjusted my skis to the suggested angle, said a quick prayer, and let gravity take me.

I went from zero to terminal velocity in a heartbeat. The HUD flashed a warning as I careened toward a jagged rock. Resisting the urge to scream and throw up my arms, I leaned left. The skis bit into the snow and I whooshed past the rock. The next series of winding turns were easier to manage, and before long, I had the basics down. I glanced back and saw the rest of my squad following in single file. We threaded through a small forest of evergreens. Thick snow dragged on my skis, but I was going too fast for it to slow me much.

My HUD blinked as we emerged back onto a bare patch of slope. *Sheer drop ahead. Recommended course of action: Stop.*

"Gee, you think?" I snapped. My guts knotted and my butt clenched. "'Let's go skiing,' they said. 'It'll be fun,' they said." My skis grated against bare rock as I hit the edge of the cliff. The world dropped out beneath me.

I looked down and spotted the thick snowbank at the foot of the cliff. It was probably about thirty feet below, but from this vantage point, it seemed more like a hundred. I bent my knees and leaned slightly forward like Elyssa had told me to do while the scaredy-cat inside screamed for me to pull the parachute tab. If I did that, there was a risk the wind would catch me and carry me way off target, plus I'd look like a wimp to all the Templar badasses right behind me.

I'd wanted to use flying carpets, but apparently, this area was warded to detect magical aircraft.

The snow rushed to meet me. I angled my skis and clenched my teeth so I wouldn't accidentally bite off my tongue. My feet hit. I sank up to my waist in the snow before bursting free and sliding face-first down the remaining twenty feet to the plateau. I lay on my back in the snow and looked up at the sky through the pine trees. Then I made a snow angel.

Elyssa stood over me and smiled. "Pretty good for your first time." She offered me a hand.

"Take me to the bunny slope." I took her hand and she pulled me to my feet.

Orchestral music drifted through the forest from the direction of the estate. I oriented myself and sniffed the air. Only the faintest hint of brimstone reach my nostrils. Either there were no infernal creatures guarding this forest, or they were doing a good job concealing their presence from me.

I twirled a finger in the air and pointed left toward the rally point where we'd meet my mother and the others. Swords drawn and senses alert, we made our way through the forest and found Mom waiting for us. Joss and Otaleon, two Darkling recruits we'd rescued from Daelissa's clutches, flanked her. Ivy busied herself making snowballs. The three Templars in Mom's squad faded into view as they stepped from concealment behind trees.

"Sense anything, Justin?" Mom asked.

"Nothing close," I said. "I'm positive there's something nasty lurking around here, though."

She nodded. "I agree. Kassallandra would never leave her flank open."

"Even though she has no idea we know about her betrayal?" Joss asked. Within a week of rescuing him, he and Otaleon had physically aged from that of teenage boys to young men in their twenties. The Darklings' memories of the Seraphim War had begun to return along with some of their fighting skills.

"All her enemies could be dead and she would still keep up her guard," Mom replied.

I listened to the faint sounds of violins for a moment. "I still don't get the midnight wedding ceremony."

"Daemos society is bound to ritual." Mom looked at me. "We are relying on those very rituals to salvage the situation."

I shuddered and prayed it didn't come to that. "Let's go."

We stalked forward. The forest floor had only a light covering of snow thanks to the thick canopy provided by the trees. I kept my nostrils peeled for any signs of danger as the wedding music grew louder.

My next step splashed into something that wasn't melted snow. Greenish goop the color and texture of rancid slime hung from the bottom of my boot like a giant-sized booger. I smelled the faintest hint of brimstone coming from the mess. Only certain kinds of dead creatures left remains like this behind—crawlers, scorps, and hellhounds. In other words, this had to be the corpse of a low-level demon spawn.

"Eww, gross." Ivy squatted next to me and poked a stick into the goo.

I held up my hand to stop the others and sniffed the air. "This explains why the brimstone odor is so faint." I knelt. "Someone killed a crawler here."

"What makes you think it was a crawler?" Elyssa asked.

I pointed to the slimy mess. "Scorps usually travel in groups, and I only see one set of remains." I looked at the trunk of the tree next to the slime and noticed a wet trail down the bark. A bit of green slime was caked to a tree branch a little way up. "It was lying in wait up there when it was killed. Hellhounds don't climb trees. Besides, Kassallandra treats her hellhounds like family and keeps them close to her for protection."

"Nice deductions." Elyssa examined the slime for a moment. "I guess this means we're not alone. Someone else had to kill this crawler."

Otaleon channeled a glowing ball of violet Murk in his hand and held it over the remains. "Who else would be out here besides us?"

"Daelissa?" Joss said, a glimmer of fear in his eyes.

As Otaleon's light moved across the dead crawler, I noticed a burned patch of earth. I created a small globe of light in my hand and ran it across the black marks. They were in the shape of a hand. I

4

found similar scorch marks running up the side of the tree. A smile stretched my lips.

"My father did this." I pointed out the burn marks. "He taught me how to summon a flaming hand from the ground."

"It definitely looks like his handiwork," Mom said. "But he doesn't know we're coming."

We'd been unable to contact my father or his sister, Vallaena, to warn either of them about Kassallandra's betrayal. Before Dad had gone with Kassallandra, he'd left a wedding invitation in my bedroom. Knowing his twisted sense of humor, I figured it had to be a joke. I was certain he didn't want any of his real family showing up while he was forced to marry the head of House Assad to keep her from defecting to Daelissa's side. The invitation had been our only clue where to find him.

"I don't know how he knows, but it's the only thing that makes sense." I stood as Otaleon extinguished the ball of light. "There's a good chance all of Kassallandra's demonic defenses are down thanks to him. Let's make the most of it."

We reached the tall stone walls guarding the estate. Yellow light glowed from the other side of the barrier, and I thought I heard a bird chirp. I cupped my hands. Elyssa put a foot inside, and I catapulted her to the top of the wall. She landed lightly on her feet, crouched, and scanned the area. A moment later, she dropped a cord down the wall. It unfolded into a stiff rope ladder. I climbed up first and looked into a lush garden filled with fruit trees and flowering bushes.

I looked over my shoulder at the snowy surroundings, and back to the greenery. My forehead pinched. Elyssa pointed to a flake of snow drifting from the sky. When it reached the air above the garden, it melted and fell as liquid water to the earth. Large wooden lanterns with amber glass hung from wooden poles lining a brick pathway. Each shone with a gentle glow. I reached a hand toward the closest one. The second my hand entered its light, I felt warmth creeping up it.

"Greenhouse lanterns," Elyssa whispered.

Hummingbirds flitted from flower to flower. Rabbits hopped amongst the shrubbery. I even spotted a few deer nibbling on leaves. A hive of bees hung from the lower branches of a tree bearing green-leaved branches on its lower half while the barren top extended too far out of the greenhouse lanterns to bloom.

I shook my head. "Who does Kassallandra think she is, Snow White?"

"She is very fond of gardens," Mom said from beside me.

I flinched because I'd been too busy taking in the bizarre scenery to notice the others had come up behind me. "Kassallandra likes gardens?

She nodded. "She has quite a green thumb."

"I can't believe that cold, hard bi—" Ivy's eyes widened, so I hastily amended my language. "Uh, I can't believe that really mean woman likes to grow things. Maybe she likes having total control over plants and animals."

"The garden looks clear," Elyssa said. She pointed at two puddles of crawler remains on the ground below, and dropped a rope ladder into the interior.

Once we reached the bottom, a disturbing thought hit me. "When I summon demons, it feels like a stack of bricks is sitting on my brain." I looked at the two puddles of slime. "I assume Kassallandra feels the same thing. Wouldn't she know immediately if someone is killing off her spawn?"

Mom stood next to me. "David once told me experienced Daemos could tether their summonings with a rune. He said it didn't entirely remove the presence from your mind, but it lightened it immensely."

"In other words," I said, "she might not notice as much, especially since she's preoccupied with getting married."

"Exactly." Mom managed a smile. "I wish mine and David's wedding had been official."

I raised an eyebrow. "Are you saying you aren't properly married to my father?"

"Does that mean we're bastards?" Ivy asked.

Mom gave her a disturbed look. "Where did you hear that word?"

"I heard Shelton tell someone they were the bastard child of a two-bit tramp." She blinked her wide innocent eyes. "I asked him what a bastard was and he told me."

Mom's eyes narrowed. "I need to have a talk with that man."

Ivy crossed her arms. "So, are we bastards, Mom?"

"Not by nom standards," she said. "Your father and I got married in Vegas after we left our families."

I gave my mother a horrified look. "You always pick such inconvenient times to traumatize me with this kind of information."

"Not really the time to discuss this," Elyssa said as the orchestral music changed to a militaristic march that was the Daemos equivalent of a bridal chorus. To me, it sounded like the forces of darkness were leading the ceremony.

Elyssa scouted ahead and returned a moment later. We followed her past two unconscious men in black suits with Lancer darts sticking out of their necks. The strong odor of brimstone told me they were actually hellhounds posing as humans. We passed another set of knocked-out hellhound men and it occurred to me that Kassallandra wouldn't be the only Daemos here with a complement of hellhound bodyguards.

I heard the murmuring of guests beyond the vine-covered wall surrounding the garden. We pressed the pendants on our uniforms and activated the disguises magically programmed into the Templar body armor. My outfit morphed into a black-and-white tuxedo. Elyssa's lengthened into a form-fitting red dress. Mom and Ivy's outfits grew into silky white gowns while Joss and Otaleon's mimicked my formalwear.

The other Templars simply switched their uniforms to black to better blend into the scenery since there was no snow in the garden.

"Guard our flanks, but only engage if you hear my signal," Elyssa told them.

They responded with precise salutes and melted into the shadows.

I peered around the corner and saw two large crowds. One was dressed mostly in various hues of blue while the other favored shades of red. The females wore long dresses with their hair worn up in elaborate weaves. The males wore suits or tuxedos that varied wildly in design. Some looked as though they were out of Victorian-era London, while others possessed a modern pizzazz. The one thing they all had in common were long robes in what I assumed were their house colors.

"We don't have robes." I looked at Otaleon and Joss. "And our tuxedos look too plain. We'll never fit in."

"The plan isn't to fit in," Mom said. "At least not for long."

A trumpet sounded and two black-suited hellhound men opened the large, oak double doors at the rear of the mansion. Kassallandra stepped outside.

"Ooh, pretty," Ivy said.

"Slut," Mom hissed, her eyes literally blazing with light.

The Maedras of House Assad wore the kind of red dress I imagined a demon princess would wear to her wedding. The top was tight and form fitting, giving ample view of her creamy cleavage. The lower part of the dress looked like layered silk with a long train held up by two little girls. Kassallandra's flame-red tresses were woven in tight braids to expose her long neck. I had to admit she looked gorgeous.

I heard someone clear their throat, and turned to see Elyssa giving me a questioning look. "Like what you see?"

I winked at her. "I like what I'm seeing now."

She smiled and rolled her eyes.

I heard a sharp intake of breath from Mom and followed her gaze. Dad exited the house behind the girls holding Kassallandra's train. He wore a dark blue suit with a fit tailored to his slim, muscular physique. His white shirt was open at the collar. He hadn't even worn a tie. His face looked sober, absent of his carefree smirk.

Mom seemed to rip her eyes from him. She gripped my hands. "Do you remember everything Cinder told you?"

I nodded. "Are we sure she'll go through with this?"

"She won't have a choice." Mom kissed my cheek and her grip tightened on me.

"Don't worry," I said. "Even if things go horribly wrong, I think Dad and House Slade will back me up." At least I hoped that was the case. If I screwed this up, Daemos social codes might prevent them from coming to my aid.

Kassallandra reached the ritual altar and offered a curt bow to a male and female standing there. The woman wore a red robe; the man's was blue. According to Cinder, they were the Paetros and Maedras of another Daemos house and would lead the ceremony.

The murmuring of the crowd dropped to a hush. My father stopped at the edge of the crowd and knelt. I had to get close to that altar without being found out.

I glanced back at one of the unconscious hellhound men and made a quick decision. I touched the Templar armor to the hellhound's suit. The disguise enchantment switched to match the bodyguard's.

Elyssa looked me up and down. "Do you really think they'll let a hellhound get close to them?"

"It's the only choice I have." I gave her a kiss on the lips and left the protection of the garden walls. The brick wall ran along the side of the crowd wearing blue. I stayed close to it and made my way down the side, looking around as if I were patrolling the place. None of the Daemos so much as looked at me. Their arrogance offered me the perfect way to hide. The faint burnt odor of succubus pheromones tickled my senses as I passed by the crowd. The last time I'd been this close to so many Daemos had been during the Battle of Bellwood Quarry in the Gloom. It was a bit unsettling.

I watched as the female ritual leader said something to Kassallandra. My father's bride took the woman's hand and pressed it to her forehead. My gut knotted as the female ritual leader raised her face to the crowd. She said, "Are there any here of worth who denounce this unification?"

Almost there. I hurried my steps and reached the front of the crowd just as the intense odor of brimstone hit my nose. Everyone else seemed to sense it at the same time.

"I denounce this traitorous whore!" A female screamed. The garden wall to my right exploded and a demon scorpion the size of a car plowed through the crowd, sending wedding guests flying everywhere.

The last time I'd seen a scorp that size had been in Kobol Prison guarding Daelissa's Seraphim resurrection project.

Something became clear to me in that instant. Kassallandra hadn't been the one helping Daelissa. This mystery woman was the traitor.

Chapter 2

A wave of bricks whooshed past my head. I dove to avoid the scuttling legs of the massive scorp. Where claws and a stinger tail would be on a normal scorpion, this monster had giant mouths full of jagged teeth. Where the eyes should be, a human face pressed against the black chitin like someone trying to escape from a black plastic garbage bag. The face screamed and the jaw-claws snapped.

A tall, thin woman with black hair ran past the scorp and kicked the stunned ritual leaders backward off the altar. Kassallandra lay stunned under a pile of bricks. I spotted my father carrying two Daemos to safety while some ran in panic and others morphed into their half-demon forms as if preparing for a fight.

The woman gripped Kassallandra's tresses and jerked her from beneath the bricks. I heard howling and rolled on my back as a large pack of hellhounds charged down the aisle at the giant scorp. The giant scorp screeched. The face trapped beneath its chitin opened its mouth wide and a swarm of small scorps crawled down the face and piled on the ground, forming a ball of legs and black exoskeletons. The ball skittered toward the pack of hellhounds. The two forces met in an explosion of fur and screeches. I tried to pick myself up off the ground when another weakened portion of the garden wall fell. I rolled on my side, but a chunk slammed on my leg. I stifled a shout of pain.

Yelps and whines filled the air. I rose to my knees in time to see the scorps churning through the hellhounds like butter in a wood chipper. A ball of fire blazed through the air and exploded against the scorps. I spotted Elyssa and the Templars herding stunned Daemos from the courtyard while Mom scorched the scorps using Arcane spells instead of Seraphim channeling. I'd learned the hard way scorps could detect incoming blasts of Brilliance or Murk and dodge them easily.

"You will die as my mother died!" the attacking female said.

I crept up behind the altar, desperate to keep the giant scorp from spotting me. The attacker looked vaguely familiar. Her long, thick hair was black, and something about her face reminded me of someone—I just couldn't put my finger on whom.

"Aerianas," Kassallandra said, her voice betraying no fear. "I thought you were dead."

Vadaemos and Orionas's daughter? That's the chick who seduced Shelton!

Aerianas flashed a manic smile and punched Kassallandra in the face. Blood sprayed from the redhead's nose. Aerianas slapped a silver collar around the other woman's neck and threw her to the ground.

By now, a horde of Daemos, hellhounds, and my group were bearing down on the massive scorp. Aerianas's dark eyes glimmered. She pressed a red gem on a circlet at her throat. Something hummed to life and the static feeling of aether pressed against me. Mom and the others bounced back as they ran into an invisible barrier.

The male ritual leader rose from the ground and tried to grab Aerianas. She flipped the Daemos over her shoulder. Before he hit the ground, she spun and kicked him hard toward the giant scorp. One of the massive claws caught the man and cleaved him in two. A thin, flexible tube shot from the scorp's underside and slurped the remains until there was no trace but a splash of crimson on the ground.

Kassallandra lunged toward Aerianas, but fell to her knees as the collar around her throat flashed. Aerianas raised her hands into the air. "Enjoy your final pain, Kassallandra. It is payment in full for hunting my mother like a dog and killing her. As for killing my father, there is no price you could pay to atone for that."

"I didn't—" Kassallandra couldn't finish her sentence as a black inky pond formed beneath her. Dozens of arms jutted from the tar-like substance, hands grasping at Kassallandra as if trying to pull her into the ground while at the same time throwing her into the air. She screamed in such pain, I had to cover my ears.

Do something, Justin!

I had to act now while Aerianas was preoccupied. Gathering my courage, I dashed forward and dove at the woman. A giant scorp claw batted me. I tumbled through the air and smacked into a blue-tinged shield. I saw Elyssa's horrified face on the other side. She pointed frantically behind me.

I regained some of my wits and rolled away just as a giant jaw claw crushed the stone pavers where I'd been an instant before. On instinct, I shot a searing beam of Brilliance at the creature, but it scuttled aside with horrifying speed for something so large. My attack splashed harmlessly against the shield.

I didn't have a wand or staff with me, but I tried casting an Arcane spell with my hand anyway. A fireball exploded from my fingertip. Searing pain shot up my arm. The scorp threw up a claw. The fireball exploded against the chitin, but seemed to do no damage.

"Anyone have a can of bug spray handy?" I shouted as I backed away from the quickly advancing monster.

"Spawn, Justin!" Elyssa called over Kassallandra's cries of agony. "Use brute force!"

I saw my dad kneeling on the ground, his face dripping with sweat. A crack formed in the ground and rammed into the shield several times. He looked up. "She's running this shield on the mansion's own aether generator. It's too strong for an earth elemental to break through."

"Can it go under it?" I asked.

He shook his head. "The barrier is a bubble."

"Where's the generator?" I asked.

He pointed to a cottage-sized brick building near the garden wall. "It's inside the shield with you."

I flipped backward to avoid another claw smash, turned, and ran to give myself some distance. As I sprinted, I reached inside for my inner demon and let it surge free from its cage. Muscles coiled around my arms, my legs, bulking me to preposterous proportions. I grew taller and felt a tail pressing against the Templar armor. The cloth grew to accommodate the extra appendage. My feet widened and the boots grew longer to allow for claws forming where my toenails had once been. I touched the seams of the armor at my ankles and wrists. The armor retracted from my feet and hands, revealing blue, scaly skin and black claws.

Piercing pain exploded in my forehead as my horns formed. Flames flickered into my eyesight. My inner demon reached the boundary between completely losing myself and retaining control. I slammed a wall of will between my remaining consciousness and the infernal spirit vying for everything I had.

Fire coursed through my veins. I spun around and faced the giant scorp. A claw lunged for me. I leapt, landed on top of it, and ran up its arm. Its other claw snapped at me. I jumped straight up, splaying out my legs to avoid losing any tender bits. The scorp's claw crunched into the chitin on its other arm, sending green gunk splashing on the ground. The creature shrieked. I landed on the other claw. The flexible feeding tube shot out from its underside. I gripped it and held the tooth-lined orifice away from me as it made sick sucking sounds. Squeezing with all my might, I crushed the semi-rigid tube and tied the end in a knot.

The scorp let out an ear-piercing screech. I jumped from the claw. Swung on the feeding tube like a vine. It took me under the belly of the beast and between two of its many legs. When I reached the apex of the swing, I flipped backwards and landed on the scorp's back. It scuttled in a circle, one claw snapping at me, but its arm was too short to reach me. Unfortunately, its exoskeleton was slick and I went down on my side. I heard a whoosh of air and rolled to the side just as the scorp's tail lashed at me. It crunched hard into the creature's own back.

Gripping a seam between the plates of chitin on its back, I managed to hang on. Rolled over. With an effort of will, I channeled a beam of destruction at the base of the tail.

"Dodge this, you bastard!" I shouted as a sudden surge of malicious glee raced through my veins. The energy sliced through the chitin. Green blood bubbled like lava from the wound. The scorp's tail lashed at me again, but the damage was done. With a satisfying crackle, the tail toppled like a felled tree and slammed into the ground. The scorp retaliated by spinning in a dizzying circle. My hand slipped until I was only holding on by my fingers. For some reason, laughter burst from me.

I think I just seriously pissed it off. My inner demon seemed amused.

There had to be a way to bring this thing down faster than cutting off its limbs one at a time. The scorp didn't exactly have a head or a brain, but if it had a vulnerable spot, it probably had something to do with the awful face on the front. Holding on with one hand, I used the other to blow chunks from the scorp's armor with spheres of destruction. Using the divots in the armor as handholds, I dragged myself closer to the dome of its head.

Even with all the noise from the scorp, Kassallandra's screams still rose above the fray. I glanced toward her and saw the infernal black arms still grasping at her body, drawing her closer and closer to the inky pond. I'd seen a lot in my short time as an incubus, but I'd never seen anything like what Aerianas was doing to her.

I reached the dome of the monster's body and gripped another chink in its armor. I saw the huge face pressing against the chitin, its mouth peeled back in a rictus of pain. Squeezing my knees tight against holes I'd burned in the armor, I pressed both of my hands together and took aim.

"Did somebody call bug control?" I shouted. Summoning all my effort, I channeled a thick beam of Brilliance right into the gaping mouth. Ecstasy flooded my senses. I felt as though I could take on an army of giant scorps.

The scorp's shrieks turned to gurgles and its body shuddered violently. I jerked back to reality. Things were about to get really messy. I turned. Ran down the thing's back. Leapt from the side. My demon-sized feet thudded into the ground but I didn't stop running.

I looked over my shoulder and watched the corpse of the giant scorp implode. It slammed to the ground hard enough to shake it. Green guts fountained across the courtyard.

Aerianas, who'd, up to this point, been so consumed with whatever she was doing to Kassallandra, looked up in alarm and saw me running at her. I had to stop her.

Or do I?

I actually hesitated. Kassallandra's death might save my father from the farce of a marriage she was forcing on him. Even so, there was no guarantee her successor would join in the fight against Daelissa. A part of me really wanted the problem to just go away. That part of me wanted to give Aerianas a thumbs-up.

Shut-up, evil Justin.

Fortunately for Kassallandra, that part of me was small.

"Stop what you're doing," I shouted in my deep demonic basso.

"Who are you?" the woman screamed.

"Justin Slade," I said. "Looks like I'm Justin time to kick your ass."

Nobody laughed.

Aerianas's face went crimson. "You're the one who captured my father. You're the reason Kassallandra was able to kill him!" The tar pit of hands bubbled down to a simmer and vanished. Kassallandra stopped screaming and fell to the ground in a heap as Aerianas turned her wrathful gaze on me.

Her thin figure burst into full demonic form within an instant. Her black dress shredded and hung from her, leaving nothing to the imagination. Aerianas's skin was smooth, purple, and devoid of scales. She easily towered over me. Black wings, like those of a bat, spread from behind her back, each joint boasting razor-sharp talons. With a flash of brilliant white fangs, she spoke in a voice like a banshee. "I will kill you, boy!"

I remembered with horror when I'd fought her father, Vadaemos. He and I had both spawned to demon form. He'd kicked my ass so hard, I hadn't known which way was up. There was absolutely no question in my mind he'd taught his daughter everything he knew. Even with all my improvements, this fight would be tough.

Aerianas blurred toward me. I resisted the urge to run and stood my ground, calling upon every ninja move Elyssa had taught me. I'd actually beaten my girlfriend in a few sparring matches and prayed to the almighty she hadn't just let me win.

Please let me have actual skill.

I twisted away from Aerianas's attack. Spun. Slammed a kick into her back. Aerianas grunted and flew forward. She face-planted with a thud and slid a good twenty feet.

"That's my boy!" I heard my father shout.

"Destroy the generator!" I heard Elyssa scream.

I turned toward the building some thirty yards away and aimed at it. My guts slammed into my ribs as something huge butted me. Sharp pain dug into my back. I tumbled along the ground and hit the shield barrier with my back. Through a haze, I saw Aerianas gloating.

Rage boiled through my veins. I leapt to my feet and braced for impact as she charged. I dodged right and tried to clothesline her with my arm. She anticipated my move, grabbed my arm, and twisted. I planted a foot into her stomach. Rolled backward and vaulted her over me. I twisted around and saw her wings catch the air. She glided to the ground and slammed her fist to the stone. The earth came alive around me. A stone hand erupted, spewing rock and dirt. It gripped my body and squeezed. Air exploded from my lungs. Rough grit tore at my flesh.

Aerianas threw her head back and laughed. "No Daemos can best me."

I struggled in the stone grip. I couldn't breathe. Couldn't move. The hand squeezed and I heard my bones creaking. *This might be it.*

"Justin!" Elyssa screamed. "Fight!"

"Get off the ground," my father shouted.

How the hell was I supposed to get off the ground with a ton of earth holding me captive? My legs were still free. I bent them and tried to leap. I heard the groan and crackle of stone, but didn't budge an inch. My legs flailed in desperation as I tried again and again to leg-press free. My oxygen dwindled. My lungs burned. Spots danced before my eyes.

Mom's voice cut through Aerianas's laughter. "Use a shield, Justin!"

I didn't know how a shield was supposed to protect me from something already holding me, but one last desperate idea came into my head. Channeling Murk, I willed it to flow from every inch of my skin. Ultraviolet energy shimmered before my eyes. The rough stone grip left my flesh. I willed it to push outward.

My brain felt as though it were being squeezed by all the force pressing against my barrier. The weight against my chest suddenly loosened. I sucked in a breath of sweet air and roared with effort. I felt the barrier expand. Heard the cracking of rock. I added Brilliance to my channeling and pushed again.

My inner demon suddenly surged with joy as if I'd just fed it puppies and kittens for breakfast. I felt heady with power. I felt indestructible. As if I could melt the world. I channeled more Brilliance and my demon side surged. *Burn! Kill! Destroy!*

Aerianas stopped laughing. I saw sweat pouring down her purple skin. Her expression of victory morphed to uncertainty. I flexed my muscles and with it, the barrier around me. With a great snapping sound, rock exploded and sprayed across the ground. Aerianas gasped and naked fear showed on her face.

"What sort of perversion are you?" she shrieked. "Monster!"

The urge to gloat was almost irresistible. I wanted to laugh in her face as I burned off her appendages one by one. *Immolate her! Char her to ash!* What the hell was wrong with me? I fought back, reasserting my will.

"Aerianas, you have betrayed Eden by fighting for Daelissa," my demon voice boomed. "Give yourself up or face annihilation." *Kill. Kill! KILL!* I felt warmth blossom in my palms, looked down and saw spheres of Brilliance growing.

"She told me I could have my vengeance!" The Daemas wailed. "Kassallandra took everything I loved from this world!"

Images of Aerianas screaming as white flames consumed her flashed through my mind. I saw myself picking her up by her throat and squeezing the life from her. I gritted my teeth and fought my demon for control. "I don't condone what she did to your mother," I said with great effort, "but your father devoured the souls of the innocent and turned you into his accomplice." I felt my arms rising. Saw the glow of destruction in each palm. Somehow my demon was controlling me. I roared and fought back.

Aerianas screamed. "I yield! I yield!"

Ecstatic joy flooded me. White flames danced in my vision. The glow around my hands surged. A scream of terror tore through Aerianas's throat. With all my effort, I jerked my arms slightly to the left just as twin spheres of destruction streaked from my hands. The energy slammed into the building with the shield generator. The brick wall turned to molten slag and an explosion sent bricks and debris scattering. A wave of sparkling magical energy cascaded into the air, signaling the destruction of the aether generator inside.

Aerianas huddled in a fetal position whimpering. Her demon form melted away, leaving the thin woman huddled in the rags of her dress. She looked up at me with tear-stained eyes. "You are a monster." Her body shook with sobs as a crowd of Daemos surrounded her.

Chapter 3

Bodyguards secured Aerianas with unbreakable diamond fiber rope.

I felt Brilliance coursing into my body and wrenched control from my demon. I snuffed out the destructive energy and shoved my demon side into the back seat once again. Seeing the mob of Daemos surrounding Aerianas, I suddenly felt protective of the thin woman. "Spare her life."

The Daemos looked at each other uncertainly.

"Do as he says," said a weak voice. Kassallandra stood at the altar, her face white as a sheet, hands clinging to the sides as if to support her.

"Holy guacamole, kiddo!" Dad stood to the side looking up at my tall demon form. He wrapped an arm around Mom. "They sure grow up fast, don't they?"

"I don't even know what to say," Mom replied, her face pale and uncertain.

Ivy laughed. "I want to grow horns and a tail, too!"

Unwilling to settle back to my human form just yet, I walked over to Kassallandra. "I believe you owe me one." My guttural voice rumbled in my throat.

Kassallandra's lips peeled back from her teeth. "This must be a very proud moment for you." Despite her weak appearance after her ordeal, her eyes turned fiery. "You have seen me humbled at my own wedding," she hissed.

"Your agony gave me no pleasure," I said, only partially lying. "I'm sorry Aerianas decided to take out her vendetta on your special day."

Kassallandra seemed torn between a desire to punch me and something else. A growl of frustration rose in her throat as she stared daggers at me. Her shoulders abruptly slumped. "You know nothing of Daemos social order, do you?"

I shook my head. "Not much."

Her red eyes locked onto mine. "You have saved more than my life, boy. You've saved my soul. Aerianas intended to banish me to the Abyss itself."

"I could have just let her finish the job." I flattened my lips as a smile threatened to break free.

"I know." She shuddered. "You've forced me into a very tenuous situation."

"I forced you?" I managed to keep my voice low. "Aerianas did this, not me."

Kassallandra looked away. "You're right." She took a deep breath and stiffened her back before looking at me. "What do you wish of me, son of Daevadius Slade?"

Finally, an easy question. I wanted to smile as the words came from my mouth, but I knew better than to risk this chance to have what I wanted. The original plan had been to challenge Kassallandra to a duel for control of her house. Although I'd still had to fight a raging Daemas, this version of events might prevent a mutiny from House Assad. "I want your loyalty without a marriage to my father. I want House Assad firmly behind me."

I could sense a struggle going on behind her steely gaze. After a long moment, Kassallandra, Maedras of House Assad did something completely unexpected. She knelt before me. "I am yours, Kohvaniss."

The crowd behind me gasped. I turned to see my father grinning like a new dad. He strode up to the altar and knelt. "I, too, am yours, Kohvaniss. The great houses stand united." He took Kassallandra's hand and they both stood, arms raised. "Daemos unitarius!"

A great roar went up from the assembly. Shouts of "Kohvaniss! Kohvaniss!" echoed in the air.

I had absolutely no idea what was going on, so I kept a neutral look on my face. It was really hard resisting the urge to give a double thumbs-up. I crossed my arms and nodded sagely as if this was exactly what I'd expected. After a moment, I held up my hands and the courtyard went deathly silent.

"Today marks a day for hope. We will hunt down Daelissa and end her tyranny." I ran my eyes across the crowd and gave them a grim smile before thrusting a fist in the air. "We will win this war!"

Cheers erupted. Some of the hellhound bodyguards broke into howls. My demon half seemed to roar with approval. I decided playtime was over and unceremoniously shoved my demon half back into his cage. My horns clattered to the ground and my body melted back to its normal form in time to receive Elyssa into my arms.

She squeezed me tight and kissed me hard. "That was impressive."

"I was a little surprised myself." I motioned my parents over.

Dad whooped and slapped me on the back. "Talk about two birds with one stone, son. I guess I owe you one too."

Mom kissed my cheek and hugged me so tight I heard my back pop. "Thank you, son."

"I guess I won't have to zap that dirty home-wrecker after all," Ivy said in grim satisfaction. She looked up at our father. "Does this mean we finally get to do a picnic?"

He bent in front of her and kissed her cheek. "It means we get to do a lot as a family, Ivy."

Her blue eyes regarded him with suspicion. "You're out of excuses for being my dad."

"I know, sweetie." He squeezed her shoulder. "I know."

"What does Kohvaniss mean?" I asked.

Dad jerked his head toward me as if interrupted from his thoughts. "In Haedaemos, my father, Baal, is Kohvaniss."

"Wait a minute." I felt my forehead pinch. "You just made me a king?"

He waggled his hand in a so-so motion. "I guess that's a rough translation." A smirk stretched his lips. "A more accurate translation would be 'supreme devourer of all souls.'"

I grimaced. "I don't devour souls."

"That's how you get to be king in Haedaemos." Dad flourished a bow.

"Be serious."

"As you wish, Kohvaniss." He bowed again.

I sighed. "What about the other Daemos houses?

Dad put an arm around my shoulder. "I think it's time to meet the other Daemos leaders." He looked at Mom, Ivy, and Elyssa. "Ladies, if you'll excuse us for a few moments."

Mom squeezed my hand. "Good luck, son."

"Let me know if anyone needs their arm twisted," Elyssa said.

I pecked her on the cheek. "Definitely."

Dad guided me to the outskirts of the crowd. A beautiful blonde woman in a flowing blue dress appeared at our sides.

"You have performed beyond all expectations, nephew," my aunt Vallaena said, her voice proud.

Dad seemed to puff out his chest a little. "We need to soften up the other house leaders so they'll join the cause against Daelissa. Think you can give us a hand?"

Vallaena nodded. "It will be difficult, but now is the time, while everyone is in one place."

I felt my forehead wrinkle. "Difficult? House Assad and Slade just called me their king. Why wouldn't the other houses jump on the bandwagon?"

"Some are cowardly. Others have grown slothful over the years."

I stopped them. "Before we launch this expedition, I need advice."

"I'd say flowers and a nice restaurant," Dad said. "You two haven't had a decent date in too long."

I scratched my head. "What in the world are you talking about?"

"I'm giving you advice about your love life." He shrugged. "A man's got to treat his woman every once in a while."

"A female is not a possession," Vallaena said with a strict look. She turned to me. "He is, however, correct that flowers and an expensive restaurant will do much to make up for churlish male behavior."

Dad laughed. "I didn't say anything about expensive— "

I put up my hands. "Shush!" I gave them both a severe look. "My dating life is just dandy, thank you very much. I'm having issues with my demon side misbehaving."

"Misbehaving?" Vallaena raised an eyebrow. "After my firm tutelage, you seemed very comfortable with it."

"When I was channeling Seraphim magic to free myself from Aerianas's rock grip, it felt like I was about to lose control." I ran a hand through my hair. "I almost blasted her to ash."

"What was the exact minute you felt that?" Dad asked.

I thought back to my efforts. "When I blasted the scorp with Brilliance."

"Destructive magic," Vallaena said. "Our demon sides revel in carnage. It is sometimes a war to maintain control."

"The struggle is real." Just when I thought I'd mastered my strange heritage, something else popped up. "My demon identifies with Brilliance, the force of destruction. I almost want to say it gains strength from it."

Vallaena touched my cheek in an almost fond gesture. "You will overcome this problem, nephew. You are my blood, my kin, and I expect no less."

"Wow, don't get all gushy, sis." Dad gripped my shoulder. "If you manifest into demon form, you'll just have to be careful if you channel Brilliance. It sounds to me like your demon side gets a real head rush from it." He shrugged. "I wish I could tell you more, but you're kind of a weirdo."

"He is unique." Vallaena offered me small smile.

Guess I'm on my own trying to figure this one out. I put on a smile. "Let's get back to Daemos politics. What do I need to know?"

"As you wish." My aunt looked around and nodded toward the female marriage ritual leader. The Daemas still seemed to be in shock. "That is Maedras Domitia Calidious. Her Paetros, Brutus, was the one the scorp devoured."

"I wish I could have saved him," I said.

Vallaena shrugged. "The two never got along very well, but losing anyone you have known for centuries is still quite a shock." She tapped a finger to her chin. "Brutus would never have joined the alliance. Domitia, however, is far more reasonable. I believe Brutus's death affords you a chance to bring Calidious into the fold. They are the third most powerful house."

I grimaced. "Should I give her some time to grieve?"

"She is in shock, not grief," Vallaena said. "Despite the interruption of the marriage ceremony, I will make sure Kassallandra doesn't cancel the festivities. Tonight is a large banquet and tomorrow

22

evening will be the grand ball. I believe that will be the best opportunity to speak with Domitia and others."

"Agreed," Dad said. "Domitia is the most important." He pointed out a tall man with platinum blond hair and an almost feminine beauty to his features. "That's Godric of House Salomon. He's a narcissistic son of a bitch."

"A rather unlikeable man," Vallaena added. "It is unfortunate the scorp did not take him as well."

"Is that his wife?" I asked, nodding toward a beautiful woman standing next to him. She wore her platinum tresses up in a mass of braids and curls like many of the woman. She had huge eyes, which should have given her an empathetic appearance, but ice-blue irises and the way she regarded everyone down her long thin nose made me dislike her instantly.

"Gwyneth, his wife and daughter," Dad said.

I looked around for a young girl who looked like the pair before I realized what he meant. "That's his daughter and his"—I made a gagging noise—"wife?"

Dad gave me a helpless look and shrugged. "Daemos don't suffer from genetic defects associated with inbreeding."

Vallaena regarded me severely. "Your ignorance about Daemos customs is something you must overcome if you wish to win their support. Do not allow your nom upbringing to taint your perceptions."

A shudder ran through my shoulders. "I'll bet Godric can really play the banjo."

Dad laughed.

Vallaena pursed her lips and stared me down. A young man ran over to us and handed her a note. She looked at it and nodded. "I must attend to some other business, but I will do what I can to facilitate your efforts." She offered me a shallow curtsy. "Kohvaniss."

"Not you too," I said.

A sly smile spread her lips as she turned and walked away.

"Does Vallaena have a sense of humor I don't know about?" I asked.

Dad snorted. "Depends on who you ask. Let's walk around a little, and I'll show you some other house leaders." He led me along until we spotted a woman in silky Oriental robes. Her skin was the color of caramel, and her hair long, silky, and black. Her jade green eyes fixed on me the moment we came into view. With a wave of her hand, she dismissed a man who'd been speaking with her and walked our way. Dad cursed under his breath. He broadcast his standard charming smile at the woman. "Maedras Yuuki Wakahisa, it is a pleasure to see you again."

She offered him a curt nod. "A pleasure, Paetros Daevadius Slade." Her wide almond-shaped eyes looked me up and down. "You are the Cataclyst I have heard so much about." She smiled faintly. "The rumors of your boldness are not unfounded, it would seem." Despite her Asian appearance, she had very little accent.

I wasn't really sure how to approach the whole Kohvaniss thing, and since she wasn't bowing and scraping, I knew pushing the matter would be counterproductive. I had to project authority without being overbearing. Or did I need to dominate her somehow? I was sadly lacking on Daemos social skills. Considering everything I'd had to learn, that was hardly surprising. I couldn't be expected to know everything.

"It's a pleasure to meet you, Maedras Wakahisa." I held out a hand.

She looked at it for a moment. "A handshake? How very Western of you."

Noob mistake, Justin. I almost took back my hand, but realized that might come across as a sign of weakness. *I'm overthinking things as usual.* I said the only thing that came to mind. "It won't bite you."

Her head tilted ever so slightly and her gaze fixed on me.

"Are you afraid to join the dark side?" I looked down at her hand. "We have cookies and a great health care plan."

Yuuki suddenly laughed, sounding very much like an excited Japanese schoolgirl. She gripped my hand and shook it. "You are very strange." She came closer and whispered in my ear. "I like strange."

I barely stopped myself from gulping and released her hand. "My girlfriend likes that side of me too."

"I am sure she would be willing to share."

"How's Tokyo these days?" Dad said, obviously trying to change the subject.

Yuuki sniffed. "Overrun with vampires. The Templar legions in Japan do nothing to curb the spread of those vile blood leechers."

"That's because they're working with the Synod," I said. "It's all part of Daelissa's plan to grow an army of cannon fodder."

She made a show of yawning. "Ah, the talk of war again. I find it rather boring."

I waved toward a pile of green goop. "It gets pretty exciting when it's on your doorstep."

Yuuki looked at my father. "I would speak with the Cataclyst alone."

He gave me an uneasy look, somehow managing to convey how much he wanted to take me aside and give me a long lesson on Daemos society. That wasn't going to happen. He nodded. "Of course."

Yuuki looped her arm through mine and led me through a gate and into the garden. "How much do you know of House Wakahisa?"

"Almost nothing," I admitted. "I haven't had a lot of time to study my Daemos heritage."

She pulled me onto a bench seat next to her. Her silky dress fell open at a slit along the side, revealing bare leg all the way up to the top of the thigh. The alluring scent of heat reached my nose. "The original Maedras and Paetros died centuries ago in the Seraphim War. I am the daughter of the former heads of our house. They were assassinated just before World War Two, as the noms call it."

"I'm sorry to hear that," I said, trying not to look at her leg, and trying desperately to ignore her succubus pheromones. "Who killed them?"

She shrugged. "I do not know, and I have never pursued the matter. My advisors believed my parents were killed because they wished to dissuade the Japanese emperor from joining with Germany."

I felt my eyes widen. "They were against the war?"

"My father did not trust Germany." She took my hand in both of hers. "I have never chosen a Paetros, though there are many who vie for the honor." Her lower hand slipped away while her top one pressed my hand against her leg. "You have the blood of the most powerful Daemos house in your veins and the magic of the Seraphim. Perhaps you could learn of your heritage first hand." She leaned closer to me and whispered in my ear. "You would be a worthy Paetros."

25

I decided ignoring the comment was the safest route. "We need allies in the war. Will you join us?"

A smirk formed a rosebud with her lips. "I have no interest in war. The two sides may destroy each other if they wish, but I have no plans to put my life in jeopardy." She slid my hand under her dress. "I can also think of more enjoyable activities than throwing away your life."

I felt a bead of sweat trickle down my forehead. Gathering my wits, I gently pulled my hand away. "As I said, I have a girlfriend."

She waved away my objection. "I know of your Elyssa Borathen. She is but a Templar. A simple soldier." Yuuki slid down the shoulder of her robe, revealing the thin straps of her dress and ample cleavage. "What is a girl compared to a woman like me?"

Anger heated my face. *This woman is playing games with me.* I stood and looked down at the succubus. "She's far more than you'll ever be. She fights by my side. She protects me and this world while you yawn and complain that war bothers you." I leaned down and let out just enough of my inner demon to ignite the flames in my eyes. "War is on your doorstep whether you like it or not, lady." I jabbed a finger toward the courtyard. "It spilled over here today. Those vampires you whine about in Tokyo are symptoms of the war in your own backyard."

Her eyes flared. "How dare you—"

I put my finger in her face. "No, how dare you talk about Elyssa like that? She's ten times the woman you are and a million times braver." I growled and felt my inner demon straining to burst free.

Yuuki burst to her feet. "You should think before talking, boy." Horns slowly grew from her forehead and her jade eyes caught fire. "You have no idea what I'm capable of."

The scent of her anger filled my nose. *That's it!* Before I could control myself, my hand gripped her neck. I pressed her back down in the seat and put my face inches from hers. "But you know exactly what I'm capable of." I wanted to threaten her, to make her join our alliance, but that would make me no better than Daelissa. Somehow, I pushed back the rage and took a deep breath. I released her neck. "If your life is worth nothing, then go back to your pitiful existence and wait for Daelissa to hunt you down and kill you." I bared my teeth.

"Or take control of your destiny and prove you're more than a waste of space."

The fire in her eyes died, and her small horns dropped to the ground. Yuuki touched her neck and stared at me for a long moment. Without another word, she stood and walked away, pulling her robe back over her shoulder as she did.

I heard the rustle of a bush and spun. Elyssa stood there, eyes large and damp. Before I could say a word she blurred toward me and pinned me against the ivy-covered wall. Her lips pressed hard to mine. Heat built in my stomach. I spun her around and pressed her to the wall. My mouth ran up her neck, across her cheek, and found her lips again. My hand ran down her leg and pulled it up against my side.

I broke from the kiss, panting. "How long have you been here?"

"Long enough." Elyssa smiled. "I wanted to make sure someone was watching your back in case it was a trap."

A laugh burst from my throat. "It was a trap, all right. Just not the kind you thought."

Her eyes turned serious. "Do you really think I'm ten times the woman she is?" Her fingers traced my jawline. "I'm just—"

I gripped her hand and pressed it to my lips. "You're all the woman I ever want and all I ever need, Elyssa." I pecked her nose. "You are my princess."

She giggled. "I love you."

"What are you doing to her, Justin?"

We whipped our heads to the side. Ivy stood a few feet away, her blue eyes huge and innocent.

I pulled away from Elyssa. "Combat training. She was showing me how I could've punched Aerianas in the face."

My sister's forehead wrinkled and her head tilted like a curious puppy. "That didn't look like combat training. It looked a lot like gross grownup stuff."

Elyssa and I burst into laughter. I walked over and gave Ivy a big hug. "Never grow up."

"Huh?" Ivy pulled away. "But I don't like being short."

I snorted and repressed another laugh. "Let's go back to the courtyard."

Dad spotted me the instant we stepped into the courtyard and walked over. "I take it things didn't go well with Yuuki."

Elyssa quirked her lips. "You might say that."

He put a hand on my shoulder and rotated me so I could see Yuuki talking to a group of house leaders. "If you want to convince more of them, you'll probably have to do some serious damage control."

Godric Salomon and Domitia Calidious glanced at me over Yuuki's shoulder, their expressions unreadable.

"How many more houses are there?" I asked.

"Two more." He pointed to a tall thin man with a narrow nose and thick black hair who was speaking with Kassallandra. "House Volkov—Ivan and Tatiana." His eyes searched the crowd. My father pointed to a man of middle height with ebony skin and a handsome, chiseled face. "That's Khamisi of House Taarkan."

Khamisi's abrupt hand gestures toward the group of people he was talking with gave the impression they were in a heated debate. His gaze swept past me and then doubled back. He gave me a good long look before returning to his conversation.

I felt my spirits sinking. I'd assumed that the support of two major houses would win me the rest. Instead, I'd alienated Yuuki and she was probably on her way to making sure none of the other houses backed me. I might have proven my worth as a fighter, but I'd screwed the pooch as a diplomat.

Unfortunately, I couldn't worry about it right now. Tonight, Elyssa and I had a battle to lead.

Chapter 4

Adam Nosti looked up from his arctablet. "Hack completed." He raised his arm and began the countdown.

"Three!"

The Obsidian Arch in the La Casona way station flickered on.

"Two!"

Behind Elyssa and me, a host of Templars and Blue Cloaks tensed and prepared for the onslaught.

"One!" Adam flicked the screen of his arctablet. A jagged bolt of energy ripped through the air between the columns, forcing a connection with an Obsidian Arch at the opposite end.

"Go, go, go!" Elyssa shouted.

Templars streamed through the arch in utter silence. Captain Takei raised his fist and jerked it down. The Blue Cloaks, three-hundred strong, rushed in, the susurrus of their cloaks the only sound they made.

Elyssa and I rode a flying carpet through the portal after our army. She piloted the rug up above the Obsidian Arch at Queens Gate for a better view.

Vampires clad in the crimson armor of the Red Cell met the Templar forces. From the air, the mass of fighting bodies looked like a sea of black pressing against a tide of blood. The Blue Cloaks broke into separate units. The group specializing in Magitsu flanked the Red Cell soldiers while those trained in spells of mass destruction unfolded platform towers and took aim at the battle mages supporting the vampires.

"I don't know why Daelissa committed her elite troops to the Queens Gate way station," Elyssa said. "She still has that Obsidian Arch in Colossus Stadium next to Arcane University."

"Well, we did kidnap her lead strategist," I said, referring to Elyssa's sister, Phoebe.

Elyssa slid the carpet to the side as a sizzling beam of light seared past us. "This is sloppy, even for Daelissa." She pointed to the empty area behind the enemy battle mages. "They don't even have an interdictor in place."

"I'm afraid it's a trap." Phoebe had certainly tricked us several times.

I spotted a group of flying carpets lift off the ground behind the vampires and head straight up for the roof of the cave. One of the carpets exploded in a ball of fire as a spell from a Blue Cloak consumed it. The other three carpets headed straight for us.

"Incoming," Elyssa said. She rotated the carpet sideways so I could get a clear view.

The battle mages on the flying carpets shot a volley of spells at us. I channeled a shield. The attacks slammed against the barrier, leaving chinks and cracks in the Murk, but it held. The attackers hurled another slew of attacks. I gritted my teeth and poured more energy into the barrier. A flaming meteor slammed the shield so forcefully it sent our carpet spinning through the air. The movement made it too difficult for me to maintain the barrier and our protection winked away.

Elyssa regained control of the carpet. I blasted another incoming fireball with Murk before it reached us. Redirected my aim, and thrust my arm toward the nearest attacker. A beam of Brilliance sliced the carpet in half. The other two carpets swooped to save their comrades before they hit the floor. This took them within range of the Blue Cloaks beneath us.

Needles of light made pincushions of our attackers. People screamed. Blood splashed and flesh turned to ash. The enemy carpets spiraled out of control and slammed to the stone floor below.

I heard a victorious roar and flicked my gaze toward the sound. The crimson forms of the Red Cell were falling back and retreating through the large doors leading into Queens Gate while their battle mages utilized portable aether generators to shield them. The

Templars pressed forward, taking down fleeing enemies while the Blue Cloaks focused their energy on taking down the aether generators.

As the last enemy made it through the door, squad leaders below called a halt. It would be too dangerous to follow the enemy through the relatively narrow opening into the pocket dimension housing Queens Gate. Our people redirected the aether generators and shielded the opening into the way station to prevent the enemy from storming back through.

Elyssa landed the carpet inside the traversion zone of the Obsidian Arch and motioned Adam Nosti through. "Great job, Adam. Do you think you can hack the arch in Colossus Stadium too?"

He shook his head. "It's a new arch and I don't have any way of looking up its magical energy signature without getting close to it." He consulted his arctablet. "I'll be in the control room. None of the other way stations know we've taken this one yet. I might be able to hack their moduli from here before they change them."

Elyssa nodded. "Let us know what you find."

"You got it." Adam headed for the control room, a skip in his step.

I chuckled. "I think that man lives for hacking."

Elyssa looked up from typing something on her arcphone. "That part of him hasn't changed since we met him."

Captain Takei and Elyssa's brother, Michael Borathen, converged on us.

Shelton walked over from a group of Blue Cloaks. "Man, we really kicked their asses, didn't we?"

I looked at the still-smoking remains of the battle mages lying scattered on the ground around us. "It was almost too easy."

"Probably because Jeremiah blew up half their army with a malaether crucible back at Kobol Prison." Shelton shrugged. "I don't think they've recovered yet."

"If they're really still so disorganized without Phoebe, we need to seize the opportunity." I looked at the shielded entrance to Queens Gate. "This way station doesn't mean squat if we can't get into the pocket dimension. We'll constantly have to worry about being flanked."

"Agreed," Elyssa said. "But the only way inside is the Obsidian Arch in the stadium."

"I wish we still had our omniarch." A wistful look came over Shelton's face. "Man, it's only been about a week and I miss the mansion already."

I felt his pain. The mansion had been our home. An omniarch in the cellar had allowed us to go anywhere we wanted so long as we could visualize it. "Maybe we can use an omniarch in the control room here."

"If we're going to act, it should be now," Captain Takei said. "It will take them time to move their forces up the mountain and to Arcane University."

"Agreed," Michael said. "We should be able to get a sizable contingent through an omniarch."

"One problem," I said. "We haven't tested any of the omniarches in this way station. They're extremely dangerous to use without extensive testing."

"Darkwater already did the work for us," Shelton said, referring to a now defunct Arcane company once owned by the late Jeremiah Conroy. "Maulin Kassus gave me a list of control rooms with working omniarches, and Queens Gate was one of them."

I felt my spirits lift. "If that's the case, we only need to decide where to stage our troops."

Captain Takei traced his wand in the air and projected a three-dimensional image of the stadium. He highlighted a thick forest bordering a large field near the stadium. "We can use the Dark Forest to shield our arrival and swing around the perimeter." He traced a line.

"How many omniarches are operational?" I asked Shelton.

He squinted as if that would help him remember. "Two, I think."

"I can have my forces through one omniarch in twenty minutes," Michael said.

Captain Takei gave him a confident smile. "I can have the Blue Cloaks through in fifteen."

"This isn't a contest," Elyssa said.

Michael flashed a rare and very small smile. "We'll see about that."

"Ten bucks says the Templars win," Shelton said.

"Oh, my." Takei shook his head. "Where's your sense of Arcane pride, Harry?"

Elyssa took a page out of my book and face-palmed.

"Let's prime the arches," I said, and headed for the control room without further ado.

The control room door led to a raised platform with a large map of the world spread along the wall. The continents only roughly matched those found on the globe today. The stars indicating the locations of Obsidian Arches didn't always line up with cities or civilization of any kind since the arches had been built long before the rise of man.

I turned left from the platform and walked down a long, wide aisle. Smaller arches, each one about the size of an elephant lined the large room. The ones to my left each bore a Cyrinthian number inscribed on the floor in front of them. The numbers correlated to a series of buttons on the side of the map. To the right was an alcove with the omniarches. Unlike their numbered counterparts, these could be used to travel anywhere a person could visualize.

"The second one and the last one," Shelton said, pointing to green markings on the floor in front of two arches.

I stepped inside the silver circle around the first working omniarch, fixed an image of one part of the Dark Forest I remembered well in my mind, and willed a portal to open there. The air between the black columns flickered and a portal split the space. Dense trees and foliage appeared across a short grassy span. One large tree in particular stood out, thanks to a giant bite missing from its trunk.

"Is that the tree the tragon bit?" Elyssa asked.

I nodded. "That monster almost took off my butt."

"Ah, the tragon," Takei said with a fond note in his voice. "We used to steal sheep from Queens Gate and throw them into the forest just so we could get a look at the fabled beast."

"Poor sheep," Elyssa said.

"I'll be right back." I stepped through the portal and paced off a good thirty feet from it, snapped a picture of the woods at that point, and returned through the portal. I walked to the last omniarch and used the picture I'd taken to open a portal. I turned to Michael and Captain Takei. "Prepare your troops for infiltration."

Takei turned to Michael. "No cheating, now."

"No need," the hulking Templar said.

Elyssa, Shelton, and I returned to the front of the room while Michael and Captain Takei rounded up their soldiers. Within a few minutes, two neat double-file lines of troops sprinted through the control room door. The black-clad Templars took the first portal while the Blue Cloaks entered the second. Shelton waved his wand and a holographic timer hovering in the air started for each contingent.

At first, the Templars moved nearly twice as fast as the Blue Cloaks since they were gifted with supernatural physical attributes, but the Arcanes must have cast a fleetness spell because they began to outpace them. Eleven minutes and thirty-two seconds later, both forces were through the portals.

"Yes." Shelton pumped his arm. "Templars barely edged them out by two seconds."

"Well, what did you expect?" Elyssa said in a curt voice.

"Hah, you were rooting for them, weren't you?" he said.

She shrugged. "I couldn't help it."

I would have chimed in with a smartass remark, but anxiety gnawed at my stomach. I went through the portal. The troops remained in a quad-file formation, two columns of Templars next to two columns of Blue Cloaks, hugging the curving forest fringe. Once we left the cover of the trees, a wide grassy field offered no cover between here and our objective.

The Dark Forest was a foreboding place anyone with common sense would avoid. Naturally, I'd been in there a couple of times, once to save Shelton, and once after I'd thrown Aunt Vallaena into a tree. Many of the trees had trunks as thick as a bus standing on one end and towered several stories high. Smaller trees and thick underbrush took up every other square inch of space. I'd only seen a few of the creatures lurking inside that dark place, and they were enough to keep me from going back in unless I had no choice.

The forest spanned a mountain peak behind Arcane University, a massive Romanesque castle with huge round towers at all four corners. Its many soaring spires met the sky to our right. To its left, the library, a long oval building with a glittering diamond dome, stretched along a landscape usually covered with lush gardens. Many of those gardens looked trampled and burnt. Almost directly in front of us loomed Colossus Stadium. Roman columns and arches supported the circular structure. It was easily five times the size of the largest football stadium I'd seen. It had to be large to support the Grand Melee, an annual event where giant golems battled equally huge robots from Science Academy across the valley.

"They really did a number on the gardens," Shelton said.

My eyes followed the swath of destruction across the grassy field and toward Greek Row where the mansion had stood only a few days ago. Daelissa's army had marched straight from the stadium to destroy my home.

Shelton, Elyssa, and I marched to the front of the formation. Michael and Captain Takei talked in low tones, their eyes on the stadium. They turned to us when we reached them.

"Waiting on intel," Michael said.

I looked at the stadium surroundings and couldn't help but reminisce about my first days here. It had been quite a shock and a pleasure all at the same time.

"I don't see many guards," Elyssa said. "They must have committed the bulk of their forces to protecting the way station."

A distant boom sounded and the ground beneath us tremored ever so slightly. A few seconds later the sound repeated itself. A silver marble zipped through the air and hovered in front of Michael. He snatched the ASE—all-seeing eye—from the air and gave it a twist. It spun in mid-air and projected a holographic image recorded inside the stadium.

Michael panned the view.

"Holy farting fairies." Shelton took off his wide-brimmed hat and ran a hand through his hair. "What in the hell are they planning?"

I couldn't tear my eyes from the video. Stone golems three stories high marched through the Obsidian Arch in the center of the stadium, vanishing to an unknown destination. Each one bristled with crystal shards capable of firing destructive spells in all directions.

Arcane university was being used to manufacture unconventional magical weapons.

Chapter 5

The color of the giant golems varied wildly. Some looked jade, others onyx, while the majority appeared to be constructed of gray granite.

The ASE dipped lower for a view through the arch. I recognized the destination almost immediately.

"They're going to Thunder Rock," I said.

Elyssa blew out a breath. "I count at least ten."

As the last monstrosity thudded through, a group of stout golems maybe a third the size of the leviathans returned through the arch, each one bearing blocks of gray granite.

"Construction golems," Shelton said. "They must be importing stone through the arch and building those monsters here."

"The stadium has all the tools they need for building golems that size," Takei said. "They can easily import the raw materials through the arch."

"I see only a skeleton crew." Michael rotated the image, marking locations of people as he went. "We need to lock down this place now before the rest of the enemy forces make it up the mountain."

"Agreed," Takei said. "I dispatched a flying carpet to keep an eye on the retreating forces so we'll know when they're on the way."

The faint sound of crackling branches and the thud of heavy feet caught my ear. This sound wasn't coming from the stadium, it was coming from the Dark Forest. The noise of the departing golems must have caught the tragon's attention. I'd used the creature to fight a giant stone golem once. Used was something of an overstatement. I'd goaded the tragon into chasing me inside the stadium and very narrowly missed becoming its next meal thanks to Elyssa knocking it out.

"Let's hit them hard," I said.

"Those construction golems have been modified," Shelton said. He pointed to large gemstones set in the faceless foreheads of the bulky humanoid shapes. "They're weaponized."

Captain Takei grunted. "He's right. We'll need to take down the golems first."

Michael rotated the recorded image. "I count six."

"We don't have any siege equipment," Takei said. "If we focus all our firepower on the leg of one golem, we might bring it down quickly, unless they've also added magic-resistant charms to them."

"Dollars to donuts they did." Shelton frowned. "There's no sense adding weaponry to those things if they don't have armor."

A distant roar echoed through the forest. I looked in the direction it had come from and sighed. "I think the answer to our problems is on the way."

"Not the tragon again," Elyssa said. "Do you know how many Lancer darts it took to knock that thing out before it ate you?"

A flock of spider-bats burst from a giant oak tree near us with shrieks of panic as the thud of breaking branches grew closer. One of the freaky-looking creatures smacked into the shield surrounding the forest and plummeted onto the ground only a few feet away, all eight of its legs twitching.

I shuddered and turned back to my girlfriend. "I'm not sick with the vampling curse like I was last time, plus I have a few more tricks up my sleeve."

The ground trembled beneath us. A group of saplings bent to the side and a red-scaled reptilian snout poked through. It sniffed the air, plumes of smoke rising from nostrils the size of manhole covers. The rest of the muzzle pressed through the foliage followed by a creature the shape of a Tyrannosaurus rex and nearly twice the size. Tiny wings fluttered uselessly atop the monster's bony, ridged back.

The tragon saw our little army and bellowed loud enough to wake a deaf corpse.

Shelton backed away a few feet despite the shield keeping the tragon inside its forest prison. He looked up at the looming beast and shivered. "You're insane if you think you can make that thing fight for us."

Lowering its head level with us, the tragon regarded me with one beady eye. Seeing its head this close gave me a better appreciation for just how massive it was. Its mouth looked large enough to swallow a car in one bite. It huffed. A blast of fire splashed against the shield. A low rumble built in its throat. Its muzzle parted to display rows of sharp teeth.

"Do you remember me?" I asked it.

The tragon growled louder.

"I think it does." Shelton shook his head. "And it ain't a happy kind of memory." He glanced toward the stadium. "All this noise is going to attract attention."

"Doubtful," Takei said. "The noise from the golems in the stadium attracted the tragon in the first place. I'm sure this isn't the first time it's come here and made a scene."

"A territorial reaction," Michael said. "It sensed something threatening in the vicinity and challenged it."

The tragon wasn't as large as the colossal golems, but it was easily larger than the construction golems. Maybe I was feeling cocky. Maybe I felt a little bit too cool for school after my fight against Aerianas. Maybe I felt like I still had something to prove. Whatever my reason, I decided having the tragon fight for us was the way to go.

The shield was designed to keep monsters in. It didn't keep people out.

So, I stepped across the line.

Before I had a chance to do anything, the tragon ate me.

Even with my supernatural reflexes, I was barely fast enough to put up a bubble shield before everything went dark. I heard teeth grinding against the shield. The tragon's mouth opened and closed as it tried to bite down on the barrier of Murk keeping me alive. It sounded like someone cracking their teeth on a jawbreaker.

I caught a glimpse of Elyssa's stunned face as the tragon opened its mouth wide and chomped down again. My view spun as the spherical shield rolled in the creature's mouth.

"How stupid are you?" I shouted. *How stupid am I?* With an effort of will, I flexed the shield, making it larger and larger until the tragon could no longer keep it in its mouth and dropped me on the ground. It took every ounce of concentration I had to keep the shield in place as I moved. Using the bubble like a giant gerbil wheel, I rolled away from the tragon.

It stalked around me like a cat looking in a fishbowl, obviously trying to figure out how to eat me. It whipped its long tail around and sent me and my shield tumbling through the trees. My concentration broke. The shield vanished. I landed on my feet just as the tragon leapt, claws extended. I dodged behind a tree. Wood splintered as the monster shredded the trunk.

I gripped a fallen tree and swung it hard over the tragon's head. It hit with a loud crack. The impact jarred my arms but did absolutely nothing to hurt the tragon. It was like hitting a person with a toothpick.

The beast reared back its head and roared. I formed a giant slab of ultraviolet murk in the air and slammed it into the monster's head. This time, the tragon staggered backwards. I threw a volley of boulder-sized Murk spheres at the tragon. Each one knocked the monster back a few yards.

"Stop trying to eat me!" I shouted.

It lunged forward. I channeled a solid beam of ultraviolet and speared it into the tragon's snout. The creature made a whimpering sound and fell against a tree, toppling it in the process. Before it could recover, I ran around the monster and used the bony spines on its back like a staircase. The beast spun like a dog chasing its tail in an attempt to throw me off.

I shot a rope of aether at the topmost spine and pulled myself forward. The tragon whipped its head and the tether jerked me forward. My feet left the tragon's back for an instant. Somehow, I locked a foot on a spine and kept myself from falling off. Using the aether rope for balance, I jerked myself back up and made another run for the tragon's head. The beast bucked and roared but I lassoed its top spine with another loop of magical energy, ran between the bat-like wings, and anchored myself.

Judging from the creature's un-tragonlike reaction when I'd nailed it in the nose, I took a slightly informed guess as to how I might maintain control of the thing. Once I took it out of the woods, I definitely didn't want it eating any of my friends or allies. I channeled a solid ring of Murk around the tragon's mouth just above the nostrils.

The creature tried to roar, but its mouth was clamped shut. The sheer power of the monster's jaw pressed against my spell, which, in turn, squeezed my head, much like when I'd fought the stone elemental Aerianas had used against me. But like an alligator—a really, really big alligator—this thing didn't have nearly the force when trying to open its mouth as it did when closing it. Its wings swooshed the air. Relative to the creature's size, they looked ridiculously small. Up close, each one spanned about ten feet— enough to knock me silly if I didn't stay out of the way.

The tragon shook its head violently. Slammed against trees. Ran in circles. Flapped its wings like crazy. I held on tight to its top ridge. I began to wonder if maybe the creature was too stupid to realize it was beaten. For all I knew, it'd keep on running and bucking until it collapsed from exhaustion. It took another several minutes, but the tragon finally stopped and stood still, a high-pitched, unhappy growl in its throat.

"Had enough?" I asked. I'd firmly anchored to the spine at the top of its neck.

It snorted and stomped the ground.

"I know your relatives, the earth dragons," I said. "We get along okay. There's no reason you and I couldn't."

It simply stood still.

"How would you like to destroy a bunch of stuff?" I asked.

Its head tilted and a parietal eye regarded me.

"I can get you out of the forest." I pointed toward the stadium. "We could go on a rampage in there."

It snorted and looked where I was pointing.

I nodded. "Destroy. Kill. Much fun."

"Do you really think it understands you?" Elyssa said from behind me.

I almost jumped out of my pants. I looked back and saw her gripping one of the spines just below the tragon's wings. "When did you come in here?"

"Just now." She shook her head and sighed. "I have a bad feeling about this."

"Imagine how Daelissa's people will feel when they see me and Trago coming."

Her forehead wrinkled. "Now it has a name?"

"*He* has a name." I patted the tragon's neck. "Let's kick some ass, Trago."

"You are the absolute worst at coming up with names." Elyssa situated herself between two of the spines. She kissed my cheek and whispered in my ear. "You're so sexy when you're wrestling giant dinosaurs."

I squeezed her hand. "If I didn't have a war to fight, I'd take you on a ride through the countryside."

She nipped my ear. "If only." A sigh escaped her throat. "Let's go. We don't have a lot of time before the army we pushed back in the way station makes it up here."

I really wanted to make out with her right then and there. How many people could scratch an experience like this off their bucket list? Unfortunately, duty called. "Giddyup, Trago." I gave the tragon a light slap on the neck.

It didn't move.

I wiggled around. "C'mon. Move. Let's go blow up some stuff."

Trago apparently wasn't having any of it. He snorted and started to walk back into the forest.

"So much for being the first tragon whisperer," Elyssa said in a wry tone.

"Seriously?" I shouted. "I offer you the chance to go ham and you just walk back into the woods? Don't you want a little adventure in your life?"

"Either it doesn't understand you, or it's a lot smarter than it looks," Elyssa said.

As the tragon pushed further into the forest, I realized we'd either have to get off and hoof it back, or figure out a quick way to turn around this reptilian tank. Since I knew the thing's snout was a tender spot, I channeled two thick coils of Murk, curving the ends and hooking them into Trago's nose. I pulled on the right rope. The tragon trumpeted with pain. Its head rotated to alleviate the pressure, but I kept pulling until it was forced to turn its entire body.

When we were headed the way I wanted, I released the pressure and the monster stayed on course. We reached the edge of the forest.

"Open the shield, Shelton!" I called down.

He swallowed hard, his Adam's apple bobbing. "I sure as hell hope you got that thing under control."

"Of course," I lied. "Total control."

Shelton waved his staff, and a section of the forest shield flickered off. I nudged the tragon forward. For a second, he didn't move so I willed the hooks in his nose to pull forward. The beast made a whining noise and stepped forward slowly, almost as if he expected to run into the shield at any moment.

The Blue Cloaks and Templars gave the creature a wide berth as it tromped past. Once he reached the grassy field, the tragon looked around. He sniffed the air and looked toward the distant stadium.

"Let's go kick some ass," I said and released the spell keeping the monster's mouth clamped shut.

A low rumble sounded in Trago's throat. He looked back at me for a moment. I figured if he had eyebrows, he would have arched one. His head flicked forward. Without warning, Trago sprang forward at incredible speed. He trumpeted a loud roar. Clods of earth flew up behind us. Every time the tragon panted, I felt heat wash across my face. I looked back and saw the bulk of our troops rushing across the field behind the tragon.

I saw two men exit through the massive archway leading inside the stadium. Their faces lit with horror and they ran screaming back inside. Trago roared. His claws clacked as he ran across the stone-paved walkway around the stadium. My mount rushed through the archway and burst into the arena. Two massive construction golems turned to face the beast. The gems on their heads glowed.

Dazzling light beams shot at my monster. At first, the lasers seemed to do nothing to the tragon's scaly hide, but wisps of smoke appeared, and he roared with pain. Trago leapt through the air, his tiny wings fluttering. I heard Elyssa gasp. I braced for impact just as the tragon's claw slammed into one golem's chest and took it down. Trago roared and a gout of ruby flames melted the golem's head to lava.

The other golem focused on us and fired a beam at the tragon's back. I shielded us, but was forced to release the spell forming the hooks in Trago's snout. My mount turned its head, seemingly oblivious to me and Elyssa, and leapt for the second golem. Elyssa and I grunted in tandem as the tragon landed on its second victim.

"I'm getting off!" she shouted.

My crotch was already rubbing raw from the constant bucking and swaying. "Me too."

The tragon slammed a claw on the second golem's chest and stood still to blast it in the face with a gout of flames that looked like a solar flare. Elyssa and I took the opportunity to abandon ship—err, dinosaur. Channeling a rope of Murk, I lowered us to the ground as Trago turned toward the remaining construction golems converging on him.

The sun disappeared in shadow. I looked up just in time to see a block of granite falling straight for us.

Chapter 6

Trago's tail swept across the ground, sending me and Elyssa tumbling out from under the block of granite. It slammed to earth inches away from us. The tragon didn't seem to notice it had inadvertently saved us as it thudded toward its giant attackers.

Battle mages standing near a half-constructed leviathan golem aimed their staffs at us and fired. Beams of energy rippled through the air. I shielded us from the first volley as we raced for cover behind a massive block of rough-hewn granite. The rest of our forces stormed onto the field. A group of demolition Blue Cloaks raced toward a construction golem as it flanked the tragon.

Trago roared in pain as energy from multiple sources lanced into his tough hide. I peeked out from cover and aimed my fist at the nearest construction golem. Focusing my supernatural vision on the laser gem, I fired a beam of Brilliance at it. The golem fired a laser at the same time. My blast met the energy. The two forces coalesced into a ball of boiling energy. I pushed with everything I had. The energy ball exploded. The laser gem shattered and the golem stumbled backward. Its huge body slammed against the tall wall beneath the stands.

My inner demon stirred. I wondered if it would be able to challenge me even if I was in human form. I braced my consciousness, but my demon side didn't surge as it had when I was manifested.

The demolition Blue Cloaks reached their target. Dodging the giant stone creature's feet as it tried to crush them, they traced runes on its knee with their staffs. One of them gave a signal, and they cleared the area. I expected an explosion. Instead, the stone around the runes crumbled as if it had lost all cohesion. The golem toppled forward and smashed into the ground with a tremendous, earth-shaking thud. A wave of earth and sod slammed into a group of battle mages and sent them screaming to their deaths as Trago incinerated them with a blast of fiery breath.

Templars threw sticky aether bombs on the legs of another golem. Battle mages fired volley after volley of deadly energy at them. One blast caught a Templar and hurled him beneath the feet of the golem. I looked away as the monstrous foot slammed down. A small contingent of crimson-clad vampires appeared from behind stone blocks and engaged another squad of Templars.

Elyssa ran to help. I raced after her, but it was all I could do to keep up. I was beyond exhausted. Hunger for soul essence clawed at my insides.

My girlfriend whipped out her sai swords and intercepted a sword thrust meant to cleave off a fellow Templar's head. She twisted the sword from the vampire's hand. Ducked. Ran him through with both her swords.

I channeled a blade of Brilliance and sliced through an attacker's sword like butter. The vampire snarled, fangs flashing, and dove at me. I moved my sword to intercept, but the blade flickered off. He slammed into me. Somehow, I managed to throw him off. I staggered to my feet just as my attacker did. My insides screamed with hunger. Survival instinct took over. My hands shot up, fingers outstretched.

A look of surprise came over the vampire's face as his hands splayed out in front of him. White light poured from the fingers of his right hand while thick oily essence flowed from the fingers of his left. Some of the numbing exhaustion left me. The vampire cried out in pain as blackened veins pressed hard against the right side of his face, while glowing white veins pulsed on the opposite. Unfortunately, feeding from a vampire was unsatisfying compared to a human. The essence seemed watered down.

I snapped to my senses and released my victim. He fell to the ground in a heap. A final cry faded away and the battlefield went silent except for a crunching noise. I turned to see Trago eating the tragon-fried bodies of battle mages.

Elyssa made a gagging noise. I echoed the sentiment. Shelton skirted wide around the monster, a grimace on his face.

45

Captain Takei approached us. "The people I sent to watch for the enemy troops retreating from the way station just checked in. Apparently, the troops evacuated through omniarch portals only moments ago."

Michael, a grim look on his face, joined us. "Any danger of them using portals to attack us here?"

"I'll have a perimeter of portal-blocking statues established," Elyssa said.

"Good idea," I said. We'd discovered the statues in an artifact warehouse in the depths of Thunder Rock. There were a variety of the statues, each one designed to block a different kind of portal. Some blocked Obsidian Arches while others blocked portals from the different realms accessible through an Alabaster Arch.

Shelton jabbed a thumb toward the tragon. "What about that? We can't just leave it roaming free."

"I'll take him back to the forest," I said. Trago crunched down on a vampire, made a rumble of disgust, and spat out the body.

A female Blue Cloak approached Captain Takei and saluted. "I have the casualty numbers, sir."

He raised an eyebrow. "How bad, lieutenant?"

"Three Templars, one Blue Cloak dead; Eleven Templars, six Blue Cloaks injured." Her eyes looked uneasily at the tragon. "I suppose the tragon is injured as well."

Takei chuckled. He motioned toward the Obsidian Arch in the middle of the arena. "See about making the arch operational, lieutenant. We'll use it to travel back to La Casona."

She snapped a salute and walked away.

I leaned against Elyssa as my knees went weak. I was almost too tired to stand, despite having fed off the vampire. I had no idea how to get Trago back to the forest in this condition. The beast snuffled in the dirt as he searched for more bodies. One of his eyes focused on me and blinked. "We might have to leave Trago loose until I get some rest," I said.

Shelton cast a wistful look in the direction of Greek Row. "I kinda wanted to see the mansion while we were here. Guess that'll have to wait."

A pang of regret hit my stomach. Elyssa and I had been living at Big Creek Ranch, aka the Templar Compound for the Atlanta area.

We'd decided to take a room in the underground complex instead of living in the house aboveground. Even though I got along with her parents these days, it would feel really weird sleeping in the same house as them. "I miss the mansion too," I said.

The Obsidian Arch hummed to life. Captain Takei waved his staff and shot up a blue flare. The Blue Cloaks lined up. Michael pressed the pendant at his collar. "Form up, Templars. We're leaving."

A Templar approached Michael and saluted. "We set up a shield across the exit to the stadium. It should contain the tragon."

Shelton snorted. "If Daelissa's people use this arch, they're in for a big surprise."

I took look at Trago as he munched on another body. "We should go before he runs out of corpses."

The troops evacuated the stadium through the portal in the Obsidian Arch. Elyssa and I lagged behind. I was tired and moving slow.

Trago lifted his bloody muzzle and looked at me as I headed toward the arch. He emitted a querulous sounding roar. I waved goodbye. "Clean your plate!" I said.

We reached the arch and Trago tromped toward us. He stopped, cocked his head to the side and regarded us as we entered the portal. We were the last through. Adam, already back at La Casona, scanned the portal with his arctablet. His eyes went huge when he saw the tragon. "What in the hell is that doing there?"

Trago, meanwhile, butted his head against an uncompleted leviathan golem. He bit the thing's leg and roared like a giant reptilian dog that had just found a chew toy. Adam made a slashing motion across his neck and the Obsidian Arch powered down with a long low hum.

"We recruited some extra help," I said as a yawn cracked my jaw. It was almost midnight in this part of the world.

Adam wrinkled his nose. "You look awful. Head into the control room and take an omniarch portal home for some shuteye."

I wanted to give a jaunty salute, but my arm refused to rise. Elyssa practically carried me into the control room. I vaguely remembered seeing the portal open before passing out.

Elyssa was already out of bed and probably going through her morning exercises when I woke up the next morning. I found a small scroll tied with a purple ribbon on her pillow. A grin stretched my mouth. I opened the scroll and read it.

Every day with you is a gift. I love you, Justin.

Elyssa and I had taken to leaving each other little notes like this. We were both so busy it seemed we hardly had any alone time anymore. We were both so tired at night, we hadn't even had a decent make-out session in a while. It was almost as if we had nine-to-five jobs and three kids.

The notification light on my arcphone blinked at me. My phone, Nookli, had been fried from a malaether explosion, but Adam and Shelton had managed to fix it. I ignored the notification indicator and wrote a note for Elyssa on a fresh sheet of parchment.

You, me, dinner and a movie. I miss having you all to myself. I love you, babe.

I rolled the note, bound it with the purple ribbon she'd used, and left it on her pillow.

With a loud groan, I flicked the screen on my phone and saw a message from Dad.

Remember the ball tonight. Dress nice and pretend you're not an ass.

I ran a hand down my face and sighed. Despite the full night of sleep, I still felt drained. It was hardly surprising considering how much I'd been through. A yawn caught me off guard. I let it ride its course and opened my email to read through a slew of reports.

Elyssa's father, Thomas Borathen, had taken troops to Australia to help Commander Taylor of the Southern Australian Legion deal with the former Northern Australian Legion, which was now in cahoots with the Synod. His liaison's email to me reported that they'd captured or killed most of the NAL leadership and were putting their troops through a truth-saying process to weed out the Synod loyalists. Their next step would be securing the Three Sisters way station, the only one in Australia with an Alabaster Arch.

I flicked to the next email, this one from Cinder, a lifelike golem created by a Seraphim named Fjoeruss, aka Mr. Gray.

The aether pods have processed ten more Darklings. Joss and Otaleon are doing an excellent job of tutoring them, but we do not have enough nom volunteers to feed them all. Please meet with me at your earliest convenience to discuss options. –C

I looked at my calendar. It was already stuffed with items. Ryland and Stacey had arranged a meeting with the lycan Alpha, Colin McCloud for tomorrow. I was also supposed to meet with Captain Takei to discuss options for dealing with Cyphanis Rax and installing a new Arcane Council.

Scrolling down, I realized every day was filled with one operation or another. We'd prioritized the Obsidian Arch way stations we needed to control for more effective logistics and scheduled the days for our military actions. It felt strange to make an appointment for fighting battles. *Killing enemies on a schedule.* All of our military actions led toward securing the Grand Nexus. As the primary Alabaster Arch in this realm, Eden, it was the only way Daelissa could open a gateway to Seraphina. Since she now had the Chalon, the key to activate the nexus, there was almost nothing standing in her way.

Thankfully, the nexus was blocked for the time being. I'd sent my friends—now Templar soldiers—to put portal-blocking statues in the way station, thus keeping Daelissa from utilizing it. Even so, it was only a matter of time before she and her minions discovered how to open the gateway. We had to secure all the way stations with Alabaster Arches before that happened.

I scanned the subjects of the other emails. Adam's sister, Felicia, had sent me a request to rescue vampires from the enemy army. Most of them were just kids who thought being a supernatural creature was the coolest thing in the world until their sires used compulsion to make them fight battles as cannon fodder.

Rescuing vampires was low on my list, so I skipped her email and tried not to feel terrible about it. Saving them meant killing the vampire brood sires, and they were just too hard to get at, especially during the heat of battle. So far, our spies were having little luck finding the lairs where the Red Syndicate leaders were hiding, and we didn't have the manpower to widen our search.

Training Darklings, however, was at the top of my list. They'd be our only hope against Daelissa and her Brightling army.

"Nookli, reschedule my ten A.M. appointment for tomorrow," I told my phone.

My phone responded at once. "Justin, there are three Indian restaurants nearby. Would you like a reservation?"

Sometimes I had to wonder if my phone was just messing with me. I repeated my request. This time, it got it right.

I looked around the gray-walled concrete room. The underground Templar barracks weren't much to look at. I remembered the mornings of waking up at the mansion. Elyssa and I would head downstairs to find a fresh batch of Shelton's pancakes and Bella's famous Colombian omelets waiting on the table. Shelton would make some smartass comment while Bella would read a tragic news story aloud and make sympathetic noises.

Cutsauce, the first hellhound I'd summoned, would run around our ankles, yipping like crazy and begging for a bite of our breakfast. Now he was hanging out with Cinder in El Dorado.

When Mom and Ivy had started living in the mansion, the place had livened up even more. I really missed having my extended family around.

I took a shower in the communal bathroom. The place was already empty by eight in the morning since the Templars didn't mess around when it came to waking up at ungodly hours. After dressing, I took the levitator—a magical elevator—up to the mess hall and grabbed some grub. Shelton and Bella were already eating there.

"Good morning, sunshine," Shelton said. "You realize you missed the morning reveille by about two hours, don't you?"

"Oh, hush, Harry," Bella said, looking at me over the morning paper.

"Is that the local newspaper?" I asked, looking at the headlines.

She nodded. "The noms are up in arms about Kobol Prison."

I read the front page. *Military Won't Say What Destroyed Choppers.* I whistled.

"Idiot battle mages," Shelton said. "The blast from the malaether crucible was enough to attract the nom military, but they still could've tossed up some interdiction spells to keep the choppers away. Instead, they blew 'em up and brought the full attention of the United States military on Kobol."

"There's an Obsidian Arch at Kobol," I said. "There was all sorts of paranormal activity, and god knows how many null cubes with cherubs left out there."

"It was only a matter of time before this war caught the noms' attention," Bella said. "Dealing with it will be difficult."

"Something should be done. What if they release a cherub?" My stomach clenched. "The last thing we need is a world full of shadow people."

Shelton took a drink of coffee and shrugged. "Ain't nothing we can do about it now. Either Daelissa or the U.S. military controls Kobol now. We'd have to invade."

The notification for a new email chimed. I flicked on the screen. It was from Christian Salazar, commander of the Colombian Templars and addressed to me, Elyssa, and the others on our command staff.

Several captured prisoners from our latest operations stated Daelissa has not made an appearance for several days as she usually does. One prisoner revealed under questioning that Daelissa may have already activated the Grand Nexus. Will keep everyone apprised of information as it unfolds.

Chapter 7

The tight feeling in my stomach went even tighter.

"What is it?" Shelton asked.

Daelissa could be in Seraphina right this moment! I turned my phone to him so he could read the email.

Bella's eyes went wide. "I thought opening a portal to Seraphina with the Grand Nexus was blocked by those statues."

"Bah." Shelton backhanded the air. "It's just a rumor. If Daelissa really went back to the motherland, we'd be ass-deep in angel feathers."

I took a few deep breaths to quell the fear rising in me. "I hope so." I took a bite of a sausage and chewed on it while my mind ran in circles. "Bella, would you get together a small group of people to monitor nom news? I need to know how aware the humans are of current paranormal events." I turned to Shelton. "Get ahold of MacLean. Ask him if his Illuminati contacts can find out how much the nom government knows."

"You should also ask Kassallandra and David," Shelton said. "From what he told me, the Daemos have a small army of informants in governments across the world."

My father, David, had once told me the same thing. A supernatural race with a master's degree in seduction could get just about any kind of information they wanted. I finished my breakfast, said goodbye to my friends, and headed for the underground hangar in the Templar compound.

The levitator deposited me in what looked like a massive underground garage. Plain boxes called sliders were parked in neat rows. Each one was equipped with flying spells much like the ones used by flying carpets, and illusion spells to make them look like nom aircraft such as helicopters or small planes. In a remote corner of the garage were two large square outlines of painted yellow dashes.

A pedestal with an arctablet fastened to it stood in front of the square.

"Justin Slade," I said to the tablet.

The screen blinked on and traced me with an array of lights. Adam, a former conspiracy theorist and master magic hacker, had written a special authentication program for the device.

"Wait time for a portal is four minutes and thirty seconds," the tablet said. A timer appeared on the screen and counted down.

I sighed, took out Nookli, and browsed the Overnet, aka the aethernet—the Overworld version of the internet—while I waited. "Man, it sucks not having my own omniarch anymore." I sent a text to Elyssa and told her I was going to El Dorado to visit Cinder. She didn't respond right away since she was probably leading some of our newer troops through training exercises right about now.

A portal flickered into being a few seconds before the countdown ended. I stepped through and into the control room at La Casona.

"Destination?" a young male Templar asked me.

"I got it," I said. Before he could protest, I touched the silver circle around the omniarch and willed it to close. The static rush of aether filled the air. I filled my mind with an image of the control room in El Dorado. The air between the arch slashed open to the exact area I'd imagined. I stepped through and willed the portal to close. It narrowed to a thin scar in the air and vanished. The control room was located deep underground beneath the dead city of El Dorado. Located in the southern jungles of Colombia, the ancient civilization had once been ground zero for the Seraphim invasion, as evidenced by giant jeweled murals slaves had built for their otherworldly masters.

I looked at the Alabaster Arch dominating the control room and wondered what would happen if I tried to open a gateway to Seraphina right this minute. If Daelissa had attuned the Grand Nexus with the Chalon, it should mean the rest of the Alabaster Arches would be attuned to the same realm.

"Hello, Justin."

I almost jumped out of my skin. I turned and saw Cinder standing behind me. He wore his standard gray suit—the same one favored by the gray men, the golems created by Mr. Gray.

He tilted his head slightly. "Ah, I surprised you. I am sorry if, as you sometimes say, I made you poop your pants."

I snorted. "I've nearly crapped myself so much lately, what's another squirt in the pants?"

"I had not realized you were being literal," Cinder said, his face attempting to mimic a concerned expression. Instead, he looked like someone who'd just bitten into a lemon. "The cupids go through an alarming number of diapers, but I'm certain I could find a pair that fit you."

It took me a few seconds to respond, because I wasn't sure if Cinder was attempting humor or actually trying to be helpful. It made me realize how hard it had to be for him in his attempts to act more human. An act of mad-scientist magic had given him sentience and emotion, but it hadn't given him an instruction booklet on using it and fitting in.

"I'll be okay," I assured him and motioned toward the control room door. "I came to talk to you about the cupids."

"Of course." He motioned toward several massive stacks of null cubes near the front of the control room. They looked as if they were made of frosted glass, but the material was designed to turn transparent or opaque to keep the horrific prisoners inside from seeing outside.

I shivered at the thought of the creatures within. The husks—I'd nicknamed them cherubs—were all that remained of Seraphim caught in the blast when someone forcibly removed the Chalon from the Grand Nexus during the Seraphim War. The Seraphim called it the Desecration for good reason, since it had wiped out everyone regardless of supernatural or mortal affiliation and turned them into shadow creatures that craved the light from any living creature they could lay their nubby little mitts on.

Cinder led me to the cubes. "We have finished sorting the cubes taken from Kobol Prison."

"Excellent." I stopped in front of the stacks. The Darkling cherub cubes were stacked to the left, the Brightlings to the right. Only one cube stood apart. A device called an affinity sphere allowed us to gauge the alignment of the cherubs inside the cubes to either Murk or Brilliance and thus determine if they were Darklings or Brightlings. The cherub in the lone cube, however, had registered right in the middle—the gray—and none of us knew what to make of it. "Any idea how many cherubs we have?"

"Indeed." Cinder paused as if accessing something. "We have seven-hundred and twenty-three Darklings, five-hundred and eighty-one Brightlings, and one anomaly. Shall we go to the cupids?"

"Sure."

We exited the room and entered the large cavern. An Obsidian Arch should have towered in the center. Instead, there were two massive leyworms—earth dragons. The red-scaled monster was Altash. I didn't know his purple girlfriend's name, so I referred to her as Lulu. We passed a trench carved in the rock by their smaller *compadres*. The cupids—infantile creatures with oil-black skin— grasped at us with nubby hands. Round, tooth-lined orifices in their otherwise faceless heads screeched with agony. "Dah-nah! Dah-nah!"

The hairs on the back of my neck felt like they were trying to uproot themselves and run away. I was happy to get past the little horrors and leave their screeches behind.

Joss and Otaleon emerged from between the scaly coils of the dragons and approached us.

"How's the training?" I asked them.

Joss looked rather pale. "It proceeds." He gagged, swallowed with effort.

"He just fed," Otaleon explained.

Nightliss told me Darklings could feed from humans, but unlike their Brightling counterparts, it was repulsive to them. Disgusting or not, feeding from humans definitely accelerated the return of the cupids back to maturity. These two had only been boys a week ago. As the angels physically aged, their old memories returned as well.

"As I explained, we have very few human volunteers," Cinder said.

Otaleon nodded. "We can't feed from a person more than once a day or we risk damage to their soul."

"Do you feel more powerful now?" I asked.

Joss's cheeks puffed out like he'd just barfed in his mouth. His face went absolutely green before he rushed a few feet away and lost his lunch—or whatever meal he'd last eaten.

Otaleon ignored the episode as if he'd seen it a dozen times before. "We're definitely feeling stronger, at least once we get past the initial nausea."

"We have several new cupids." Cinder watched Joss with a neutral face. "I am worried we will be unable to bring them to maturity quickly enough to counter those Daelissa revives."

Daelissa had been reviving husks at her own facility in Kobol Prison. We'd destroyed half the prison, but not the part housing her facility. Even so, we'd stolen the majority of the husks she'd stored in the loading bay. Unless the U.S. military had taken over the building, it was possible her aether pods were pumping out more cupids every day.

"Have you found Maulin Kassus?" I asked. The man had tried to kill me in the past, but thanks to Altash, I'd captured him. Unfortunately, I'd had to make a deal with the scoundrel since he knew how to make the aether pods, and also had a lot of other useful information. I'd last seen him when Daelissa attacked the mansion, but nobody had seen him since.

"I saw Kassus enter the portal back to the mansion when we were evacuating the cubes," Cinder said. "He returned, but disappeared sometime thereafter."

Either he'd chosen the confusion as a convenient time to make a run for the hills, or someone else who had a gripe with the former leader of the Black Robe Brotherhood had done away with the man.

Kassus wasn't the immediate problem anyway. I paced up and down a few times trying to figure out where we could find noms who not only knew the Overworld existed, but would be willing to allow supernatural beings to feed from them. Felicia Nosti's boyfriend, Larry, came to mind, but he was only one person. He'd been accidentally exposed to supernatural elements and had to take something Elyssa jokingly referred to as Overworld rehab, where noms were told in no uncertain terms that they couldn't reveal the existence of the supernatural to others.

A light bulb blinked on in my head.

My fingers snapped a second later. "What about the people the Templars put through Overworld initiation classes?"

Cinder touched his chin. "That is an interesting proposal. From what Katie told me, many of those exposed were rather willing to have vampires drink their blood."

"Vamp groupies," I said with a grimace. "Who knows, maybe having Seraphim feed from them will sound more glamorous." I looked at our environs and wondered how difficult it would be to convince anyone to come to a strange place like this so otherworldly beings could feed on their soul essence. Then I remembered the strange places I'd gone during my Kings and Castles LARP—live-action role-playing—days. Lovers of the supernatural were a hell of a lot harder to scare off than typical noms.

I looked at Cinder. "Do you have access to the list of exposed noms?"

"No," he replied. "The list would reside in the Custodian archives."

The Custodians were an independent department of the Templars assigned to clean up supernatural messes and keep them hidden from the noms. Unfortunately, their operations had been fractured after the split between Thomas Borathen and the Synod. It just so happened that I knew someone in the Custodians even if we weren't BFFs.

"Let me make a few phone calls," I said, and paced away a few steps. I quickly found the number I needed.

"Superintendent Gaetano speaking," said a female with a saucy Italian accent.

"Grand Poobah Slade here," I replied.

"What have you destroyed?" she asked in a wary tone. "My resources are limited."

I chuckled. "Amazingly, I haven't destroyed anything you need to worry about, Fausta."

She let out a breath. I heard someone speaking in the background. "No, that is all wrong. Cover the fang marks and arrange the bodies like I showed you to make it look like a mugging."

"Look," I said, "I probably caught you at a bad time—"

"It is always at a bad time," she snapped. "There are vampires running rampant thanks to this war you are fighting. There are too many of them for their brood sires to keep under control, and they're treating noms like cattle to be slaughtered." Her voice rose to a near shout. "Do you know how many murders we've had to cover up these past few days? I am—" I heard her teeth clack. She sucked in a deep breath and let it out. "I apologize, Justin. I thought I could handle anything, but the hidden underbelly of this war is terrible."

"I know." I didn't know what else to say. I was blowing things up while Daelissa's minions did whatever they could to keep snowballing their forces. Fausta and her comrades had to clean up the toxic waste afterward. I wasn't sure if the Custodians still under Synod jurisdiction were doing the same thing or not. "I have what is hopefully a simple question."

"I will help you if I can."

"The Darklings need noms to feed from."

Faust growled. "Where are you going with this?"

"Do you have access to the list of noms who had to attend those rehabilitation classes for people exposed to the supernatural?"

"You want to force these people—"

I cut her off before she took off on a rant. "Absolutely not. I want to ask for volunteers. Since they already know about the Overworld, I won't be exposing innocents."

She went silent for several seconds. "I suppose your plan is not insane."

"High praise," I replied dryly. "Can you help me?"

"I have a small database of exposed noms, perhaps forty."

"That's it?"

"I do not have access to the main Custodian database."

My heart sank. "Let me guess. It's in their headquarters surrounded by death traps and dinosaurs."

"You are very melodramatic for a man." Fausta sounded almost amused. "The Custodians are not at war with one another like the Templars, even if my division is not officially recognized."

"What are you saying?"

"I have contacts within the bureau. Perhaps someone would be willing to copy the database for us."

"Ah," I said. "Spies. I like it."

"I will ask around. In the meantime, I will send you my list." She sighed. "Please be careful with my rescues. I do not want to hear of any mistreatment."

"Rescues?"

"It is what some of us call the noms we save."

I scratched my head. "Sounds like you're saving puppies from the pound."

"Exactly," she said in a tight voice. "They are very much like innocent puppies when it comes to the Overworld."

I couldn't disagree. "Thanks, Fausta."

"Goodbye, Grand Poobah Slade." She disconnected.

A moment later, I received an email with the database of rescues. I called Felicia Nosti.

"Justin!" she squealed.

"Hey, Felicia. I have a favor to ask."

"Anything for you."

I laid out the basics of the volunteer program in a nutshell and then explained how she could help. "I think a lot of the people who volunteer will be vampire groupies."

"Vamp tramps," she said in a disgusted voice. "They'll jump at the chance to let supers feed on them."

"You're also a vampire and an attractive woman, so—"

"You think I'm attractive?" she asked in a hopeful voice.

I repressed a sigh. In a sense, Felicia was my rescue. The way she saw it, I'd saved her from Maximus and also saved her from dying to the vampling curse even though I hadn't been the only one participating in the operation. She viewed me as her knight in shining armor.

"Of course you're attractive," I said. "I think you can convince more people to participate because you're a cute vampire."

"Oh," she said in a slightly disappointed tone. "Want me to use compulsion?"

"Absolutely not," I said.

"Good." Her voice lightened. "You're such a great man, Justin."

I decided it was safest to ignore her praise. "I'll send you the list. Let me know how it goes."

"You got it."

I sent her the database after I ended the call, and updated Cinder and the others on the progress.

"This is excellent news, Justin." Cinder approximated a smile.

Joss and Otaleon didn't seem overjoyed. They exchanged uneasy glances.

Admittedly, the thought of dozens of nauseated Darklings barfing all over El Dorado made me a little queasy. "Do you have any idea why it's so hard for Darklings to feed?" I asked them.

Joss shrugged. "We tried it during the first war, but it was too hard."

"We were fighting so much it was hard to find time to feed," Otaleon added. "It might take a Brightling a few short minutes to consume a human, but since we are constantly fighting nausea, it takes us nearly an hour to reach the limit with a human."

"How do you know when you've hit the danger zone?" I asked.

"You can feel it," Joss said. "It is like feeling a bottle of water lighten as you consume it."

"How long does it take a human to recover?" I asked.

"It depends on the human," he said. "Happy people recover very quickly. Those who are prone to sadness are much slower."

"Is there any way to sweeten the essence?" I asked.

The two Darklings looked at each other. Otaleon spoke. "I am sorry, Justin. I don't think there is any way to make it pleasant. Even if you procure more humans, it is unlikely we and our brethren will ever be able to feed enough to match the Brightlings in power."

Chapter 8

I hated hearing the hard truth, but I'd learned that complaining about it didn't solve the problem. I decided it was time to put myself in Joss and Otaleon's shoes so I could understand where they were coming from.

"Do you have a human I can feed from?" I asked Cinder.

He tilted his head. "You wish to feed?"

"I need to test something." I had a suspicion, but needed to know for sure.

"I believe so," Joss said. He entered the gap in the dragon coils and returned a moment later with an old man.

"Howdy there," the man said in a lively tone. "What can I do ya fer?"

"I'm Justin," I said, offering my hand.

He grinned and gave my hand a strong shake. "I'm Abe. You must be the guy everyone keeps talking about."

I smiled. "That depends on if what they're saying is good or bad."

He winked. "I really appreciate this opportunity. I was wasting away in a retirement home when my granddaughter told me I could serve our great country." Abe chuckled. "Sorry, I meant the world. I served in Vietnam, so I know about war, son. It took a tremendous toll on me, but your people here have cured most of my ills and given me a purpose in life."

I felt my eyes moisten, and cleared my throat to ward off the surge of emotion. "I appreciate your help more than you could imagine."

He saluted. "Makes me proud, son."

"We don't salute around here," I said with a smile.

"Hah. My granddaughter said you weren't all that formal."

"Who is your granddaughter?" I asked.

His chest puffed out. "Katherine. She's training to be a Templar, and I sure am proud of that little girl."

I looked at Cinder. "Do I know a Katherine?"

"I believe you know her by her nickname," Cinder replied. "Katie."

"I never knew her name was Katherine." I also wondered if she'd asked permission from anyone before exposing her nom grandfather to the supernatural. Then again, did it even matter at this point? The whole world was going to be exposed if we didn't stop Daelissa. There were plenty of people like Abe who felt old and useless. We could give them a chance to feel important again. Another idea occurred to me even though the Custodians would hate me for it. "Do you have other friends who'd like to help save the world?"

Abe's eyes lit with pleasure. "Son, I could get you a whole platoon if you want."

I rubbed my hands together like an evil genius who'd just come up with the best world domination plan ever. "If you could do that, it would be amazing."

"I'm on it, sir."

I turned to Cinder. "Help Abe recruit more volunteers. Make use of the omniarch to go where you need to go."

"How interesting," Cinder said. "I will be delighted to help."

Abe's grin stretched from ear to ear. "Now, was that why you wanted me out here, or can I help you with something else?"

"I need to test our feeding procedure," I said.

He held out his left hand. "Be my guest."

I held out my hand and let instinct take over. Smoky ultraviolet wisps flowed from his fingers and into mine. At first, I felt nothing more than a tingle. My right arm twitched as it tried to rise. Since I could access both Brilliance and Murk equally, it seemed my body wanted to feed from both sides of the spectrum. I forced it to keep feeding from only the dark.

A moment later, I felt as though I'd been riding in the belly of a boat on storm-tossed seas after eating a slab of salt pork with a side of boiled okra. My gorge rose and it took tremendous effort to keep my breakfast down. The more I fed, the worse I felt. I cut off the feed. I let my right arm extend. Milky white essence trailed from Abe's fingertips into mine.

The nausea slowly subsided until it was gone. Within a few minutes, I felt heady, giddy, and almost drunk. My left arm tried to rise, but I forced it down and flooded myself with Brilliance. I sensed a strange lightness in Abe's aura and released him immediately.

He staggered back a foot and shook his head. "Whoa. I ain't never felt that during a drain."

"Your eyes are white," Joss said to me. "I have seen this before when Brightlings feed."

I felt high on power. I felt as though I could rule the world or destroy it as I saw fit. It reminded me of the feeling I'd once had texting someone while I was drunk. At the time, it had seemed my words could fix everything when in reality they'd further demolished all my hopes and dreams. If this was what Brightlings felt when they fed from humans, it was no wonder they'd enslaved the world. It was no wonder Daelissa was insane.

At the same time, I knew exactly how to protect the Darklings from nausea. I had Joss bring out two more noms and tried to show him and Otaleon how to feed from both sides of the spectrum. Try as they might, neither one of them could draw more than a tiny trickle of Brilliance. I finally tried something Mom had once done to help me.

During a battle in Australia, the enemy had tried to detonate a malaether crucible. The explosion would have demolished the local Templar headquarters. Ivy had detonated the bomb prematurely, but we'd been at the fringe of the blast. I'd shielded us, but hadn't been strong enough to maintain it for very long. Mom had put her hand against my back and bolstered my spell with her own energy.

I tried to do the same with Joss as he fed. Pressing a hand to his back, I sent Brilliance coursing into him. After a few minutes, his green face turned a normal shade of olive, and he looked at me in surprise.

"I don't feel sick anymore."

I did the same for Otaleon with identical results.

"How interesting," Cinder said. "It appears balancing the two types of essence are the answer."

"I can't be here to help everyone," I said. "For that, we'd need Brightlings."

"Surely there must be a way for us to learn to feed as you do," Joss said.

There was only one other Seraphim I knew of who might be able to do so, but he and I weren't on friendly terms. On the other hand, I'd been planning to visit him in a last-ditch effort to form an alliance, even if it seemed like a lost cause. It seemed I had no choice but to move up my schedule and plan a visit.

I turned to Cinder. "Let me know how the recruiting goes. Give the new volunteers any healing they need." I had a feeling most of them were receiving crappy healthcare in veterans' hospitals or nursing homes.

"I will speak with Meghan and tell her to expect more patients," Cinder said.

"Thanks." I nodded at the others. "I'll be in touch." I shook Abe's hand and the hands of the other two volunteers. "Thank you for everything you've done. Maybe we can save the world after all."

Abe grinned. "We've got your back, son."

I took out my arcphone, took a picture, and used Adam's app to schedule a portal to take me back to the Ranch. After a ten minute wait, a portal appeared. I stepped through back to La Casona, and opened another portal back to the Ranch. Once there, I phoned someone I hadn't spoken with for some time.

"Mr. Slade," said a nasal, nerdy voice. "What can I do for you?" Lornicus didn't seem the least bit surprised by my phone call.

This golem was the most lifelike creation of Mr. Gray's I'd seen. Unlike the gray men, his skin was a natural peach tone. Unlike Cinder, Lornicus used emotion as fluently as any person I knew. He could also be something of a supercilious ass.

"I'd like to speak with Fjoeruss. Can you arrange a meeting?"

"I'm afraid he is quite busy, Mr. Slade." Lornicus mumbled as if looking up the schedule. "Ah, yes. His calendar is simply packed."

I felt my jaw clench and forced it to relax so I could talk without sounding angry. "In case he hasn't noticed, there's a war going on."

"He is very much aware of the conflict between you and Daelissa."

I waited for him to continue, but my pause was wasted. "It's not just between me and Daelissa. Some of her minions blew up a fleet of military helicopters and she's preparing to take over the world. Last I checked, Mr. Gray lives in Eden along with the rest of us."

"Mhmm. I'm familiar with the conflict at Kobol Prison." Lornicus sounded unimpressed. "What is it you wish to discuss, Mr. Slade?"

"I'd rather do it face-to-face."

"As I said—"

Anger flashed-fried my manners. "Don't make me hunt him down."

Lornicus made a tutting noise. "Such bad manners. Surely you've learned that honey catches more flies than vinegar."

He wants me to wheel and deal as usual. "Is there something you want?"

"Information, as usual, is highly prized, provided you have anything of interest."

"What will I receive in return?"

Lornicus made a pleased sound. "Face time with Fjoeruss."

I decided to go with the most shocking news I had even if it wasn't a certainty. Mr. Gray would certainly be interested to know Daelissa had the Chalon and might have already slipped into Seraphina. "It just so happens I have some very interesting news. If you want to hear it, you'll have to wait until Fjoeruss is present."

"Such vague assurance is unacceptable. I may already possess the information."

"I guess you'll just have to wait, then." I shrugged. "If it turns out the information is redundant, I have plenty more where that came from." Mr. Gray had a network of golem spies, many of whom looked like real people even if they didn't have much of a personality to fall back on. We had measures in place to detect them, making me feel confident Lornicus wouldn't already know what I planned to tell him.

Lornicus said nothing for a long moment. "Very well, I will arrange the meeting and text you the information."

"I'll be waiting." I disconnected and took a deep breath to ease the knot of tension in my chest. If simply meeting with Mr. Gray required a payment of information, how much would it cost to ask him how he fed on both sides of the spectrum? I didn't like the way Lornicus rigged the pay scale, but there wasn't much I could do about it.

I went to the war room. With Thomas and the other Templar leaders out on various missions, the place was empty for once. I reviewed footage from our most recent conflicts, and studied the map of Obsidian Arches. We controlled a little over half a dozen, though most were of little strategic value. Out of all the Alabaster Arch nodes, we controlled only El Dorado and soon, I hoped, also the Three Sisters in Australia.

Daelissa might be in Seraphina.

The thought itched in the back of my mind, but I didn't dare do anything to investigate the rumor on my own. If I went to El Dorado and the arch there did open to the Seraphim home world, there might be guards waiting on the other side. Then Daelissa would know that we knew and, knowing would be half the battle—at least for her. I needed to put together a strike force. If the Alabaster Arch opened to Seraphina, and if there were Brightlings waiting on the other side, we had to put them down quickly.

I could only hope that any Brightlings on the other side hadn't fed from humans and wouldn't be nearly as powerful as Daelissa. I took out the tablet and began plotting our next move.

"There you are," Elyssa said.

I flinched and looked up to see her standing at the door. "Sorry. Did you text me?" I glanced at my phone and saw a missed text from her.

She walked over and kissed me. "I figured you'd be in here."

I sighed. "All this responsibility makes me feel like I'm nineteen going on fifty."

"Believe me, I know exactly what you're saying." She dropped into a seat next to me and took a sip from a foil blood bag. "Dealing with these noobs all day makes me want to scream." She shook her head. "Even with our recruits, I don't know how we'll get the numbers we need to match the Synod if it comes down to an all-out battle."

"Considering all the vampires they have, it would be impossible to match them man for man."

"I know." Her lips quirked into a wistful expression. "I'd take a trained Templar over a dozen untrained vampires any day, but they outnumber us by a lot more than a dozen to one."

"Is there any way to increase recruitment?"

"Even if there were, we don't have the personnel to train them all."

I bit my lip in thought, stood, and paced. There weren't any easy answers in this conflict. "I'm running into a similar problem when it comes to feeding the Darklings."

She raised an eyebrow. "How's that operation going?"

I shrugged. "I guess if you consider a few nauseated Darklings a success, then we're doing great." I told her about my plan to recruit vets and noms who'd been exposed to the supernatural.

Elyssa's eyes lit. "Hold on a second. What if we could recruit those same vets into the Templars?"

I felt my forehead wrinkle. "These guys are super old. They'd have to go into battle using their walkers."

She laughed. "Not if Nightliss blessed them."

"Would they revert to youth again?"

"I don't know what would happen."

It wasn't a bad idea, but there were plenty of other issues I could think of off the top of my head. "Some of those vets have mental issues. Some of them have seen horrible things."

"I'd be willing to bet many wouldn't want to fight either," Elyssa said. "If it were up to me, I'd recruit straight from the nom military. Unfortunately, that's just not an option."

I told her about the possibility of Daelissa already being back in Seraphina and my idea for seeing if we could open a portal to Seraphina. If the Grand Nexus wasn't attuned to anything, the other Alabaster Arches would simply open a portal to it. If it was attuned to another realm, then the other arches would open a gateway there.

Elyssa's lips curled into a grimace. "We are so screwed if she's already back there."

"No doubt." My phone chimed, letting me know it was time to go back to Kassallandra's crib in the Swiss Alps for the formal ball. It would be my last chance to recruit more Daemos, so I had no choice but to put on my best face.

I held out my elbow for Elyssa. "Shall we go get gussied up?"

She groaned, sucked the blood pack dry, and then looped her arm in mine. "Let's do this, Prince Charming."

I wiped a fleck of blood from her lips and kissed her. "As you wish."

Chapter 9

Daelissa

Waterfalls sparkled down the side of Mount Hein far below the cottony clouds of the skyway carrying Daelissa, Qualan, and Lanaeia toward Zbura.

The capitol city of the Seraphim Empire sprawled across the great plateau spanning the mountaintop. Where it had run out of room, alabaster houses dotted the steep slope. Large islands of earth called skylets hovered in the air around the mountain. Each skylet had been uprooted from the ground by the immense tides of aether flowing through Seraphina. The same currents of aether now suspended them. Eden lacked so many wonders of home. Her throat knotted with joy to see her fair land again.

Even with the skyway, the journey from the Grand Nexus, where it resided atop the Cliffs of Eternity, had taken longer than expected to finally reach this place.

I am home, but everything has changed.

Zbura had been a quarter this size the last she'd seen it. It most certainly had not possessed the great crystal palace dominating the highest point near the mountain peak. A plain government building for the Trivectus had formerly occupied that land.

Despite the differences, Daelissa could barely contain her glee.

"The city among the clouds," Lanaeia said in a quiet voice. Her eyes took in the fluffy halo a third of the way down the mountain. "It is so different than I remember."

"Of course it's different," Qualan snarled. "We have been gone thousands of years."

Lanaeia tucked a lock of her glossy white hair behind an ear and ignored the other Brightling's outburst. "I think the palace is lovely."

Daelissa had left her human entourage back at the gateway to Eden, but brought the two revived Brightlings with her. She could already feel the madness fading from her mind as her home realm restored her. Even so, she felt a familiar ache in the palm of her right hand. She'd practically gorged on soul essence before leaving Eden. She flexed her hand and examined the small scars on her palm. *The pain is of no concern.* She returned her gaze to the city. *Raising my army is all that matters now.*

The moving cloudbank of the skyway took them above the palace. If Skazaeleus was still in power, he would likely be there.

She willed the skyway to take them to the palace doors. A cloud parted from the main path and descended at a steep angle, upsetting a triangular formation of doves. The cooing of the doves was the only other noise besides the wind at this altitude. As the cloudbank carried them closer, the sounds of the city seeped through the calm. Unlike Eden, there were no sounds of automobile traffic or industry. The city had no roads, only pedestriums on the ground and the skyways above. Machines did not play a major part in life on Seraphina—at least not in the human sense. Instead, everything was aided by channeling through gemstones.

"Why did we never build skyways in Eden?" Lanaeia asked. She knelt and ran a hand through the billowing mist.

"I believe we once did," Daelissa replied. "It is why so many noms believe we lived in a cloud city." She expected Qualan to make a disparaging remark, but he was lost in his own world again, judging from the tears streaming down his face. The Slade boy had incinerated his twin sister, Qualas, so she could hardly blame the man—the seraph—for his grief.

It had been too long since she'd spoken Cyrinthian or thought in native Seraphim terms. She would have to adjust some of her vocabulary. In Eden, she found herself referring to even male Seraphim as men when, in fact, they were seraphs, while females were called seras. In the old days, referring to a Seraphim as a man or woman was a mortal insult.

The skyway deposited them outside the palace gates instead of inside as Daelissa had expected. She took a deep breath to calm her mind in anticipation of the madness, which usually consumed her when presented with an obstacle. Instead, cold logic remained firmly in control. She felt a smile stretch her lips. It was a delight to be rid of the chaos.

A line of Seraphim waited outside the gates and stretched down the walkway for a good distance. Guards in translucent crystal armor stood watch while an officious bureaucrat in red robes listened to citizens petition for an audience with the royal court. He wore a bored look on his face and turned away a family with a whisk of his hand.

"Next," he called.

"This reminds me of the way nom royalty treated their subjects." Lanaeia wrinkled her forehead. "It appears Skazaeleus has adopted their methods."

"Come." Daelissa strode to the head of the line.

The guards stepped forward to stop her.

"You would do well to step back," she said in Cyrinthian.

The stone-faced guards said nothing but drew Brilliance-forged swords of glowing white crystal.

She ignored them and looked at the bureaucrat. "Take me to Skazaeleus."

The Seraphim's eyes widened. "You dare call the emperor by his name?" He pointed a finger at Daelissa. "Arrest her."

Anger heated Daelissa's cheeks, but she held her hand. "Do you know who I am?"

The bureaucrat sneered. "I know who you are not, and that is all I need to know."

"You have just killed yourself." Daelissa looked to Qualan. "Dispose of him."

The bureaucrat hardly had time to utter a response when Qualan unleashed a burst of Brilliance that burned a gaping hole in the Seraphim's chest.

The guards froze at the sight and the waiting crowd burst into a frenzy of screams. Seraphim scattered. Some took to the skyway while others ran down the winding paths in the city. Daelissa threw up a shield as the guards recovered and thrust their swords at her. She bound the hilts with ropes of Brilliance and jerked them from their grasps.

The two seraphs channeled rays of destruction at her shield, but their efforts were pitifully weak. If Daelissa were any ordinary Seraphim they could have cut her down, but centuries of feeding from humans had enhanced her. She was no mere Seraphim, but a goddess.

I am the Divinity.

"Take me to Skazaeleus or I will annihilate you both," she said in a cold voice.

The seraphs bared their teeth and tried to cut through her shield, all to no avail.

Daelissa blurred from behind her shield and backhanded the closest guard. He flew backward and slammed against the crystal gates hard enough to crack them. She gripped the arm of the other seraph and squeezed it hard enough to make his bones crack. He screamed and fell to his knees.

She leaned over him. "I ask you one last time, you pitiful speck. Take me to Skazaeleus."

He groaned. "As you wish, mistress."

"You will call me Divinity." She released him.

"Y-yes Divinity." Holding his arm against his body, he staggered to his feet.

By now, the crowd had completely dispersed, aside from a single seraph who looked at Daelissa with adoring eyes. "You have returned at last," he said falling to his knees. "Seraphina, our fair Daelissa has arisen!"

At least I have not been wholly forgotten. Daelissa felt a blush creep over her cheeks. She motioned the seraph to approach. He did so, bowing and scraping the entire distance. She lifted his chin to face her. "I give you a holy mission."

He groaned with pleasure. "Speak, and it will be done, Divinity."

"Spread the word that I am back. Soon we will purge Eden of the vermin plaguing it and take it for our own." She pressed a hand to his forehead and blessed him. His eyes glowed white, marking him in such a way others would have no choice but to believe. Only Seraphim who had spent a great deal of time in the human realm could bless others. Since the way between realms had been closed for so long, the ability would have long ago faded from Seraphim living here.

"At once!" The seraph sprang to his feet and raced away.

She turned back to the guard. "Proceed."

The guard glanced at the still form of his comrade on the ground before the gate, but seemed to realize Daelissa would brook no more delays. He channeled a thin ray at a gem on the white crystal gate and it silently swung open. The seraph led them down a shimmering path the color of platinum. It wound through a garden filled with flowers and vegetation Daelissa recognized as being native to Eden. Though the two realms shared common plant and animal life, it was obvious most of this had been imported long ago.

Lanaeia oohed and touched a turquoise rose. "This garden is so lovely." She stopped to run her fingers across the broad ivory leaf of another plant. "I could be happy wandering this place for days."

Qualan slapped her hand and shoved her forward. "Keep moving, you little fool. We don't have time for such nonsense."

Lanaeia's eyes welled with tears. "You cruel brute. What value is all the world when you cannot stop to appreciate its beauty?"

He gripped a handful of her hair and jerked her close to his snarling face. "There is only beauty in power."

Daelissa resisted the urge to backhand them both across the garden. "Stop with your bickering and move before you injure my calm."

Qualan released Lanaeia's hair and offered a slight bow to Daelissa. "As you command."

With his sister no longer around to keep him occupied, I must keep an eye on him. Qualan had never been particularly ambitious, but now that he was without his other half, he might look for other ways to fill the hole in his life. He might try for her power. *He is still no match for me.*

The path ended at a wide courtyard that led to the palace stairs. Two more guards waited at the doors. Judging from the consternation on their faces when they saw the injured guard, they knew something was wrong.

"Halt!" they shouted in unison.

Daelissa clenched her teeth tight to repress the outrage at this treatment. Somehow, she stopped herself from killing them both. Since she was no longer on Eden with easy access to humans, she needed to conserve her power.

"She is clear to pass," their guide said.

"I do not see signed papers," the taller of the two guards said. "Without them—" His sentence broke off in a scream as Qualan raked a thin beam of Brilliance across the seraph's cheek.

"I could just as easily kill you," Qualan said. "Let us pass."

Instead, the other guard called out for help. Within seconds, another dozen guards raced from inside the palace, their crystal swords blazing.

Qualan burst into laughter and levitated as glowing spheres of destruction blossomed in his palms. The guards looked on in open astonishment. Very few Seraphim were strong enough channelers to levitate, and fewer still could summon so much destructive energy.

"Lay down your swords or die!" Qualan roared.

The guards attacked. Several of them aimed their swords and fired white rays at Qualan. He shielded himself easily. The guards who chose to attack with their blades slammed against the shimmering barrier. Some slashed at it to no effect.

"Pitiful ants," Qualan said. He dropped his shield and laughed with joy as he butchered the guards where they stood. Steaming flesh and entrails exploded from the first group of guards. Qualan raked the others with searing beams, laughing all the while, his eyes shimmering with delight.

Daelissa heard retching and turned to see Lanaeia on hands and knees. She pursed her lips in disgust. This girl was nothing like her parents. Perhaps a few weeks under Qualan's tutelage would fix this.

The gate guard had ducked into a ball. He looked up at the slaughter, eyes full of terror. "How is such power possible?"

"Easily," Daelissa said. "Join my army in the march on Eden and such power will be yours."

"I had though Eden a myth," he said in a quiet voice. He looked up. "Are you truly the Daelissa from the legends?"

I have been away long enough to fade into legend. Daelissa almost laughed at the absurdity. "I am indeed." She stabbed a finger toward the doors to the palace. "Now lead us onward."

Qualan pulled Lanaeia from her knees and prodded her forward, making the girl walk through the worst of the carnage. "This is beauty." His voice reverberated with pure pleasure.

She squeezed shut her eyes and almost tripped over the gutted torso of a dead guard. "It is horror!"

They walked through the palace leaving behind a trail of bloody footprints. The crystalline structure engulfed them in its enormity. The floor was made of pure alabaster, and the walls boasted ornate columns of pure energy supplied by aether wells in the floor. The energy lit the crystal from within.

It must look wondrous at night.

A fierce grin lit Qualan's face as he inspected one of the aether wells. "Such waste. I love this place already."

Preserved remains of humans and animals alike occupied an adjacent hallway like museum displays. Tapestries and murals from Eden decorated the great halls leading to the throne room. Daelissa recognized some of them from her early days on Eden when she had hoarded whatever fascinated her and brought it home. It had been a time of discovery for her and her closest friend, Alysea. Little had she known the person she trusted most would betray her.

At last, they reached the throne room. A great crystal seat infused with Brilliance glowed atop the stairs. The crystal rose in spires that protruded at every angle much like the feathers of a peacock. Rays of pure white shined from the tips of each shard, giving the illusion of a sun. The throne, however, was quite empty. Behind the great seat, a mural of Skazaeleus dominated the wall. He wore a glowing crown and held his arms out as if to encompass the world.

A seraph in red robes sat on smaller chair, which occupied a landing halfway up the stairs. He looked as bored as the bureaucrat Qualan had killed.

Daelissa growled deep in her throat. "Where is Skazaeleus?"

The seraph's eyes went from Daelissa to the guard and across the others in the group. "This is very irregular."

"Daelissa has returned," the guard said. "Please take us to the Emperor."

The bureaucrat laughed. "Daelissa? What fairy tales have you been reading?"

The guard trembled. "Please do not provoke her. Her servants have already killed more than a dozen guards." He fell to his knees and cried out, "By all that his holy, please show her to the Emperor!"

The seraph's eyes turned uncertain. He looked to the left. Daelissa followed his gaze and saw more murals, each one a smaller replica of the ones in El Dorado. The seraph regarded the one resembling her. He looked from the depiction and back to Daelissa.

Some sort of wisdom must have intruded into the bureaucrat's mind, because he simply nodded and stood. "I am Tovaard. I will take you to him." He glanced at the guard. "Remain here."

"At long last, someone I do not have to kill," Qualan said in a mocking tone.

"Thankfully," Lanaeia said in a quiet voice.

Tovaard led them through a small door behind the throne and onto a skyway, which angled up a long corridor. They soon reached a large, curved room with a window overlooking the city. It was evident they were in one of the towers. Tovaard turned left and walked to a large platinum door. He extended a finger and charged a small gem in the center of the door with Brilliance.

A chime sounded.

A moment later, the door slid open and a female Seraphim—a sera—in the gray tunic of a Darkling servant answered the door. She bowed and kept her eyes firmly fixed on the floor. "How may I serve, Magister Tovaard?"

"Get your master, you filthy Darkling," Tovaard said, his lips curling in disgust.

"At once." She vanished inside and soon returned with a plump seraph in white robes.

"What is it, Tovaard?" The seraph's eyes scanned the group. "You know how busy I am."

"Greetings, Minister Kjoeriss," Tovaard said. "Daelissa has returned."

Kjoeriss's eyes flared with surprise. He narrowed his gaze and looked Daelissa up and down.

Daelissa realized she had finally hit her limit with these lackwits. "How many fools must I go through to reach Skazaeleus!" Daelissa shrieked. She shoved past Kjoeriss. He plowed into a bench with a loud grunt. Daelissa stormed through the foyer and several rooms until she reached a hallway. She heard laughter from one room and tested the door. It was locked. She looked at Qualan and pointed toward the obstacle.

He blasted a hole through it. Surprised screams echoed as Daelissa burst inside to find a harem of scantily clad seras inside.

Skazaeleus was not there. She stepped back into the hallway and marched to a door at the end. Qualan repeated his destructive performance.

She stepped inside.

The bedroom boasted a massive bed in one corner and a balcony overlooking the city beyond. A shimmering blue pool ran the length of the right wall, outside to the balcony, and seemed to end at a sheer drop off the mountain itself. It was in the pool she spotted a seraph leaping from the water and racing toward a sword. He was not Skazaeleus.

"Who is this?" Daelissa said.

Tovaard raced into the room, panting. "It is the Emperor, Daelissa."

She felt her brow crease. "This is not Skazaeleus."

"Who is this sera?" the man shouted as he drew a crystal blade. Unlike the guards' swords, this one glowed brightly. It had obviously been charged with far more Brilliance than the norm.

Kjoeriss staggered into the room, blood trickling down the side of his head. "May I present Emperor Skazaeleus the Fourth," he said in an unsteady voice. "Your majesty, may I present Daelissa."

The Emperor's eyes flashed with disbelief. "What is the meaning of this, Kjoeriss? Do you mean to betray and assassinate me?"

"Sheathe your sword," Daelissa commanded. "Have your servants provide us with food and wine."

The Emperor looked long and hard at Daelissa. Fear joined the uncertainty in his eyes, but he reluctantly sheathed his sword. "Tell the servants to fetch all Daelissa asks for." He charged a gem on the wall. Yellow light suffused the air around him and the water evaporated from his body.

Kjoeriss shouted commands and within moments, a veritable feast lined the long table outside on the balcony.

Daelissa sat at the head of the table with Qualan to her right and Lanaeia to her left. The Emperor moved as if to sit at the other end of the table, but Daelissa motioned him to sit next to Lanaeia instead. Tovaard and Kjoeriss hovered nearby, obviously uncertain about whether they were invited to join them or not.

"Who here can tell me what has happened since the war?" Daelissa said.

"Which war?" Skazaeleus the Fourth looked uncertainly at his advisors. "Everything I have ever heard about you was deemed legend or myth. Many of the older Seraphim died during the Second and Third Darkling Insurrections—"

Anger warmed Daelissa's face. "There were two more rebellions?"

"The first happened seven-hundred years ago," Kjoeriss said. "The second and third each occurred about a hundred years apart after that."

"Wrong," Qualan said in a haughty tone. "Your third rebellion would actually be the fourth."

Daelissa rose to her feet without meaning to as her anger flared to outrage. "Find me someone who knows Seraphim history. The ignorance at this table is sickening."

Kjoeriss held up his hands defensively. "I know of no one so ancient."

"Ancient?" Daelissa hissed in her coldest tone. "Are you calling me ancient?"

"Absolutely not!" the seraph said, dropping to his knees. "You are immortal."

Tovaard cleared his throat. "Mistress—"

Qualan blurred across the room and gripped the seraph by his robe. "She is the Divinity. You will refer to her as is her due."

"My apologies, Divinity," Tovaard said in a quavering voice. "I will send out a memo at once to notify everyone of your proper title."

Daelissa granted him a smile. "You may now speak."

Qualan released him and walked back to the table.

Tovaard seemed to reach inside himself for more strength and continued. "Divinity, our lifespans are typically not much more than a few centuries. This is why we know of no one who might know your history. The university was destroyed during the First Darkling Insurrection, and much of our historical records were lost."

Centuries? Daelissa was aghast. Seraphim had been immortal, some countless millennia old when she was a child. What had happened to her people? She directed her gaze at Kjoeriss and Tovaard. "You will search the land for someone who knows the history." She turned to young Skazaeleus. He only slightly resembled the seraph she had known. Though she had no personal love for the seraph she had appointed as regent, a pang of nostalgia made her yearn to see him.

He is dead.

She collected her thoughts and spoke. "I will allow you to remain emperor, but you will send forth a public decree stating that I am the Divinity and as such, the ruler of Seraphina."

He looked as though he wanted to interrupt her, but held his tongue.

Daelissa continued. "Assemble your army, Emperor. We depart for Eden five days hence."

His eyes went round. "But Divinity, I cannot possibly assemble—"

Qualan stood and channeled destruction around his fist. "All things are possible, fool. All you require is motivation."

Skazaeleus shrank away, hands held defensively. "I need no extra motivation." His voice rose to a high-pitched whine. "I will assemble the army at once, Divinity. I swear it!"

Daelissa smiled. In a matter of days, her millennia of plotting and planning would finally see fruition.

Chapter 10

Despite a social coaching lesson from my father, I felt way out of my depth at Kassallandra's ball. The house heads were a cliquish bunch of snot-bags though it was obvious they didn't trust or even like each other in the human sense. Daemos had a strict hierarchy somewhat akin to a caste system. The Paetros and Maedras were the heads of house with those of Anae status a close second.

Anae Vallaena flowed in and out of conversations with house leaders as easily as she did those of her social standing. Daemos of Benae and Cenae status wore colored silken armbands to identify them and rarely seemed to stray from their groups. I'd once been considered Castratae—outcast—but apparently, my new deodorant had saved the day.

I watched a group of brightly dressed Daemos waltz to the music of an orchestral ensemble on a stage near the front of the ornate marble dance hall. The setting looked as though I'd stepped straight into the pages of a fairy tale ball. Unfortunately, this was the last place Cinderella would meet her Prince Charming.

"It is, of course, a matter of house strength," Vallaena said to Godric Salomon.

Her words pulled me from my trance.

"By what measure?" Godric asked in a haughty tone.

"Perhaps the only measure of import in these troubled times." Vallaena regarded him grimly. "I would not suppose there are many who could face such a fierce opponent as Daelissa, at least not alone."

His icy blue eyes regarded her coldly. "If the objective is to goad me into risking my house, such time is wasted."

"We are strong," his wife, Gwyneth, protested. "We are not as numerous as House Assad, but quality is often found in lower quantities."

"I agree," Vallaena said, touching my arm. "I know one of surpassing quality."

"How sweet," Yuuki Wakahisa said as she walked into our group. Her eyes went back and forth between me and my aunt. "The mother deer teaches her fawn to forage for leaves."

Vallaena smiled. "It is regrettable he must use his mind to navigate treacherous waters, Maedras Wakahisa, especially while some rely solely on body parts requiring no thought whatsoever to gain favor."

I blinked a couple of times before I finally figured out the insult.

Yuuki's sensual smile seemed to indicate she enjoyed the verbal joust. "It is a shame those with perfectly lovely appendages are unwilling to employ them. Perhaps the favor of one house would have already been gained."

Gwyneth tittered as she looked me up and down. "He is not unpleasant on the eyes."

I felt myself blush and tried to hide my discomfort. If my observations were accurate, Gwyneth seemed the least socially refined of the bunch. The key to the interaction seemed to be using a lot of passive verbs as opposed to directly stating something about someone as she had done.

Vallaena replied to Gwyneth with another thinly veiled insult that seemed to question her worthiness to sleep with me. This drew yet another rejoinder from Yuuki. After listening to them go on for several more minutes, I had to wonder if the primary requirement for Daemos socializing was learning how to throw insults in someone's face without them even realizing it.

Do I even want these people fighting by my side?

My victory over Aerianas hadn't seemed to sway Godric or Yuuki, and my words certainly hadn't and wouldn't, especially since I wanted to call them all warthog-faced buffoons. I still had more Daemos muckety-mucks to meet with, and getting to the point was like reaching around my elbow to scratch my ass. If they all took this long, the war would be over before I managed to convince just one.

This is a waste of time. I almost blew out a breath of disgust, but held it in.

"Really?" Gwyneth said with a laugh. I suddenly realized she, Yuuki and Godric were staring at me.

"And not a word of defense spoken." Yuuki smirked as though she'd scored major points on the cut-down meter. "The truth often lies in one's silence."

The urge to backhand her across the ballroom floor was overwhelming. I'd obviously missed whatever they'd said, but it didn't matter. These Daemos weren't worth the time it would take me to convince them and I decided to let them know just how I felt. To make my words even more insulting, I used a British accent. "The more words I hear from certain lips, the more I realize the universe does have a sense of humor." I let a small smile curl my lips. "In fact, it seems there is ample space to waste on trivial beings."

Yuuki's eyes widened as if she were barely holding back an angry retort.

"Contemptuous halfling bastard," Gwyneth said. "How dare a mere Castratae—"

Godric gripped his wife's arm so tight I saw his knuckles whiten. He bowed to me. "My apologies, Anae Slade. She has had more than her fair share of drink."

I met the Daemos's icy eyes and noted a hint of fear in them. *What is he afraid of?* With Yuuki, I'd already seen that physical threats wouldn't coerce these people into joining me. I felt like I was in a lake with alligators circling beneath the dark waters and no land in sight.

"Surely there is no need to challenge Paetros Salomon to a duel for publicly questioning your social standing," Vallaena said. "It was merely a slight—nothing worth a Paetros losing his house."

Godric's eyes narrowed at Vallaena. "Surely not," he said in a cold voice.

If I could've taken Vallaena aside and asked for advice, I would have, but I didn't want it to look like I was completely ignorant. I translated Vallaena's statement. *Gwyneth insulted me, so I can challenge Godric to a duel. If I win, I remove him as Paetros of his house. That scares Godric.*

Yuuki, Godric, and others in their positions reminded me of snooty old aristocrats. If there was anything I'd learned from reading *Pride and Prejudice* in school, it had been that those sorts of people were nothing without their status. More than anything, they feared being social outcasts.

Removing Godric as Paetros would be devastating to him and Gwyneth.

When in doubt, bluff.

I settled the coldest gaze I could muster on Godric. "Perhaps a duel would be productive. All this talk makes me yearn to destroy something."

"You cannot be serious," Godric said.

"As Anae Slade and the son of Paetros Slade, he is within his rights," Vallaena replied. "Maedras Salomon offered him grave insult, which could damage his social standing."

"How very clever," Yuuki said with a sly smile. She raised an eyebrow and regarded me with what looked like newfound respect— or wariness.

"Perhaps it's time for new leadership in House Salomon," I added, trying to keep up the pressure. "I'd like a house of my own." I looked at Vallaena. "Would House Salomon become House Slade if I were the Paetros?"

"You would have the right to take a new surname if you desired," Vallaena said.

"I could change my last name to Unicorn if I wanted?"

She lifted an eyebrow. "Of course."

Godric's chin trembled. His face turned an angry shade of red. "Surely there is another way to solve this situation."

I turned to face him. "How else will I retain my social standing if we do not duel?"

Gwyneth whimpered as Godric squeezed her arm even tighter. "I believe I know a way."

An almost euphoric rush burned through my veins. "Explain," I said, barely able to contain a smile. *Am I starting to enjoy these social games too much?*

Godric's jaw tightened as he mumbled something.

"I'm sorry," Vallaena said. "I could not quite hear that."

"I said, I will acknowledge Anae Slade as Kohvaniss."

"That will mean you join the alliance against Daelissa," Vallaena said, giving him a very solemn look.

"I am very well aware of the consequences," Godric said in a stony voice.

Yuuki regarded me through heavy-lidded eyes, as if what was happening now was even better than an all-you-can-eat Swiss chocolate buffet attended by shirtless male models.

"Then let's get it out of the way while everyone's here." I almost extended a hand so we could shake on it, but remembered Yuuki's response when I'd done that to her.

"Do we have a pact?" Vallaena asked.

Godric released Gwyneth's arm and held out the flat of his hand toward me. "We have a pact."

Vallaena looked at me expectantly, so I held out my hand the same way. Godric pressed his palm to mine. I felt a tingle and saw a flash of blue flame as he withdrew. The orchestra finished their latest piece and the dancers clapped politely.

"I believe that is your cue," Vallaena said to Godric.

He scowled, but walked to the stage and held up his hands before they started playing again. All eyes turned to him as he cleared his throat. "House Salomon has long been known for its wisdom."

Scattered applause echoed in the great hall, probably from all the Salomon fanboys.

Godric nodded and continued. "Kings of yore depended on the wisdom of Salomon, and even today, many Overworld citizens come to us seeking aid." He raised his chin and looked upon the crowd like a king to an audience. "After much deliberation, it has become evident to me that Eden once again requires the services of House Salomon." He held out a hand toward me. "The Kohvaniss himself has asked for guidance and wisdom. With Eden in the balance, I could not refuse."

More applause sounded around the room, this time with a bit more enthusiasm.

Paetros Salomon regarded me with a smile that could have deforested a river basin. "Anae Slade—Kohvaniss—House Salomon stands ready to serve against Daelissa's hordes."

"Even when he's lost he makes it sound like he's won," I muttered to Vallaena.

She leaned close. "He must save face. If he were disgraced in any way, his house might not follow his lead."

I repressed another sigh and listened to Godric drone on and on about the great things his house had done. He made it sound like they saved puppies and kittens on a daily basis.

Yuuki looped her arm around mine and spoke into my ear. "You are cleverer than you led me to believe, Anae Slade, but you still have not won the support of House Wakahisa." She released a warm breath into my neck. "Dare I ask what you have in store for me?"

I felt the hairs on my neck rise, though I couldn't say for sure if it was from arousal or fright.

If I had good sense, it would definitely be from fright.

Low-ranking Daemos parted to reveal Maedras Domitia Calidious walking purposefully toward me. She offered a curt nod to Yuuki who responded in kind.

"Might I borrow the charming Anae Slade?" Domitia said in a tone that was more statement than request. Her amber eyes sparkled by the light of the chandeliers.

"Gladly," Yuuki replied. "Though I would love to *dominate* him, I must not be selfish."

I cringed at the way she said the word "dominate". Even the thick porridge I called a brain picked up on the double entendre not-so-subtly hidden within.

Yuuki released my arm and just as suddenly found my father lurking nearby. "Ah, Daevadius. Don't you look magnificent this grand evening?"

Domitia took my arm in a strong grip and led me a safe distance away. "I never had the pleasure of thanking you for saving my life."

I almost spurted out my standard response of, "Hey, no problem." Caution kept my mouth shut. I tried to think of something a character in a Shakespeare play would say. "Verily I say unto thee, it was an honor."

Her forehead crinkled. "You have been listening to the supposed elite running their mouths it would seem." She smiled. "Don't worry. My Brutus was the same. He loved nothing more than being a pompous ass." She sighed. "You'd think after centuries of being disgusted with someone's behavior it would be easier to accept their absence."

I dropped the Shakespearean act. "Losing someone you've been with is hard no matter what," I said. I wanted to ask if this meant she'd join the fight against Daelissa, but decided to let her speak.

She walked us outside into the cool air beneath a brilliant half-moon. A few partyers stood outside talking. Some Daemos in their half-demon forms were doing headstand keggers. I felt my eyes widen at the spectacle.

Domitia tsked. "Young Cenae who have no worry about propriety." She sighed. "Sometimes I wish I could shed the façade of civility and join them."

"You're different than the others," I said, deciding to be as straightforward as she'd been with me.

She shrugged. "I can be. She stopped and gave me a solemn look. "But we aren't here to talk about trivial matters. We are here to talk about our very survival."

I returned her serious look. "That's a good way to put it."

"We are close to House Assad in power and numbers." A young Daemos whooped as he downed a flaming cocktail and she glanced his way. "Maedras Kassallandra and I have rarely seen eye-to-eye. If I acknowledge you as Kohvaniss, will you assure me none of my people will fall under her command?"

This was something I'd discussed at length with my father and Vallaena, so I had an answer ready. "Thomas Borathen, the honorable Supreme Commander of the Templars, will plan strategy and command the troops, though I have the final say in all matters. I will make sure the hierarchy of command doesn't place any Daemos house above another unless that house specifically requests it."

Her lips curled into a small smile. "You are young, but I see you wisely listen to council. I find those terms acceptable."

"Can I count on your acknowledgement tonight, then?"

"Of course." She paused. "The minor houses should follow suit, even that insufferable twit, Yuuki."

I snorted and quickly covered my mouth.

She burst into a full-throated laugh. "I see you share my feelings on the matter."

"Let's just say she reminded me of some girls I went to high school with."

"I am only somewhat familiar with the nom educational system, but if the females there are anything like Yuuki"—she shuddered—"it must be a dreadful place indeed."

"Terribad," I agreed.

We spoke a few moments more and returned inside. Domitia took the stage and more or less repeated Godric's performance, giving a speech about how the alliance would benefit from House Calidious. I noticed Ivan Volkov exchanging resigned glances with Khamisi Taarkan, and the two went to the stage and joined hands with Domitia as if that had been their plan all along.

Dad came up behind me and slapped me on the shoulder. "You are something else, son." He nodded his head toward Yuuki. "Now that everyone else is onboard, she'll look like a fool if she doesn't join."

As if she'd heard us, Yuuki cast a smoldering look my way. I couldn't tell if she was angry or aroused. She ran her tongue across her lips and smiled.

Dad chuckled. "Better watch out for her."

"Why, is she going to try to kill me?"

He shook his head. "Worse. She'll try to bed you. There's nothing she likes better than a Daemos who can best her in politics."

"Seems more like playground antics to me." I let out a deep breath as Yuuki took to the stage and acknowledged me as Kohvaniss. "Wow. I can't believe we did it."

"Like I said, there's something about you that draws people together no matter how stubborn they are." He regarded Yuuki. "Or how slutty."

The Daemos leaders left the stage to resounding applause. A Daemos with a Cenae armband approached Domitia and whispered something in her ear. A look of alarm came over her face, but she quickly covered it.

Dad stiffened. "Something's up."

I felt my back tense as Domitia approached.

"Let us enjoy some night air," she said, and headed for the exit. We walked with her.

Once we'd walked a ways into the courtyard, she turned and spoke in a low voice. "As you know, Paetros Daevadius, representatives from several houses have been questioning Aerianas."

"I thought she was being uncooperative," Dad said.

"She was, but she finally broke." Her lips pressed tight. "She admitted the reason why she came on this suicide quest to kill Kassallandra alone without help from Daelissa is because the mad Seraphim is no longer in Eden."

My chest constricted as my worst fear gripped my heart. "She's in Seraphina," I said.

Domitia gave a grim nod. "The Grand Nexus is operational. Daelissa has returned home to gather her army."

Chapter 11

Dad and I found Elyssa, Mom, and Ivy in the ballroom.

Elyssa gripped me in a tight hug. "You did it!"

"These people are boring," Ivy said in a whining voice. "Can we go?"

Mom smiled at me. "I'm so proud of you, son."

I wished I could bask in the glory of the moment, but now was not the time. "Domitia just told us something awful. Aerianas confirmed Daelissa is in Seraphina."

Their smiles vanished.

"Ooh, can we go?" Ivy clasped her hands together. "Daelissa used to tell me how beautiful Zbura is, and how they have these sky roads made of clouds you can ride."

"I'm afraid that's out of the question," Mom said, though she had a longing look in her eyes.

"Because we'd get blasted?" Ivy asked, eyes wide and innocent.

Dad ruffled her hair. "That about sums it up." He looked at me. "Her absence explains why we haven't been seeing the sort of resistance we should have during our latest encounters."

I put a hand to my chin and thought. "She hasn't been back for thousands of years. The political situation there might not be conducive to her raising an army."

"She's still strong from sapping humans," Mom said. "Daelissa will use absolute force to bring the empire to heel, should it still exist."

I could think of only one way to handle this, and it was the hard way. "We have to take the Grand Nexus and close it before she returns."

"Agreed," Elyssa said. She looked at Mom. "Is there a chance she could return via another Alabaster Arch?"

Mom nodded. "A slight chance. They are scattered all over Seraphina, though, so it's unlikely she would take a different one. The Grand Nexus is closest to the capitol city of Zbura, but even using the skyway, it would take her some time to transport troops there."

"Let's call a meeting at the Ranch," I said. "We'll need our entire army to attack the Grand Nexus."

Dad grimaced. "I'll bet Daelissa has all her forces there. It's going to get nasty."

Vallaena approached our group, her face grim. "I have heard about Aerianas's confession. I assume you know about Daelissa?"

"Yeah," I said without much decorum. "Can you and Dad invite the house heads to a meeting at the Ranch tomorrow?"

Vallaena seemed to puff up a little as if I'd given her a really swell assignment. "We will do so immediately."

"We're on it, son." Dad flashed a quick grin. "This is going to be fun."

My aunt quirked an eyebrow. "Your idea of fun is unsettling." She headed toward the crowd. "We should get started."

Dad winked at me and followed his sister.

"I've already messaged my father," Elyssa said, tucking her phone away in a small red purse. "He suggested we hold the meeting in La Casona since we can use the omniarches to transport everyone there."

The logistics of gathering so many people was going to be a nightmare. I hoped we were up to it. A yawn cracked my jaw. "We'd better go get some sleep. We're going to need it."

"Ivy and I will be staying with your father at the Slade estate." Mom kissed my cheek and did the same with Elyssa. "We'll see you two tomorrow."

I gave Ivy a hug and a kiss. "Goodnight, sis."

"Night, bro." She gave Elyssa a hug, stepped back, and gave her a solemn look. "No yucky grownup stuff with Justin, okay?"

Elyssa giggled. "No promises."

I took my girlfriend's hand and walked outside. Once there, I used Adam's app to schedule a portal to take us back home. "I really miss the mansion."

She sighed. "Me too." Elyssa took both my hands and looked at me. "I know we're young, but maybe it's time to do something really scary."

I raised an eyebrow. "It seems like hardly a day goes by where we don't already do that."

Elyssa laughed and kissed my nose. "What I mean is, maybe we should find our own place to live."

My heart skipped a beat. "I don't know why, but that sounds terrifying and wonderful all at the same time."

"I know, right?" She moved a hand to push a lock of hair behind her ear.

I stopped her hand. "That's my job, babe." I tucked the hair away and smiled. "See? I'm an expert."

"Are you trying to change the subject?"

I shook my head. "No, it sounds wonderful, but—"

She raised an eyebrow. "But what?"

"I really liked having everyone in the same house. It was like having a huge family"

"I miss that too." She wrapped her arms around my neck. "What do you miss the most?"

"Breakfast with everyone."

Elyssa smiled. "I loved the group meals, but I miss playing Scrabble with Bella."

I snorted. "Not me. Bella always seems to win." I ran a hand down her back. "If we could find another place like the mansion, would you be interested in that?"

She gave me a serious look. "You do understand the mansion was a fluke, right? We can't just waltz into another estate that size and claim it as our own."

"Finding another one with its own omniarch would be a challenge too." I blew out a breath. "It sure was nice being able to go anywhere we wanted at a moment's notice instead of waiting like this."

As if in answer to my complaint, a gateway shimmered into being. I took Elyssa's hand and stepped through to La Casona. A moment later, we stepped through the omniarch back to the Templar compound. During the entire short trip, I wondered what it would be like to live with just Elyssa. We got along great, but our lives were so busy, we rarely had a chance to be a normal couple.

Would things change if we survived the war and lived together?

As if sensing I was thinking about her, Elyssa squeezed my hand and kissed my ear. "I love you," she whispered.

"Love you back," I replied. My heart swelled. "Let's go do some gross grownup stuff."

Elyssa's fair skin blushed. "Thought you'd never ask."

My phone rang. I almost ignored it, but noticed it was Cinder. "What's up?" I put him on speakerphone.

"I apologize for calling so late," Cinder said, "but this is about your hellhound."

Elyssa gave me a concerned look.

A lump of ice formed in my chest. "Is he okay? Did a dragon eat him?"

"Cutsauce is in good health and spirits," Cinder said.

I heard Cutsauce yipping as if to confirm the statement.

I felt my forehead pinch. "What do you need to tell me?"

"After the evacuation from the mansion things were very busy. This is why I did not notice until recently that Cutsauce was wearing a collar."

"I never put a collar on him," I said.

"Precisely," Cinder said.

If I hadn't put a collar on him, who had, and why?

"What does the collar look like?" Elyssa asked.

"It appears to be plain leather."

A yawn hit me. After I fought it off, I said, "It doesn't sound like it's anything sinister. You can remove it if you want."

"I will do so immediately." Cinder called Cutsauce. I heard a couple of excited yips followed by a disappointed growl. No doubt, the little hellhound had expected some petting.

"Thanks, Cinder." I winked at Elyssa to let her know I hadn't forgotten our earlier conversation. "I'll talk to you tomorrow."

"Justin, wait." Cinder's deadpan voice betrayed a hint of urgency.

I stopped my thumb from disconnecting the call. "I'm really tired—"

"There is something written inside the collar."

My sleepy brain perked up. "I'm listening."

Cinder continued. "It says, 'look to the first pillar of resurrection.'"

"What the hell does that mean?" I scratched my head and looked at Elyssa.

She pursed her lips. "It means we need to go to El Dorado."

We were still in the underground hangar. "We'll schedule another portal," I told Cinder. "Give us a few."

"If you'd like, I can ask someone to open an omniarch portal from here," he replied. "The Templar Arcanes just today certified two of them safe for travel."

"Thank god." I managed a smile. "I wasn't looking forward to a twenty minute wait."

"Oh, please," Elyssa said. "Twenty minutes to travel thousands of miles isn't that awful."

I shrugged. "First world problems."

She laughed and kissed my cheek. "More like Overworld problems."

"I will ask one of the Arcanes here to open a portal," Cinder said.

"I'll send you a picture." I hung up and took a picture of one of the sliders in the hangar. Without warning, I swept Elyssa into my arms and gave her a deep kiss. She melted in my arms. I ran a hand through her hair and gave a gentle tug before coming up for air. "All I want is a date night with you. We can't seem to catch a break."

"I'm with you." She smiled and pressed a hand to my face. "That's what matters to me."

"What about flowers and dinner at a nice restaurant?"

Her violet eyes sparkled. "Well now, I didn't say you couldn't get me flowers."

Unable to resist the lure of her full lips, I pulled her back to me.

"Greetings, Justin and Elyssa."

We jerked apart and looked at Cinder where he stood on the other side of a portal.

"I did not mean to disturb your mating ritual." He offered us a plastic smile.

Elyssa straightened her mussed hair. "It wasn't a mating ritual."

"We were just making out to pass the time," I said, trying not to laugh. I looked at an object in Cinder's hand. "Is that it?"

He handed me the collar. "Indeed it is."

Elyssa read the message. "First pillar of resurrection. Meh, that's easy." She marched straight past the golem and left the control room.

Cinder and I exchanged a look and hurried to catch up to my girlfriend. She went to the aether pods. Each device consisted of two bands of thick silver spinning around each other like a gyroscope with a Tesla coil to either side, providing the pod with aether directly from the ley lines running through the earth beneath them. Null cubes with cherubs inside hovered in the center of the silver bands, each one glowing with tremendous amounts of aether.

Elyssa went to the pod on the far left and knelt next to the Tesla coil. Cinder and I knelt next to her and looked at the base of the coil. A single word was inscribed in the metal.

"Illuminare," Elyssa said. She wrinkled her nose. "Isn't that illuminate in Latin?"

"I believe so," Cinder said.

"The aether pod is already illuminated." I pointed to the glowing cube inside the silver circles. I turned to Elyssa. "Are you sure this is what the inscription in the collar pointed to?"

"Unless the aether pod at the other end is the first one." She shrugged. "It seemed pretty obvious that these are resurrection devices, and the first pillar would be the Tesla coil powering it."

"As this was the first pod constructed," Cinder said, "I would agree with your hypothesis."

"Well, illuminare didn't do squat—" I stopped speaking as a thin beam of light projected from the top of the Tesla coil and widened into a two-dimensional image.

Elyssa gave me a smug look. "I guess it just took the right person saying the word to activate a spell."

I might have responded with a smart-assed remark, but was too busy looking at the image floating before us. "I know what that is," I said.

"Holy cow, is that the Chalon Jeremiah stole from us?" Elyssa said.

I took a picture of the holographic image. "I think I know why my voice activated this spell." I ran back to the control room with the others on my heels and went to one of the omniarches where the floor was marked with green paint to indicate it wouldn't kill us the instant we used it.

Using the image of the Chalon and the blue cloth it sat on, I opened a portal. On the other side of the gateway stood a shelf with a Chalon nestled in the same blue cloth from the image. "This is Jeremiah's secret vault," I said.

"The picture was the key to get inside." Elyssa moved as if to step through and then stopped herself. "Do you think he disabled the protective wards?"

"I will check," Cinder said, and stepped through.

"No!" I shouted, but it was too late.

Thankfully, Cinder didn't disintegrate or explode. Instead, he looked around, his usually expressionless face assuming the wide-eyed look of a child set loose in a toy store.

"Justin, this place is remarkable. I really must take the time to examine it in its entirety." He turned and tilted his head. "I believe it is safe for you to proceed."

Elyssa took my hand. We looked at each other and stepped through. When nothing happened, I released her hand and drew in a breath of relief.

We stood in a room at least the size of an airplane hangar. The vault stretched on for hundreds of yards to our left. To the right, it terminated in a rock wall about twenty yards away.

"I've been here before," Elyssa said. She walked to the left and picked up a snow globe sitting on the shelf above the Chalon. A smile lit her face.

"Is that a special snow globe?" I asked.

She shook the globe, releasing a white flurry inside. "It makes it snow in Sheboygan."

"Where?" I asked, scratching my head.

She shook it again. "It's a city in Michigan. Ivy played with it when we were in here."

I noticed several other snow globes on the shelf just above the one where it had been. "Cool. I wonder what cities those snow globes go with."

Elyssa wrinkled her forehead and looked at the globe in her hand. Her eyes widened. "Oops."

"Oops what?" I took the globe and looked at the label. It said *Atlanta*. I gave her a stern look. "You realize you probably just caused a snowpocalypse, right? Ninety percent of the population in Atlanta can't drive worth a crap in the snow."

"Justin, come here," Cinder said.

I almost dropped the snow globe, sending yet another fresh flurry into the air above the city. I peered in at the lifelike representation of the Atlanta skyline. "Sorry, guys." I put it gently back in its spot and went to Cinder where he stood looking at a shelf.

"I believe these are for you," Cinder said and pointed at a shelf full of red jewels. A scroll of parchment behind the jewels had my name written on it.

I unrolled it and read the neatly quilled note.

Justin, in case anything should happen to me, I wanted you to have access to my vault. The red jewels next to this parchment are called flame jewels. If you heat them with an open flame, they will project an image much like the ASEs of today do. On these jewels, you will find diagrams and other information about the Grand Nexus. I do not have time to catalogue everything for you, but I suspect Cinder will happily do so.

Though we did not get off to a very good start, I am glad we became better acquainted. If I am, indeed, dead, I feel Eden is in good hands with you as her protector.

Your friend,

Jeremiah

I took a deep breath to push away the regret lodged in my chest. Jeremiah—Moses—might be dead, but he was still looking out for Eden. I turned to Cinder. "Can you organize the information on these flame jewels in time for tomorrow's meeting?"

Cinder's smile of joy actually looked genuine. "It would be my sincere pleasure, Justin. So much information. So much valuable history. This will be exceedingly interesting."

Elyssa snorted. "I think he's in heaven."

"Be sure to send over any vital information about the Grand Nexus to Thomas Borathen the minute you find it," I said. "He's coordinating the assault."

Cinder nodded. "I will prioritize anything I discover about the nexus."

As much as I wanted to stick around and snoop, I was dead tired. "We'll leave the portal open and take the other omniarch back to our room."

Cinder looked up from one of the flame jewels. "I'm sorry. Did you say something?"

I chuckled. "Good night, Cinder."

"Good night, Justin." He held a jewel in one hand. "I really must find a candle."

Elyssa and I left via the portal. We stepped to the other usable omniarch and opened a portal directly into our bedroom at the Templar compound. Once through, I closed the portal. Elyssa and I changed into our favorite sleepwear and dropped into bed. As much as I regretted it, all the gross grownup stuff I wanted to do with her would have to wait.

I kissed Elyssa. "Once we win this war, we're going to take a long vacation."

She snuggled up to me. "And then what?"

"Huh?" I gave her a puzzled look. "I hadn't really thought past that."

"Typical guy." She smiled to show she was just kidding. "Do you ever think about our future?"

"A little, I guess." I'd been so consumed with surviving the present the future seemed like a faraway magical destination. "I think about being with you and doing things for fun instead of constantly running for our lives."

Elyssa's expression turned serious. "I think about being with you for the rest of my life." Her eyes seemed to focus on something distant. "I think about marriage and how many kids—"

"Whoa, kids?" I arched both eyebrows. "We're not even in our twenties yet. Can we live a little before chaining ourselves to rug rats?"

"I'm not in a rush." She pecked me on the nose. "I just want to know your thoughts."

I squeezed her hand. "I want to spend forever with you. I want you to be the mother of my children." I ran a hand across her fair cheek, loving the way her smooth skin felt to my touch. "I just want us to enjoy us before we embark on that adventure."

A beautiful smile stretched her lips. "That's all I wanted to hear." She kissed me. "I love you."

"Sweet dreams." I closed my eyes and felt sleep tugging at consciousness. Tomorrow would be a very busy day.

Jeremiah had lent us a helping hand from beyond the grave. I hoped we could put his information to good use.

Chapter 12

There were so many people at the meeting the next day, it seemed like a full-blown conference.

If I'd known there'd be this many attendees, I would've ordered a few hundred donuts.

Commander Salazar's Templars had converted part of the large warehouse containing the La Casona way station into a room with seating for about a hundred people. A rectangular table with room for five sat on a platform at the head of the room.

As a certified nerd, I'd been to Dragon Con on multiple occasions and felt like I was about to participate in a panel. Unfortunately, this wasn't about some fantasy television show—it was about real life shiznit flying at high velocity toward a very large fan.

Captain Takei led the Arcane military delegation inside the conference room. Zagg, my former history professor and current friend entered a moment later with a small entourage of people I recognized as teachers and students from Arcane University.

He walked toward the front of the room and shook my hand. "Hey, Justin, looks like I'm the duly appointed leader of the Arcane civilian forces."

"How's the situation at the school?" I asked.

He shrugged. "Looking better, but I'd really like to know what Cyphanis Rax did with the missing staff." Zagg's face darkened. "I should be back to teaching history right now instead of planning for war."

I glanced toward the doors as Colin McCloud, the lycan Alpha entered, followed by my friends Stacey and Ryland. I turned back to

Zagg. "If we don't fight, Arcane University might never have students again."

"Believe me, I know." He made a fist. "You know what makes me even angrier?" Zagg didn't wait for an answer. "Jeremiah's death. He could have answered so many questions I have about the history of the university or even the dawn of man."

"Don't give up hope." I told him about the amazing gift Jeremiah had left for us.

"He left a huge vault with records in it?" Zagg said, eyes wide. "Oh, man, you've got to let me in there. Can you imagine what we might find?"

"You and your civilian Arcanes can help Cinder sort through everything." I let the idea sink in for a moment.

Zagg only needed a split second. "Definitely! I'll start right after this meeting."

I saw Cinder enter the room and motioned him over. "You have anything for me?" I asked.

The golem handed me an ASE. "The flame jewels are very interesting predecessors of the ASEs. I was able to directly record from their projections and convert the information into the more current format, but I believe, with someone's help, I could compose a new spell to directly copy the information."

"Now you'll have plenty of help." I waved a hand toward Zagg. "He and his Arcane volunteers will pitch in."

Cinder managed a stiff smile. "I enjoyed working with Professor Zagg to save the world on earlier occasions. His help will be quite valuable."

Zagg grinned. "I can't wait."

I held up the ASE. "Did you get the information to Thomas?"

Cinder nodded. "About an hour after you left, I sent all vital data to his assistants. They assured me he would have immediate use of the information."

I palmed the marble-sized orb. "Excellent."

I left Zagg and Cinder deep in conversation about the best way to catalogue everything in Jeremiah's vault and headed toward the front of the room.

Some of the newly recruited Daemos made their grand entrance just then. Godric reached me a split second before Yuuki did.

"We are here to serve, Kohvaniss," he said.

I offered a brief nod to Godric. "Thank you for coming, Paetros Salomon." I turned to Yuuki. "It's a pleasure to see you again, Maedras Wakahisa."

"House Wakahisa stands ready to serve," Yuuki replied in a voice loud enough to project across the room.

I wasn't sure if this was some way to gain face, and I really didn't care. I just smiled and let the other house heads do their thing. The only ones who didn't seem concerned with the pomp and circumstance were Domitia and Kassallandra. My father, of course, simply gave me a thumbs-up when he entered the room and took a seat at the head table next to Captain Takei.

Kassallandra looked stunning as usual in a silken red dress. Her flaming hair hung in loose curls about her bare shoulders. She approached after the other house heads had taken seats in the front row of chairs.

"I feel I must thank you again for saving my soul," she said in a quiet voice. The fiery Daemas actually looked somewhat demure for once. "Eternity in the Abyss is a fate far worse than death."

"Is that where Abyssal demons live?" I asked.

Her eyes flashed with alarm. "How do you know of them? Even though Daemos can summon many creatures from Haedaemos, none would dare summon an Abyssal."

"Why is that?" I asked.

She took my hand and pressed it between both of hers. "Please, tell me why you ask such a thing."

"I summoned one to defend the mansion when Daelissa attacked." It had been all I could do just to maintain control of the mysterious being.

Kassallandra blanched, which was saying a lot since her skin was fairer than an Irish girl's in the winter. "They now know of you." Her eyes locked onto mine. "You must never summon one again."

I tried not to show surprise at her reaction. "I won't."

She regained control and returned to her standard regal countenance. "Very good. I must go take a seat now." Kassallandra turned and took a seat next to the aisle with Domitia as the neighbor to her left. Apparently, the Daemos leaders were sitting in order of house power.

The room filled up rapidly. I spotted Shelton and Bella near the back next to Ivy and Mom. Nightliss entered and sat next to Mom as well—a move I found confusing since she was the Templar Clarion. Then again, we didn't have a lot of room at the front table. I decided it was time for me to take a seat at the head table, though I wasn't sure which seat to take. After looking at the setup, I decided to go for the gold and take the one in the center. I had called the meeting; therefore, it stood to reason I'd be leading it.

I just sat down when Commander Thomas Borathen walked through the door with Commanders Salazar, Taylor, and Olson behind him. Jeremiah had converted Olson to our side, and the man had delivered a sizeable contingent of Templars to our cause. Even so, we were still soundly outnumbered by the Synod. The Templar commanders sat near the front of the room, but only Thomas took a seat at the head table to my right.

Colin McCloud got up from his seat at the end of the table and came over to me. "It's a pleasure to finally meet you." His Scottish brogue reminded me of MacLean, though it was evident this man worked a bit harder to keep it under control.

I stood and shook his hand. "I can't tell you how happy I am to have the lycans onboard."

"I'd had enough foolishness with the conclave," he said with a growl. "After Yuria Assad voted to change the rules so Rax didn't need a supermajority to pass his bloody Unity Initiative, I knew the government was completely compromised and even more useless than before."

Just to my left, Dad laughed. "Aerianas blackmailed Yuria to make her vote that way."

McCloud's ears twitched like a wolf's. "Blackmail, eh? I'm not familiar with this Aerianas you speak of, but I don't doubt there were some dirty dealings going on."

"Like you said, the Overworld Conclave is nothing but a shell," I said. "The time for playing by their rules is long gone."

"Agreed," McCloud said with a toothy grin. "I'm looking forward to sinking my teeth into something real."

I returned his grin. "Hopefully Cyphanis's ass." It suddenly occurred to me that I shouldn't talk that way to the lycan Alpha, but McCloud barked a laugh.

"Damned right, Mr. Slade." His canines seemed to lengthen as he spoke. "You may be young, but you're speaking my language." McCloud patted me on the back. "I'll take my seat so you can get this meeting underway."

By now, every chair in the audience chamber was filled, and there were even people standing near the door. I recognized only a handful of attendees, but our truthsayers had vetted everyone before allowing them entrance. My stomach fluttered, and I folded my arms behind my back to hide the slight tremble.

This is the big time.

I was just about to signal for them to close the door when two creatures that looked like floating brains with tentacles—minders— drifted inside. I felt my forehead wrinkle at these unusual attendees.

Minders lived in the Gloom—the shadow version of Eden—and their only job was to process dreams from people in the real world and convert those dreams into aether—magic. Every person in Eden had a minder in the Gloom. If a person died, their minder would slowly fade away unless it came to the real world and fed directly from the thoughts humans or supers. As far as I knew, the orphaned minders didn't have much initiative and generally did what they were told, which was why I felt a little uneasy at the sudden appearance of two of them.

One of the minders floated toward the front of the room. I descended the platform and went to meet it. I heard a hiss of surprise from someone as the minder extended a tentacle and touched my head.

What's up, bro? The voice sounded exactly like mine.

Minder Justin? I thought back to it. *I had no idea you were coming.*

I decided it was worth the investment to take a break from dreamland and see what we could do to help. I assume you've put all the orphaned minders to work so far?

We even set them up on a great retirement plan, I told him. I looked at the other minder. *Whose minder is that?*

He flashed the image of a grin to me since minders had no faces. *Who do you think? It's Elyssa's minder. We really hit it off. She's got a great set of tentacles, doesn't she?*

I repressed a grimace and smiled. *I'm not sure if I should be creeped out or not.*

His laugh echoed in my head. *Considering most minders don't date, it is a little weird. Ever since you and I met, and since Elyssa made contact with Minder Elyssa, we've changed. Normally we don't have a lot of personality, but it would appear making physical contact with our corporeals changes us.*

I looked around at the questioning stares of some of the attendees. They, of course, couldn't hear the conversation and probably thought I was locked in thrall. I caught a concerned look from Elyssa and flashed her a thumbs-up. *I'm glad you two came. Maybe we can catch up after the war.*

Let's kick some ass, bro. He flashed the image of us shaking hands, and then detached his tentacle from me. He and Minder Elyssa drifted to the back corner, much to the dismay of the people standing there. Some of them shuffled away while others just stared.

Minder Justin was probably laughing his non-existent ass off.

I went to the podium, cleared my throat, and addressed the room. "Once upon a time, there was a Brightling Seraphim named Daelissa who came to our realm. She and her fellow Seraphim discovered that by feeding on human soul essence, they became incredibly powerful." I looked across the room and saw I had everyone's attention. "The Brightlings enslaved humans and made them build entire cities as monuments." I spun an ASE—all-seeing eye. It projected a holographic image of El Dorado and several other ancient cities Zagg and Cinder had discovered in our historical archives.

After letting the images soak in, I continued. "Daelissa and her companions used their slave armies in war games. Thousands of people died." The ASE switched to an image of Jeremiah Conroy. "Then a new breed of human emerged." I saw a few confused looks. Jeremiah's face morphed from that of a gray-haired man with a goatee and top hat to an olive-skinned man with dark hair and a grim countenance. "Though many of you knew him in his contemporary guise, Jeremiah was, in fact, Moses, the first Arcane. Some of you may have heard of him as the founder of the Arcane Council, Ezzek Moore."

This drew a round of gasps from some corners of the room. His other identities had not been widely known. "Moses convinced Baal, king of Haedaemos that the Seraphim were a threat to all the realms. Baal sent his son, Daevadius, to become the first Daemos on this earth. After that, the great houses of Daemos rose to defend Eden."

Godric and some of the other house heads looked rather smug as I talked them up. After speaking with Dad about this presentation, he'd convinced me to put the Daemos on a pedestal since it would make them lose face if they didn't perform up to the legendary standards I set for them.

The holographic slideshow flickered through images of the house leaders in order of prominence.

"After a long and brutal war, the alliance of Daemos, Arcanes, humans, lycans, felycans, dragons, and Seraphim Darklings assaulted the Grand Nexus, the prime gateway between Eden and Seraphina. Unfortunately, Daelissa's army of Brightlings, Flarks, vampires, and other magically altered humans who'd aligned with her were too strong."

I paused for effect. The room was so quiet you could have heard a mouse fart. "Someone managed to reach the nexus and plucked the Chalon—the key to the nexus—from its socket. It erupted in an explosion of magical energy that drained the light from every creature in the vicinity. The chain reaction traveled through all of the Alabaster Arches, draining anyone near them." I caught a troubled look from Nightliss and my mother. They had been at that battle. "Any Seraphim caught in the blast were turned to husks. Humans and other supers were turned to shadow beings, which consumed the light from anyone they touched. Daelissa and her minions were thought to be husked or dead. For thousands of years, the survivors of the Seraphim War thought Eden was safe."

The ASE switched to a recording taken when Daelissa had destroyed the mansion. Meteors streaked through the air and slammed into the ground, leaving trails of fire in the forest behind the mansion. It zoomed in as the last part of the mansion toppled over to show Daelissa and Qualan burn Moses to a statue of ash. A being of light emerged from the gray remains and ascended into the heavens while Daelissa and Qualan futilely tried to blast it with Brilliance.

Even some of the uppity Daemos gasped at the sight. I saw tears in Ivy's eyes and suddenly wished I'd asked Mom to keep her out of this meeting. *Too late now.*

I forged ahead. "Daelissa did not die. The fate of Eden lies in the balance." Judging from the grim faces in the room, my point had hit home. "The Grand Nexus is once again operational. Daelissa is in Seraphina as we speak, gathering her army, and preparing to invade. That is why we must act now." I brought down my fist on the table to add emphasis. "We must storm the Grand Nexus and remove the Chalon properly so it does not create a second Desecration. Daelissa will be trapped in Seraphina. Eden will be safe."

"Hell yeah!" Shelton yelled.

Bella covered her face in embarrassment.

I put on my best fierce grin and said, "Are you with me, champions of Eden?"

A roar went up from the assembly. Even the Daemos got into the spirit, pumping their fists. Kassallandra, teeth bared, and fire in her eyes, stood. "The houses of Daemos are with you, Kohvaniss."

Captain Takei stood from his seat at the table near me and saluted. "The Arcanes are here to serve."

"The lycans answer your call!" McCloud stood and raised a fist.

Thomas Borathen, a grim smile on his face, stood and pounded a closed hand to his chest as he looked at me. "The Templars stand ready to serve."

A huge man whose face bore an uncanny resemblance to that of a lion stood. "The felycans are with you."

The assembly burst into cheers.

I raised my hands for silence, and the room grew still. "Let's get down to business."

Chapter 13

Located beneath Chernobyl, Ukraine, the Grand Nexus had remained hidden for millennia. I had never been there, though I'd sent Katie, Ash, and Nyte on a mission to block the nexus with the portal-blocking statues.

Thomas Borathen projected a holographic image of the Grand Nexus. The first thing I noticed was how huge it was. In fact, the layout of the way station was completely different from the standard design of all the other arch way stations. Most were designed with a large cavern dominated by an Obsidian Arch. If it had an Alabaster Arch, it was located in the control room along with rows of smaller arches and omniarches.

Due to the size of the Alabaster Arch known as the Grand Nexus, it had been placed in the same cavern as the Obsidian arch, though there was ample space between the two. The giant circles of silver surrounding each arch were separated by perhaps twenty yards, according to the diagram. The smaller numbered arches, the omniarches, the control modulus for the Obsidian Arch, and the world map were located to the west of the main way station.

The main way station was shaped like a hub with four corridors radiating out to a ring around the entire complex. I had to blink my eyes a couple times when I saw the measurements for each of those corridors. I'd been worried about fitting an army into the nexus, but the place looked as if it would easily hold our forces.

I realized Thomas had been talking for the past few minutes and tuned back in.

He traced a laser pointer around the outer ring. "The external corridor is much smaller than the main corridors. Jeremiah's information suggests it is also blocked by rubble from the first war. Since we only have images of the south corridor"—he indicated the bottom corridor—"that is where our forces will enter and congregate. Scouts will patrol the perimeter on flying carpets and deliver intel should we need to adjust our positioning."

Thomas continued to detail the assault and the responsibilities for each faction. Thanks to all the information left by Jeremiah, we had precise details on the layout and size of the nexus.

"Is everyone clear on their assignments?" Thomas asked when he finished his briefing.

Godric Salomon stood. "Commander Borathen, your knowledge of battle tactics is renowned, but entering enemy territory without a clear understanding of their numbers or capabilities entails undue risk, wouldn't you agree?"

Thomas regarded the Daemos, his expression neutral. "I would not say it is undue risk. We already have an excellent assessment of their capabilities because we captured their head strategist." He flicked an ASE into the air. It hovered and projected a three-dimensional image of a tall metal rod. Four copper rings were evenly spaced along its length, which terminated in a copper orb at the top. "As I said earlier, one of our greatest concerns are these magic interdictors which could render our Arcanes powerless. We have been busy making tokens which allow spell casting while inside an interdiction field, but at this late date, we won't have enough to go around." Thomas braced his hands on the table and leaned forward. "This makes the Daemos role more important than ever. If there are interdictors, it is up to your people to take them down."

Godric swelled a little, running a hand through his lustrous platinum locks like a preening girl. "I had thought as much. House Salomon has imparted wisdom to leaders throughout the ages. I am glad to have helped." He sat down next to Gwyneth. She pursed her lips and tilted her head up.

She's looking so far down her nose, I can see her boogers.

I looked at Dad. He met my gaze and rolled his eyes.

"We thank you for your wisdom," Thomas said. "Are there any further questions?" He waited barely two seconds before banging his fist on the table and declaring, "This meeting is adjourned. The arch operators will send you to your rally points so you can gather your forces."

The room broke into a multitude of conversations. I felt a hand on my shoulder and glanced left to see Dad.

"Are you loving Daemos politics yet?" he asked.

I sighed. "Godric has a way of inserting himself into everything. He didn't give Thomas a single suggestion but acted like he'd just won the war by opening his big mouth."

Thomas apparently overheard me. He turned to us. "One must often suffer fools to execute a campaign."

My father barked a laugh. "Reminds me of the first Seraphim War."

"Perhaps you'd be willing to share a tale or two," Thomas said.

I masked my disbelief with a straight face. Elyssa's father had at one time despised all demon spawn because he'd believed they'd lured Templars into a trap at Thunder Rock and slaughtered them. As it turned out, Vadaemos, the suspected culprit, hadn't been responsible. Daelissa had framed him in an attempt to sow discord in the Overworld Conclave. Thomas had accepted that not all Daemos were evil, but this was the first time I'd seen him actually be friendly to any Daemos but me.

"We have a few hours while the troops assemble," Dad said. "I know a great place here in Bogota where we could grab a *cerveza* and talk about the old days."

Thomas nodded. "We have twelve hours before the troops will be assembled, and another ten before the attack commences. I could use a brief respite from duty."

Dad slapped him on the shoulder. "I'll lead the way. Let me tell my wife where we're going."

"I'll do the same and meet you outside," Thomas replied.

Dad headed toward Mom and Ivy.

Thomas turned and extended a hand toward me.

I recovered from the shock of him and my father planning a boys' night out and accepted his grip.

"I don't know how you united the Daemos," Thomas said, "but I am very impressed."

"I'm not entirely sure either," I said.

He leaned toward me and lowered his voice. "The battle of the nexus will be our greatest challenge yet. We will spare nothing to close the gateway."

"I understand."

"Good." He paused as if considering something and finally voiced it. "If anything should happen to me, I want you to know that I'm glad Elyssa has you."

My next breath caught in my throat. Thomas Borathen wasn't one to get sentimental. "I'm so glad to have her too," I said.

He laid a hand on my shoulder. "Take care of her, son." With that, he turned and left.

Elyssa came up to me a moment later, her forehead wrinkled. "Something strange is in the air." She looked at our fathers as they left together. "Since when does my dad go drinking beer with anyone?"

I shook my head in amazement. "Since when does he call me son?"

Elyssa gripped my arm, her eyes lit with delight. "Are you serious?"

I nodded. "I'm a little freaked out."

"Me too." She blew out a breath. "We have twenty-two hours until operation commencement and I, for one, would like to spend it alone with you."

"Date night?" I said. "Gross adult activities?"

She pressed her soft lips to mine, pulled away, and smiled. "Oh, yes."

"I've been dying to investigate the pocket dimension here at La Casona." I pulled her closer and kissed her again. "With how often we've been here, it's amazing we never checked it out."

Elyssa's face lit with a delight smile. "There are some awesome—"

My phone buzzed.

We glanced at it. There was a text message from Lornicus. *Fjoeruss will speak with you. Please meet me at this address in one hour.* The golem obviously knew I had access to an omniarch because the address was in Shanghai, China. He'd included the picture of a spacious lobby with marble floors.

Elyssa and I exchanged concerned looks.

"How does Chinese food sound?" I asked.

She sighed. "It's never ending, isn't it?"

I wrapped an arm around her shoulders and squeezed. "I can ask him for more time."

"Absolutely not." She seemed to steel herself. "If there's even a remote chance we could recruit Fjoeruss, we need to take it."

"Don't get your hopes up." Even as I said that, I imagined his armies of gray men fighting alongside us. I had no idea how many he had, but even they would pale compared to what Fjoeruss himself might be capable of. Realistically, I knew just getting him to help me teach the Darklings how to feed on both Brilliance and Murk was a long shot. "Let's go tell my mom where we're going."

Elyssa narrowed her eyes with suspicion. "Maybe we should bring some backup."

"That would probably be a deal breaker." I held up my hands before she protested. "Don't worry, I'll figure out something. Maybe we could leave the portal open with a rescue force ready to rush through at a moment's notice."

"That would be a good idea."

I found Mom talking to Elyssa's mother, Leia, with Ivy standing to Mom's side. The three were laughing about something but Mom and Leia broke off with guilty looks when they saw us.

"What's so funny?" I asked.

"Did you really throw your poop at the monkeys?" Ivy said with a giggle.

I felt my face grow hot.

"Ooh, this sounds interesting," Elyssa said. "I definitely want to hear this story."

"No." I shook my head vehemently. "You really don't."

Ivy, unfortunately, obliged. "Justin went to the zoo when he was three and he saw a monkey throw poop. So he reached into his diaper and threw his poop right back, but he missed and got it all over some man's pants." She burst into fresh giggles. "And then he starting yelling, 'stinky monkey!'"

Elyssa, Mom, and Leia all exploded with laughter.

I buried my burning face in my hand and shook my head. "Most embarrassing story ever."

Leia gave me an understanding look. "About as embarrassing as the time when I left four-year-old Elyssa in the bathtub so I could grab shampoo from another bathroom. She decided to run naked downstairs with her toy sword while her father was speaking with his lieutenants."

"Mom!" Elyssa said, her fair skin turning pink.

Leia shook her head. "To top it off, she declared that she was her father's little ninja."

It was my turn to laugh.

"I did something like that when I was living with Jeremiah," Ivy said. "He and Bigmomma wouldn't get me a puppy, so I snuck out of bed when he had guests over and told them I'd blast them to ashes like Daelissa taught me if he didn't get me one. I blew up the dessert table just to show them I was serious." She grinned. "It was funny." Her face turned sad. "I still didn't get a puppy."

Mom looked mortified, but quickly covered with a smile and a total change of subject. "We were going to get some food in La Casona. Would you like to join us?"

"Actually, we have to pay someone a visit." I felt the lighthearted moment slip away. "Fjoeruss."

"Fjoeruss?" Mom said in a shocked voice. "Why in the world would you see him?"

I told her about my plan to help the Darklings feed. "I suspect with all his talk of balance and gray he might know how Darklings can feed on both the light and the dark."

Mom's eyes grew worried. "Perhaps, but he never gives information for free."

"I'm hoping it'll be an even exchange of information." I squared my shoulders. "I really have no choice but to try."

"We need backup in case," Elyssa said. She turned to her mother. "Can you arrange for a rescue force in case things get hairy?"

"Of course," Leia replied, her usual reserved expression back in place.

"I'll be standing by as well," Mom said.

Ivy piped up. "Me too!"

I hugged my little sister. "Now I feel safe."

She kissed my cheek. "I won't let anyone hurt my brother."

We met Mom, Leia, Ivy, and a squad of Templars at one of the omniarches twenty minutes later. It was time to enter the wolf's den.

Chapter 14

I opened the portal using the picture provided by Lornicus.

The golem stood on the other side, a friendly smile on his square-jawed face. He wore a black suit with a red tie and his silvery hair was slicked back. "Mr. Slade and Miss Borathen, how pleasant to see you again," Lornicus said in his nerdy voice. He looked past me at Mom and the Templar squad. "My, my. Were you expecting a trap?"

"Just precautions," I said, and stepped through with Elyssa by my side.

He nodded. "You have nothing to fear so long as you behave."

I looked at the massive atrium stretching around us. A twisting shell of glass encased walkways that wound between plots of grassy earth, each with neatly sculpted trees and bushes. Rounded columns with glass elevators vanished into the upper section of the superstructure where I imagined offices must be. I whistled. "Fancy digs."

"Thank you," Lornicus replied. "It was an exciting project."

"Does Fjoeruss own this entire building?" I asked.

"That is not what you came to discuss," Lornicus said. "Let's save further questions for the meeting."

I pshawed. "Geez, you'd think I just asked whether Fjoeruss prefers boxers or briefs."

"All information is valuable, Mr. Slade." Lornicus led us toward one of the elevators.

I decided to keep further remarks to myself.

We stepped inside. The golem slipped a card through a reader. The doors closed and the elevator zipped upward. As we rose, the glass car offered a stunning view of Shanghai as the last rays of the sun touched the city. Two impressive skyscrapers loomed next to this building, one shaped like a wedge with a rectangle cut from the top, while the other looked square and dull in comparison. We soon rose higher than the building's two neighbors, and the view vanished behind a blank gray wall. A moment later, the elevator stopped with a ding.

The doors slid open to reveal a wide, round office with clear views of the city in all directions. Short walls made of what appeared to be dark mahogany boasted tapestries and paintings. Glass cases held vases and other decorative pieces. I wondered if some of those dated back to ancient times, or if they might even be magical artifacts.

Mr. Gray—Fjoeruss—stood by one of the windows looking out at the city. He turned to face us and offered a brief nod to Elyssa. "Good day, Miss Borathen." He looked identical to Lornicus, but unlike his golem assistant, his voice was deep and commanding. "What did you wish to discuss, Mr. Slade?"

I held back a shudder. Seeing a man who looked identical to my friend Cinder was always unsettling, especially knowing this man— this Seraphim—had created him. "I need your help."

"Perhaps you could be more specific." Fjoeruss motioned toward a set of four leather divans spaced around a table. "Have a seat."

He's certainly being friendlier than I expected. Elyssa and I sat down. Fjoeruss sat across from us, but Lornicus remained standing next to the elevator doors.

I leaned forward, bracing my arms on my knees. "As you know, Seraphim have an affinity to either the Brilliance or the Murk."

He raised an eyebrow. "Of course."

I continued. "You, however, seem to have an affinity for both, or perhaps a way to feed from both spectrums."

"I'm waiting on the point, Mr. Slade."

I'd been thinking a lot about how to phrase my next question so Fjoeruss wouldn't know my plans. "Can you teach me how to feed from both the light and dark?"

Fjoeruss crossed a leg and regarded me for a moment. "Which hand do you write with?"

My forehead scrunched. "My left. Why?"

"Could you teach yourself to write with your right hand?"

"Sure." I flexed my right hand. "It might take some time."

Fjoeruss waited a moment, as if hoping I'd get his point.

Amazingly, I caught his meaning right away. "You're saying it could be taught, but it takes time." My heart thudded into my stomach's basement.

"Precisely." He motioned to Lornicus. "Fetch one of the prisms."

"At once, sir." The golem opened one of the glass cases, removed a crystal pyramid, and brought it to Fjoeruss. I noticed it had the Cyrinthian symbol for light on one side, and the symbol for dark on the other. It appeared to have symbols on all sides, but I couldn't make them out.

"The other option is to use one of these." Fjoeruss touched the pyramid to the palm of his hand. It seemed to stick there like a magnet. He rotated it so the light symbol faced me. "If I were to feed on Murk, this prism would reverse the spectrum and draw Brilliance instead. He twisted it so the dark symbol faced me. "This would do the reverse."

My heart took the elevator from my stomach and rose with hope, but I kept my neutral expression. "How many of these do you have?"

"Hundreds." He tilted his head ever so slightly. "At one time the Brightlings used them in a misguided effort to change the affinity of Darklings. Brightlings can naturally withstand enormous amounts of light essence, but Darklings will go quite mad if they are force-fed a singular diet of Brilliance."

I knew my next question would give away my intent, but I had no way around it. "Are they for sale?"

He shrugged. "To me, they are useless trinkets. I have never required their assistance as I have a natural affinity for balance."

"Is that a yes?"

Fjoeruss plucked the prism from his palm and held it between a thumb and forefinger. "So, you wish to have Darklings feed on Brilliance." He wrapped his hand around the crystal. "I must admit I cannot understand why you want to drive them mad. I assume you have run into the problem most Darklings face when feeding from humans."

I didn't answer. Then again, I probably didn't need to. Elyssa met my eyes, but kept her facial expression in check.

His gray eyes lost focus for a moment. "Ah. Perhaps if they balance their feeding between both spectrums, they will not be so sickened." His gaze settled on me. "You seek to counter Daelissa's revived Brightlings with more powerful Darklings."

"Balance," I said, trying not to betray the disappointment in my voice that he'd figured out my plan. Then again, he'd had plenty of clues to work with and he wasn't an idiot. "If the Darklings can match her revived Brightlings, then we can at least achieve a stalemate."

A knowing smile faintly curved his lips. "Perhaps." He flicked the prism at me.

I caught it and felt surprise flash across my face.

"That one is free, Mr. Slade." He leaned back in the divan, causing the leather to creak, and crossed his arms. "For you to earn the rest, you must give me truly remarkable information."

Here goes nothing. "The Grand Nexus is working. Daelissa is in Seraphina."

Fjoeruss's face went absolutely blank—not surprised blank, but completely unanimated. I turned to look at Lornicus and saw a look of utter shock on his face. Elyssa gripped my arm and squeezed it.

"Seraphina?" Lornicus said in a strained voice.

Fjoeruss apparently recovered from his surprise. "Are you certain?"

I turned to see a very concerned look creasing his forehead. "Aerianas confirmed it."

"Aerianas is alive?" Lornicus said. His hands gripped the back of my divan.

I squinted at the golem and turned back to Fjoeruss. "I find it hard to believe you didn't know that." Holding the prism between my thumb and forefinger, I held it up. "I think I've earned more of these."

"Your plans are clear to me now," he said. "With Daelissa in Seraphina, there is nothing to prevent you from attacking the Grand Nexus and taking it offline." He rose to his feet. "Daelissa would be trapped in Seraphina, and you would have free reign here in Eden."

Elyssa and I stood and backed away ever so slightly. I kept sight on Lornicus from the corner of my eye.

"You make it sound as though I'll take over the world myself."

He shook his head. "Not precisely, but close enough. You would, no doubt, purge the Overworld Conclave of the current leaders and replace them with people of your own. Rules would be rewritten. A great deal would change."

"Daelissa controls the Conclave now, in case you hadn't noticed." I looked between him and Lornicus. The golem simply watched and said nothing. "Wouldn't it be better if I took that from her?"

"The new variables you've introduced have changed the game." Fjoeruss paced toward the window. "I need time to calculate the outcome."

"You promised me those prisms," I said. "Are you reneging on our deal?"

He flicked his gaze toward me. "I may have promised you the prisms, Mr. Slade, but I did not say when I would deliver." He nodded toward the door. "Leave, and I will have them delivered."

"You've got to be kidding me," Elyssa said.

"I need them now." I put some steel in my voice.

Fjoeruss settled the full weight of his gray gaze upon me. At one time, he might have scared me poopless. I'd seen too much and done too much to be as scared as I should have been. This Seraphim was smarter than Daelissa and wily as a coyote. I had never seen him fight with his magic and no idea what he was capable of.

I have no choice. I stepped toward him and held out my hand as if he'd just hand me more prisms. "Honor the deal, Fjoeruss."

"For your own safety, Mr. Slade, I suggest you leave." Fjoeruss looked at Lornicus. "Show them out."

"I'm not moving until I get those prisms." I hoped Elyssa was signaling our rescue squad. As if in answer, an alarm beeped from somewhere in the room and a holographic display appeared above a desk, showing my mother and a group of Templars storming through the portal in the lobby.

Lornicus touched his fingers to his wristwatch. "Poorly conceived, Mr. Slade. Do you think this building is unguarded? Tell your rescue party to retreat." A group of gray men formed a blockade in front of my mother.

I looked back at Fjoeruss, but his face once again looked blank. I began to wonder if he might be insane and was simply covering it up. "Nobody's going anywhere until I get those prisms." My chest constricted, and I hoped Mom and the others could fight off the horde of golems. The four elevators in the penthouse chimed. The doors on each one slid open and disgorged a gaggle of gray men.

Steel rang as Elyssa freed her sai swords from their sheaths. I did a quick headcount and figured there were at least twenty super-strong golems coming for us.

"Don't make me do this," I told Fjoeruss. "Things are about to get really messy if you do."

He shook his head. "No, Mr. Slade. You are the one making me do this."

I smiled grimly and shrugged. "Your loss." With that, I drew in power, aimed both hands at the oncoming golems, and channeled a blast of Murk. The ultraviolet force blasted the golems back, smashing them against the short mahogany walls. Others crashed through the windows, flying out into the night sky to fall hundreds of stories to the asphalt below. Glass cases shattered and the wooden walls cracked and broke. Wind howled into the penthouse from the broken windows.

I spun toward Fjoeruss who, once again, had a blank look on his face. I bound him in chains of Murk and held him off the floor. Elyssa flipped backwards. Twisted Lornicus's arm behind his back and slid the blade of her sword under his chin.

"Don't move, golem," she said in a fierce whisper.

Fjoeruss simply stared at me from his prison of glowing Murk. Something was very wrong with this picture. I'd expected some magical response from the Seraphim, but he'd done absolutely nothing. I noticed the blank look on his face once again, and something registered in my mind. His face wasn't merely blank, it was unanimated. Whatever I had captured wasn't the real Fjoeruss.

The truth hit me like a ton of bricks. I spun toward Lornicus just as a haze of gray energy engulfed Elyssa and froze her in place.

"There never was a Lornicus," I said. The murk holding Fjoeruss squeezed tight and tore him in half. As expected, there was no blood. He'd been a golem.

Lornicus clapped his hands. "Very astute, Mr. Slade." He shrugged. "I have found it useful to hide my true identity in case anyone wished to move against me."

I drew in power and prepared to defend myself. "You once told me you have spies everywhere who look real and can act real within limited specifications. I guess this golem was one of those."

"Indeed." Orbs of gray energy coalesced in his hands. "You have grown in power."

I formed spheres of Murk and Brilliance in my hands and held my arms out to my sides. "I'm not the weak kid you once kidnapped."

"So it would appear."

"What have you done to Elyssa?"

He glanced at her still form. "She is merely held in place. Do not force me to do the same to you."

"Then give me the prisms."

Lornicus—Fjoeruss pressed his lips together. "I need more time, Mr. Slade." He stared at me for a long moment. "There's another reason I can't have you closing off the Grand Nexus just yet."

I couldn't think of any good reasons to keep it open unless he wanted Daelissa to win. "Tell me."

"Perhaps we could talk under less tense circumstances." He straightened and the gray energy in his hands evaporated.

I nodded toward Elyssa. "Release her."

He backhanded the air, and the translucent gray cloud around her vanished.

Elyssa stumbled backwards and sucked in a breath. She recovered and tensed. "You son of a—"

"No need for profanities, Miss Borathen." Fjoeruss smiled as Lornicus had.

I released the energy in my hands, but continued to fill my aether well just in case he tried something sneaky. A gust of wind from the broken windows picked up a stack of papers and scattered them around the room. "Call off the attack on my Mom and the others."

"Already done," he said.

I glanced at the holographic security display and saw dozens of still gray-suited bodies lying on the floor around Mom and the others. The rest of the golems had backed away and the two groups stood facing each other.

"Are you going to spill your guts?" I said. "I don't have all day."

His expression turned serious. "As the battle for the Grand Nexus began, someone very important to me begged me to abandon Daelissa."

"Did you listen to them?" I asked.

He shook his head. "I had not embraced balance. She believed we existed for a reason and it was not to enslave those weaker than us."

She? Did Mr. Gray have a girlfriend?

"Sounds like a wise woman," Elyssa said.

"Indeed." His gaze seemed to latch onto something in the past. "I was the last line of defense for the Grand Nexus, but since we were crushing the opposition, it appeared there would be no need for my services. A portal opened and she stepped out of it."

"Who is this mysterious 'she'?" I asked.

"Melea." His voice sounded dull, as if speaking the name took all the emotion from him. "At first I thought she'd changed her mind and decided to fight in the battle. Instead, she disabled me. Although I could not move, I could still see and hear everything." His eyes seemed to focus back onto the present. "She told me neither side should win. That the only way to achieve balance was to remove both sides and she had figured out how to do it."

"Remove both sides?" Elyssa said. Understanding blossomed in her eyes. "That would mean—"

Fjoeruss nodded. "Even as I worked to break the spell immobilizing me, she pushed me through the portal she'd used to reach me. I watched as she held her hand to the Cyrinthian Rune. It rose from its socket on the Grand Nexus. She gripped it and channeled a weave I hadn't seen before. It began to sever the connection between the rune and the nexus. Before she could complete her task, the gateway to Seraphina opened and a group of Flarks overpowered her."

"She fought them as they dragged her through the gateway to Seraphina." Fjoeruss's lip curled with anger. "Dark energy crackled around the rune. Melea shouted that she forgave me." His eyes saddened. "The portal she'd pushed me through closed and that was the last I saw of her."

"She caused the Desecration," I said. "Lornicus—you—once told me nobody knew who'd done it."

"I saw no advantage in revealing it," he said.

"Melea went to Seraphina," I said. "That's why you don't want to close the gateway. You want to find her."

"Precisely."

"What if we let you go through before we disable the nexus?" I asked. "It might be tricky, but it's worth a shot."

"Hold on a minute," Elyssa said. "Who was this woman to you?"

Fjoeruss, his gray eyes troubled, didn't answer at first. Finally, he said, "My sister."

Chapter 15

Fjoeruss had dropped a bomb. Unfortunately, reuniting him with his sister might be impossible. Provided we could even fight our way to the Grand Nexus, opening a portal to Seraphina would take time we didn't have. What if Daelissa were waiting on the other side with a Seraphim army?

Elyssa dropped another bomb. "Your sister isn't in Seraphina."

I yanked my gaze her way. "How in the world—" I suddenly realized she was right. When we'd stolen null cubes with imprisoned husks from Kobol Prison, we'd had the help of a man named Jenkins. He'd been using an affinity sphere, which could detect whether the imprisoned husks were Brightlings or Darklings. One cube hadn't responded to the test. He'd called it an anomaly because the sphere had turned neither white nor dark, but gray.

"Why do you say this?" Fjoeruss regarded us with suspicion.

"The Flarks must have brought her back through the gateway from Seraphina at the last minute," Elyssa said. "Does your sister have a gray affinity like you?"

He nodded. "She is the only other like me, at least that I know of."

I felt a victorious grin stretch my face. "How would you like to make a deal? You join our side, and I'll give you back your sister."

Fjoeruss's gaze hardened. "If this is a trick, Mr. Slade, you will pay dearly."

By freezing Elyssa with equilibrium, he'd proven that he fought differently than Daelissa. I'd once frozen a torrent of Brilliance like ice with the force of stasis. While I knew how to channel it, Fjoeruss had centuries of experience more than me. In other words, I didn't take his threat lightly.

"It's not a trick," I replied in an even tone. "Will you join us or not?"

His jaw tightened. "If you are telling the truth, it appears I have little choice."

"You already tried to break one deal with us," Elyssa said. "How do we know you won't do it again?"

Fjoeruss crossed his arms. "The terms of the deal were not broken."

"You used a technicality to delay delivery," she said. "In my book, that's as good as breaking it."

"Let's go downstairs," I said. "I want to speak with my mother and make sure everyone is okay." I didn't wait for a response and headed for the elevator with Elyssa by my side. When I turned to press the button, Fjoeruss sullenly followed us in.

I hit the button for the lobby. We watched the magnificent nighttime view of the city flash past as the elevator swiftly carried us to the bottom level. When we stepped out of the elevator, Mom rushed forward and hugged me.

"I was so worried," she said. Her blue eyes went hard as diamonds when she saw Fjoeruss. "I should have known he would betray you."

Fjoeruss held out his empty hands. "I betrayed no one. Your son simply disagreed with a deal we brokered."

"You and your deals," Mom said. She turned to me. "Be very careful how you craft deals with this devil. Even on Seraphina he was quite wealthy because he knew how to gain the advantage in any contract he made."

"I can see that now," Elyssa said.

Mom scowled at him. "Even in mine and Daelissa's circle of friends, we had a nickname for him."

"Are you truly going to dredge up the past?" Fjoeruss said. His voice sounded more like Lornicus's nerd accent than the commanding baritone he'd used since breaking from his deception.

Mom waved her hand at the huge building. "The past? You appear to be the very same even in the present." She turned to me. "We called him Trickster, and for very good reason."

The man had disguised himself as Lornicus by hiding as himself in plain sight. He'd tried to make shady deals with me while my mother was held prisoner by the Black Robe Brotherhood, holding out for an advantage even when he knew she might die. His deceitful deal for the prisms further proved my mother was right to doubt his word.

"I gotta say, the shoe fits." I tried not to gloat now that I held an advantage over him, but it was hard. The more I thought about how he'd refused to help me with my mother, the less I wanted to let him have his sister back. Then again, his sister sounded like a decent sort, if a bit misguided. "At least the mystery of who pulled the plug on the Chalon is solved."

"It is?" Mom looked at me with surprise.

I jabbed a thumb at Fjoeruss. "His sister did it to keep either side from winning."

"Your sister?" She looked confused for a moment, but seemed to shake it off. "I guess we can see how that turned out."

"It only delayed the inevitable," Fjoeruss said, his body language and voice back under control. "I can see your memories of those days are still incomplete."

"I remember enough," Mom replied, though doubt was plainly written on her face.

"I want the prisms now," I told him. "I'd also like to know how many golems you have. We're going to throw everything we have at the nexus."

"First, I would like to see proof you have my sister."

I shook my head. "First, the prisms."

He stared at me with a dark look for a moment before tapping on his watch. "Very well."

"Prisms?" Mom asked.

I showed her the one Fjoeruss had given me.

Her upper lip curled in disgust. "What use do you have for those things? Once they were used to force Darklings to feed on Brilliance in an effort to 'correct' their orientation. It drove them mad."

"Now we can use it for balance," I said. "Feeding from humans sickens Darklings, but if the essence is balanced between Murk and Brilliance, they're unaffected."

Mom sighed. "I hope they work."

Several minutes later, a gray man carrying a large briefcase stepped from an elevator. He stopped next to Fjoeruss, balanced the case in one hand, and presented it to his master. Fjoeruss undid the latches and opened the lid. About fifty of the small prisms were held in place by thick gray foam. Fjoeruss unfolded the foam to reveal even more. I counted the rows and columns, did some quick math, and estimated there to be about two hundred.

I nodded. "Thank you."

Fjoeruss folded the top layer back into the briefcase, closed it, and his golem handed it to me. "Proof about my sister, if you please."

A group of gray men bearing the crushed bodies of their fallen comrades entered the lobby. I was shocked when Chinese janitors stepped from another elevator and began cleaning up the remains of the other golems. Before I could admonish Fjoeruss, it occurred to me they might be golems as well.

If so, they looked really convincing. One of them was going bald and had a beer belly while another looked like a little old lady. What gave them away was the dead look in their eyes. They bent to their task without question or conversation, faces devoid of any emotion. Then again, if I were called in late at night to clean up bodies, I might look the same way.

I motioned Fjoeruss toward the portal. "Right this way."

Elyssa watched the janitorial golems work. "You must save a bundle on labor costs."

"Millions," Fjoeruss said, and stepped through the portal.

Once everyone had stepped through the gateway and back to La Casona, I deactivated the portal. Using a well-memorized image, I opened a portal to the cavern in El Dorado just outside the control room. Mom and Elyssa stepped through first, followed by Fjoeruss and me.

He paused to stare at the giant dragons in the center of the cavern. "Impressive," he said, his voice once again similar in tone to what he used as Lornicus.

Looking at Altash and hearing Lornicus's voice only reminded me of the hell I'd gone through to save my mother. I'd needed blood from Maulin Kassus to open the diamond fiber prison holding Mom. Fjoeruss had told me he could easily get the blood, but would only do so at the price of one cupid.

I took a deep breath to quell the anger and buried my emotions with a placid façade. "In here." I led the group into the control room and to the stacks of null cubes. I set the briefcase with the prisms next to the wall.

"You are more clever than I thought," Fjoeruss said, a note of admiration in his voice. "When I heard about the Battle of Kobol Prison, I thought it a tremendous blunder on your part." He gazed at the stacks of cubes. "Instead, you feinted with your queen in order to steal all the enemy's pawns."

I ignored his praise since it was probably an attempt to fish for more information. In his guise as Lornicus, he'd used a similar tactic. Most people like to talk about themselves, and I was no exception. If you pump them up a little, they're more likely to brag. Knowing what I knew now, I intended to weigh everything I said in his presence. He was extremely perceptive, as evidenced by his ability to guess our plans for the Grand Nexus from a few small clues.

I found the affinity sphere sitting on its pedestal to the right of the Brightling cubes. "This shows us the alignment of the husks in the cubes." I demonstrated by measuring a Brightling. The sphere turned white. I did the same for a Darkling, and the sphere turned deep ultraviolet. "Observe this cube," I said, and let the affinity sphere do its thing. Within seconds, it turned medium gray.

Fjoeruss hissed a breath through his teeth. "This is not a trick?"

I rolled my eyes. "Who do I look like—you?"

He stared longingly at the cube, seemingly unable to take his eyes from it. "You will revive my sister if I agree to help you close the Grand Nexus?"

"No," Mom said. "You must help us to defeat Daelissa."

His gaze remained on the null cube with his husked sister. "I assume trapping her in Seraphina counts."

"It does." Mom stepped beside him. "We cannot trust you with simple assurances. I don't for a moment believe you wouldn't try to find a loophole to get out of any agreement that didn't suit you."

"Draft whatever contract makes you comfortable." Fjoeruss directed his gray gaze at Mom. "I will keep my word and help Mr. Slade end his war."

"It's not my war." I gave him a look of disbelief. "If anything, it's Daelissa's war."

"War is war, Mr. Slade." He crossed his arms. "When will you revive my sister?" Fjoeruss's gaze caught on something behind me and tightened.

"My creator," Cinder said in a calm voice.

I turned to see my golem friend standing in the control room doorway.

"I would dearly love to look at your spark," Fjoeruss said. He walked toward Cinder and extended a hand. "I am Fjoeruss." Aside from Fjoeruss's peach-colored skin, the two looked identical.

Cinder shook the Seraphim's hand. "I would prefer you not open my head, but it is a pleasant surprise to meet you." He tilted his head. "Should I refer to you as Dad?"

Fjoeruss chuckled. "That might be somewhat awkward." He released Cinder's hand and looked him up and down. "I see you still dress in gray. It would appear much of the original programming still drives your spark."

"There are certain urges which are hard to ignore," the golem said. "Justin has told me you have golems with natural skin tone. Would it be difficult to change my skin color so it is not so"—he looked at his pallid hands—"lifeless?"

"I'm sure we could come to an agreement," Fjoeruss said.

Mom quickly stepped to Cinder's side. "Be very careful making deals with this man or you might end up losing your spark to him."

"Man?" An amused smile slipped over Fjoeruss's lips. "You've spent too much time among the mortals, Alysea. Do you also refer to Daemos as men and women?"

"You're sidestepping the point," Mom said. "What is your price for giving Cinder normal-looking skin?"

"A chance to examine his spark." Fjoeruss held up his hands. "The golem will come to absolutely no harm. I promise."

"You just barely finished making a deal to revive your sister in exchange for help against Daelissa, and you're already wheeling and dealing again," I said. "Looks like an addiction to me."

"You still have not answered my question," Fjoeruss said to me. "When will you revive my sister?"

"I will have her put into an aether pod with the very next batch if you'll grant Cinder his request for natural skin."

Cinder shook his head. "No, Justin. I believe that would be a very unfair deal for you."

Fjoeruss raised an eyebrow. "How so?"

"First, I should apologize for eavesdropping." Cinder looked at me. "I stood in the doorway and listened to the terms of your agreement with Fjoeruss. Although you did not agree to a timeline for reviving his sister, I believe you could glean valuable information from him by adding certain conditions."

I saw Fjoeruss stiffen and knew he hadn't expected Cinder to show such business acumen. I had to admit, I was a little surprised myself. Although the golem had issues pretending to be human, he was excellent at finding and disseminating information.

"What conditions?" Fjoeruss asked.

"I think it would be very beneficial to our cause if you would share how you create golems." Cinder approximated a shrug. "Though I have seen golems made of stone, wood, and even metal, only yours simulate real people. How do you make lifelike flesh? How do you make them act of their own accord without constant input?"

The Seraphim regarded Cinder with an almost proud look on his face. "Rather than have me change your skin to a natural hue, you would learn the very secrets of creation itself."

"In this way, my selfish request could instead be used for the common good." Cinder turned to me. "Does this sound acceptable, Justin?"

I had to admit I didn't like the idea of using someone's sister as collateral for a deal, even if that person was Fjoeruss, a person who'd tried to kill me in the past.

Mom made the decision for me. "It sounds like an excellent deal."

"Even if I gave you the secrets, you would be unable to use them," Fjoeruss said. "It requires someone with my particular affinity to create such lifelike facsimiles."

"What about someone like me?" I asked.

He pursed his lips. "You have demonstrated an ability to channel both Murk and Brilliance, so it would not surprise me if you are capable."

"It doesn't sound like you lose anything if you tell us the secret to making gray men and their more lifelike brethren." I felt a rush of gratitude toward Cinder. If I could close this deal, I could make an army. "If I agree to put your sister in the front of the line for revival, will you also divulge those secrets?"

"You are not the same boy who asked me for help when his mother was kidnapped." A pleased smile crept over Fjoeruss's lips. "Using my sister in such a way is rather ruthless."

A pang of guilt knotted in my chest. I did feel kind of bad. *But not that bad.*

"Your sister caused the Desecration," Elyssa said in a low, angry voice. "She sacrificed thousands of lives so she could get what she wanted. I suggest you look at her example if you want to define ruthlessness."

Fjoeruss's lip curled into a snarl. "My sister was a brave, caring soul. She wanted an end to the conflict. If only I had listened to her sooner!" He flinched, as if suddenly realizing he'd said too much.

His outburst gave me a hint of insight into the way he operated. Fjoeruss wasn't simply intent on maintaining the status quo—he wanted to maintain peace at any cost. "Everything you've done up to now has been in your sister's name, hasn't it?" I asked.

The Seraphim pressed his lips tight and turned to me. "I will agree to your price. Draft the contract and let's be done with it."

I could tell from the look on his face I wouldn't be getting any more informative freebies right now, so I nodded, turned to Mom. "Please create the contract."

She excused herself and took a portal back to Big Creek Ranch.

"Cinder, would you give me a tour of this facility?" Fjoeruss asked after Mom left.

Cinder looked at me. "Is this permissible?"

I nodded. "I doubt there's much here he doesn't know about already." I slapped Fjoeruss on the back. "Plus, he's part of the team now, right?"

The Seraphim looked at me from the corner of his eye. "Do not assume such familiarity with me, Mr. Slade. I am partnering with you on a temporary basis, nothing more." He offered a sarcastic smile. "There will be no lasting friendships from this venture."

I shrugged. "Your loss, dude. I think you could use a few friends in this world instead of being the guy nobody trusts." I looked at Cinder. "I'll be here if you need me."

"Very well, Justin." Cinder turned and left with Fjoeruss in tow.

Elyssa squeezed my hand and squealed with delight. "We did it, didn't we?"

I gazed at the doorway. "We did something." For some reason, the excitement had faded. Would Fjoeruss keep his word, or would he cite some technicality and leave us hanging out to dry?

Only time would tell.

Chapter 16

As Fjoeruss spoke with Cinder, Elyssa and I took a stroll to the dragons. Altash, his long lean muzzle resting on the floor, regarded me with a parietal eye. Things were approaching a climax about ten hours from now and there was one major faction I hadn't convinced to join our cause.

Jeremiah had been on friendly terms with the dragons, and Altash had once spoken to me. I hoped that meant he would talk to me again. The problem was, I didn't exactly know how to broach the subject.

Keeping it simple seemed best, so I went direct. "We need your help fighting the war against Daelissa."

I heard a low rumble and suddenly Lulu's giant purple head shifted toward us to the right. It was definitely creepy having a giant eye looking at us from both sides.

Elyssa gripped my arm. "Did they say anything?"

I shook my head. A couple of deep breaths settled my nerves. Since I wasn't sure who wore the pants—err scales—in the family, I looked back and forth to make eye contact with both of the dragons. "We need to shut down the Grand Nexus for good. The dragons fought in the first war. Will you help us end this one quickly?"

Lulu seemed to regard Altash. He snorted. She snorted back. He vibrated the air with a growl. Lulu's pupil shrank. She picked up her head and moved it away back to its original resting position.

"Is that a yes?" I asked.

WE CANNOT. The loud words echoed in my head.

Elyssa and I jumped and shouted in surprise at the same time.

Altash curled his head back onto his snakelike body. Our brief audience was over.

My pulse was racing. Elyssa pressed a hand to her heart.

"He needs to lower his voice," she said.

I felt my jaw tighten as I looked at the lazy dragons. I was tempted climb up Altash and kick him in the snout until he agreed to help us. Unfortunately, he was many times larger than the tragon and I'd only succeed in hurting my foot.

"Why won't you help us?" I shouted. "At least explain it to me!"

No explanation came.

I blew out a frustrated breath and turned to Elyssa. "Have you seen Slitheren and his gang around?" Slitheren and the leyworms like him were a smaller, different breed of dragon from Altash and Lulu, but he was still plenty big.

"Cinder told me the smaller dragons were out on their rounds." She bit her lower lip. "There's no telling when they'll be back."

Leyworms seemed to be responsible for maintaining ley lines, the magical power conduits running through the world. How exactly they performed such tasks remained a mystery. The smaller leyworms seemed to do all the work, judging from how much Altash and Lulu lazed around.

"Let's see if we can find them anyway." We spent better part of an hour wandering through the various tunnels and holes in the nearby vicinity, but failed to locate any of the gang.

Mom finally returned with a very long scroll drawn up by a Templar legal expert.

Elyssa grimaced when she saw it. "Looks like something a nom government would write."

My eyes swam just looking at all the neatly quilled verbiage on the yellowed parchment. "I'm getting a headache." I returned it to her. "Will it hold up?"

Mom nodded. "This Templar has done hundreds of deals with Daemos over the years. As I'm sure you've observed with your father, they are known for trickery. If anyone knows how to confine the Trickster to a contract, it would be this woman."

"Are you sure?" I asked.

"I believe even he will be hard pressed to find a loophole in this document." She rolled the parchment. "Both you and he will need to sign it."

We found him talking to Cinder near the bank of aether pods in the main cave. Altash's red, scaly head rested on the floor behind them, providing a surreal backdrop. As I watched Fjoeruss and Cinder talk, several alarming thoughts ran through my mind. What if Fjoeruss still had control over Cinder? What if he'd reprogrammed my friend without me knowing? I had no idea if that was possible. Altash's parietal eye blinked open and seemed to stare at me for a moment.

Not a word was said, nor a sound made, but something told me the huge dragon was looking out for Cinder and wouldn't let anything happen. I braced myself in case he planned to say something. Altash had spoken to me once through telepathy, and it was like the mental version of an old person texting in all caps at the top of their lungs. I didn't like anyone, much less a giant dragon, yelling in my head. Aside from my rambling thoughts, I didn't receive any mental communications.

I met the leviathan's gaze. *Yeah, you just keep on being stoic, big fella.*

Altash closed his eye and resumed being lazy. Ever since we'd created the aether pods, the dragons hadn't consumed any more husks and projectile vomited them back out once they were restored as cupids. They really didn't seem to do much except sleep and occasionally open their eyes to watch us.

Fjoeruss saw us coming and looked at the scroll in Mom's hand. He took it from her without a word and read it. I fiddled with a game on my phone while I waited and waited some more. When he finally finished reading, he chuckled. "Very thorough, Alysea. Whoever designed this agreement did an impressive job."

Mom held a quill out to him. "Ready to sign?"

Fjoeruss channeled a hovering gray tabletop, placed the contract on it, and signed. He handed the quill to me. I was thankful my time at Arcane University had taught me how to write with a quill even if my signature looked like a spaghetti noodle had collided with a ball of yarn. I signed and handed the quill to Mom.

She looked it over and nodded. "The deal is sealed."

Fjoeruss waved a hand toward the aether pods. "Cinder tells me this batch will be done within hours. I would like my sister put in a pod the moment one becomes available."

I checked the time. It was already super late, and we had a battle to fight the next day. "Agreed. Can you do that Cinder?"

"I would be happy to, Justin." Cinder turned to Fjoeruss. "I was interesting meeting you."

The Seraphim gave him a nod. "Consider my offer. I promise no harm will come to you."

Cinder tried on a smile. "I will, though I admit my sense of self-preservation makes me hesitant."

"Now, for business." Fjoeruss folded his arms across his chest. "What role will I play in this assault on the Grand Nexus?"

Elyssa took out her arcphone. "I conferred with my father. He'll need the number of your golem forces, their strengths, and weaknesses."

"The gray men, as you call them, are not all alike." Fjoeruss looked at his watch. "I have an elite force of two hundred who would be a match for the vampires' Red Cell. Another hundred are less physically capable, but crafted to withstand magical attacks and disable Arcanes." He flicked the screen on his watch. "The rank and file consist of two-hundred golems that are a match for most common vampires." He gave us a wry look. "Though after today, I am short by the eighteen you destroyed."

"Five hundred golems? Is that it?" I'd expected him to have thousands of the things. On the bright side, he didn't have thousands of lifeless beings ready to obey his every command or he might have taken over the world for himself by now.

"Those are the forces I can most readily commit." He pressed a button on the watch and the screen blinked off. "I have experimental units, but they would be unsuitable for an operation in such tight quarters."

"Such as?" Elyssa prompted.

Fjoeruss seemed hesitant, but finally spoke. "Let us say they rival even the behemoths one might see at the Grand Melee."

I whistled. The golems at the Grand Melee could range up to three stories high. "I think you're right. As large as the Grand Nexus way station is, it's already going to be packed with our forces."

Elyssa was busy tapping away on her arcphone. It chimed a couple times as she received text messages. She looked up. "I have your units slotted with the lycans. You'll be responsible for taking down any vampire forces present."

"What are the enemy's numbers?" Fjoeruss asked.

"At this point, we're not entirely sure," Elyssa said. "Daelissa's forces seemed small and uncoordinated during our operations to take back Obsidian Arches. Since we captured her lead strategist, we don't know if they've pulled back to the nexus, or if we'll arrive to find only a token force."

"We've planned for the worst," I assured Fjoeruss.

He stroked his chin. "I should hope so. I find it rather disappointing you haven't done a better job with reconnaissance."

"We didn't want to tip our hand by opening portals and sending through scouts," I said. "With the element of surprise, we might win this battle handily."

I motioned everyone back toward the control room. "I'll send you wherever you need to go with an omniarch to ready your forces."

Elyssa showed Fjoeruss something on her phone as we walked. "La Casona is your rally point and this is the number of the arch operator. He can arrange an omniarch portal wherever you need one."

"I already have an Obsidian Arch at my disposal," he replied as he tapped the information into his watch. "I will send my units through to the La Casona Obsidian Arch if that is acceptable."

She nodded. "It is."

We arrived in the control room.

Fjoeruss stepped up to one of the functioning omniarches. "I will use the arch myself." He stopped and turned to me. "Once my sister is in a pod, I will transmit the instructions for creating my special breed of golems."

"I might need some lessons to go along with that," I said.

"Perhaps. It will take time and patience." Fjoeruss touched a thumb to the silver circle around the omniarch and sealed the magical circuit. He turned toward the arch, and activated it. A room with the tapestry of a woman in a pink dress hanging from the wall appeared. He turned to face us. "Don't attempt to use this tapestry to open a portal to this location. I change it with every use."

I gave him an unconcerned look. "Wouldn't dream of it."

"Until tomorrow," he said, and stepped through the portal. It winked off a second later.

"He changes it?" Elyssa arched an eyebrow. "Talk about paranoid."

I turned to Cinder. "You're not going to let him mess with your brain are you?"

The golem gave me a blank look. "I do not have a brain." He touched a finger to his forehead. "Though, in a general sense of the word, I suppose my spark is like a brain." He shook his head. "I decided it was not wise to let him study me. To him, I am likely still just a tool."

I gripped his shoulder. "To us, you're a friend, and we don't want to lose you."

Elyssa touched his other shoulder. "Exactly."

"Why have I been given no role in the assault?" Cinder almost managed to look a little hurt at being left out.

I had a good reason. "Your work here is far too important to interrupt. Come over here." I led him to the briefcase with the prisms where I'd left it near the null cubes. I opened the case and showed him the small crystals. "These might help the Darklings feed without becoming sick."

Cinder took one and held it between his thumb and forefinger. "How interesting. Will you show me how they work?"

"Right this way." I headed back into the cavern, walked to the dragons, and into the large space between their coils. The space in between was partitioned by stone walls molded from the cave floor by smaller leyworms. One area was a nursery for the newly reborn Seraphim. An adjacent area was filled with bunk beds for the older ones. Joss and Otaleon were inside this area. Joss was reading a thick book entitled *Science and You*. Otaleon was fiddling with a deck of cards.

The two Darklings stood when we entered.

"Are we to take part in the assault?" Joss asked. He looked eager.

"Maybe," I said. "Cinder, can you fetch one of the nom volunteers?"

"I'm here," Abe said, coming around the corner. "I heard you all talking and was feeling nosy." He smiled.

I returned the smile. "We'd like to test something again, if you don't mind."

"Go right ahead, son."

135

I showed Joss the prism. "Put this this in your right hand with this symbol facing Abe." I showed him the symbol for light.

Joss put the object in his hand. As with Fjoeruss, it seemed to adhere to his skin. He gave it a wondering look. "What next?"

I waved a hand toward Abe. "Feed."

The Darkling's fingers twitched. Abe's hand rose toward Joss's and white soul essence trickled out slowly through one finger. More essence began to stream from his other fingers until he was feeding at a normal rate.

Joss's eyes went wide. "I—I seem to remember this device." He narrowed his eyes as if reaching for distant memory, then shook his head. "I cannot quite remember why I recognize it."

"These were used by Brightlings to force Darklings to feed on Brilliance." I motioned to his other hand. "Feed with your left."

He raised it. Abe's left arm rose toward his and smoky tendrils of Murk drifted from his fingers and into Joss's.

"This is amazing," Otaleon said, eyes bright. "How does it feel, Joss?"

"Incredible." Joss's right eye glowed white, while his left glimmered with ultraviolet. "I feel so strong now."

I handed the briefcase to Cinder. "This is how they need to feed from now on."

Abe's knee's wobbled, and I gripped Joss's arm. "That's enough for now."

The Darkling flinched, but stopped feeding. "My apologies, Abe. The feeling was so wondrous, I forgot myself."

Abe leaned against the wall. "No problem, son." He looked at me. "We put the word out for recruits, and, boy, have they answered the call. This place is gonna stink like a veterans' hospital in no time."

I laughed. "We'll make sure our healers take care of everyone. You'll obviously want to be in top shape for feeding."

Abe wiped a bead of sweat from his forehead. "Tell me about it."

Joss clenched his fists. "I feel as if I could take on Daelissa herself, Justin." His eyes lit with determination. "I want to take part in the assault."

"As do I," Otaleon said. "How long do we have until it begins?"

I checked the time and held back a groan. "Eight hours until assembly. Are there enough volunteers for you two to feed from?"

"I believe so," Otaleon said.

Cinder checked his arcphone. "There are four who should be recovered enough from the last feeding."

"I gotta admit, this double feeding takes it out of me faster," Abe said. "Better keep a close eye on the fellas while you're doing it."

Joss walked over to the man, put a hand on his shoulder and looked him directly in the eye. "We will exercise utmost caution, my friend."

Abe grinned. "Good man—err—angel."

I looked at Cinder. "Do we have any more Darklings who are ready for prime time?"

"Not yet." He checked his arcphone. "It will be at least another week before our first batch reaches maturity."

I didn't like that it was taking so long, but once we had more volunteers, I hoped we'd be able to field our new batches more quickly. I got Joss and Otaleon's attention. "Elyssa and I need some shuteye. Meet us at La Casona in eight hours, okay?"

"We will," Otaleon said.

Elyssa and I said our goodbyes and walked back between the dragons' coils and into the main chamber. Cinder followed us.

"I wish you luck," he said. "Please, be careful."

"We will," Elyssa said, stifling a yawn.

"I also request that you kick ass and chew bubblegum." A slightly manic grin stretched his mouth.

I kept a straight face. "I assume you got that little nugget from Shelton."

He nodded. "I keep a record of his colorful sayings so I can use them when appropriate."

"Good idea," Elyssa said with a smile.

She and I waved goodbye to Cinder and headed back into the control room where we took an omniarch portal back to the Templar compound. I was dead tired and tomorrow was going to be a brutal day.

Chapter 17

La Casona was a madhouse.

I could only imagine what the other way stations looked like. Templars clad in black Nightingale armor raced around taking care of last minute tasks as the countdown to the assault reached T-minus thirty minutes. Several Templars-at-arms distributed swords and other equipment. Templar Arcanes tucked rolled-up flying carpets beneath their arms so they could hover in the rear ranks and cast spells over our front lines.

Elyssa and I overlooked the activity from a flying carpet of our own. "He's not here yet," I said.

She bit her lower lip. "I hope he hasn't wriggled through another of his loopholes."

"I wouldn't be surprised." I looked down at a large group of people who weren't nearly as color coordinated as the sea of black uniforms around them. "At least it looks like we have plenty of lycans."

"Are those felycans?" Elyssa pointed at another smaller group standing well away from the werewolves.

Massive cats with bristling fur and bony protrusions on their spines were curled up on the floor behind the strangers. "I think so, because those oversized housecats behind them are definitely moggies." I spotted the huge lion man from the meeting. He seemed to be the one in charge.

Elyssa's eyes flashed surprise. "I'm surprised there are so many."

I spotted Stacey walking across from the lycans to her fellow felycans. Even with her preggers bulge, she still managed to walk in the most seductive way, hips swaying, her body moving with liquid, feline grace. She even captivated the eyes of a few Templars. Stacey clapped her hands and got the attention of her kitty comrades. I couldn't make out what she said thanks to distance and the general hubbub of activity, but whatever it was seemed to galvanize the felycans.

Some of them roared like lions even in human form, causing some lycans to howl in response.

I elbowed Elyssa in the ribs. "Brings a whole new meaning to cat calls, doesn't it?"

She groaned. "Maybe you can defeat Daelissa with bad jokes."

"If only."

A trumpet sounded. There was a flurry of activity and suddenly the mass of Templars melted into neat formations. The lycans and felycans were a lot less organized, but an OCD Templar had thoughtfully marked the floors where those two groups should line up, making it a paint-by-numbers exercise.

A klaxon sounded and a low hum filled the cavern as the Obsidian Arch powered on. The space between the towering arch columns flickered between white, gray, and black. The humming noise wound higher and higher until, with a loud crackle, the air within the arch split open. Three platoons of gray men appeared on the other side.

Without a shout of command, the perfectly aligned formations marched through.

The first platoon was comprised of golems in their standard gray business outfits complete with dark sunglasses and slicked-back silvery hair. They merged into a double-file line at a position marked by Templar organizers.

Elyssa breathed a sigh of relief. "I guess your Mom's contract held up."

A knot of pressure in my chest loosened a little at the sudden appearance of Fjoeruss's forces. "Thank god." I felt my forehead wrinkle as the next group of gray men marched through.

The golems in this platoon wore gray trench coats and matching fedoras. Their clothing glittered as if coated with sequins. Futuristic guns hung from leather holsters at their waists.

"What the heck are they supposed to be?" I said. "Disco cowboys?"

139

Elyssa squinted. "I think their clothing is made of diamond fiber."

"Ah." I magnified my vision. "They must be the anti-Arcane golems."

"Those guns sure look weird." She looked at me. "Looks like something from one of your space movies."

"More like something from a black-and-white sci-fi movie from the fifties." I was really curious to see what they did.

The members of the third and last platoon emerged from the arch portal. These golems wore gray leather outfits with burgundy lightning symbols on the sleeves. Black leather gloves and tall matching jackboots completed the outfit. Curved sabers with sparkling hilt guards hung from both sides of their sword belts.

"Diamond fiber sabers," Elyssa murmured. "Wow. I can't imagine how expensive and difficult it was to make those."

"More difficult than making the trench coats?" I asked.

She nodded. "Diamond fiber is almost indestructible, so you can't sharpen it. You have to layer the blade, and even then, it's nearly impossible to give it a sharp edge before the spell resistance kicks in."

I'd seen diamond fiber used in all sorts of capacities. Unfortunately, the magical resistance that made it so strong also made it somewhat useless for people who used spells because it interfered with magic. I assumed the anti-Arcane golems could wear the diamond fiber clothing because they didn't use magic.

"I have a feeling Fjoeruss might be into cowboys and pirates." I suspected if I could make golems like he did, I might build armies of my own toy soldiers.

Elyssa chuckled. "They're like full-sized dolls for grown men."

Fjoeruss flew through the arch on a large carpet. He saw us and glided to our position as the Obsidian Arch powered down with a low hum. "Is the assault ready to commence?"

"Better almost late than never, huh?" I said.

"I am a very busy person," Fjoeruss said. "It behooves me to be efficient with my time."

A voice boomed across the cavern. "Leadership, take positions."

"Guess that's us," I said, giving Fjoeruss a pointed look.

He didn't seem the least bit fazed. "I will follow your lead, Mr. Slade."

I directed our carpet over the heads of the troops and took us through the control room door. Most control room doors were hidden by illusion and only wide enough for two people to walk through side-by-side. In advance of this operation, Commander Salazar's people had remodeled the doorway so an elephant could fit through the thing. I swooped through easily and zipped down the center aisle to a niche filled with omniarches.

We held position on our carpet, hovering across the aisle from the omniarches. Fjoeruss stopped to our left. Commander Salazar arrived a moment later on his rug and was followed by a carpet bearing Colin McCloud. Stacey and Ryland appeared on a carpet of their own a moment later.

I waved at my friends. "How in the world did you get felycans to help?" I asked Stacey.

Ryland barked a laugh. "Might wanna wait and hear that story later."

"A bloody nightmare," Stacey said, gracing us with a smile. "I believe it will be worth it."

"Mutants," Fjoeruss said under his breath.

My super hearing, however, heard it just fine. "I don't appreciate you calling my friends names."

"Simply an observation," Fjoeruss said without a hint of shame. "Though we Brightlings were responsible for creating vampires, it is interesting how humans mutated into magical beings on their own."

"Call it what you will," Stacey said. "I consider it evolution."

Another trumpet echoed in the main way station outside. Templars activated each of the three functioning omniarches across the aisle. Portals winked on. Through the gateways, I saw a cavernous hallway lined with ornate marble arches and a black marble floor veined with white. A massive statue loomed in the center of the corridor. The middle portal looked upon the front of the statue while the other two portals viewed it from diagonal angles.

"I think it's rather ironic we used Daelissa's statue as a reference for our portals," Elyssa said.

Fjoeruss grunted. "I suppose it is rather poetic."

"Forward troops advance," boomed the voice of the head coordinator.

Templar troops swarmed into the control room in ranks six soldiers across. As the line reached the first portal, the first two columns veered into it. The middle two columns entered the center portal while the last columns entered the portal to my left. Within minutes, the Templar force was through.

The coordinator sounded another command. "Leadership, advance!"

I took us through the portal. My vision warped as if looking from inside a fishbowl for a split instant as we entered the traversion tunnel and just as quickly snapped back to normal as we reached the other side thousands of miles away. Fjoeruss emerged from a portal thirty yards to our left while the other carpets came through the right portal.

Climbing higher, I took us to a position twenty feet above the troops. Looking at the arched ceiling hundreds of feet overhead, I felt like a Lilliputian might while walking into the house of a giant. Even the massive statue of Daelissa reached only halfway to the ceiling. The corridor was at least a couple hundred yards wide, and far too long for me to even guess its length. Other large statues lined the hallway. My eyes caught on one that bore a striking likeness to Fjoeruss.

As I gaped like a tourist, I spotted scouts racing ahead while, far behind us, Templars in the rear ranks set up pedestals with symbols on them and transmitted the pictures to our troops located around the world. Portals blinked open in front of each of the paintings. Blue Cloaks streamed through one, while other Arcanes came through another. A sortie of flying carpets zipped through another portal and hovered above the Blue Cloaks. I saw Shelton and Bella on one of them.

After the Blue Cloaks were through, my father and Aunt Vallaena led the Houses of Daemos into the corridor. Kassallandra, Domitia, Godric, Yuuki, and the other leaders followed in order of power. Each house head carried a flying carpet.

I took us over to Dad and Vallaena and landed the carpet on the floor. "Ready for this?" I asked him.

He walked between me and Elyssa, wrapping an arm around our shoulders and squeezing. "You bet." He surveyed the crowd. "I gotta say, this is pretty damned amazing, son. I'm proud of you."

Vallaena smiled at me. "You have come so far, nephew."

I grinned. "Seems like just yesterday you were chasing me down with your hellhounds at Arcane University."

Her eyes almost seemed to mist at the memory. Vallaena leaned forward and kissed me on the cheek.

I gave her a surprised look. "What was that for?"

"For rising to the challenge and proving your worth." She looked at Elyssa. "I must also admit that this young woman has done more for you than I thought possible." She squeezed my hand. "I know I have been somewhat overbearing in the past, but it was necessary."

I saw battle coordinators on flying carpets flashing the signal that indicated we would be marching forward soon and realized just how big and dangerous this operation would be. I gripped Vallaena in a tight hug and gave her a peck on the cheek. "Thank you," I said. "Stay safe."

Vallaena's lips curled into a smile. She turned to Dad. "I told you he likes me."

Dad snorted. "At least somebody does." He gave me and Elyssa another quick hug. "Stay safe, kiddos. I guess we need to get into position."

I saw Godric floating on his flying carpet. He gave me a cold look before turning away.

"We'll see you soon," I told Dad and Vallaena. I took the flying carpet bearing Elyssa and me back into the air and headed for the command positions.

"There's your mother," Elyssa said, pointing toward a carpet with Mom and Ivy on it. They were hovering next to Joss and Otaleon. Nightliss stood on a carpet of her own with a worried expression on her face.

"What's wrong?" I asked the petite Darkling.

Nightliss frowned. "Nothing in particular. I believe I am suffering flashbacks."

Mom nodded. "It's like déjà vu all over again."

"The outcome will be different," I said, projecting a confident smile.

Ivy wrinkled her nose as she looked at the army beneath us. "This place stinks. All the body odor drifts up here."

"Probably not body odor," I said. "Just a lot of nervous farts."

Ivy grimaced. "Eww!"

143

The battle coordinators flashed another symbol and the back half of the army responded by marching backward to make more room as lycans arrived from La Casona. Instead of forming columns and rows, they pooled into smaller packs, as did the felycans and moggies who came through shortly after.

I scanned the corridor. "I'm really surprised there's no response from the enemy yet."

"It is a bit strange." Elyssa peered through a set of magnifying spectacles. "I know we're being quiet, but moving so many soldiers makes enough noise to alert anyone with one ear."

The gray men were the last to arrive. They formed neat square formations on the eastern side of the corridor.

The south corridor was filled for hundreds of yards in either direction by our army. Even with so many soldiers, there was still a wide aisle down the middle of our forces in case we needed to shuffle their order for any reason. The Daemos and Blue Cloaks were in the rear to the west and east, respectively. The shifters—lycans and felycans—were in front of the Blue Cloaks while the gray men stood before the Daemos. Templar soldiers and Arcanes were at the forefront.

The battle coordinators flashed the symbol to advance. The front ranks of Templars marched toward the entrance to the nexus way station several hundred yards down the corridor.

I looked at Fjoeruss and nodded my head toward the statue in his likeness. "I love what you guys did with the place. Makes me want to drop to my knees and do some worshipping."

He cast a sour look at the statue. "I did not request a sculpture raised, but Daelissa felt the desire to decorate after these annexes were built."

"How long did it take to build the corridors?"

"Not as long as you might think." He glanced at Nightliss. "We had a large workforce of Darklings build the corridors and the hub. It took several decades for the basic structure, and several more to embellish them."

Nightliss's lips peeled back. "It was the building of this place that caused my people to revolt. Little did Daelissa know that she built the very Darkling army that opposed her."

"Indeed." Fjoeruss looked unimpressed. "Your sister has never appreciated irony, so I doubt she ever blamed her own lack of foresight for the war."

"Though my memories may never again be complete, I now remember the day Daelissa enslaved me and brought me here to help build this grand monument." Nightliss jabbed a finger toward the huge statue of her sister. "If I could, I would topple it over on her."

Elyssa's eyes flashed wide. "Ouch. I've heard of sibling rivalry, but it doesn't sound like you and Daelissa ever got along."

Nightliss shook her head vehemently. "Daelissa discovered her affinity a day before mine came to me. Even before then we had never been close. Our parents always spoiled her. It was no secret they preferred the blonde hair and fair skin she shared with our mother."

Fjoeruss looked at her appraisingly. "It will be interesting to see if you have it in you to kill your own sister, should the opportunity arise."

More symbols flashed as our troops neared the entrance to the nexus.

"It's time for us to advance," I said and moved my arm forward.

"I'm nervous," Joss said as we flew over the moving troops. He touched his stomach.

Fjoeruss stared at Joss. "You've been feeding from both essences, I see."

"How do you know that?" Joss asked.

"The eyes," Fjoeruss replied.

Otaleon narrowed his gaze. "I know you from somewhere."

"I'm sure you do." Fjoeruss turned to me. "They just flashed the symbol for my troops to move out. It is best I accompany them." Before I could answer, he flew away.

"I have a bad feeling about him." Otaleon's eyes stayed on Fjoeruss. "Something in the past tickles my mind, but I cannot remember it."

"Agreed," Joss said. "It is unsettling."

I clapped my hands together to get their attention, and to cover my own nervousness. It felt like I had a flock of hummingbirds fluttering in my stomach and occasionally pecking my heart. "Fjoeruss used to be one of the bad guys. Technically, he's not really good now, but he's contractually bound to help us."

"Plus, we have his sister," Elyssa added.

Nightliss looked confused. "Fjoeruss has a sister?"

I told her about the null cube with the gray affinity and the contract we'd made with him.

"It sounds like you were very busy last night." Nightliss gave me a sympathetic smile.

Mom sighed. "I'd hoped to have a girls' night, but instead it turned into more work."

I looked Joss and Otaleon up and down. "Aside from nerves, how do you feel?"

"Powerful," Joss said.

Otaleon nodded. "I feel ready to take on the Empire itself."

I quirked an eyebrow. "Empire?"

"Ah, the Seraphim Empire." He smiled. "An old memory of the uprising intruded."

"So here's where all the elite hang out." A carpet with Shelton and Bella banked around us and skidded to a stop a few feet away.

I grinned. "I was wondering where you were."

"Apparently, we never got slotted with anyone, so I said screw it, grabbed a spare carpet, and followed the Daemos through." He rubbed the back of his neck and looked around. "Man, does it stink up here, or is it just me?"

"Harry!" Bella slapped his shoulder.

"It's nervous battle farts." Ivy pinched her nose. "I think those felycans ate too much broccoli beforehand."

Mom gave Ivy a shocked look.

Shelton snorted. "Yeah, guess we're flying in the fart zone up here."

The battle coordinators showed the symbol to halt. Our army paused a hundred yards from the entrance to the Grand Nexus way station.

I looked toward the opening and wondered what lay inside the main cavern. It felt like the calm before the storm.

The sound of scurrying feet filled the corridor. I looked toward the disturbance. The walls at the far end of the hall appeared to be crawling. I magnified my vision and saw a wave of Nazdal, their misshapen humanoid forms loping along the floors, the curved walls, and ceiling.

Some wore chains manacled to their wrists or necks. Their heads were huge, mouths like great gaping sores with clusters of sharp teeth protruding at all angles. The creatures came from a realm called Sturg and they were nasty opponents. They soaked up the life force of the dying, gaining strength, size, and even magic resistance with each feast of the fallen.

A growl escaped my throat. "I thought we'd killed most of them."

Elyssa cursed. "They must have brought in fresh reinforcements from Sturg using the Grand Nexus."

I saw the flutter of wings as hundreds of dark forms filled the air behind the Nazdal.

A trumpet sounded and the lead platoons of Templars advanced toward the oncoming horde.

"What are those things?" I asked.

Elyssa shook her head and handed me her spectacles. When I peered through them, my butt puckered. Humanoids with giant webbed wings like those of bats soared through the air while hundreds of Nazdal clambered across the walls and ceilings around them. It was only when I sighted bared fangs did I realize the affiliation of the flying creatures.

Vampires.

Chapter 18

"Flying vampires?" My voice shot up an octave.

I'd read horror stories about vampires who could morph into bats and fly away, but having encountered plenty of vampires, I'd never once seen any turn into bats, much less grow huge black wings and fly. If Daelissa and her kind were capable of turning humans into vampires, could she also have given them this ability?

"I wonder if Serena had something to do with these winged vamps," Elyssa said. "That crazy Arcane would experiment on her own mother, given the chance."

I knew this to be true from my experience as a "guest" of Serena's in her Gloom Fortress at Bellwood Quarry. The kooky Arcane had fed humans to a cluster of minders she called the brain. Maybe she'd come up with a potion for vampire wings.

"As if regular vampires weren't enough, now we gotta deal with these mofos," Shelton said.

Bella looked worried. "I just hope they aren't stronger than normal vampires."

A chorus of howls rose from below as dozens of lycans morphed into massive humanoid wolf creatures. Some remained in human form while others shifted into super-sized wolves. The felycans shifted as well, some changing into half-cat, half-human, and some turning into oversized cats of prey. The huge felycan man turned into a saber-toothed feline of immense proportions.

Shelton watched the spectacle with big eyes. "Holy fur balls. That cat could take down a wooly mammoth."

I spotted Thomas Borathen on a levitating command platform near the front lines. The platform was about twenty feet wide and constructed of enchanted titanium. It held ten people, but it wasn't nearly as fast as the flying carpets. Thomas shouted commands and the other people on the platform relayed the commands to the various units.

"I'm moving us up," I told Elyssa.

She gripped my arm. "We're supposed to wait here."

"These flying vampires weren't part of the plan. I can blast them out of the air."

Elyssa's eyes hardened. "My father is well aware of your capabilities, Justin. He's also aware that you are a finite resource. If you use all your energy on this first wave, what happens if there are more?"

I heard my knuckles crack as my fists clenched of their own volition. Our first wave rushed to meet the dark cloud of Nazdal and vampires. My heart seemed to freeze in my chest. So many people were about to die, and there was nothing I could do to prevent it. I released a breath and tried to force the tension out of my chest.

"You're right. I just"—I sighed—"I hate all this death."

Elyssa kissed my cheek. "I know, baby. I know."

I grabbed a spare set of spectacles from my utility belt, took our carpet higher, and watched the battle unfold. I heard a swooshing noise and felt wind against my right side. Glancing right, I saw a sortie of Blue Cloaks zip past on their carpets and head into the oncoming storm.

A Nazdal the size of a horse led his army of crooked, crawling humanoids. He bellowed. Spittle sprayed from his lipless mouth. Huge chains hung from an iron band around his neck and from manacles on his biceps. The chains were a sign of authority to the twisted creatures.

The first wave of Templars crashed into the Nazdal army. I heard the creak and clatter of catapults. Hundreds of glittering shards flew from within our ranks and landed among the fighters.

"What was that?" I asked.

Elyssa grimaced. "It's how my father decided to handle the Nazdal life-leeching ability."

"How?"

"Is he using soulstones?" Shelton asked with a look of horror. "Those things are banned for a good reason."

"Soulstones?" I asked.

"They trap soul essence at the moment of death." Shelton made a face and spat over the side of his carpet.

"Hey, watch it up there!" yelled an Arcane below as he wiped his face.

Shelton looked over the side of his carpet. "Sorry!"

"The soulstones will keep the Nazdal from leeching the life force from the dying?" I asked.

"They should," Elyssa said. She looked at the fighting. "It looks like the Templars have soulstones in their utility belts, too."

"Those things are evil," Shelton said. "You know who uses them?" The question was obviously rhetorical, because he didn't wait for an answer. "Necromancers do. I couldn't list a single one of them I'd bring home and introduce to my mother."

"Will the souls of our people be trapped in the stones?" The mere idea horrified me.

Elyssa nodded. "Only temporarily. Breaking the stone releases the soul."

I looked back through the spectacles. Silver Templar blades slashed through smaller Nazdal like wheat. I saw a look of confusion on the huge Nazdal as his people died. I'd fought his kind before. They soaked up life force instantly and grew almost as fast. The manacles had release latches on them that would snap open so they wouldn't choke the wearer as he grew. This guy was just realizing something wasn't kosher.

The Nazdal leader slashed at two attackers and sent them flying backward. Blue Cloaks zipped overhead and shot him with spells, but they didn't do much to singe his spell-resistant hide. The Blue Cloaks broke off their attacks on the Nazdal and regrouped just before the wave of flying vampires reached them. A formation of Templar Arcanes rose on flying carpets at the last minute.

Surprise flashed on the faces of the first few vampires at the sudden swell of numbers in the flying Arcane ranks. Hundreds of spells burst from staffs. A searing yellow beam burned off one vampire's wing and sent him spiraling into the fighting mass of Templars and Nazdal below. Crackling green energy leapt from vampire to vampire like an electrical current. Every affected vampire fell from the air like a zapped bug.

One Arcane sent a flurry of blue energy discs singing into the morass. Vampires screamed as the spell tore through flesh, bone, and wing. Despite the onslaught of spells, there were simply too many vampires to stop and the wave of darkness crashed against the Arcanes.

Lycans and felycans poured into the mix. The giant prehistoric cat leapt high into the air and took down three vampires with one massive claw strike. He landed on a large Nazdal and ripped the thing's throat out before it could even swipe at him. Before the downed vampires could recover, his giant claws beheaded them in one fluid slash.

I heard Shelton gulp. "I'm glad that thing is on our side."

A flurry of movement in our ranks caught my gaze. I watched a group of Arcanes load silver spheres onto catapults. They waved their wands. The arms of the catapults swung forward and launched the spheres far into the air.

Flashes of brilliant ultraviolet light blinded me for a moment. Scores of vampires fell from the air, their skin blistered and horribly sunburned. I watched them plunge to the ground in the middle of the ground fighters. Allies and enemies dodged falling bodies. Silver swords flashed, and blood sprayed.

The giant Nazdal was still alive, but dozens of his fellow monsters lay dead around him. His huge, clawed hand slammed into a Templar. The soulstone on the Templar's belt flashed as his body sailed through the air and flopped lifelessly to the floor.

I felt sick to my stomach.

More Nazdal, vampires, and Templars fell. More soulstones flashed as they captured the life essence of the dead. Despite the staggering enemy casualties, our people continued to die. I saw several Blue Cloaks plummet from their carpets as vampires swooped from above and slammed into them. One vampire grabbed a struggling Arcane from his carpet. With a vicious snap, he buried his fangs in the Arcane's neck and flew up toward the vaulted ceiling. The Arcane's struggling body went still. A moment later, the vampire dropped the lifeless body above the Templars. The corpse crashed atop one of our fighters.

More of the larger Nazdal joined the fight at the front lines. They began to tear a hole in our defenses. A clowder of moggies funneled into the breach. Some of the mutant housecats were as large as grizzly bears. They ripped into the larger Nazdal as if they were squirrels. The head Nazdal grabbed a moggie and crushed its head like a walnut. Gouts of blood exploded across the throng.

A thunderous roar rumbled across the chamber and dino-cat leapt through the air. His golden fur was matted with gore, and some poor vampire's trousers fluttered from one of his razor claws. The huge Nazdal turned to the sound and intercepted the big cat. The two rolled across the marble floor. Pools of blood made the surface slick and the combatants slid several yards, slamming into smaller Nazdal and scattering them like pebbles. Even with the spectacle binoculars, all I could make out was a blur of claws, fur, and flesh.

The Nazdal threw the huge cat away from him and staggered back on all fours. The iron manacle around his neck clattered to the floor. Blood streamed from claw marks all along his body. The saber-toothed cat landed on his feet and looked at his enemy. His tongue lolled as he panted from the exertion. Blood trickled down a bare patch of skin.

Templars, lycans, and smaller Nazdal fought all around them. Stricken vampires and the occasional Arcane plummeted from above even as the two huge creatures once again advanced on each other. The big cat suddenly slipped on a pool of blood. The Nazdal seized the opportunity. In a blur, he leapt for the falling cat.

I sucked in a breath and heard Elyssa gasp.

The huge feline recovered easily, making it obvious he'd just faked his fall.

"What a feint," Elyssa said with appreciation.

I whistled. "Pro jukes."

The Nazdal could do nothing to undo his mistake. He twisted in midair, talons outstretched. The saber-tooth dodged and swatted with a massive claw. The Nazdal's body splashed into a pool of blood, sending a crimson tide splashing in all directions. His decapitated head thudded to the floor and rolled to a stop.

"Yeah!" Shelton yelled. "Thunder Cats go!"

Two of the large Nazdal leapt onto the saber-tooth's back. They sank their pointy teeth into the cat's hide. The saber-tooth roared with pain. A ten-foot tall wolf-man gripped one of the Nazdal by the scruff of its neck and ripped it off the cat before slamming the creature so hard against the marble floor, its head exploded like a watermelon. A huge wolf leapt and tackled the other Nazdal. The two tumbled across the floor.

So much carnage! With everything I'd seen, I still felt a little sick to my stomach. Even so, I couldn't tear my eyes from the battle.

The saber-tooth blurred to the fallen Nazdal. Its right claw slashed. The stricken Nazdal fell apart like sliced deli ham. The lycans howled and formed into a pack. I spotted multiple packs racing through the confusion of battle. Ignoring the smaller Nazdal, they hamstrung any of the larger ones wearing chains. Without the ability to soak of the life force of the fallen, the smaller Nazdal retreated. The creatures were naturally strong, but not as strong as the were-creatures hunting them now.

The roar of battle in the cavernous corridor grew almost unbearable as every sound echoed from the hard surfaces. Even more unbearable was standing, watching, and waiting. *I need to help.* Scores of dead and wounded littered the corridor. I spotted crews of healer Templars removing our casualties whenever the opportunity presented itself. They placed the bodies on flying carpets and took them to the rear of our formation and through one of the portals.

The original omniarch portals had been closed. New portals had been reopened in a straight line across the back of the corridor, each one marked with a destination. If disaster struck, those portals would be our only way to retreat since the tunnels into this place had been sealed eons ago.

Shelton winced and looked away from his binoculars. "Oh, damn. That guy was really kicking ass."

"Who was?" I asked.

Bella rubbed his arm and looked at me. "One of the Templars we'd been watching."

"He took down about twenty Nazdal, and one of those stinking vampires dropped dead on him right when he was fending off two of those crawling bastards." Shelton bared his teeth. "I want to roast those effers alive right now."

"I'm right there with you." I looked back through the spectacles and watched as the saber-tooth retreated from battle. Blood poured from multiple wounds, and he looked ready to collapse. A team of healers intercepted him and, with great effort, hauled the huge cat onto a flying carpet and evacuated him.

The saber-tooth morphed back into a large man as the healer rug flitted beneath us and into a portal.

"Was he still alive?" Bella asked.

"Hope so," I said.

The swarm of flying vampires seemed noticeably thinner as I turned my gaze back to the battle. Fresh waves of enemies appeared at the far end of the corridor. I saw ordinary vampires on foot. Battle mages in the tight, black cloaks of the Black Robe Brotherhood appeared on flying carpets. Behind them came Exorcists, some dressed in the old-fashioned loose robes their order had once favored. Others wore the modern form-fitting robes mandated by their former leader, Phoebe Borathen.

I looked at our command platform. Thomas Borathen wore a grim smile on his face.

"What does your father know that I don't?" I asked Elyssa.

She swung her spectacles his way. "We're winning."

A trumpet sounded a quick series of notes. My Templar communicator blinked three times.

Shelton whooped. "Tighten your butt-cheeks, boys, we're going in!"

Fresh Templars swapped out with those at the front lines. The new soldiers held large black shields that spanned the corridor from wall to wall. Our air force of Blue Cloaks and Templar Arcanes formed lines and began spamming spells at the remaining vampires. The Nazdal forces couldn't withstand the pressure. The vampires fell back.

Our entire army pushed forward with a roar.

I felt the urge to rush to the front so I could spam a few spells of my own, but Elyssa would probably knock me over the head if I broke formation.

Our forces closed to within fifty yards of the corridor exit before the fresh waves of vampires and battle mages reinforced the enemy lines. Beyond the end of the tunnel, I saw obsidian and alabaster shimmering in the brilliant yellow light of the way station.

So close!

A female Templar on a carpet flew up to us. "Commander Borathen must speak with Omega Group."

"At once," Mom said, and directed her carpet toward the command platform.

Elyssa and I followed. Omega Group was the designation for those of us responsible for babysitting Mom while she safely removed the Chalon from the Grand Nexus. At one time, she'd been the only one capable of removing it since it required a voice with perfect pitch to sing in the musical language of the arch builders.

Thomas nodded at us as we arrived. "We need to close the arch now. Even though I'm confident we could demolish the rest of the enemy forces, it will take time we don't have."

Elyssa gave him a troubled look. "Are you afraid Daelissa will come through?"

"One of our scouts reported that the Grand Nexus was activated not long after we arrived." He barked a command to one of his battle coordinators and turned back to us. "I fear someone went through to warn Daelissa."

"Any idea who?" I asked.

"Serena was spotted by advanced scouts earlier." Thomas consulted a tablet. "We believe it was her."

"I'm more than ready to fight," I said.

Shelton punched a fist into his palm. "We all are."

"Excellent." Thomas looked at another coordinator. "Bring up the battering ram."

The coordinator tapped out the command on his arctablet. "Order relayed, sir."

Thomas pointed to a diagram of the way station on his arctablet. It looked like the blueprints to a space station. "Daelissa's people have portal-blocking statues inside the way station. We've tried opening omniarch gateways with images from our scouts, but none have worked."

"How could they know about the portal blocking statues?" I asked.

Thomas motioned to an arctablet secured to the table by a flexible arm. On it was the picture of a man standing near the Grand Nexus. I recognized him immediately.

"Maulin Kassus," Shelton growled.

"Apparently, he felt he had enough valuable information to keep Daelissa from killing him," Thomas said. "I mistakenly thought his sense of self-preservation would prevent him from returning to her service."

"You and me both," I said, feeling a little nauseous. "He must've been the one to tell Daelissa about the portal-blocking statues so she could use the Grand Nexus even after we blocked it."

A large force of Blue Cloaks on flying carpets formed up to the right of the command platform. One of them saluted. "Lieutenant Hertz reporting for duty."

Thomas pointed to the way station diagram. "We're in the south corridor here." He highlighted the bottommost of the four spokes in the blueprint. "Our scouts have defused a path through the wards guarding the east corridor." He traced a finger toward the corridor on the right. "There is a contingent of flying vampires and battle mages guarding the end of the corridor. The Blue Cloaks will ram a path for you." He ran his finger into the central hub. "Once there, proceed directly to the Grand Nexus and guard Alysea while she removes the Chalon. The Blue Cloaks will help."

"What if the backside of the army turns around and comes at us?" Shelton said.

"We'll do our best to keep them busy," Thomas replied. He blew out a breath. "Waiting any longer is too great a risk."

"I agree," Mom said. "I'm ready when everyone else is."

Ivy punched the palm of her hand and scowled. "I was born ready."

"We will guard you well," Nightliss said. Joss and Otaleon nodded in agreement.

Shelton took a compact rod from the holster on his belt and flicked it out into a full-length staff. "Let's kick ass and chew bubblegum."

"I don't think you're saying that right," Elyssa said.

I snorted. "And now you've got Cinder saying it all wrong too."

Shelton shrugged. "Who cares how you're supposed to say it if it sounds good this way?" He spun his carpet around. "Let's do this."

The formation of Blue Cloaks turned. "We're ready," Hertz said.

Heart pounding with adrenalin, I turned my carpet south. "It's go time."

Chapter 19

We flew at top speed over our army, past the line of portals, and into the outer ring corridor. It was slightly smaller than the grand hallway we'd come from, but rubble blocked the tunnel to the west. The ceiling had also collapsed to the east, but a gap allowed us to fly our carpets through.

The corridor beyond was dimly lit and littered with debris. Fallen statues lay across our path. Chunks of rock from the broken ceiling above had destroyed much of the tile floor. I understood why Thomas hadn't tried to flank the enemy with this corridor. It would take our land units hours to navigate through this mess.

We hadn't gone far when I noticed a human skull. It wasn't the only one. There were bones everywhere. Most looked human, but there were several that might have belonged to animals or other creatures I'd never seen before.

"This place is a graveyard," Shelton said in a hushed tone.

Ivy made a face. "Creepy."

"From the first war," Mom said, her eyes sad. "The bones of many departed friends lie in this tomb."

Shelton looked over his shoulder at her. "Let's not add ours to the mix, okay?"

We passed through the ribcage of something huge and long.

Elyssa touched one of the bones as we passed it. "This must have been a leviathan dragon."

Bella shuddered. "I'd hate to see what killed this massive creature."

We passed over several gaping holes that seemed to go straight into the earth. I examined one. "The dragons that survived must have tunneled down."

"Including the ones that saved me and Nightliss," Mom said. She shook her head. "So much of that battle is still a blur."

"Time for silence," the Blue Cloak leader said. "We're approaching the east tunnel."

The last marble arch before the east corridor lay broken across our path. We had to weave through narrow gaps in the blockage to make our way through. I almost jumped out of my skin when a shadowy form stood from behind a jumble of stone once we emerged to the other side.

Elyssa didn't seem surprised. "Report, scout."

He saluted. "The enemy diverted all but a handful of troops to the main fight." The scout displayed a map of the hallway on his arctablet. He pointed to several red blips. "There are thirteen flying vampires and three battle mages."

"No Nazdal?" Elyssa asked.

"None." He panned the map to show the central chamber. "After eliminating the hallway guards, take the path down the right side of the main chamber to avoid a contingent of battle mages. We might be able to take them out, but it's possible they could signal for reinforcements before we do."

I noticed a large red square on the left side of the way station. "What's that?"

The scout grimaced. "A battalion of Red Cell just arrived via the Obsidian Arch along with several dozen battle mages with interdictors."

The Blue Cloaks exchanged unsettled looks. Hertz spoke. "Any plans to take them out?"

The scout shook his head. "Not from my end. Commander Borathen probably has something in store for them."

"Ain't that just dandy," Shelton said. "Good thing I brought along some of those token rings that allow me to channel."

Bella smiled sweetly. "I also packed clean underwear for you, just in case."

A couple of the Blue Cloaks snickered but quickly recovered their detached demeanor.

I wasn't amused. My stomach tightened with every second we wasted. "We have all the information we need. Let's move out and get this done before Daelissa brings home the bacon."

Hertz saluted. "Yes, sir."

It felt really odd being called sir by someone so much older than me, but I simply nodded and said, "Thank you, lieutenant."

The scout boarded a carpet and tailed behind as we headed for the large, arched entrance to the east corridor. We peered around the marble column buttressing the curved span. A mural depicting a battle between massive but primitive armies decorated a large stretch of the wall. Beyond that, I saw humans on display in clear cases. Many wore animal furs. Broken pottery and destroyed marble was strewn all around the cases.

Ivy's eye brightened. "It's a museum."

"In a manner of speaking, yes." Mom's voice was harsh. "These humans were magically preserved while still alive."

Shelton grimaced. "Museum of horrors."

"How did the displays survive?" Elyssa said as she looked at the ruins behind us.

"The cases are made from an early predecessor of diamond fiber." Mom shook her head sadly. "The humans inside may still be alive, but I know of no way to remove them."

Bella shivered. "How awful."

As terrible as these living displays were, I didn't want to waste time contemplating them. I scanned the corridor and spotted movement about a hundred yards ahead. "I see the defenders."

The hallway guardians had apparently seen us, too.

The vampires flapped their leathery wings and hovered, while the battle mages rose on flying carpets. As we closed in, I saw uncertainty in the eyes of the battle mages and decided to exploit it.

"Surrender and join us," I called out. "No harm will come to you."

The battle mages looked at one another. For a moment, only the beating of vampire wings broke the quiet.

"There will be no bargains," one of the vampires said. His skin was so pale it looked blue and cold as ice. His long black hair was pulled back in a ponytail and he wore a satin vest with a ruffled shirt beneath it.

Shelton took off his wide brimmed hat and made a show of inspecting it. "Before we start killing each other, where in the hell did you get the wings?"

The vampire smiled, revealing pointed teeth. Fangs extended from beneath his upper lip and grew three inches before stopping. "We are the first of our kind, human, not like the weak, flightless, blood leechers of today."

I gave him a stony look. "Our forces are annihilating your superior buddies in the south corridor."

A skeletally thin woman laughed. "Those creatures are not our kin. One of the Arcanes used our blood to mutate those pitiful leechers into something resembling us."

"We outnumber you," Hertz said. "I ask you one last time to surrender."

The leader vampire moved so fast, even my supernatural vision had trouble keeping up with him. He gripped Hertz and threw him from his carpet. Only Mom's quick thinking kept the Blue Cloak from plummeting to his death. She flung a strand of aether and caught him.

The vampire pivoted and flew at me. I felt his iron grip squeeze my throat. Felt my feet leave the carpet as he threw me. His hand left my skin. My arms flailed, hands grabbing at thin air. Sparks flew as Elyssa's swords intercepted attacks from the skeletal female. I flung a rope of Murk and snagged the carpet. Using my momentum, I swung beneath the carpet and up over the other side, landing behind the vampire.

Elyssa parried another blow from her attacker. I cupped both hands and shot a white fireball at the vampire's backside. The explosion knocked her forward. Elyssa leapt straight up, legs splayed to the side as her attacker stumbled forward and fell from the carpet with an angry shriek.

The remaining vampires were already swooping in for an attack. I conjured a shield of Murk. They slammed into it like ravens against a window. My shield cracked and the carpet slid back a few feet before I brought it under control.

I saw Bella fighting off the battle mages with the aid of the Blue Cloaks. Shelton, a look of intense concentration on his face, flicked his fingers on his arcphone.

"Now is not a good time to be playing video games," I yelled.

The other vampires circled us, wings flapping, red eyes glowing. "It appears you are more than you seem," the lead vamp said. "Your blood smells rich."

The scrawny woman flew into position next to him. "Come, Sarkin. Let us feast upon him."

I made a fist and held it up. "The only thing you'll be feasting on is a knuckle sandwich."

Elyssa put her back to mine and braced herself for the next attack. "These guys are a lot tougher than their descendants."

Twin beams of Brilliance lanced into the chests of two of the vampires. The impact sent them tumbling backwards through the air. I looked back and saw Mom and Ivy taking aim at the next vampires. Rather than spiraling to the ground in a ball of flames, the two vampires recovered. Though their clothes were blackened and burned, their pale flesh beneath looked unharmed.

Sarkin's lips peeled from his pointy teeth in a smirk. "The amount of Brilliance used to give us our gifts also protects us from it."

The woman cackled. "You cannot kill us!"

"Yeah?" Shelton shouted. "Try this on for size, bucktooth." He slammed his staff on the carpet and shouted, "Solaris!"

Yellow energy swirled around the top of his staff, coalescing into a brilliant miniature sun. One of the vampires streaked toward Shelton and suddenly screamed as his skin flaked off like ash. He exploded into a cloud of gray soot. Bones scattered and fell. Two more vampires too close to the blaze instantly combusted.

Sarkin and the others shrieked in anger and fled, their cries fading into the distance.

The three battle mages suddenly knew the gig was up and threw their hands into the air. Several Blue Cloaks secured them with diamond fiber straps and left them on top of one of the clear cases.

Shelton wiped sweat from his forehead. "Knew I had that spell somewhere. Glad it worked."

"I always thought vampires being instantly incinerated by sunlight was just a myth," Elyssa said.

"These ancient ones must be more sensitive than their modern kin." Bella looked at the slowly drifting cloud of vampire ash. "I wonder if a stake through the heart would kill them."

161

"Good luck getting close enough," Shelton said. "I never saw a vampire move that fast."

"I've seen Sarkin before," Ivy said.

Mom's eyes widened. "When?"

"After Daelissa put you in the astral prison, she started bringing all sorts of weirdos to Jeremiah's house." Ivy pursed her little lips. "Sarkin brought that skinny woman once. Her name is Priscilla."

"That woman needs to eat more carbs," Shelton said. "She's all leather and bones."

I took a quick headcount. We were down three Blue Cloaks. I spotted the Templar scout's broken body on the floor below and grimaced. Shelton's miniature sun rotated slowly as it drifted in the general direction of the main chamber ahead.

I cleared my throat to break up the conversation about the vampires. "Let's go. Sarkin might regroup."

Lieutenant Hertz tried to salute and winced. "Move out."

We flew as fast as our carpets would take us through the ruined hall. In addition to trapped humans, I saw all manner of ancient animals entombed in the diamond cases, even mammoths. The Seraphim apparently like to collect animals as trophies as much as humans.

I stared longingly at one of the massive creatures. "Any chance I could cut a mammoth out of these cases?"

Elyssa laughed. "The tragon wasn't enough?"

I looked at her over my shoulder. "My dream is to collect all the dinosaurs."

Ivy pinched her nose. "I'll bet they stink."

The main way station opened up before us and our conversation died away. I felt like a mosquito compared to the enormous grandeur. A great dome decorated with murals of Seraphim sparkled above us.

"Is that you, Mommy?" Ivy pointed her finger toward a mosaic of two blonde Seraphim surrounded by a tribe of kneeling humans.

Mom's face flushed. She closed her eyes and sighed. "Yes, dear. I'm afraid it is."

My stomach knotted at the sight of Mom and Daelissa's first encounter with humans. Mom's gaze seemed troubled as she stared at it.

Our group veered right and stayed low behind rows of smaller arches to avoid the remaining guardians. The towering presence of the Grand Nexus grew larger and larger. We finally reached it.

"Form a perimeter," Hertz told his people.

Shelton and Bella joined the Blue Cloaks. Mom and Ivy flew to the arch. I glided us in behind them and parked at the foot of the structure. The Chalon, a small orb etched with intricate lines, rested in a socket about chest height.

The distant sounds of battle echoed from the south. I saw flying forms in that direction, but rows of arches blocked my view of the land troops.

Mom took a long drink of water from a bottle and hummed a few notes. She drew in a deep breath and released it. "Here I go." She extended a hand toward the Chalon. It popped from the socket and hovered beneath her hand. The silver circle embedded in the floor around the arch flashed as it sealed itself to magic.

"Is the arch still attuned to Seraphina?" I asked. I hoped it was still set to Sturg.

She nodded.

I groaned. "Would it be faster to attune it to another realm before you attempt to remove it?"

She shook her head. "It would take nearly the same amount of time."

I shut my mouth so she could get started.

Mom closed her eyes and began to sing. I'd heard this unearthly tune before when Mom had tried to remove the Chalon from the Shadow Nexus—a version of the Grand Nexus in the Gloom. The arch builders used a musical language to grow the arches from stone. Mom was using the same language to properly remove the Chalon from the nexus. To force it out would cause another Desecration.

I heard shouting and saw the Blue Cloaks preparing to fight as the battle mages the Templar scout had warned us about ran our way. I hoped the platoon of Red Cell soldiers didn't come as well. The battle mages seemed to realize they were outnumbered and abruptly changed course.

"They're going to warn the others," I said. "We can't let them do that."

"I've got Mom's back," Ivy said. "Go get 'em!"

Several Blue Cloaks left formation and pursued the battle mages. I directed mine and Elyssa's flying carpet to follow at top speed. Our group closed the gap in no time since the enemy was on foot. The mages turned and fought. Deadly spells sizzled through the air. One of the Blue Cloaks cried out and fell from the carpet. A smoking hole gaped where his stomach had been.

His comrades retaliated. A blue energy disc hummed from the end of a Blue Cloak's staff and sliced the legs from one of the enemy mages. Another Blue Cloak flipped from his carpet. He spun his staff. Deflected a bolt of deadly energy and cracked the end of his staff against the attacker's Adam's apple. The battle mage went down coughing blood.

The Blue Cloak ducked beneath an attack from the remaining mage. He flicked his wand and stabbed it up through the soft flesh of the mage's chin. The mage gurgled. Brilliant green light burst from inside his mouth. His eyeballs boiled in their sockets and gray matter sizzled from his ears. The Blue Cloak withdrew his wand with fluid grace and wiped it off on the dead man's cloak before the body hit the ground.

"Wow," Elyssa said. "That Magitsu is crazy stuff."

I shuddered and looked away. I'd seen some awful stuff in my time, but watching anyone's brains erupt from their ears was something I didn't care to see. "Let's get back to Mom."

A brilliant red flare streaked up toward the southern portion of the dome and exploded. I spotted a small group of Exorcists standing in the wide aisle between the smaller arches. One of them raised a wand and fired another red flare.

We reached the nexus. Mom was still singing. I almost asked her how much longer she had, but knew from experience attuning the Chalon took several minutes.

"We're going to have company very soon," Elyssa said.

She'd no sooner said it than a platoon of Red Cell marched into view. The elite vampire warriors marched in precise formation. Each wore red armor that protected them from most magic attacks and each was a force to be reckoned with in hand-to-hand combat. We were down to eight Blue Cloaks plus the five of us. Mom wouldn't be able to help.

We didn't have a chance in hell of holding them off.

Chapter 20

Having a huge force of elite vampires marching toward our indefensible position motivated me to think really hard about how I could keep us alive long enough for Mom to unseat the Chalon and save the day.

I briefly considered resealing the silver circle around the nexus with a physical barrier, but quickly realized I couldn't do that without interrupting Mom's work. I turned to Ivy. "Stay here and guard Mom. We're going to help against the vampires."

"Wait, Justin." Ivy ran up to me, her blue eyes round as she looked at the oncoming force. "Maybe I should help you too."

I shook my head. "If someone sneaks up on Mom while we're dealing with the main force, she'll be in big trouble."

Ivy frowned. "Jeremiah had to blast a guy in diamond fiber armor once." She looked at the encroaching force now only a couple hundred yards away. "The guy thought he was invincible, so Jeremiah heated the floor underneath him and cooked him inside his suit."

"He made you watch?" I asked, aghast.

"No, he made me look away, but I peeked." She grinned. "How else can I learn stuff if I don't watch?"

"Watch Mom." I ruffled her hair. "And thanks for the advice."

"Anytime, bro." Ivy ran back to Mom's side.

Elyssa squeezed my arm. "Your sister probably needs therapy after all she's seen."

"Her therapist would need therapy afterward." I rotated the carpet toward our pitifully small group of defenders and urged it to top speed. I heard Hertz barking commands as we approached.

He turned to me. "This probably won't work for long, but we're going to shield as much ground as possible and hold it."

Shelton shook his head. "Ain't no way in hell we'll be able to hold up a shield against that many vamps across such a wide space."

"If only we could drop the ceiling on them," Bella said, looking at the dome far above. "But it would take too long to fly up and cut chunks loose."

I waved my hands to get everyone's attention. "New plan. We're going to heat the floor."

Hertz raised an eyebrow. "Heat the floor?"

I nodded. "Diamond fiber might protect against damage, but it transmits heat so long as it's not from a magical source."

Shelton snapped his fingers. "Like what you did against the Flark."

Flarks were naturally resistant to magic. I'd shot one of the shapeshifters with a fireball, but it had splashed harmlessly over the creature's skin. The only way I'd been able to harm it was by melting the stone ceiling and floor around it, indirectly burning it with magic.

Hertz nodded. "Everyone focus on the same area. We'll heat it faster."

"Agreed." I drew in aether and pointed to an area thirty yards outside the silver circle. "Let's start there."

On the count of three, the Blue Cloaks, Shelton, Bella, and I unleashed a torrent of energy into the stone. It began to glow after a few seconds. We shifted our aim, tracing across the floor until we'd covered a swath too wide for vampires to jump over and long enough that they'd have to take several minutes to detour around it. Sweat broke out on my forehead. Some of the Blue Cloaks coughed as the air heated and shimmered like the desert. The vaulted ceilings allowed much of the heat to rise or we probably would have suffocated ourselves with hot air. It was already like breathing inside a heated oven.

We finally had to back off and recuperate. The enemy force, apparently aware we were up to something, had picked up the pace and closed in fast. I knew from my high school physics class that the stone floor would retain the heat for quite a while. Vampires might be tough, but even they wouldn't be able to walk across a two-thousand-degree stone floor.

The front ranks of the Red Cell troops abruptly stopped as they hit the hot zone. I'd kind of hoped the back ranks might push the formation forward into the superheated rock, but the vampires were too well trained and stopped on a dime. A vampire with four fang badges on his shoulder narrowed his eyes at us. He motioned to his left and right. Two soldiers broke formation and ran along the perimeter.

"Won't take them long to march around it," Shelton said, his eyes following one of the enemy scouts. "What then?"

I glanced back at Mom. The Chalon was rotating faster and faster. It wouldn't take much longer. We just had to buy enough time. The enemy scouts returned within minutes. The Red Cell leader split his forces, pointing the groups to either side of our heat barrier. It was easy to see how the two forces would converge and crush us. Our only option would be to pull back into a tight formation so I could shield our group.

With Ivy's help I could probably hold a shield for several minutes, depending on what forces the enemy brought to bear on it. I'd have to be careful not to cut the Chalon's connection to the arch with my shield, or risk causing another Desecration.

A huge explosion erupted to the south. The Red Cell leader stopped barking orders and turned to look. A flurry of winged vampires rose into the air and retreated west. I saw a large force of ground troops running beneath them.

Shelton raised a fist and whooped. "They're running!"

I met the sharp gaze of the Red Cell commander and shouted, "You should retreat now while you can. Our forces will be here any minute."

His cold eyes bore into mine. "Not before we kill you all."

Not the answer I was hoping for. I flashed my teeth with a confident smile. "Have it your way. I'll simply shield us from your attacks until our main force arrives."

"You're Justin Slade?" he said, his tone indicating it wasn't quite a question.

"The one and—" I'd hardly started to speak when the entire front row of Red Cell soldiers flung silver daggers at me. I yelped and somehow channeled a shield an instant before they reached me. One made it through. The hilt slammed hard into my shoulder and I almost

167

lost my concentration. The rest of the daggers pinged off the barrier and clattered to the floor.

"You dirty butt nuggets!" Shelton roared.

"Are you okay?" Elyssa asked as she inspected my shoulder.

I looked around and saw that everyone else was still standing. The Blue Cloaks had cast shield spells of their own.

"I'm fine," I said, shooting eye daggers at the vampires.

"A pity," the Red Cell leader said. "You should have made killing you easy. Now we'll have to do this the hard way."

Anger built in me as I looked at him. *If he wasn't covered from head to toe in magic-resistant armor I would*—That was when I realized the vampires didn't have their faces covered. Either their armor didn't grow to cover the face like Nightingale armor did, or they simply didn't think they needed their faces covered. Either way, an exposed face was all I needed right this instant. I shot out a tendril of Murk. Before the commander could make another overconfident remark, the strand pinched his nose. I jerked him forward onto the superheated rock.

Elite vampire leader or not, he screamed bloody murder and did a hotfoot dance but was unable to break my tether. With a horrendous croaking sound, he fell face-first onto the rock. Steam and smoke boiled up where his flesh hit the stone.

Shelton waved a hand under his nose. "Smells like barbequed bloodsucker in here."

Facemasks abruptly covered the exposed faces of the remaining vampires. One of them with three fang badges on his sleeve held up a fist, twisted it sideways. The entire formation beat a hasty retreat to the west, doing their best to catch up to the rest of the army.

Mom's singing suddenly stopped. I turned to look and saw her holding the Chalon in her hand. Ivy threw her arms around her while Mom cried out, "We did it!"

Jagged bolts of aether arced between the columns of the Grand Nexus. With one last crackle of defiance, the great arch went dark. The gateway to Seraphina was out of order.

Cheers erupted from the Blue Cloaks. Shelton grabbed Bella's hand and the two danced in a circle. "We are the champions!" Bella shouted before gripping Shelton by the collar of his leather duster and planting a long hard kiss on him.

Elyssa and I looked at each other, our eyes wide with disbelief.
"It's over?" she said.

I could hardly believe it. The Grand Nexus was closed. Daelissa was gone for good. I grabbed Elyssa around the waist and spun her around. "We did it! We won!"

"Victory kiss!" she shouted.

Her soft lips met mine. The cheering and distant sounds of battle faded until we finally had to breathe.

Despite our victory, there was one vital thing we had to take care of. I grabbed the Blue Cloak leader. "Get my mother, sister, and the Chalon to safety." I waved a hand at the rest of my crew. "We'll rejoin our forces and help them with the remaining enemies."

Hertz saluted with his uninjured hand and grinned. "Excellent work, sir."

The other Blue Cloaks snapped salutes at me before breaking into more cheers.

Mom and Ivy ran to me and gripped me in a tight hug.

"I can't believe it's over," Mom said.

Ivy cast a wistful look at the nexus. "I still kinda wish I could've seen Seraphina."

I doubt that will ever be possible. My inner nerd regretted missing out on exploring strange new worlds, but knew it would be folly to reopen the arch to fight a Seraphim army. I kissed her forehead. "Maybe one day."

She quirked her lips and looked down. "Yeah, maybe."

The Blue Cloaks spirited Mom and Ivy away on their carpets while Shelton, Bella, Elyssa, and I raced toward the bulk of our army, now engaged in pursuit of the enemy forces. Before long we'd tracked down most of them, though hundreds had gotten away through an omniarch. We found a disabled portal-blocking statue nearby and sent scouts to find any others hidden throughout the sprawling complex.

I found Thomas talking to the other Templar commanders. Taylor and Olson were all smiles as they greeted us.

"I can't believe it," Taylor said. "We saw the Red Cell forces marching on you, but we couldn't break the blockade."

"Fjoeruss did it with his golems," Olson said. "One of them ran into the middle of a group of defenders and exploded."

"It was the break we needed," Thomas said. He let out a breath and the weight of the world seemed to leave his shoulders.

Michael appeared. Blood spattered his armor and his sword looked like he'd butchered a herd of cows. "So far we haven't found any of the faction leaders."

"No Cyphanis or Bara Nagal?" I asked.

"What about Serena?" Elyssa asked.

"Our scouts think she and a small force entered the nexus as the battle began." Thomas folded his arms and managed to look a bit smug. "I hope they don't mind Daelissa feeding on them, because they're all she'll have for the foreseeable future."

I felt a slap on my shoulder and turned to see Dad and Vallaena along with several of the other Daemos house heads. He and Vallanea had cuts and bruises, though not nearly as much blood spatter as Michael. Kassallandra and Domitia also bore injuries. Godric and Yuuki looked as if they'd never seen a minute of battle, though they both wore self-satisfied looks.

"House Salomon congratulates you on our grand victory, Kohvaniss." Godric nodded at me.

Yuuki bit her lip suggestively. "A grand victory indeed. Perhaps the Kohvaniss would like to celebrate."

I felt Elyssa tense next to me and hoped she didn't slice the Daemas to ribbons.

"A celebration is rather far off," Thomas said. "There is still the matter of the Overworld Conclave. We have many important decisions ahead of us."

"What to do with the vampires, for one," Godric said. "I suggest removing them from the Conclave entirely. We will be better off for it."

"Oh, yes, let's create a huge power vacuum," Dad said, his voice heavy with sarcasm. "I'm sure all the disenfranchised vampires won't mind."

"They have done it to themselves." Godric's chin rose so high, I thought he might break his neck. "Otto Strassman and his lowly leechers deserve no power in the new arrangement."

"Let's shelve this talk for later," I said, already sick of hearing Godric's snooty voice. "The Overworld is a mess right now and it's going to take a while to sort it all out."

"House Slade agrees," Dad said before Godric could open his big mouth again.

I turned to Thomas. "Commander Borathen, how do you suggest we handle the immediate issues?"

"We need to reign in all rogue enemy units such as the Synod and the vampires, and bring them firmly under control before we pursue any political resolutions." He showed us an arctablet with a list of names. I recognized several as the leaders of the rogue factions. "Once we force unconditional surrenders from them, it will make our efforts much easier."

"This will only continue the war, not end it," Godric said.

Kassallandra frowned at him. "There is wisdom in Commander Borathen's words. I suggest we heed them."

"If we don't bring them to heel," Dad said, "we could end up letting this conflict drag on for ages."

Godric opened his mouth to speak when a klaxon boomed throughout the way station. The hubbub of conversation died away as the klaxon sounded again. A Templar scout on a flying carpet zipped toward us.

Eyes wide, he leapt off and saluted Thomas. "Sir, the Grand Nexus is activating."

"Activating?" Godric said in a high-pitched voice of disbelief. "You must be mistaken."

Thomas didn't hesitate. He climbed aboard the command platform, which hovered nearby, and shouted commands at his coordinators. He turned to us. "Gather your forces and make all haste to the nexus."

Shelton and Bella appeared with Stacey and Ryland in tow.

"Did I hear right?" Shelton said. "The Grand Nexus is powering on?"

My heart went tight. "Do we have any portal-blocking statues for it? Please tell me we have one!"

Elyssa gave me a helpless look. "The only ones we had were the statues Katie and the others put here originally. We don't have any more."

The Templar forces were already marching in tight formation toward the nexus. The Daemos and lycan troops followed closely behind, though I saw Godric loitering behind.

We ran to our carpet. Elyssa hopped on behind me and we rose into the air. I rotated the carpet and shot toward the nexus along with several formations of Blue Cloaks and Templar Arcanes. We arrived just as the air within the arch columns flickered into a view of another realm. An army of Seraphim with blazing white swords and crystal armor stood in formation on the other side.

Someone roared a command and the Seraphim army invaded.

Chapter 21

Daelissa

The Divinity Scepter floated within a crystalline case. A small orb rotated within a jeweled setting at the top of the slender crystal rod. Daelissa did not remember such a scepter and wondered if the original Skazaeleus ordered it crafted for her as a gift before the Desecration.

"It is lovely," Lanaeia said.

Qualan grunted and strode around the small room of artifacts located in the south wing of the palace. He looked as if he wanted to smash everything to bits with his bare fists.

"Legend has it this was crafted from a part of the Elder Gate itself," Banj explained. Tovaard had found this wrinkled old historian for her, hopeful he could fill in the gaps after her exile to Eden. He claimed to have documents proving Daelissa had really existed. Until her arrival back on Seraphina, he'd been considered an eccentric old fool. He was still old but no longer a fool.

Daelissa found his age disgusting. *Such decrepitude is unnatural!* "What is this Elder Gate?" she asked.

"The arch upon the Eternal Cliffs." Banj dabbed at a puddle of drool forming on the corner of his mouth. "This is the gate Daelissa—you—and the elders used to travel between worlds."

"The Grand Nexus." Daelissa did not appreciate being called an elder, but apparently, she, Qualan, and Lanaeia were the oldest Seraphim in this realm.

"I believe I know what happened," Lanaeia said. She sat at a table next to a bookshelf. The useless sera had been poring over Banj's documents for the past four days. "The nexus was closed during the

Desecration, but since it was still attuned to Seraphina, some part of the backlash traversed our realm and changed our people. This is why they now age."

Qualan spun on his heel and gave her a scornful look. "You're saying the Desecration on this side of the nexus took away immortality?"

"My father, Bjoerrinn, was an advisor to the original Skazaeleus. He often complained that the regent liked to author his own decrees rather than have scribes do it for him." Lanaeia pointed at the magically preserved parchment. "I recognize his handwriting. These are pages from what may have been his journal."

Banj's eyes lit with excitement. "That explains why these documents were discovered in the Tomb of the Emperors." He touched Lanaeia's arm. "Tell me, my dear, did you know the first emperor well?"

"He was no emperor," Daelissa snapped. "He was a regent appointed by me to oversee the realm in my absence." She opened the crystal display case and took the scepter in her right hand. It felt perfectly ordinary. "He failed me miserably." Her grip tightened, sending a sharp pain radiating out from her palm.

Banj nodded. "After the Elder Gate—"

"Grand Nexus," Daelissa said in a sharp tone.

He bowed. "Yes, Divinity. After it was closed, the Darklings grew bolder. It was during the second uprising that they drove the Brightlings from the far southern land of Pjurna and claimed it as their own."

"Without humans to feed from, the Brightlings lost their power advantage," Lanaeia said. "This empowered the Darklings."

Qualan smashed a fist against the table causing Lanaeia to shriek and flinch away. "We will crush the Darklings and put them back in their place."

Lanaeia looked at him with wide eyes. She took a deep breath and held up another parchment. "Skazaeleus wrote that he held contests to find the fairest voice in the land. He made them sing to the scepter for some reason."

"Indeed," Banj said. "Many thought he was insane. For centuries after his death, his successors carried on this legacy. It was said that only one with a perfect voice could awaken the Divinity Scepter."

"How odd," Lanaeia said. "It sounds like a fairy tale."

Tovaard appeared at the doorway. "Divinity, the army is almost at the Grand Nexus."

Joy lit Daelissa's heart. "Then let us go!" She slashed a hand through the air at Lanaeia. "Stay here and read to your foolish heart's content. You are ill suited for much else."

"May I have her?" Qualan asked. He gripped a handful of the sera's hair and jerked her head back to expose her throat. "I believe I could turn her into a warrior."

A tear trickled down Lanaeia's face. "You are no warrior. You're nothing but a brute."

Qualan roared and drove her face into the table. "A brute? I am a prince!"

Lanaeia sobbed. Blood pooled on the table beneath her face.

"Please," Banj said, placing himself between Qualan and the sera. "Some are simply not made for war, my prince."

"Indeed," Qualan said, wiping his bloody hands on the old seraph's robes. "They are the ones who will bow and scrape to the rest of us."

"Well said." Daelissa graced Qualan with a smile. "Let us go. We have a realm to force to its knees." She almost tossed the scepter away, but decided to keep it. It was rather lovely to look upon, and the color complemented the blue in her eyes. She paused at the door and looked at Lanaeia. "Pick yourself up and come."

The sera's bruised face was slowly healing, but Daelissa saw something in her eyes that would never heal. *Good, good. Perhaps you'll soon learn power equals protection.*

Lanaeia rose without a word and followed. Banj gave her one of his handkerchiefs.

"Be careful, sweet sera," he told her.

Skazaeleus was waiting for them at the entrance to the Imperial Skyway. Unlike the public ones, this skyway could be directed to go anywhere and was much faster. It had taken the imperial troops only hours to travel from the palace grounds to the Grand Nexus.

Minister Kjoeriss and several other members of the royal retinue waited with the Emperor. Daelissa, Qualan, Lanaeia, and Tovaard stepped onto the skyway.

"Let us make all haste," Daelissa said.

Skazaeleus the Fourth bowed. "Make it so," he told the operator.

The cloudbank began to move. It gathered speed and height as it went until Zbura dwindled to a speck behind them and the land receded far below. Daelissa stood near the edge and watched her kingdom sail past beneath them while the others sat on plush divans and sipped wine. She turned to look at her entourage.

Lanaeia sat by herself near the back. She made no move to wipe crusted blood from her face, nor did she express any emotion. Her nose was still slightly swollen and purple. It was obvious she hadn't fed from humans for very long before making this journey. Otherwise, she would be fully healed by now.

Qualan's dark eyes glittered as he looked at the young sera. "It will be fun breaking that foolish sera."

Daelissa smiled at him. "Perhaps you will one day make something of her."

Emperor Skazaeleus shifted uncomfortably in his royal armor. Unlike the enchanted cloth armor favored by the Templars, this armor was made of thin crystal scales. While it would certainly disperse the weak attacks of the Brightlings in this world, it would do little to stop the power of Seraphim fed on the essence of humans.

At last, they reached the Eternal Cliffs. The crystal armor of the Seraphim troops glittered in the sun like hundreds of diamonds on the plateau below the Imperial Skyway. The cloudbank broke free of the Imperial Skyway and descended. Daelissa spotted a commotion below. Her gaze picked out a familiar woman at the center of the fray, surrounded by imperial soldiers.

What is Serena doing here? I told her to wait.

The instant the cloudbank settled to the ground, Daelissa strode to the soldiers around Serena. "Free her. She is my servant."

"At once, Divinity," a young lieutenant said. He bowed and backed away without looking up from the ground until he was a safe distance away.

Serena's eyes widened when she saw Daelissa. "The enemy is attacking the Grand Nexus! I tried to tell these fools they needed to invade at once, but they wouldn't listen to me."

Daelissa bared her teeth. "Activate the nexus immediately!"

Serena ran to the empty socket where the Chalon would sit. This side didn't require the Chalon since the other side already had it. The

Arcane held her hand over the socket. The arch hummed as it drew aether from the ley lines below. The air between the arch columns flickered. The thrumming noise of the arch abruptly wound down as if it had lost all power.

"No!" Serena shouted. She held her hand above the socket, but nothing happened. Eyes wide and full of fear, she turned to Daelissa. "They have removed the Chalon."

Ice formed in Daelissa's chest. "They what?"

"We're trapped in Seraphina." Tears formed in Serena's eyes.

"Trapped?" Qualan stormed to her, gripped her by the throat, and lifted her from the ground. "How could you let this happen you idiot?"

Serena made a choking noise. "Tried...invade..."

"Put her down," Daelissa commanded.

Qualan growled and dropped her.

The short Arcane stumbled to her knees gasping. "I told them to invade." She sucked in another breath and managed to climb to her feet. "I came here immediately and told your people hours ago. They wouldn't listen."

Fire burned through the icy dread in Daelissa's heart. "Who did you speak with?"

Serena pointed to the Lieutenant. "Him."

Qualan covered the distance in an eye blink. Grabbed the lieutenant, and flung him across the rocky ground to land at Daelissa's feet.

He held up a hand. "Please, Divinity, I did not know this human was authorized to command us."

Daelissa clenched her scepter. "You have cost me everything!" She swung the scepter hard. It smashed into the seraph's head. Again and again, she pummeled his skull until the crystal shattered. With a final scream, she drove the splintered shaft into the base of the seraph's neck.

Laughter burst from Qualan's throat. "Truly, he has learned his lesson, Divinity."

As Daelissa rose, she looked at her bloodied hands. Skazaeleus looked at her with naked fear on his face, as did some of the nearby soldiers. She could no longer take her army to Eden. Her plans to scour her enemies from that realm were vanquished. Fury boiled beneath her skin. She wanted blood. She wanted to obliterate Justin Slade as she had Moses.

"Mistress."

Daelissa looked down and saw Serena combing through the scattered brains of the dead lieutenant. The Divinity bared her teeth. "Were you not a human I could feed from, I would kill you this instant."

Serena held up something small and coated with gore. "Where did this come from?"

"Is it a bit of bone? An eye?" Daelissa almost slapped it from the woman's hand. "How should I know?"

Serena wiped it on a clean part of her dress and held it up.

Daelissa recognized it. "It is the orb from the Scepter of the Divinity."

Insane giggles erupted from Serena. "This is no mere orb."

Freed from the intricate setting atop the scepter, Daelissa realized how clever the original Skazaeleus had been. The Chalon on this side must have fallen from the arch after the Desecration. Unable to attune it without Alysea, he had hidden it.

"This was why Skazaeleus the First sought a perfect voice," Lanaeia said. "He thought someone else could attune the Chalon."

"Pah!" Serena gripped the orb. "It must be in the nexus to be attuned."

"Then by all means activate it," Qualan said.

Serena placed the orb near the socket. Nothing happened. She took an arcphone from her satchel and projected an image of Alysea.

Daelissa felt her lips peel back at the sight of the traitor. Unfortunately, she still needed the services of her former friend.

The holographic image of Alysea began to sing. A few minutes later, the Chalon snapped into place like a magnet. Serena's eyes brightened. "If it is not already attuned to Eden, it will take me several minutes to do so using a recording I made of Alysea when I held the Slade boy and his father captive in the Gloom." She giggled again, eyes almost manic. "The key to all the realms is ours."

Daelissa's heart lightened a thousand fold. Giddy laughter sprang from her lips.

Qualan raised his arms in the air and roared. "We will have Eden!"

"Troops form up!" Skazaeleus shouted.

The military commanders took up the call. Before long, the imperial army stood in neat columns, ready to march through.

"The Chalon is already attuned to Eden." Serena caressed the hovering orb with her hand. "All I need to do is activate it."

Daelissa stepped atop a personal cloudbank that operated much like a flying carpet. She felt a smile stretch across her face. "Then by all means, let us invade."

The Grand Nexus hummed to life. A moment later, the gateway tore through the ethereal divide between the realms to reveal an army of Templars. Surprise flashed across the faces of the rebels.

Skazaeleus floated nearby on his own cloudbank. He held an amplification crystal to his throat and boomed the first command of the real war. "Attack!"

Chapter 22

The air in my lungs froze as the Seraphim army rushed to meet ours. The enemy soldiers wore sparkling armor that appeared to be made of glass or crystal. Each held swords of the same material that glowed with an inner white light, as if infused with Brilliance.

The first wave of Templars engaged the Seraphim. Silver swords shattered when they met the shining swords of the enemy. Arcanes fired spells into the Seraphim ranks but the armor seemed to soak it up and glow brighter.

Seraphim soldiers cleaved through the Templar lines like paper, losing only a few of their own. Although we held a numbers advantage, the area around the nexus was too small for all our forces to fit. I saw lycans and Daemos unable to reach the front lines as more and more Templars fell to the relentless advance of the invaders.

A wave of enemy soldiers flew through the gateway on small clouds. Blue Cloaks took up positions. The new attackers aimed their swords at the Blue Cloaks and fired white beams from them. Our people threw up defensive shields or dodged the attacks on their flying carpets.

The Blue Cloak who'd used Magitsu to kill the battle mages earlier swooped beneath the enemy attacks and leapt to the cloud carrying one of the Seraphim. He ducked beneath a swing of the sword and pressed his wand to the back of his attacker's knee. Light flashed, and the inside of the crystal armor glowed bright, as if the spell were ricocheting off the inside of the armor.

The Seraphim screamed and plunged from his mount into the sea of invaders below. The Blue Cloak leapt from the cloud back to his flying carpet in time to avoid several death beams from the attackers' swords.

"We've got to do something," Elyssa said. Horror gripped her face as she watched Templars fall.

A trumpet sounded and our forces began to retreat toward a large space where they'd be able to regroup. But even as they marched back, the enemy forces advanced, taking down our people left and right.

It was too much to bear. I flew our carpet low and blasted a searing wave of Brilliance into the midst of the Seraphim soldiers. Their crystal armor cracked and shattered, unable to absorb the full power of my attack. Screams rose from their ranks as they fell. There were far too many for me to kill, but their march faltered.

I saw Joss and Otaleon blasting the enemy with ultraviolet beams as they flew overhead, giving our troops even more space. Otaleon managed to ravage a couple of soldiers with a thin beam of white destruction.

Brilliance speared through the gateway in the nexus, narrowly missing the two Darklings. A cloud bearing Qualan burst through. His face bore a look of rage and delight as he unleashed another blinding bolt at Joss. "Filthy Darklings! Come face me!"

Joss and Otaleon were already in dangerous territory flying so close to the enemy. I waved my arms to get their attention. "Fall back!"

Otaleon blocked another attack from Qualan with a shield as Joss wheeled the carpet around and flew after us.

I fired a flurry of beams from my fingers at Qualan, but they all flew wide, or dispersed before reaching him. He roared when he saw me and launched into pursuit. The rest of the Seraphim army came through the portal as our troops made more space. Another cloud zipped through, this one bearing Daelissa. I spotted the elfin girl, Lanaeia, on a flying cloud of her own. Her face looked bruised and bloody. The two of them flew at us. Daelissa balled her fists, pressed them together, and discharged a beam of white light into our troops.

Our people screamed as pure destruction cut them down. I tried to shield some of them, but I was out of position to render much aid. Daelissa's cold eyes settled on me. The cloud bearing her came straight for us. Qualan launched another attack. This one caught Otaleon on the shoulder.

Their carpet spun out of control. A Blue Cloak flew his carpet close, leapt to theirs, and stabilized it. Joss gripped Otaleon to keep the Darkling from falling off the carpet as the Blue Cloak flew them toward the southern corridor where our troops were retreating.

Although it was hard to maintain a moving shield, I was plenty good at making a stationary one. Just as Qualan took aim again, I threw up a small shield right in front of his head. He cried out in surprise as his face slammed into the barrier. The cloud flew from beneath his feet, and the Brightling tumbled backwards into his own troops.

Unfortunately, the fall wasn't nearly enough to kill him.

"Run all you want, Justin Slade," he screamed at the top of his lungs, "I will kill you!"

The Seraphim troops had fallen well behind our people by now, but it was due more to our own dead blocking their path than the speed of our retreat. The angels were incredibly agile, however, and managed to navigate the bodies of our fallen without tripping over them.

The bulk of our troops reached the south corridor about fifty yards ahead of the Seraphim. I spotted Thomas on his command platform and raced to him.

"What now?" I asked.

His face seemed set in stone. "We hold."

I saw Daemos and lycans moving to the front lines while ranks of the elite gray men took positions to the right. The Daemos morphed into demon forms while the lycans shifted into their beast forms.

The front row of Seraphim soldiers balked when they saw what they had to fight. Qualan, once again on his cloud, flew overhead.

"Attack!" he shouted. "Destroy them!"

He fired a thick beam at our front lines. I intercepted his attack with a barrier of mirrored Murk. It reflected his attack to the side. The base of a massive column supporting the corridor entrance exploded into shards. A great rumbling sounded and the entire right side of the entrance cracked.

"Retreat our units!" Thomas shouted.

A trumpet sounded and our rear guard moved back.

Cracks ran up the wall. Huge chunks of marble rained down. One slab thudded into the Seraphim front lines. Another took out a squad of gray men. Still another hit the Daemos as they raced backwards. Our forces moved farther and farther back until we were near the statue of Daelissa. We watched as the ceiling and walls collapsed in on themselves, blocking the corridor while a thick dust cloud billowed toward us.

Heart in my throat, I flew our carpet to the Daemos. I scanned the infernal forms until I spotted a huge red demon, my father, carrying a wounded, blue-skinned female. Her lower body looked as though it had been crushed. Blood flowed from her mouth.

I leapt from the carpet and raced over as Dad called for help, his demon voice low and guttural. The female slowly reverted to human form. I realized, with a shock, it was Vallaena. A group of healers raced over, but after one look, they simply shook their heads.

"Heal her!" Dad roared, his voice rising in tenor as he shifted back to human form.

"Too late, brother." Vallaena coughed and a fountain of blood erupted from her mouth. She saw me and smiled. "I am proud of you, Justin." She drew in a harsh breath. "You are dearer to me than you know…" Her voice trailed to silence. Her body slumped.

Dad pounded the ground hard enough to leave cracks in the marble. "No!"

I stared at her still form in disbelief. *Aunt Vallaena is dead?* We hadn't been close, but she'd been there for me. She was the one who'd taught me how to unlock my Daemos abilities. She'd persevered through my stubbornness and pushed me to be the best. I looked at her face, so calm in death.

"No." It was the only word I could muster.

"Pity," Godric said from behind me. "I do not understand why someone of her social rank would risk the front lines."

I looked and saw the Daemos standing on his own flying carpet. His clothing still looked as clean as when he'd arrived. I heard a roar and something flashed through the air. Dad gripped Godric by the throat, carried the Daemos off the carpet, and slammed him hard into the floor. His fists blurred. Godric cried out and went limp.

Dad wiped the blood from his hands on Godric's shirt and stood. He spat on the unconscious Daemos. "Cowardly scum."

Kassallandra strode from the mass of other Daemos. She placed a hand on Dad's shoulder. "Your sister was brave and noble. She was not the only of our kind to die this day. Having seen the Seraphim army, I am sure she will not be the last."

Dad gave her a grim look. "No matter how many of us die, this time we end Daelissa."

Somehow, I ended up staring at Vallaena again. I found myself next to her on my knees, my hand stroking her silky hair. Though Jeremiah and I had bonded during his last days on Eden, I hadn't lost someone so close to me before. I leaned down and kissed her on the forehead.

"Rest easy," I whispered. Anger burned in my heart. "I will win this no matter what."

A trumpet blasted four staccato notes signaling a retreat through the portals. As the dust settled and revealed the choked passageway, I saw that we would not finish this war today.

Meghan Andretti appeared with a group of healers. She placed a black cloth over Vallaena's body. "I'm so sorry, Justin."

"Thanks," I mumbled.

She looked toward the tunnel and shook her head sadly. "All the dead beyond those walls." A shiver ran down her back. "May they rest in peace."

A hand settled on my shoulder and pulled me to me feet. "Shake it off, kiddo." Dad bared his teeth. "Let's go home and clear our heads. We've got a bitch to kill."

I nodded numbly. "I need a minute."

"We all do after today." He gave my shoulder a squeeze and walked away.

I stared at the destruction around me. Elyssa appeared from somewhere and gripped me in a tight hug.

"I thought we won," I said, hardly able to believe the turn of events. I looked at Elyssa. "Tell me this is a bad dream."

She kissed my forehead. "We need to go home and rest."

A pair of healers carried Vallaena's body away. I saw dozens of flying carpets bearing the dead floating toward the portals. How many more victims lay beneath the rubble?

"Go ahead without me," I said. "I—I just have to think."

Her forehead creased. "Why here?"

I shook my head. "Please. I'll be along soon."

Elyssa kissed me again and followed the dead to the portal. I saw rescue crews pulling survivors from the rubble and ran over to help. One man was trapped beneath a huge slab of marble. Only another pile of stone had prevented the slab from crushing him. I channeled Murk and lifted the slab enough so Templars could pull him out. We patrolled the wreckage. Our supernatural hearing allowed us to locate several more entombed allies and free them.

I lost track of time as we moved from one victim to the next. We liberated more corpses than we did survivors. We even found two dead Seraphim soldiers. We were finally about to call off the search and leave through the portals when I heard a faint whimpering near the wall.

"We're here to help," I said. "Can you tell me who you are?"

There was a brief pause in the crying. "I am nobody. Just leave me," said a female voice.

I slashed a hand in the air. "Never! I refuse to give Daelissa one more soul today."

She sniffed. "I am hardly worth the trouble."

Leaning toward the sound of her voice, I said, "Every life is worth the trouble. Hang on, we'll have you out soon."

I was dead tired from so much channeling. My hands and arms were filthy, bruised, and crusted with blood. My inner demon clawed at my insides. I needed to feed. For some reason, the hunger and pain felt good. It kept my mind off our spectacular failure. More importantly, it reminded me I was alive.

I tried to channel a wedge of Murk to move debris from the area where I heard a woman crying, but my legs turned to jelly and I almost fell over.

"We've got this, sir," said a familiar voice.

I turned to see Hertz and his crew of Blue Cloaks. I managed a smile. "Thanks."

Tell us what you see, Kanaan," Hertz said to the man I recognized as the Magitsu master.

The man studied the pile of rubble for a moment. He was tall and appeared to be of mixed Asian and Caucasian descent. He ran a hand through his thick black hair and knelt next to a thin slab of marble that didn't seem to be part of the pile trapping the female.

"Here is the weak point," he said in a calm voice. He pressed his wand to a seam between the stones, and whispered a word. A small part of rock fell from the slab. It shifted ever so slightly and freed a boulder from its weight.

Hertz and the others were able to pull the boulder free with a couple of spells, revealing a small cave. I saw a bruised, dirty foot. Kanaan examined the pile again, removed another small bit of rock, and the Blue Cloaks were soon able to remove the enough of the pile to reveal the person trapped.

A filthy girl blinked her eyes at us. A sharp bit of shrapnel jutted from her thigh. Crusted blood glommed her silvery hair. I knew who she was immediately.

Lanaeia.

Chapter 23

I braced myself for a fight but only managed to stagger backwards in exhaustion.

Tears streaked through the dirt on Lanaeia's face. The elfin Brightling squeezed her eyes shut. "Just let me die. I am worthless."

Kanaan inspected her thigh. He pressed his hands to the wound around the jagged stone. "There is no way around it. This will hurt." He pressed a hand to her forehead. "Prepare yourself."

She closed her eyes and nodded.

Kanaan jerked the sharp stone from the wound. Lanaeia cried out in pain. She gripped Kanaan's arm and pressed her face against it, sobbing. He watched her, but said nothing. A Templar healer cleansed the wound and pressed a wad of what looked like gray bubblegum over the hole.

"That will keep it from getting infected," the healer said. She looked at Lanaeia. "Are you a Daemas?"

"I am your enemy," the girl replied. "I am a Brightling."

The healer flinched back and a couple of the Blue Cloaks drew wands.

I'd seen Lanaeia fight and knew she was more than capable of handling herself. Either she was too exhausted to fight, or she really meant what she'd said about dying, because she didn't raise a hand to defend herself.

Kanaan never moved. He pushed Lanaeia's damp hair from her face and looked at her, as if seeing into her soul. "She is not like the others. You have nothing to fear from her."

Hertz and the Blue Cloaks relaxed. They apparently trusted the man explicitly. The healer didn't seem quite as sure, but made no move against the injured Brightling.

Lanaeia's silver eyes looked questioningly at Kanaan. "How do you know? I might be very dangerous."

He smiled. "You are very dangerous, just not in the way others might think." He stood and helped her stand.

She limped, but her supernatural healing had obviously started mending her injuries. "Thank you."

"How did you end up under the rubble so close to our side?" I asked.

She looked at the floor. "I wanted to be away from Qualan. For him it is always about hurting and murdering. He killed so many of our kind in Seraphina." Her eyes drooped with sadness. "I thought your people might kill me or take me prisoner. Either way, I would be far away from that evil seraph."

"Seraph?" I asked.

She tilted her head. "A male Seraphim. A female is a sera."

I groaned. "I'll probably keep using human terms like man and woman. Did you know a female lycan should be referred to as a bitch?" I waved my hands. "Talk about suicide."

A couple of the Blue Cloaks chuckled.

"I am comfortable with your decision," Lanaeia said. "Will you take me prisoner?"

"That depends." I already knew from experience not all Brightlings agreed with Daelissa's policies. Maybe once I knew more about Lanaeia, I could make a judgment call about her. "Will you tell me what you know about Daelissa's plans and how she managed to open the Grand Nexus from the other side?"

She looked at Kanaan. "Will you be there?"

The Magitsu master raised an eyebrow. "You should be able to walk on your own shortly."

"Yes, but you make me feel safe." Her silver eyes grew large and pleading.

I looked at Hertz. "Can I borrow your guy for a little bit?"

The lieutenant nodded. "Of course." He looked at Kanaan. "Behave yourself."

"He's a wild man," another Blue Cloak said.

Kanaan didn't look amused. "I will accompany the lady if it makes her more comfortable."

"It does," Lanaeia said and smiled sweetly.

I looked at the massive pile of rubble blocking the way to the Grand Nexus. Daelissa wouldn't have to break through if the omniarches and Obsidian Arch on the other side worked. For all I knew, her troops might already be gone. I thought about leaving a guard to watch this place, but saw no point. There was nothing of value on this side of the wall.

We headed toward the lone remaining portal, which had been left open for us, and returned to La Casona.

Hertz shook my hand before he and his men headed for their quarters. "Don't worry, sir. We'll still win this war."

"I know. Thanks." It was incredibly hard to muster anything resembling enthusiasm after the debacle at the Grand Nexus.

I opened a portal to the Borathen Templar compound and went through it with Kanaan and Lanaeia.

"You look very young," Lanaeia said looking me up and down. "Why do the others follow your orders?"

I shrugged. "Must be my good looks."

She seemed briefly confused before enlightenment lit her face. "You are Justin Slade."

I remembered all the daggers the Red Cell soldiers had thrown at me and almost didn't answer the question. On the other hand, Kanaan had declared her safe and, since the Blue Cloaks trusted him, I could probably trust him.

"That would be my given name." I looked at her. "It also happens that you're my cousin."

Her silver eyes widened even further. "Of course. You are Alysea's son."

I led them to the war room. Thomas and Elyssa were there with Commanders Taylor and Olson. All eyes turned to us when we entered the room.

Elyssa rushed to me and gave me a firm hug. "I was getting worried about you, but Meghan told me you were helping recover survivors from the rubble."

I pushed a dark lock of her hair behind an ear and kissed her. "I had to do something." I turned toward my guests and introduced them to everyone. "This is Lanaeia and Kanaan."

Elyssa stiffened. "Isn't that the girl from Kobol Prison?"

I nodded. "I think she's okay."

Taylor nodded at the Magitsu master. "It's an honor to see you again, Kanaan."

"I was surprised but pleased to learn you were with the Blue Cloaks, Master Kanaan," Thomas said. "It was my understanding you had left them."

"I refused to serve with Cyphanis Rax giving the orders," Kanaan said. "Once Captain Takei told me he had joined forces with you, I reconsidered."

"I'm glad we have you," Commander Olson said.

I wrinkled my forehead and looked at the Blue Cloak. "How does everyone know you?"

"Perhaps that is a story for another time," Kanaan replied. He helped Lanaeia into a seat. "I will vouch for this Brightling."

I wondered how he could be so sure, but now wasn't the time to ask him.

"Why should we trust you?" Elyssa said to the Brightling girl. "You tried to kill us at Kobol Prison."

Lanaeia's eyes turned sad. "I was only looking for my family when your group attacked me."

I held up my hands. "Let's put that episode in the past and get to the present." I dropped into a chair since my legs were killing me. "Tell us everything you know, starting when Daelissa revived you."

The Brightling nodded.

"May I suggest we refresh ourselves first?" Kanaan said.

I looked down at my filthy clothes. Lanaeia looked as bad as I did, and Kanaan wasn't much cleaner. I nodded. "A shower and some food would be great."

"Would you accompany Lanaeia, Master Kanaan?" Thomas asked.

"I will," he said.

We left and took the levitator down to the barracks levels.

"I already took a shower, so I'll accompany Lanaeia," Elyssa said when we reached the communal showers. "I'll procure some fresh clothes for you, Master Kanaan."

He held up a hand. "Just Kanaan is fine, Miss Borathen."

She smiled. "Just call me Elyssa." I could have sworn her eyes were a little brighter than usual.

Kanaan gave her a short bow. "Thank you." He stepped into the shower room.

"That guy must be part incubus," I said, noting the smile still on Elyssa's face.

She giggled. "I guess there's something alluring about the dark, mysterious type, especially one with his reputation."

"He is very handsome and stoic," Lanaeia said. "He makes me feel secure."

I looked at my girlfriend. "I've never heard of him. Who is he?"

"Something of a legend." She squeezed my hand and kissed me on the lips. "Go clean up. I'll fetch clean clothes for Lanaeia and Kanaan."

"You trust me here alone?" Lanaeia said.

Elyssa nodded. "No peeking in the boys' locker room though."

Lanaeia blushed deep red. "I would never do such a wicked thing."

I snorted. "You're definitely not Daelissa's type."

Her eyes widened. "Daelissa likes to look at unclothed males?"

A laugh burst from Elyssa. "I think he means if you blush just thinking about peeking in the men's locker room, you're probably not evil."

"Oh." Lanaeia pursed her lips. "That is quite a relief."

Elyssa handed her a towel. "I'll be back soon."

By the time we were all clean, my insides felt like I'd imbibed a bottle of drain cleaner. My incubus side was desperate to feed.

"Your irises are white," Elyssa said, alarm on her face. "Feed off me before you rampage in the middle of dinner."

I switched to incubus vision and saw my girlfriend's brilliant halo shimmering around her body. She'd obviously fed on blood recently. I latched onto her with ethereal tendrils of my own essence, and slowly drew in sustenance. It took all my self-control not to gorge myself. Doing so usually led to highly inappropriate behavior.

We met the Templar commanders in Thomas's private dining quarters and ate. The atmosphere was grim, and few words were spoken, even though I was bursting at the seams with the desire to discuss our next moves. Unfortunately, I had no idea what to do next. With the Grand Nexus closed off, and no idea where Daelissa would take her troops from there, the future was filled with uncertainty.

Once we were done eating, Thomas turned to Lanaeia. "Please tell us what you know."

The girl patted her lips with a napkin. "I will start in the far past. My parents sent me to Eden hoping I would achieve some modicum of greatness as had the other Seraphim who ruled this realm at that time." Her eyes saddened. "I had no desire for their bloodlust or cruel games. I merely wanted to learn about the mortals. I was at Thunder Rock with my parents during the Desecration. Needless to say, I do not remember anything until the time I became self-aware after my revival."

Lanaeia's hands trembled. "I was among the first to be revived along with Qualan and Qualas. I remembered their cruelty and tried to avoid them whenever possible." She gripped her hands together to stop them from shaking. "After the battle at Kobol Prison, we went to Queens Gate where Daelissa's minions attacked your mansion. A man named Kassus put a statue artifact somewhere beneath your mansion to block omniarch portals." She regarded her hands. "He bragged about how he betrayed your trust. He also told her that the Grand Nexus was likely blocked as well."

"It was," I said, looking at the others. "We didn't know until recently about his betrayal."

"He is a hateful man," Lanaeia said. "I felt terrible watching as they killed Moses. During the first war, I often heard stories of him and hoped he would be able to stop Daelissa's conquest." She looked at me, eyes fierce. "I feel no shame admitting that when you killed Qualas, I felt no sorrow."

"That girl and her brother are cray cray," I said.

She nodded. "Yes, very cray."

"Please continue," Thomas said.

Lanaeia took a sip of water. "After the mansion was destroyed and Moses was dead, Daelissa sent minions looking for you while some of us went to the Grand Nexus."

Thomas leaned forward. "Who went with you?"

"Serena, Kassus, Qualan, myself, and, of course, Daelissa." She tapped a finger to her chin. "There were others, but I do not remember them all." Lanaeia paused as if in thought and resumed her story. "Once in Seraphina, we took the skyway from the Eternal Cliffs to the capital city of Zbura."

"Skyway?" I asked.

"It is a moving path of clouds in the sky." She flattened her hand and glided it through the air as if demonstrating. "We also use small cloudbanks much like flying carpets."

"That was what Daelissa was riding," Elyssa said. "How do they work?"

"We'll discuss how they function later," Thomas said. "Please continue with your story."

Lanaeia told us how Daelissa and Qualan had forced their way into the palace and commanded Emperor Skazaeleus the Fourth to ready his troops. We were surprised to learn that the Desecration had somehow affected Seraphim lifespan and that there was also a Darkling nation.

"The Desecration didn't appear to affect Seraphim strength or ability," Thomas said.

Taylor looked pensive. "Once they feed on humans, they'll only grow stronger."

"How did Daelissa reopen the Grand Nexus?" Elyssa asked.

"There was an ancient scepter supposedly created by the first Skazaeleus," Lanaeia said. "From the documents I read, the Chalon on the Seraphina side of the nexus fell from its socket during the Desecration. He had no way to reattach or attune it, so he put it in his private art collection and named it the Divinity Scepter."

"With a name like that, there was no way Daelissa wouldn't take it," I said.

Olson leaned back in his chair. "Her troops could go anywhere from the nexus. I don't see how we can prevent them from feeding on humans."

I told him about the prisms we were using so revived Darklings could feed on both essences. "We should have more human volunteers helping us, but we don't have nearly as many Seraphim as Daelissa has."

A smile broke on Elyssa's face. "No, but I know where we can get an army."

I caught on to her meaning. "The Darklings in Seraphina."

Taylor snapped her fingers. "We control several Alabaster Arches." She took out an arctablet, projected a map, and turned to Lanaeia. "Do you know where the Darkling nation is?"

"Pjurna." The elfin girl pointed to Australia.

My hopes rose. "We control the Three Sisters." I stood up. "We can travel there tonight and go to Seraphina."

Thomas didn't look as enthused. He turned to Lanaeia. "Do you think the Darklings will help us?"

She shrugged and shook her head. "I do not know. Skazaeleus and his people did not offer much information about them."

I pushed my chair back. "It doesn't matter. We need an army and they have one."

"Even so, you're too valuable to send as an emissary," Thomas said. "Perhaps your mother—"

"No." I slashed a hand through the air. "She's a Brightling. Nightliss would be far more effective."

There was a knock on the door.

"Come," Thomas said.

A Templar entered. "Sir, the nom news is reporting something you should see." He placed an arctablet on the table and projected the broadcast from one of the twenty-four hour news networks.

A grim newscaster looked at the camera. The image of a small town with *Mystery Disease?* in large green letters splashed across it hovered over his left shoulder.

"According to the last official word we received, there are three-hundred confirmed dead in Lithia Springs, Georgia," he said. "Our very own Jan Vincent is on the scene."

The still image over his shoulder switched to a live video feed. A young, blonde woman smiled and nodded. "That's right, Dave. The bizarre snow storms which ravaged the metro area drove many people in this small community to seek shelter in the local high school gym. We were on our way to cover a story about it when a large military convoy passed us."

Elyssa and I exchanged guilty looks. *We caused that snowstorm with the snow globe in the vault.*

"What sort of vehicles were in this convoy?" Dave the newscaster asked.

Jan turned and pointed toward a cordon of military vehicles blocking a small two-lane road. Snow covered the ground, but the road had been cleared. Most of the vehicles looked like regular Humvees, though a couple had machine-gun turrets on top. "So far, I've been unable to get a comment from them, except that the CDC is on the way to the scene."

A ghastly moan sounded. Jan's eyes locked on something behind the camera. She screamed and leapt back. The camera view panned to show a man crawling on his hands and knees out of the snowy woods bordering the road. He looked up. Blackened veins ran down his face and his eyes swirled with darkness.

"Help," he moaned, reaching toward the camera.

Another woman appeared from off camera and knelt next to the man. She turned him over on his back and gave him some bottled water.

"Don't touch him," Jan shouted. "He's infected!"

The woman directed a fierce glare at Jan and turned back to the victim. "What happened to you?"

The camera zoomed in on the man's pallid face. "Angels," he wheezed. "Angels of death." A final breath rattled from his throat and his body went still.

Chapter 24

"Did he say angels?" Newscaster Dave asked.

Jan stared at the dead man, her mouth hanging open.

"Jan?"

She shuddered and looked at the camera. "Yes, Dave. Whatever sickness killed this poor man obviously causes hallucinations."

Thomas paused the playback. "How old is this news broadcast?"

"The Custodian monitors sent it over less than twenty minutes ago," the Templar said.

Taylor stared at the frozen image. "Where is Lithia Springs?"

"Just outside Atlanta," I replied.

"There's no question a Brightling fed on that man." Elyssa's lips curled in disgust. "From the casualty reports, it sounds like Daelissa's entire army fed there."

"Why Lithia Springs?" The more I thought about it, the more it seemed an odd place for Daelissa to take her army.

Thomas projected a map from the arctablet and scrolled it. "It's not far from Thunder Rock."

"Daelissa knew her army wouldn't be at full strength until they fed on humans," Olson said. "Unlike Seraphim allied with us, she has no compunction letting her troops feed on unwilling subjects."

I stared at the map. "She could have taken her people to any city, but she brought them here." A sick feeling built in my stomach. "There's only one target that would bring her to Atlanta."

"The Grotto?" Taylor said.

I shook my head. "She has Thunder Rock so she doesn't need the Obsidian Arch way station at the Grotto." I traced a line across the map all the way to Decatur. "She's coming for the Ranch."

Thomas's eyes narrowed. He stood. "Justin is right. Daelissa wants to uproot the headquarters of the resistance."

"Is she just going to march her army across Atlanta to get to us?" Olson said.

"Daelissa probably feels invincible right now," Thomas said. "Unless she has sensible military advisors, she probably sees no danger in taking her forces wherever she wants."

"What about the nom military?" Taylor said. "Do you think they'll pose a threat to her?"

"Unlikely." Thomas highlighted several points on the map. "These are the closest bases. They may dispatch aircraft, but it will take land units much longer to reach the city."

After having seen a group of battle mages take down a small fleet of military helicopters, I knew most nom aircraft wouldn't be a match for Seraphim. "What do we do?"

"We can't force a battle in the middle of the city. The number of casualties would be enormous." Thomas scrolled the map. "If we want to save lives, we'll need to attack Thunder Rock."

"How will that save lives?" Lanaeia asked. "Daelissa has many soldiers stationed there."

"It will force her to turn from Atlanta and fight us," Thomas said.

"We need to include our allies in this discussion," Olson said. "Our soldiers melted like butter to those Seraphim warriors."

"Their crystal swords shattered ours." Elyssa bit her lower lip. "If we don't have swords, we can't fight."

"Their armor and weapons are infused with aether," I said. "Whatever that crystal material is seems to hold the energy like a charge."

"Our people brought in the bodies of two Seraphim soldiers." Thomas brought up a picture of one of the swords. "We believe this material is forged with Brilliance, which is also why it can hold an aether charge."

I blew out a breath. "The Seraphim soldiers aren't going to need those swords much longer."

"Justin's right," Elyssa said. "Once they feed on enough humans, they'll be far more powerful."

I turned to Lanaeia. "Any idea how much they need to feed on humans before they turn into super Seraphim?"

She shrugged. "It can take weeks or months. I do not think it is a matter of how much one feeds on humans, but how consistently one feeds over time."

"In other words, the power accumulates," Thomas said.

"I believe so." Lanaeia tucked a strand of hair behind her ear. "When I first came to Eden, I fed sparingly on humans because I did not wish to harm them. After a few months, I discovered my abilities were on par with many who gorged themselves on human essence."

Thomas turned to the Templar who'd shown us the news broadcast. "Send an emergency broadcast to the faction heads. We need to meet immediately."

The Templar saluted. "At once, sir."

"Can I have a look at one of those crystal swords?" I asked Thomas.

He nodded. "They're in the armory."

"I'll take him." Elyssa rose and took my hand.

"I would like to accompany you," Kanaan said.

"Of course," Elyssa said.

Lanaeia stood. "May I come as well?"

"Yes, fine," I said impatiently. "Let's get a move on."

When we stepped outside, it was like entering a winter wonderland. Since our quarters were underground, I hadn't actually gone for a stroll and seen what shaking the snow globe had done.

Elyssa's hand tightened on mine. "We doomed all those people to death. They wouldn't have been gathered in the gym if this snowstorm hadn't hit their town so hard."

"How could you be responsible for a snowstorm?" Lanaeia asked as she shivered in the cold. "Is it not winter here?"

"A magic snow globe caused the storm." That was something I certainly never expected to say.

Elyssa pressed her face to my shoulder. "A whole town, Justin. My god, what have we done?"

"Such an outcome would have been likely even without the snow," Kanaan said. "Those same people would have been out doing their daily business when the army marched through." He looked up at the gray sky. "This storm may save lives. It will keep humans indoors and perhaps save them from Daelissa's soldiers."

Elyssa looked at him with a spark of hope.

I squeezed her tight. "It was an accident, babe." I kissed her forehead. "Kanaan's right. I'll bet a lot of people got out of town or stayed indoors when the storm hit. That means thousands of people won't be on the roads between us and Daelissa."

She looked at the snow-covered ground and begrudgingly nodded. "Maybe you're right." Elyssa seemed to steel herself and strode forward. "I can't let it affect me now."

We walked to the large barn and took a levitator underground to the armory. After the Synod, the ruling council of the Templars, declared Thomas a traitor, he'd been forced to significantly broaden his scope of his legion's duties. A year ago, the underground portion of the compound had been little more than a few holding cells since, in the past, most prisoners were moved to centralized compounds run directly by the Synod. Now it was a veritable labyrinth running through the bedrock hundreds of feet below the surface.

We rounded a bend in the wide tunnel and came to a warehouse the size of a wholesale discount club. Shelves filled with all sorts of gadgets both mundane and magical loomed behind a transparent barrier of diamond fiber. A Templar with horn-rimmed glasses looked up from an arctablet.

"Can I help you?" His head jerked back when he saw Elyssa. He jolted to his feet and saluted. "Yes, Sergeant Borathen?"

Elyssa rolled her eyes. "Stop brown-nosing, Roger. That's what got you desk duty in the first place."

Roger sighed and deflated, shoulders slumping. "Sorry." He swiped a finger to the diamond fiber barrier and a door swung open.

"If you're a Templar, why do you need glasses?" I asked him.

He took them off and held them out so I could see through them. "They're not prescription. I just like the way they make me look."

"Glasses are so peculiar," Lanaeia said, taking them from him and putting them on.

Roger's eyes turned dreamy. "Wow, you look totally geek chic." He narrowed his eyes as if trying to figure who she was. "Are you a Templar?"

Elyssa raised an eyebrow and crossed her arms. "Where's the equipment we took from the Seraphim soldiers?"

"In the testing section," Roger said. "Just take a left—"

Elyssa nodded. "I know where that is, thanks." She plucked the glasses off Lanaeia's face and handed them back to the clerk.

"They are lovely spectacles," the Brightling girl said.

Roger practically drooled as he looked at her. "Thanks. Maybe later—"

Elyssa clapped her hands. "Back to work, Templar!"

He jerked back and saluted. "Yes, Sergeant!"

My girlfriend motioned us to follow her and took off at a brisk pace.

"Are you usually so quiet?" I asked Kanaan as we walked.

He carried himself with a casual grace that left no question in my mind he could respond to any threat in a heartbeat. "I prefer to listen rather than speak."

I waited for him to say more, but he remained silent. "I've tried listening before, but I like the sound of my own voice too much."

Kanaan smiled. "There's no shame in that."

I almost asked him if he'd teach me the wax-on, wax-off technique and maybe toss in some crane-kick lessons, but a loud bang startled me from my smartassery. I looked forward and saw a person in a black lab coat hammering away on one of the crystal swords with a sledgehammer. She stepped back and made a notation on an arctablet.

"Hello," Elyssa said.

The woman shrieked, jumped, and dropped her tablet. It stopped just shy of the floor and floated back up to her. She stared at it a moment before snatching it out of the air. Out of the corner of my eye, I saw Kanaan holster his wand.

Elyssa gave the woman an apologetic look. "I'm sorry, Leanne, I didn't mean to startle you."

Leanne took a deep breath. "It's okay. I was so engrossed in examining this sword I didn't hear you approaching."

"Have you discovered anything so far?"

She nodded and consulted her tablet. "It appears to be made from steel like any other sword, but the forging process turns it translucent and makes it incredibly strong."

I took the sword off the table and hefted it. The handle was wrapped with soft leather. When I ran a finger along the flat of the glowing blade, it felt like warm metal. "Is that why it breaks ordinary swords?"

"May I?" Leanne held out a hand.

I transferred the handle to her.

She walked to a bar of steel secured between two clamps. Using both hands, she swung the sword. It flashed when it struck the bar. Tiny white scars glowed in the stricken metal. She pointed to the marks. "The sword discharges destructive energy when it hits. As you can tell, it stressed and weakened the metal here."

Elyssa ran a finger over the damaged material "We need a counter."

"I don't know what to tell you," Leanne said. "Only diamond fiber could resist this kind of energy output, and we couldn't possibly forge enough swords out of it anyway."

Kanaan inspected the steel bar. "When something is struck"—he slapped the heel of his hand into the other palm—"it absorbs the energy of the strike." In one precise blow, he karate-chopped the steel bar where the sword had weakened it, snapping the metal like a twig. "If an object cannot absorb the energy, it breaks."

I almost called him Captain Obvious, but decided now was a good time to listen and not speak.

He took the sword and looked at the blade. "This sword's strength comes from its ability to absorb great amounts of energy." He held it to Elyssa. "Please hold this out for me."

She took it and held it in a defensive position. "I'm ready."

Kanaan removed the lower half of the steel bar from the clamp. He swung it and delivered a vicious blow to the sword. Elyssa's arm hardly even moved but Kanaan's arms jerked back as if she'd struck the bar.

She looked surprised. "I hardly felt the blow."

He nodded and showed us the bar. Fractures laced the steel where it had hit the sword. "The impact is absorbed and returned to the origin."

I whistled. "No wonder. How are we supposed to fight back against that?"

"Oh, it's much worse than you think," Leanne said. She took the sword and leaned it against the table, backed away, and looked at Kanaan. "Hit it with a spell."

He flicked the wand from its holster and pointed it at the sword. A jagged bolt of blue energy struck the sword. The blade glowed a little brighter, but the sword didn't even move. Kanaan knelt and examined it. "It absorbs the energy from spells. I had surmised as much when observing how their armor functions."

Leanne twisted her lips with a regretful look. "Their armor is made from the same material."

"Let me try something," I said. I took aim with one finger and channeled Brilliance into the blade. It glowed brighter and brighter until the metal began to rattle against the floor. I stopped and watched as energy leaked from the blade like white flames, warming the air around us.

"It has a limit," Elyssa said. "But our Arcanes would be hard pressed to reach it. Their spells aren't as powerful as Seraphim channeling."

I thought back to the battle. "When I hit the enemies with one strong burst, their armor cracked and broke immediately."

"It could not absorb it quickly enough," Kanaan said.

I nodded. "If I trickle energy slowly until it's full to bursting—"

Elyssa's eyes widened. "It could cause an explosion."

"Would you humor me and channel Murk into the blade?" Kanaan said.

"Sure." I extended a finger and trickled ultraviolet into the translucent metal. The white glow abated after several seconds until the sword was suffused with gray.

Kanaan picked up the sword and gently tapped it against the workbench. It shattered like glass.

"Brilliance and Murk neutralize each other," I said.

"They form a delicate balance," Kanaan said. "It corrupts the metal alloy and makes it fragile."

I looked at the broken shards. "This is helpful, but it'll take forever to infuse the blade and armor of every soldier with Murk, even if all our Darklings pitch in."

"It is a beginning," Kanaan said simply. "Now we know."

"And knowing is half the battle." I said pursed my lips and attempted a wise look.

Elyssa punched me in the shoulder. "Now is not the time to start quoting after-school cartoons."

I gave her a hurt look to cover an impish grin. A thought occurred to me. "Kanaan, how did you kill that one Seraphim when you put your wand to his armor?"

"I cast the spell into the gap between scales." He pointed to a pile of the crystal armor on the workbench. "Like most rigid materials, it must leave gaps to allow movement. When I cast the spell, it refracted within the armor. I suspect the inside of the armor is not enchanted for absorption."

I grunted. "I suppose that's good for close combat, but I'm not as agile as you."

He nodded. "It is not a tactic I would recommend to others, even those skilled in Magitsu."

Leanne brought in another set of armor and placed it next to the first. "I'll keep plugging away at it. Maybe I'll figure out something useful."

"We're about to attack Thunder Rock," Elyssa said in a grim voice. "Do your best to discover something quick."

She nodded and pulled out a wand. "I won't let you down." She looked at Kanaan. "You've got a great Zen aura going on. I dig your style."

He offered her a curt nod of his head. "Thank you."

I gave him a sideways look. "I want whatever body spray you're using. Maybe you should turn that Zen charisma on Daelissa and teach her to make love, not war."

"Justin," Elyssa said in a warning tone.

Kanaan simply smiled.

We went back through the warehouse, up the levitator, and to Thomas's dining quarters. It was empty, but a helpful Templar told us everyone was gathering in the war room. I would have helped myself to a second helping of roast beef, but settled for a couple of apples to munch on. We reversed course and went to the meeting. Mom and Dad were there along with leaders of all the major factions. I spotted Nightliss next to Mom and walked over to them.

"Justin, I am very sorry about your Aunt Vallaena," Nightliss said.

Dad flinched when he heard the name but didn't say anything.

"Thanks." I took her aside. "I don't know if anyone mentioned the plan to ask the Darklings in Seraphina for help, but we might need your ambassadorial skills."

"Alysea told me about the plan." She gave me a worried look. "It has been so long since I've been home. I don't know how useful I will be convincing them to join us."

"We don't have much of a choice." I blew out a breath. "I have a terrible feeling about attacking Thunder Rock."

"As do I." She touched my arm. "Whatever happens, you must not risk yourself."

"I don't think I'll be able to help that."

She gave me a sad look. "To think we almost won."

I squeezed her hand. "I know." A melancholy feeling weighed me down. "I know."

Thomas called for quiet and the conversations in the room died away. Everyone took seats around the table. He remained standing. "Daelissa is marching for this compound."

Stunned looks greeted this announcement.

"We prepare and face them here," Colin McCloud said, baring his teeth. "We'll wipe the floor with them on your home ground."

"I'm itching for some payback," Dad said.

Cries of agreement went up around the table.

I saw Fjoeruss looking calmly around the table, but I couldn't tell if he agreed or not.

Thomas held up his hand to quiet everyone. "Unfortunately, it's not as simple as that." He projected a map of Atlanta and highlighted the town Daelissa had attacked. "Our scouts report that the Seraphim are advancing in a line that will take them through the city, feeding on humans as they go. If we allow them to continue, the casualties will be staggering."

"Do you suggest we march to meet them?" Fjoeruss said.

Thomas shook his head. "No." He drew a line to the south. "We stage an attack on Thunder Rock and draw her forces there."

"Suicide," Colin McCloud said. "We don't know what forces she has stationed there, or what defenses she'll have."

"It will merely be a feint," Thomas said. "If we draw them back to Thunder Rock, it will give us time to prepare our defenses." He drew a new line from Thunder Rock to the Ranch. "Their return course will likely take this path through the southern part of the metro area. The Custodians have put emergency protocols into effect to vacate the noms. With the streets now mostly clear of snow, that should allow the humans clear passage."

"Emergency protocols?" Dad asked.

Thomas projected a television broadcast above the table with newscaster Dave.

Dave smiled. "The cold from the snowstorm apparently has given the communities of East Point, Decatur, and several other parts of southern Atlanta even more unwelcome surprises this winter. Gas leaks in stressed pipes have caused officials to evacuate people from several affected areas." A map of Atlanta appeared with several pulsating red markers on it.

Thomas paused the broadcast. "The Custodians faked those incidents. We need to buy as much time at Thunder Rock as possible to allow the humans to clear the corridor."

"Tricky." Dad smiled. "It would lower the collateral damage."

Captain Takei made a thoughtful sound. "If we are to prepare a strong defense, we can't send all our forces to Thunder Rock. The logistics would be too demanding."

"If we send a small strike force, Daelissa might suspect it's a diversion and keep marching for us," Commander Taylor said. "We need her to think it's a fully committed assault."

"I might be able to help with your problem," said a tired voice from the doorway.

All eyes turned to see who spoke. I turned in my chair and saw the person who'd once commanded the enemy forces.

Phoebe Borathen.

Chapter 25

"Who's this?" McCloud asked.

Elyssa gasped. "Phoebe?"

Her sister gave a tired smile. "Nightliss cleansed me of Daelissa's tampering. Now that I know the error of my ways, I want to help."

Thomas froze for a moment and leaned down to converse with Nightliss. She looked none too certain herself.

"That's Luna," Captain Takei said. "She was Daelissa's chief strategist."

Murmurs went up around the room.

Nightliss stood. "Quiet, please."

"I'd be bloody interested to know why that woman is here," McCloud said.

"I am Luna no longer," Phoebe said.

McCloud put a hand to his heart. "Ah, well what a relief. Why don't you come sit in on our top-secret meeting then, lass?"

"Why is she walking free through your compound?" Captain Takei asked Thomas.

Thomas looked at Phoebe. Uncertainty flickered through his face but vanished behind a wall of resolve. "During the American Civil War, I lost my daughter and two sons battling vampires. My daughter was taken by Daelissa, her mind implanted with falsehoods to turn her against me. Over the decades, those falsehoods festered and grew. True, she was leading Daelissa's forces, but Nightliss has managed to heal her damaged memories."

Captain Takei looked uncertain. "How can you be sure she is free of Daelissa's influence?"

I spotted every woman's favorite Magitsu master leaning against a wall in the back of the room. He watched the proceedings with a neutral expression. I stood. "Kanaan, what do you think?"

Takei raised an eyebrow. "How could he know if her mind is free?"

I motioned toward Lanaeia. "He took one look at her and said she held no evil in her heart. Maybe he can do the same with Phoebe."

A smile broke on the captain's face. "He said that, did he?"

I felt my forehead wrinkle. "Why's that so funny?"

"It was merely a gut feeling," Kanaan said. "I'm no mind reader."

I gave him a dirty look. "Well, that's good to know."

A female cleared her voice loudly. I turned toward the noise. Nightliss stared at the assembly with narrowed eyes and hands on her hips. "I have been working nonstop with Phoebe. Though she is still weak and tired from the treatments, I am confident her mind is once again her own." She directed a glare at Takei and raked it over McCloud as well. "If you have any doubts, you can take it up with me."

"Oh, my." Takei gave her an apologetic smile. "I will take your word on the matter."

McCloud gave her a tooth-baring grin. "I'd much sooner stay on your good side, Clarion."

Nightliss folded her arms and looked slightly less peeved. "Now that the objections have been cleared, perhaps we should let Phoebe speak."

Phoebe looked like the perfect combination between Elyssa and their mother, Leia. She had black hair, fair skin, and was Elyssa's height. Phoebe's nose, however, was more like Thomas's, and her lower body was a bit thicker than Elyssa's. The last time I'd seen her, she'd been convinced her family had intentionally abandoned her and her brothers to their deaths over a century ago. Thankfully, we'd managed to capture her and subsequently discovered the tampering Daelissa had done to her mind.

"Come to the front and speak," Thomas said. His voice sounded rough.

Phoebe made her way toward him. She moved slowly, and it was obvious removing Daelissa's influence had taken a physical toll on her.

I felt Elyssa's hand tighten on my forearm. I met her moist eyes. "Are you okay?" I asked.

She wiped a tear gathering in her eye and smiled. "I'm just happy."

I freed my arm, wrapped it around her shoulder and squeezed. *At least this is something we can be happy about.*

Thomas leaned toward Phoebe and whispered something in her ear. She nodded and whispered something back my supernatural hearing couldn't pick up. I suspected he'd asked her if she was up to this. Considering how effectively she'd managed Daelissa's troops against us, I prayed she was.

"I watched an ASE recording of the battle at the Grand Nexus provided to me by Nightliss," Phoebe said, getting straight to business. "I'm still analyzing it for weaknesses in the Seraphim fighting technique, but with their superior armor and weapons, I'm afraid we'll have to resort to trickery."

"Do you plan to trick them into removing their armor?" McCloud asked.

She shook her head. "You need a diversion that looks like a full-scale invasion. I know how to make it look like one."

I snapped my fingers. "Just like you did during the attack on the Australian Templar legion."

She gave me an apologetic look. "Yes." She opened her hand to reveal an ASE. It projected what it had recorded as a three-dimensional holograph. "Using about a hundred of these, I was able to make our force of battle mages look magnitudes larger than it actually was."

"The question is, will Daelissa's forces fall for it?" I asked.

"You'll need an initial show of force," she said. "I'd suggest a battalion at least two-hundred strong to strike the first blow."

"How many ASEs will you require?" Thomas asked.

Phoebe bit her lip. "In order to make them think we have a full army, I'd need several hundred."

"We don't have that many," he said. "Ever since our split from the Synod, we haven't been able to spare Arcanes to make them." He tapped something on his arctablet. "According to inventory, we have one-hundred and fifty-three not in service."

"That poses a problem." She folded her arms, a pensive look on her face.

The solution seemed pretty clear to me. "Why don't we record formations of four people for each ASE? Heck, we could record an entire army and have it project that."

"The ASE wouldn't be strong enough to project a full-sized recording of an army," Phoebe said. "At most, it can project two people at full size."

"How many could it handle at half size?" I said.

"What good would that do?" McCloud asked. "We won't frighten them with an army of midgets."

I shrugged. "Maybe if we dressed them up as clowns we would." That raised a few eyebrows. I waved my hands. "Sorry, bad joke."

"I personally find clowns terrifying." Phoebe flashed a smile. "To answer your question, an ASE could project about ten people at half size."

I did some quick math. "An army a thousand strong would work."

McCloud's forehead wrinkled. "But, midgets!"

"Everyone hold your thumb and forefinger in front of one eye." People shifted in their chairs and exchanged confused looks, but eventually complied. I repressed a grin. "Now, holding your thumb and forefinger a few inches from your eye, look at the person's head across the table and pinch it."

McCloud chuckled as he pretended to pinch Thomas's head. "I think I see where you're going with this."

"Everything is a matter of perspective." I put on my most devious look. "We simply need to position the holographic troops in a place that makes them look full sized from a distance."

Phoebe pursed her lips. "I think that would work."

"We need to include every Darkling and Brightling we have in the real strike force." I held up a hand before anyone could object. "We pack a strong punch for such a small force, and once Daelissa gets word that Nightliss, Alysea, and I are hitting her, I guarantee she'll turn her army right for us."

"I can't agree to that," Thomas said. "If anything should happen to you, this war is lost."

I stood and pressed a fist to the table. "I absolutely disagree." I met the gazes around the table. "Even without me, you are still stronger than Daelissa. She fights for one thing only—power. There is nothing more hollow than power. It fills you with an insatiable need you can never fill." I touched Elyssa's shoulder. "We fight for the ones we love and the realm we hold dear. Eden is our home. We will never let Daelissa take her from us."

"Aye!" McCloud shouted and pumped a fist into the air. "We'll give her a nip in the arse and send her packing."

"Hear, hear!" Dad said.

Cheers erupted around the table.

Brave words, but are they true? I hoped we could follow through.

"I think Mr. Slade is right," Phoebe said after the cheers died down. "All our available Seraphim should initiate the attack."

"I'm going with several wolf packs," McCloud said.

Dad stood. "I'll commit however many Daemos we need."

Nightliss rose. "I will be by your side, Justin."

"As will I," Mom said.

Phoebe looked a bit dazed as her gaze wandered around the room. "It's settled then." She turned to Thomas. "Commander, can you disperse the ASEs among the various factions and have them record groups of ten soldiers?"

"Immediately," he said. "We don't have time to spare."

One of Thomas's advisors came forward and whispered in his ear. His face turned grim. "We have even less time than I thought. Daelissa has hit another suburb of Atlanta and is pillaging its citizenry even as we speak." He handed his assistant the tablet. "See to these orders immediately." Thomas turned to us. "Assemble your squads and meet in the hangar. Commander Salazar's people will open portals to La Casona within thirty minutes." He stood. "Dismissed."

The crowd in the room diminished quickly. I saw Thomas speaking with Phoebe but the other commanders drew his attention away.

Elyssa stared at her sister. "Now that she's cured, I don't know what to say to her."

I stroked her fair cheek and smiled. "Why don't you start with something simple, like hello?"

Elyssa giggled. "Such sage advice. I'll give it a try."

Thomas gripped Phoebe's hands and spoke with her a moment before leaving with his entourage of Templar leaders. Phoebe looked across the table at us, violet eyes filled with uncertainty. She looked so much like Elyssa I had to blink a couple of times to see the differences again.

Elyssa walked around the table. Phoebe met her halfway. Without a word, they gripped each other in a tight hug. Tears trickled down Phoebe's cheek.

She pulled away from Elyssa and said, "Thank you for saving me, sister."

Elyssa wiped away tears of her own. "Anytime, sis."

Phoebe looked at me. "It's no wonder I couldn't win battles against you. You really know how to encourage the troops."

I shrugged. "I guess when you talk as much as I do, something inspiring is bound to pop out every once in a while."

"You two are a couple?" Phoebe asked Elyssa.

Elyssa beamed a lovely smile at me. "He's all mine."

"I'm glad to see you on your feet," said a deep voice. I looked toward the source and saw Michael Borathen filling the doorway with his hulking form.

Phoebe regarded him for a long moment. "I'm sorry. You are?"

"Your brother, Michael." He shrugged. "I should have introduced myself sooner, but Nightliss was rather adamant about us leaving you alone."

Phoebe gave him an apologetic smile. "Nightliss ordered me not to leave my bed, but when I heard about what had happened at the Grand Nexus, I had to see if I could help. To see if maybe I could reverse some of the damage I've done." Her lips pressed together in a wistful look. "I just wish I could offer more than simple tricks."

"We need help figuring out how to overcome the Seraphim armor and swords," I said. "Maybe you could help Leanne in the armory examine them."

Michael grunted. "You certainly aren't ready to go into the field."

"If I can be of help, I will." She sighed. "I will examine the Grand Nexus battle recordings as well and see if I discover anything that might help."

I folded my arms. "I'm just glad I don't have to get my ass kicked by you anymore."

She giggled. It reminded me of Elyssa's laugh. "You could use more practice, though I believe you never used the full extent of your powers against me."

"He won't kill if he can help it," Elyssa said.

"For that, I am immensely grateful." Phoebe gathered her arctablet from the table. "I will go to the armory and see what assistance I can provide."

Michael offered her his elbow. "I'll be happy to show you the way."

She took his arm and looked up at him. "I don't know why I didn't see it before, but you look so much like your brothers. I wish you could have met them."

"Goodbye." I waved. "Thanks for not beating me up this time."

Phoebe laughed and waved goodbye as Michael led her out of the door.

Elyssa gripped me in a tight hug. "Was that real? Did I really hear my long-lost sister laugh?"

I kissed her forehead. "As real as the fart I just cut."

She lightly slapped my chest. "Be serious for two seconds."

I kissed her cheek. "Heck, I'll even shoot for three."

We ran down to our quarters, put on our Nightingale armor, and met the others in the underground hangar bay. Mom, Nightliss, Joss, and Otaleon stood at the front of a large mixed contingent of Daemos, lycans, felycans, and Templars. Lieutenant Hertz led a force of Blue Cloaks toward us.

"How's the arm?" I asked him.

He rotated it. "The healers patched me up. I'm good to go."

"Excellent." I handed him several ASEs. "Have your people record themselves in groups of ten."

"You want action shots?" he asked.

I shrugged. "Whatever makes it look convincing."

He nodded. "We're on it."

I dispersed ASEs to the other factions and watched as they recorded footage. We might have a lot of duplicate holographic soldiers, but hopefully the enemy wouldn't realize that until it was too late. Before long, the hundred ASEs were filled with video and hovering nearby, waiting for me to deploy them.

"Where's Ivy?" I asked Mom.

"I don't want her along on this mission," she said. "I know she can take care of herself, but this is extremely risky."

Fjoeruss walked in with a formation of elite gray men. He strode over to me. "Am I to accompany the Seraphim contingent?"

"Can your golems take care of themselves?" I asked.

"Yes." He met a glare from my mother. "Is something bothering you, Alysea?"

"Despite the contract, I am ever on guard against you," Mom replied in an even voice.

Fjoeruss's expression remained impassive. "As always, I will adhere to the letter of the contract."

Mom flashed a sarcastic look. "A contract, to you, is a puzzle to be untangled and rewoven into an advantage. If only you had a care in the world other than yourself."

"Such hurtful words, Alysea." Fjoeruss smiled coldly. "As it happens, I do care for my sister."

I held out my hands to ward off any more insults. "Don't make me put you two in separate corners, okay?" I huffed. "We have a difficult battle ahead and we can't have any distractions."

Mom looked a little ashamed and hurt. "I'm sorry, son."

Fjoeruss simply shrugged and took a position in the back of our Seraphim formation.

Thomas came over to me. "Justin, the troops will be under your command for this operation. I'll remain here and ready our main force to defend the compound."

I nodded. "Once Daelissa takes the bait, how long should we wait before escaping through portals?"

"Wait until you see her army. If you retreat too soon, she might realize the trick and turn her troops back toward Atlanta." He looked at an arctablet. "According to the news, the evacuation from the southern part of the metro area is proceeding. The longer you delay Daelissa, the fewer the nom casualties."

"Understood."

Thomas shook my hand. "Good luck, Mr. Slade."

"Same to you, sir."

Templars standing next to the two portal zones marked by yellow squares painted on the hangar floor raised their arms. Portals sliced the air vertically and blinked open horizontally.

I turned to Elyssa. "Call the troops to order, please."

She turned and bellowed in a commanding voice, "Attention! Form up!"

Dad turned to the Daemos under his command and relayed her orders. Colin McCloud loosed a blood-chilling howl, and his packs gathered, the felycans organizing behind him. I saw the huge felycan man say something to McCloud and press a hand to his shoulder before forming up with others of his kind. I felt encouraged watching the friendly exchange—a stark difference from their attitudes at the Grand Nexus.

I held up my arm and swung it forward. "Move out!"

The battalion split into two equal rows and raced through the portals until everyone was in the control room at La Casona. The Templars stationed at the omniarches closed the portals and opened new ones to the outskirts of Thunder Rock. I gave the signal and, once again, our people threaded through the portals.

I waited until the other factions made it through before motioning my Seraphim squad to follow. We ran into a field choked with the remains of weeds and clumps of snow. Several hundred yards separated us from the mounds of rock and earth guarding the border of the quarry pit. A forest of pine trees surrounded the field. The cold wind rattled dead leaves and burned the air in my lungs.

Using a program on my arcphone, I brought the hundred ASEs with the recordings of our fake army through the portal behind us. I switched them to loop playback mode and sent them to hover another fifty yards in front of the tree line behind us. Our virtual army flickered into being. Up close, it didn't look very convincing, especially since most of the soldiers stood only as high as my stomach. The tall weeds made them look even shorter.

I scrambled the location of the ASEs to hide the duplicates the best I could.

"How do they look?" I asked.

Dad put a hand to his chin and stared. "I think dressing them up as clowns might have worked better."

McCloud looked at the mounds of earth around the quarry pit several hundred yards away. "From that distance, they'll look big enough." He knelt and peered over the weeds. "Have the ASEs raise the holograms off the ground a couple of feet. The weeds will hide the fact that they're not on the ground."

The idea was so simple I wished I'd thought of it. "Great idea."

Once I made the adjustments, our virtual army looked a whole lot better. I hoped it was enough to fool the enemy.

I rubbed my hands together to ward off the cold and put on my most confident smile. "Take your positions, people. It's time to poke the hornets' nest."

Chapter 26

Elyssa led the Templars into the tree line to our left while the lycan and felycan forces melted into the forest on the right. The Blue Cloaks set up illusionary blinds and hid behind them, ready to strike when the enemy showed its ugly face.

I led my Seraphim entourage to the earth embankment bordering the quarry. We walked up the side and peered over the ledge. A road wound down the sides of the granite cliffs and ended at a gaping pit where a lake had once been. With the lake bottom gone, it looked like a black pit of doom. Aside from a few guards walking the perimeter, there didn't seem to be much activity. Unfortunately, this angle offered a limited view of the pit.

The drop to the road below was about ten feet. I motioned to the others and lowered myself over the ledge. Stray bits of gravel rattled down the ledge. The guard patrolling nearby turned toward the noise. I blurred at him and knocked him out with one quick strike. His designer shirt and jeans gave away his affiliation as a vampire. I gagged and bound him with diamond fiber rope.

"Why not simply kill him?" Fjoeruss said.

I put the unconscious vampire behind a rock on the side of the gravel road. "He's no longer a threat." I knew plenty of killing lay ahead of me. Sparing even one life we didn't have to take didn't balance that, but it made me feel a little less like a monster.

Fjoeruss stared at the body but said nothing more on the matter.

We continued in plain sight down the road. I wasn't concerned about the guards on the opposite side seeing us since we were about to intentionally attract a lot of attention. We reached the lip of the pit. The last time I'd seen this place, it had been filled with water.

Daelissa's agents had since drained the lake and turned Thunder Rock into a functional way station.

Nightliss gasped as she looked down. "Are those golems?"

The rest of us followed her gaze. Giant stone monsters stood in rows upon rows along one side of the enormous pit. Scores of enemies walked below. I saw Exorcists, battle mages, and Synod soldiers among them. Across the floor from the others was a formation of red uniforms I quickly identified as Red Cell soldiers.

I felt a sinking sensation in my stomach as I nodded. "Those are the giant golems they were building at Queens Gate."

"We won't be able to do much damage from so far away," Joss said.

I gauged the distance to the cavern floor at several hundred feet. Even with our combined might, magical attacks would disperse by the time they traversed the space to do much harm. I examined the cliff wall beneath us. "We don't need to hit them directly." I walked to the side and found a ledge jutting from the cliff. "Let's drop a few tons of rocks on their heads and see what they think about that."

I focused a beam of Brilliance at the ledge. Mom added her effort to mine. Lava bubbled from the cut. With a loud crack, the earth broke free and tumbled into the pit. Joss and Otaleon levered two boulders from the side of the road with ultraviolet tendrils of Murk and sent them rolling in right after.

Shouts and cries echoed from below as people scrambled out of the way of the falling rocks. I wedged a jagged beam of Murk into the cliff side, releasing a small rockslide. The guards on the road across the vast pit cast spells at us. Their efforts fell well short of the mark. Flying carpets loaded with battle mages rose from below, and enemy squads boarded large, flat levitators to bring them to the top.

"Time for us to go," I said.

I ran to the road ledge behind us, leapt, caught the edge, and pulled myself to the top. The others followed suit. Fjoeruss simply levitated the distance. We climbed up the rest of the switchbacks until we reached the top. By the time we cleared the earth embankment, the flying carpets were already closing in fast.

I motioned my group to take cover behind a boulder.

The first carpet rose over the gravel mound. A volley of spells from the hidden Blue Cloaks slammed into it. The carpet caught fire and left a smoky trail as it vanished beyond the lip. The next enemies were more careful, rising as a group a distance away from where their comrades had gone down in flames.

I saw the whites of their eyes as they caught sight of the virtual army behind us. I knew better than to give them time to gawk.

"Open fire!" I shouted.

We sprang from our hiding place.

Mom sliced a carpet in half with a beam of Brilliance. Nightliss and the other Darklings slammed ultraviolet orbs against other riders. Fjoeruss gripped another carpet with stasis, causing it to stop in place. The riders, however, kept going. Their screams of terror ended when they hit a slab of granite.

I spun a cloud of Murk into a gust of wind and hurtled dust toward the attackers to keep them from getting a better look at our holographic allies. Fjoeruss channeled a beam of Brilliance into my wind. Veins of white encircled the ultraviolet. The breeze gathered impetus, forming a funnel.

The battle mages on the carpets shouted in dismay as my breeze suddenly erupted into a full-blown twister. It dragged flying carpets inside. Some were hurled out with the riders still bonded to their carpets. Other mages weren't so lucky. The tornado tore them loose and tossed them in all directions.

"How the hell did you do that?" I yelled at Fjoeruss over the roar of the wind.

He raised an eyebrow. "There is far more to our abilities than brute force, Mr. Slade."

I gave him a look of disbelief. "I'd call a tornado pretty damned brutish, dude."

Fjoeruss flung a ball of gray smoke toward the body of a screaming battle mage. The spell stopped the man in midair. Astonishment had barely registered on the man's face when Fjoeruss unleashed a bolt of Brilliance and incinerated him.

I cringed. "Would you like another side of irony with your previous statement?"

Another sortie of carpets rose. I channeled a stream of cold Murk at the ground and envisioned it rotating. A small weak funnel rose. Using Fjoeruss's example, I wove heated Brilliance into the mix, willing the two forces to spin. Like a match to gasoline, the magical weave exploded with a life of its own. It grew exponentially until it threatened to drag my allies inside. I hit it with a gust of Murk and sent it spinning into the oncoming enemy.

"One should use caution when dabbling with nature," Fjoeruss said. "The concomitant interaction could be rather deleterious."

I gave him an uncaring look. "One should also be careful using too many ten-dollar words in a sentence." I watched like a proud parent as my tornado sucked in a wave of attackers and spat them out.

My arcphone buzzed. I spared a glance at the screen and saw a text message from one of Thomas's assistants.

Queen Bee is returning to the hive. ETA twenty minutes.

Twenty minutes, I'd learned, was an eternity when you were trying to hold off superior forces, though it seemed like an eye blink when you were in the thick of a battle. The first tornado Fjoeruss and I had created reached the earthen embankment around the quarry and roared down into the pit until it vanished. The second twister veered away and tore through the field to the west, leaving the battlefield altogether.

A wave of enemies appeared to the east. They formed up but made no move to attack.

"Can you fog the air a bit?" I asked Fjoeruss.

He wet a finger and held it in the breeze. "The air is too dry. It would be difficult to draw enough moisture for fog."

I viewed the gathering enemy through a pair of spectacles. A small group consisting of a vampire, a battle mage, and an Exorcist huddled together in conversation. They occasionally peered at our army and were obviously deciding whether to attack or dig in.

Unfortunately, twenty minutes gave them plenty of time to see our army for exactly what it was. I lowered the spectacles and channeled another stiff breeze to cloud the air with dust.

"I would caution against another tornado," Fjoeruss said. "It could very well turn on us."

The communication pendant on my armor beeped and Elyssa's voice spoke. "Justin, they're sending scouts into a flanking position to get a better look at our soldiers. I've already dispatched people to intercept and the lycans have done the same."

"We have to hold out twenty minutes," I told her.

She went quiet for a moment. "What if we split the ASEs and sent them into the forest out of sight?"

I snapped my fingers. "That might work. They'll think we plan to flank them and might entrench their current position."

"Exactly." She murmured a command to someone. "I have my people on it. Let's pray this works."

Clouds scudded overhead, gathering into ominous gray mountains in the sky. A bolt of lightning speared into the woods to the west. Thunder rumbled and a funnel cloud dove into the tree line north of the quarry.

I looked through my spectacles. "It looks like someone over there is messing with the weather."

"It would take several battle mages to change the weather," Mom said.

Fjoeruss pointed toward a group of people standing at the front of the opposing force. "It would appear they already have Seraphim here."

"They're so young," Mom said. "They must have been recently revived."

I focused my spectacles on the group. A male and female Darkling channeled a funnel of air with Murk while several Brightlings charged the air with destructive energy. I noticed two battle mages prodding the Darklings with their wands. Judging from the distressed looks on the Darkling's faces, they were under painful duress. My jaw tightened. "They're forcing the Darklings to channel for them."

Nightliss gasped. "We must do something to help them."

"Impossible," Fjoeruss said. "Need I remind you that we're here as a diversion. A rescue attempt would be suicidal."

"Don't you think I know that, Trickster?" Nightliss's voice seethed with such contempt, she almost sounded like her sister, Daelissa, for a second.

Gray eyes void of emotion, Fjoeruss simply gave a curt nod. "Good."

Sometimes the man made me think he was a soulless golem.

A great wind rose from the north sending leaves, dirt, and debris into our faces. I turned my face from the cold gust and saw the last traces of our holographic army melting into the trees. Freezing rain bit into my exposed neck and scalp since I hadn't covered my head or face with the Nightingale armor. Lightning crashed all round and the air vibrated with the deep basso of thunder.

"Fools," Fjoeruss said, his voice filled with contempt.

I turned back and saw the enemy Brightlings fighting to push a two-story tornado toward us. Even with the air current blowing toward us from the north, the twister bucked and bent as if trying to go a way of its own choosing. The bulk of enemy forces were already retreating from the growing tempest. The cold air suddenly turned warm against my face as the Brightlings channeled more and more heat into their creation.

Nightliss gripped my arm. "We cannot allow them to hurl that toward us." Pain filled her voice. "We must fight back even if we harm the Darklings."

I didn't like the idea of harming the capture Darklings any more than she did, but she was right. We had no choice. I turned to Fjoeruss. "What's the best way to push back?"

He narrowed his eyes as warm rain began to beat down on us in earnest. "We need to create a cold front to neutralize the temperature differential. That may disperse the tornado." Fjoeruss looked over the others. "I believe we might have a chance since there are more of us who can channel Murk."

"Since I can't channel Murk, I'll bolster Justin," Mom said. She pressed a hand to my back, sending a chill of aether tingling up my spine.

Fjoeruss looked at Nightliss, Joss, and Otaleon. "Imagine an arctic cold flowing from you and into the air. I will stabilize the current." He looked at me. "You will push the air with all your might."

"Let's do it," I said.

The three Darklings thrust out their hands. Aether suffused the air with an ultraviolet glow. Ice crystals formed and sparkled. The warm rain turned colder and colder until it was sleet. A moment later, small bits of hail pelted us. Drawing upon all my power, I willed the cold air to move and circulate. I pushed it north with a wave of Murk. Fjoeruss sent threads of gray flowing through the air current. It seemed to bind the airflow together into one cohesive force. The enemy's tornado howled south towards us. Our cold front hit it.

The tornado shrank ever so slightly. The enemy Brightlings responded. Superheated currents of Brilliance lanced into the tornado, causing it to grow again. I added more energy into the wind powering our cold front. The enemy once again reinforced their efforts. The air erupted with a tremendous boom of thunder. Lightning struck the ground over and over in the open field between us and the opposing Seraphim.

I had to close my eyes against the blinding light. The afterimages of jagged lightning bolts danced behind my eyelids. A tremendous rush of wind pulled at me and roared in my ears like a train on horse steroids. I peeked through slitted eyelids and saw a monstrous tornado fighting to break free.

Like a rebellious teenager, our monstrous creation ripped from its bonds and began to lay waste everything around it. Since it was still in the field between us and Thunder Rock, it threw out dust, gravel, and dead plants in all directions. It grew from three to four stories tall and drifted north back towards the enemy.

"Stop channeling," Fjoeruss said. "It's too late to stop it. You'll only feed it now."

We released the channeled power. I lost sight of the enemy as debris filled the air. Brilliant veins of destruction threaded through the maelstrom, presumably as the opposing Brightlings tried to send it our way.

Sweat dripped down my forehead despite the freezing cold. Mom's hand left my back and my knees turned to jelly. The storm gathered strength. Lightning sprang in all directions from the dark gray turbulence. I wearily pushed to my feet and looked at the others. Joss and Otaleon leaned on each other for support. Nightliss lay on the ground. Blood trickled from multiple cuts on her face. I felt warm liquid on my cheeks and touched one. A jagged bit of rock poked from the skin. In all the confusion, I'd forgotten to extend the armor facemask.

I touched the collar so it would grow over my head and face, but nothing happened. *All the channeling probably short-circuited the enchantment.* Mom pulled Nightliss to her feet.

"It's coming our way!" Mom cried over the roar of thunder and wind. Her blonde hair lashed about her face with a life of its own.

Looking up at the monstrosity, I couldn't tell if it was actually moving toward us, or simply growing. "Retreat!" I shouted at the top of my lungs. "We've done what we needed to do."

My group started moving toward the portals near the tree line a hundred yards behind us. I touched the communicator pendant at my collar. "Everyone move back. We're getting out of here." The communicator hissed with static. I listened but couldn't hear if anyone responded. "Damn it, I think our comms are down."

"The others will know to fall back," Fjoeruss said in a maddeningly calm voice.

I tried to see through the dark blanket of debris where Elyssa's squad should be but couldn't see a thing through it. I waved the others toward the portals. "Go! I'll catch up."

My knees wobbled as I strode forward into the howling wind. I heard someone shouting behind me, but pressed on. *Elyssa is out there.* Dirt flew into my mouth. Wind-tossed shrapnel slammed me from every direction. The armor deflected most of it, but my unprotected head felt the sting of every tiny blow.

An uprooted tree flew at me from the darkness. I fell to my knees as it bounced once, twice, and flew feet over my head. Drawing upon every ounce of strength left to me, I pushed forward. Something black flew at me. Before I could dodge, it slammed into me. I felt the earth sliding against my back. Weeds poked into my scalp.

I'm going to go bald before this is over.

Someone groaned. I looked up at a masked Templar.

"Are you okay, sir?" a male voice asked.

"I'm just peachy! Where's Elyssa?"

"We were falling back but a gust of wind threw me." He pushed himself off me and pulled me to my feet. "The others should be right behind me."

The din seemed to abate ever so slightly. Somewhere behind me, I heard howls. *Please tell me the lycans are falling back.* A group of dark figures staggered in from the dark. One of them gripped me in a tight hug.

"Justin, why aren't you wearing a facemask?" Elyssa's voice was unmistakable.

I almost cried with relief. "It's not working." I turned toward the south. "Let's go!"

The wind lessened further. I turned and saw the deadly tornado ripping through the trees to the east. It seemed to pick up speed as it headed in the direction of Kobol prison. Before we took another step, a brilliant light evaporated the remaining haze. My butt cheeks clenched at what was revealed.

The Seraphim army.

Chapter 27

"Run away!" I shouted. "Run for your freaking lives!" I took two steps and stumbled. Elyssa slung my arm over her shoulder and woman-handled me to my feet.

I managed to time my steps with hers and we picked up speed.

"Justin Slade!" screeched Daelissa. "Turn and face me, coward!"

"Go away!" I yelled without looking back.

A searing bolt of Brilliance the width of a finger plowed a small furrow in the ground inches to our right. Another slammed into the back of a Templar running to our left. The armor smoked. The man screamed as the white-hot beam exploded from his chest and sent his lifeless body tumbling.

"I will annihilate you, Slade!" roared the insane voice of Qualan. "I will avenge my sister upon your burning corpse!"

Scorching heat bit into my back. Elyssa jerked me from the path of the deadly beam. I saw a second attack from the corner of my eye. When Elyssa moved me to safety, she put herself directly in the line of fire. I smelled smoke. I tried to pull her away but everything happened too fast. She screamed.

Time seemed to slow. I looked at Elyssa as destruction ripped from the front of her armor. Blood sprayed from her chest. We stumbled and fell. The ground rushed to meet us. Agony carved a hole in my heart. Rage and instinct took control. Without thinking, I loosed my demon half. My body burst with muscle. A taloned hand I barely recognized as my own caught the ground before we hit. The other hand scooped Elyssa into my arms.

I felt heat building between my shoulders. My demon tail catapulted us away from the deadly strike as the heat became unbearable. I saw lycans, felycans, and Daemos racing across open ground ahead of us, the red demonic form of my father in the lead.

One-by-one, they raced through the portals. My father saw us and veered our way. His flaming eyes went wide and he dove just behind me. I turned my head and saw twin beams of Brilliance intersect him. He roared with pain and slammed to earth.

"Dad!" My voice emerged as a basso roar.

Something big and purple streaked past. Kassallandra scooped my father's huge body from the ground like a sack of flour and dodged another searing attack. Less than fifty yards away I saw Daelissa on a flying carpet. Her blonde hair whipped around her face and her eyes glowed white. A maniacal smile spread across her face.

"It is only a matter of time," she yelled. "You cannot escape me forever, boy!"

Qualan flew a carpet beside her. His face was locked in a vicious scowl as he channeled pure death at us.

I looked forward. The portal was so close. Ten steps. Five. Two. I passed through and into the La Casona control room.

"Close the portals!" Kassallandra shouted.

My legs could take no more. I slowed, stumbled. Another Daemos caught me before I fell.

"Justin." Elyssa's voice was weak. Blood bubbled from her mouth. She gasped for air.

"Someone help her!" I cried. "Help her!"

Elyssa's hand touched my cheek. "Always…love…you." Her hand dropped and her body sagged in my arms.

"Save her!" I roared. My voice echoed throughout the control room.

"We're here." Two Templars with healer badges tried to take Elyssa's still form. "You have to let her go, sir."

I tried, but my arms were like rigid steel bands.

"Son," Mom said, coming into my view. Tears poured down her face. "You have to let her go."

I forced my arms open. The healers whisked her away. Tears sizzled in my eyes. I felt my body shrinking back to normal. "Save her," I said in a tortured whisper. "Save her."

Mom gasped. "David!"

I looked and saw Kassallandra helping healers handle my father's manifested form even as it reverted to human. He was unconscious, but seemed to be breathing. Burn marks scored his chest where the armor was burned away. "He saved me," I said. "Elyssa saved me." A harsh breath shook my body. I didn't dare say the next thing that came to mind. *They might die for me.*

Christian Salazar appeared at my side. He looked grim. "Your assault drew Daelissa where we wanted her, but she's already turned back towards the Ranch."

"Is Thomas ready for her?" I asked.

"As ready as anyone can be under the circumstances." He held out a hand.

I took it and he pulled me to my feet. I had to lean against him to remain standing. "I have to feed. Do we have any human volunteers?"

"Several." He raised an eyebrow. "Do you mean to feed your demon side or Seraphim?"

I bared my teeth. "Both." My mind flashed back to Elyssa's still form. Grief tore through my stomach. I let it boil into rage.

"Sir, I don't think—"

"Do it," I said in a cold quiet voice. "Now. Please."

He pursed his lips. "As you command." Commander Salazar helped me cross the control room. My legs ached with every step, but not as much as my heart. We walked through the main way station. Templars were everywhere, but the usual civilian population of travelers was almost non-existent. That was hardly surprising given the political situation in the Overworld.

We entered the doors leading into the La Casona pocket dimension. In all the times I'd been to the way station, I'd never entered the actual town. It looked much like the city of Bogota. Cobblestone roads wound between brick houses with terracotta shingles. Christian took me into the first house on the left.

Elyssa and I were supposed to go on a date here before— I pushed the thought from my mind.

Christian spoke a few words to a Templar. The man nodded and vanished through a door. He returned a moment later with five people. Three were middle-aged women. The men, one tall and blond, the other short with a shaved head, appeared to be in their twenties.

"What kind of super are you?" one of the women asked.

227

"This must be one hungry dude," the tall man said with a slightly worried look.

The short man simply smiled as if he didn't understand English.

"This is Justin Slade," Christian said.

Their eyes widened.

"*The* Justin Slade?" the tall guy whistled. "What can we do for you?"

I'd already latched my demonic essence into a short blonde woman. I was ravenous, but managed to keep my emotional energy level.

"Just sit and relax for now," I said. It was impossible for me to relax, but I did my best to fake it. Within minutes, I felt my psythus—demon belly—cease its complaining. My skin itched where it began to heal from the cuts and bruises sustained during the tornado. I looked at the tall guy. "Just let me know if this becomes too much."

He swallowed. "Sure." A nervous chuckle escaped. "I'm used to dhampyrs drinking my blood. I've heard you're part demon, part Seraphim."

"That's right." I held out my left hand, palm facing down toward the tall guy. His hand rose of its own accord. Inky essence trickled from his fingers and into mine. I raised my right hand, causing his to do the same. Milky white poured from his fingers to mine.

"Ooh, that's pretty," the short blonde said. "Does it hurt, Mitch?"

The tall guy shook his head. "Nah, but it does make me feel a little fuzzy around the edges."

"*Bueno?*" asked the short man.

Mitch nodded. "*Si, bueno.*"

After a couple of minutes, the veins on Mitch's face began to stand out, so I motioned toward the short man and fed from him.

"How's the fight going?" Mitch asked as he watched his short comrade's arms rise to meet mine.

"Not well," I said. It was difficult to keep a scowl off my face. "I'm going to face Daelissa which is why I need to feed right now."

Mitch grimaced. "I hope you kick her ass."

"Why is she so power hungry?" the blonde asked. "I'd give anything to have just a little bit of your power. It seems all she wants is more, more, more."

"Ain't it just like a woman?" Mitch said with a smile on his face.

The thin brunette to the blonde's right rolled her eyes. "She's more like a man than a woman. I think world domination would be boring. Just give me limitless access to all the shoes in the world and I'll be a happy girl."

I finished feeding from the short man and moved to the buxom brunette next to him. "How did you end up volunteering?" I wasn't really interested, but it was less awkward making conversation while I consumed their soul essence.

"I was attacked by a vampire and the Custodians brought me in for Overworld orientation a few years ago," Mitch said. "A day or so ago, they sent out word they needed volunteers for feeding. I had to attend another orientation about what kinds of supers would be involved." He chuckled. "Man, I thought vampires and werewolves were crazy. When I found out there were Seraphim, it blew my mind."

The short man grinned and nodded. "Seraphim."

The blonde touched her chest. "I was hoping for vampires myself, but you're pretty hot."

I faked a smile. "Thanks. I moisturize."

She giggled. "I was here on vacation when the vampires blew up a convoy of trucks right outside La Casona." Her eyes widened. "They told me some crazy vampire named Maximus was trying to kill the Templar leader."

"I was here when that happened," I said. The memory wasn't a warm, fuzzy one, because I'd been imprisoned by Maximus during the ordeal and used as a blood slave.

"Vampires got me into this mess, too," the thin brunette said.

The buxom woman smiled. "It was an incubus for me." She sighed. "Best sex of my life."

The blonde laughed. "TMI, Charlene."

I repressed a grimace. "I appreciate you all volunteering for this."

Mitch gave me a thumbs-up. "You're the ones risking your lives for the rest of us normal joes. I was happy to lend a hand however I could."

I rotated to the thin brunette. By the time I finished feeding from her, I felt flush with energy. I stood. "Thank you, everyone. I believe I'm full."

The blonde looked disappointed. "Aw, I really wanted to see what it felt like."

I forced a smile. "I fed my incubus side from you."

Her eyes widened. "Oh, maybe that's why my nipples got so hard all of a sudden."

The others burst into laughter. The short man seemed confused and looked at Mitch who seemed all too happy to translate.

I thanked them again and left. Once outside, I ran to the doors leading from the pocket dimension and back into the way station. Even though I felt ready to take on the world, exhaustion still gnawed me around the edges. I found Christian. "What's the ETA on Daelissa's army reaching Thomas?"

"Perhaps forty minutes," he said. "They're moving quite rapidly since there are very few humans in the path the Custodians cleared." My heart pounded painfully as I asked the next question. "How is Elyssa?"

His lips pressed tight. "Perhaps you should speak with the healers."

My legs went weak. "Is she okay?"

"She's alive." He gave me directions to the healing ward inside La Casona itself.

I rushed back through the doors into the pocket dimension and raced just down the street from the volunteer house. The two-story building was attached to two others just like it in the fashion of row houses. I entered without knocking.

A petite young woman in blue Arcane healer robes looked up from a desk. "Can I help you?"

"I'm here to see Elyssa."

Her forehead pinched. "Oh." She stood and walked around the desk. "Are you family?"

I nodded. "How is she?" I couldn't hide the pain in my voice.

"Come with me." She led me upstairs to a long wide hall. Other healers, obvious by their blue robes, rushed to and fro, as did people dressed in tight, white robes. She turned into a room with a single bed in the middle. A dimly glowing barrier shaped like a glass lid covered the lone occupant.

I rushed forward and looked down on my love. She lay on her back, eyes closed, face at peace. Only a blanket lay over her. A neatly cut hole in the cover revealed the grievous wound. Hot tears burned my eyes. "Why is there a shield around her?"

"It's a preservation spell," she said. "The damage to her heart is severe, I'm afraid."

"She needs blood." My voice trembled. "She can heal herself."

"Even a dhampyr needs a beating heart to assist the healing process."

I spun on her. "Her heart isn't beating?"

"Please, sir, calm down." She took a step back.

"Commander Salazar told me she was alive!" My voice broke.

"Only by the barest thread," the healer replied. "She is beyond our help."

Chapter 28

I gripped the healer by the shoulders. "She's not beyond help. Do something. Heal her! You have magic, damn it!"

Her brown eyes flared with pain. "Please, sir, you're hurting me."

I released her and took a step back. Tears blinded me. I couldn't live without Elyssa. What good was all the world without my true love in it? One of the last things Jeremiah had told me echoed in my mind. *You and Elyssa remind me of me and my Thesha.* Daelissa had killed his wife. Had she done the same to Elyssa?

We're supposed to get married. We're supposed to have kids one day. What about our lifetime of adventures? *Oh my god, it's all gone. She's going to die and I'll be alone in this miserable world.*

Someone rubbed my arm. I looked up in confusion and saw the healer trying to comfort me. "What?"

"We think a Darkling can heal her," the healer said. "We'll find one and everything will be okay."

"Nothing is okay." I looked at Elyssa and wished more than anything I could touch her. Instead, all I could do was press my hands to the barrier keeping her alive.

"I've already spoken to the Clarion," the woman said. "She's still healing from the battle, but has promised to help when she's recovered."

"Nightliss said she could help?" I asked.

The woman narrowed her eyes. "You're Justin Slade, aren't you?"

I nodded.

"Oh." She took a step back. "Sir, we'll do everything in our power to heal her."

My eyes locked onto the burnt skin on Elyssa's chest. *Daelissa did this.* The sight fueled my rage. My inner demon awoke. *Kill. Destroy!* I was tempted to completely free it and loose my rage on Daelissa's Seraphim army. I would surely die, but I might have my revenge.

My fists clenched tight. I turned to the healer, uttered a hoarse word of thanks, and left. Marching down the street, I thought of all the ways I could kill Daelissa. I had plenty of power, but she had more and an army at her back. Even worse, she had revived Seraphim who'd been feeding from humans for some time now and could counter me.

I went back to the way station and walked into the control room. Stepping up to an omniarch, I told the nearby operator to open a portal to the Ranch. He saluted and complied with my request. I stepped through the gateway and into the underground hangar. Aside from the Templar standing near the marked off arrival zones, no one else was there.

"Where is Commander Borathen?" I asked him.

He touched his communicator pendant. "Mr. Slade requests the location of the commander."

"One moment," a voice replied. After a brief silence, the voice spoke again. "Inform Mr. Slade the commander is in the war room."

The Templar looked at me. "Sir, the commander—"

I slashed a hand through the air. "I heard." It took me two minutes to get to the war room. Thomas was inside with Taylor and Olson. Their faces looked grimmer than usual.

Taylor's face brightened when she saw me. "Mr. Slade, what are you doing here?"

I jumped straight to the point. "I'm here to help."

Thomas looked at the other commanders. "A moment, if you please."

They left the room.

"What's wrong?" I said.

His serious blue eyes bore into mine. "How is she?"

"Alive." My voice trembled. "They think Nightliss can heal her."

He nodded. "Why are you here?"

"I'm ready to put a hurting on Daelissa."

"Are you really?" He leaned back against the table and folded his arms. "You're probably seething with rage right now. You probably want to kill Daelissa no matter the cost."

"You're probably right." I felt a volcano of hatred burning in my chest. "She needs to die for everything she's done."

"What about you?" he asked.

I raised an eyebrow. "What about me?"

"Do you need to die?"

"I don't need to, but I'm willing."

Thomas stood and paced a short distance before turning to me. "I love Elyssa with all my heart. The fatherly side of me is beyond anger. If it controlled me, I wouldn't hesitate to do everything I could to wrap my hands around Daelissa's throat and choke the life out of her." He took a deep breath. "I'm a commander. I'm responsible for hundreds of lives." His eyes met mine. "If I lose sight of the ultimate goal, all of us might lose our lives."

"Clear a path to Daelissa for me," I said. "That's all I need."

"We'll be lucky to hold out for an hour before we have to retreat," he said. "Clearing a path to Daelissa is out of the question."

It took everything I had not to slam my fists against the table hard enough to reduce it to splinters. "You don't even think you can save the Ranch?"

He shook his head. "All of our Seraphim forces are out of commission." Thomas pointed at me. "You shouldn't be here either."

"I fed," I said. "I'm topped off and ready to go."

"You might be powerful, Justin, but even you need sleep and rest to be back to full strength." He looked at the strands of my torn Nightingale armor. "Your armor looks like it's ready to fall apart."

"I'll change into fresh armor."

Thomas walked over to me, gripped my shoulders and looked me directly in the eye. "Without more Seraphim, holding onto the Ranch is impossible. Engineers are already setting up a new base in a secret location. It'll take time, but in the long run, it's for the best."

"Elyssa grew up in that house." I pointed straight up. "Daelissa took our home from us in Queens Gate. She took Jeremiah. She took Vallaena." I choked on my aunt's name. "What if she's taken Elyssa from us?"

"The decision is yours." Thomas released me and stood back. "You think long and hard about what Elyssa would want. If you don't know the answer, then maybe you don't love her as much as you think you do."

His words stabbed me in the heart like a dagger of ice. Elyssa would want me to fight, but she'd also want me to stay alive and save lives. Daelissa wanted me dead. I would have to live just to spite the bitch. "I'll stay and help. Tell me how I can best serve."

Thomas looked satisfied. "With the time you bought us, we started evacuating all non-essential personnel and equipment to El Dorado."

I looked at the floor. "If only we could get the dragons to help."

"You asked, but they obviously don't see it in their interests to help." He picked up an arctablet and looked at blueprint of the compound. Red blips blinked in various locations. "We've laced everything with nom explosives and destructive spells. If the Seraphim take this place, we should be able to take a few of them down with it." He sighed. "I don't like to lose the place I call home, but sometimes a step back is a step forward."

"If you're going to destroy the Ranch, why not use a malaether crucible on the enemy?" I asked.

He shook his head. "Unleashing a magical nuke so close to nom populations would be a terrible mistake. Besides, we don't have any at our disposal."

Thomas's communicator buzzed and a voice spoke. "Sir, enemy forces are at five miles and closing."

"Thank you, lieutenant." He looked at me. "Let's inspect the final preparations."

We stepped into the hallway. Taylor and Olson were examining a blueprint on an arctablet.

Taylor looked up. "The armory has been emptied except for the practice equipment. It would take too long to move it all.

"Practice equipment?" I asked. "Do you have icers and soggers?"

"Tons of them," Olson said. "Why?"

"Turn the pastures into bogs with the soggers," I said. "It won't stop the Seraphim, but it'll slow them down."

"Good idea," Taylor said. "I recall you using a similar technique to defeat the battle mages at our compound."

I shrugged. "It worked the first time. At least we'll make the bastards get dirty."

Taylor spoke into her pendant and told her people my plan.

"I'll go to the armory and help," I said. "Maybe I'll hold onto an icer and nail Daelissa in the face with it."

Olson chuckled. "In that case, grab a scorcher for me."

I left the commanders and took the levitator down to the armory level. The diamond fiber shield guarding the area was gone as was the guard. I followed the signs to the practice equipment. Along the way, I heard voices and detoured toward them.

Leanne and Phoebe were examining a piece of Seraphim armor.

"Don't you think I tried that?" Leanne said in a disgusted voice. "It sucks up normal spells like a sponge."

"Shouldn't you two have evacuated by now?" I asked.

Phoebe jerked her head toward me. Her eyes instantly saddened. "Justin, are you okay?"

Looking at someone who could have passed for Elyssa's twin punched me in the gut like a sledgehammer. *She looks like her, but to me, she's still a stranger.* It took a moment before I could safely speak without bursting into tears. "I'm doing okay."

"Elyssa is still alive, right?" Leanne asked.

I nodded. "Look, we can talk about her condition later." I told them about my plan with the soggers.

"Yeah, I remember hearing about that tactic against the battle mages during our assault on the castle." Phoebe grimaced. "I'm sorry. I know it must make you angry to think about my role in those battles."

It did, but I shook it off. Now was not the time. I'd take out my burning rage on Daelissa. "We're allies now. I need you to put that superior intellect to good use." I motioned toward the Seraphim armor. "No luck with that, I take it?"

Leanne shook her head. "We figured out why the Seraphim keep such tight formation."

Phoebe put two sets of the armor next to each other. "If a spell hit this armor, this second set absorbs a portion of the spell as well."

"They act like a circuit," Leanne said. "As long as they're within a couple of feet of another armored soldier, they can absorb all sorts of spells and disperse the energy among them."

"It's not like they need the extra protection," I said. "One set of armor seems to absorb most spells without a problem."

"We talked about how channeling Murk weakens the armor," Leanne said. "If you could channel enough, it would flow from one set of armor to the other since they're all interconnected."

I shook my head. "There's no way I could channel that much power. I'd need a small army of Darklings to help."

Her shoulders slumped. "I know. Maybe once we revive more Darklings it'll be an option."

"They won't need their armor by the time we have enough Darklings," Phoebe said. She groaned and gave me a wondering look. "How you've kept her at bay as long as you have is amazing."

I ignored her praise. "Would nom weaponry harm the armor?"

"I tried a blowtorch and a gun on it," Leanne said. "It soaked up the heat and repelled the bullets."

"We'd have to saturate the armor with enough kinetic energy to cause it to shatter from the inside." Phoebe bit her lower lip and instantly reminded me of the way Elyssa looked when focusing on a tough problem. I swallowed against the lump in my throat. "Even though Nightliss removed her sister's negative influence from my mind, I still have the 'blessings'"—she made air quotes—"she gave me."

I ran a hand across the cold translucent armor. "How did you concoct the plan to assault the Australian Templar compound?"

"I ran simulations about how the Templars would respond to a split assault." She shrugged. "It stood to reason they'd commit their normal soldiers to defend against vampires, and split their Arcanes to defend against magical attacks from the front. My only limitation was the small number of battle mages at my disposal." Phoebe pushed a lock of hair behind her ear. "I used the Templars' own battle tactics to make them weaker. Without all of their Arcanes fighting the vampires, it gave that assault a better chance of succeeding. Once the magic interdictors were in place, it would have crippled the Arcanes and our superior numbers might have won out."

"What kind of simulations?" I asked.

"They're kind of like the video games the noms like to play." She slid a finger across an arctablet and showed me a program with an overhead view of virtual soldiers fighting each other. "Sometimes I pick up on patterns by staring at the simulations."

"You have the overhead videos of the Seraphim army from the Grand Nexus, right?"

She nodded. "Their pattern is fairly predictable. They adhere to a tight trapezoidal formation to maximize the benefits of their armor. The side of the formation under attack spreads out to allow the soldiers to swing their swords."

I drew upon my LARP days, thinking about the various weapons different players used. "Do they all use swords or do they have pike men and other units?"

"This particular army is comprised only of swordsmen." She projected the image of a Seraphim soldier. "Since their swords can also discharge Brilliance and other absorbed energy, it gives them a unique battlefield presence."

"They're arrogant in the superiority," I said. "It's no wonder the Darklings in Seraphina managed to break the yoke of Brightling oppression."

"The Darklings may very well use similar battle tactics." She placed a hand to her chin. "While Brightlings can use their abilities to heal, the Darklings are far superior in that capacity. It probably gave them an edge."

I backhanded the air. "None of this helps us defeat the Brightlings."

"We simply have to find a way to use their advantage against them just as I did with the Templars." Phoebe sighed. "It's harder than I thought it would be."

I heard the sounds of crates being moved and looked down an aisle. I saw Templars carrying boxes of soggers toward the exit. "I need to go help."

Phoebe snapped her fingers. "Since the Seraphim keep such a tight formation, turning the ground to a bog should have a good chance of slowing their advance."

"It's not much, but I guess it's all we have." I touched the armor one more time. "Will this fit me?"

"We can try," Leanne said. She took the first breastplate. It was far too short for me. The other one didn't fit any better.

I took the sword and swung it. I knew I'd do much better having my hands free to sling magic and set it down. "You two should get what you need to the evacuation point. Things are about to get ugly." I gave them the number to my arcphone. "Call me if you think of anything."

Phoebe hesitantly touched my shoulder. "Be safe, Justin. I think Elyssa would want that."

I closed my eyes and pictured Elyssa's still form. "I know." I stepped back, turned and walked away.

On the way to the levitator, I grabbed a box of soggers. I followed a line of other Templars carrying the sogger crates and rode the levitator to ground level with them. Once we reached the top, the Templars broke into groups.

A man with a tablet shouted orders for each group and sent them to a different pasture to soak the earth with the soggers. After the last group left, I walked to him. "Which direction is the Seraphim army coming from?"

He did a double-take when he saw me. "Oh, Mr. Slade. I didn't expect you to be helping us."

I took a deep breath. "Direction, please?"

He showed me a diagram of the compound. "According to our scouts, they're coming straight up this highway as the most direct route."

I felt my eyes stretch wide. "That's Ponce de Leon Avenue."

"With the various tactics employed by the Custodians to evacuate the area, we're hoping there won't be many noms in the way." He switched to a live-video feed from a remote ASE.

The Seraphim army marched six abreast down the four-lane highway. I instantly recognized where they were. "They're less than a mile away." At the speed they were marching, it wouldn't take them long to reach us. "May I?" I gripped the tablet.

"Of course, sir." He released it.

I switched back to the map and traced a line. *Daelissa is all about brute force.* She'd push her troops straight at us. That would take her past a mall and right through the rear pastures. "How many soggers are being deployed in this field?" I tapped it with a finger.

The man looked where I was pointing. "We knew that would be her preferred route, so I sent half our soldiers to saturate it. It should be a boggy mess by the time they get here."

"Justin?" Phoebe's voice startled me.

I spun. "What are you doing here?"

"I can't let you go alone." Phoebe wore Nightingale armor and had two katanas sheathed diagonally across her back.

My heart stopped at the likeness to her sister. *Stop thinking about it!* I shook it off. "You should—"

"Don't even think about telling me to leave." Her violet eyes sparkled with ferocity. "I don't plan to get up close and personal with the Seraphim, but I will be sure you make it out alive."

A group of Templar Arcanes walked past. Two familiar figures burst from the group.

Bella gripped me in a tight hug. "Justin, what are you doing here?"

"You should be recovering," Shelton said. "We wanted to come with you to Thunder Rock but"—he made a helpless gesture—"things got so crazy around here we ended up pitching in."

"How's Elyssa?" Bella asked, worry plain on her face.

"She's being taken care of." I didn't feel like getting into details right now. It was all I could do to stop thinking about her. "Are you evacuating with the others?"

"We're joining with the Templar Arcanes to hold them off as long as possible." Shelton held my gaze. "You don't look right. Are you sure you're okay? We heard everyone took a good beating during your assault."

I ran a hand down my face. "I don't want to talk about it right now." I gripped his shoulder. "Just make sure you get out of here in one piece."

He poked a finger into my chest. "*You* be careful. We can take care of ourselves."

Bella squeezed me one more time. "Please don't overexert yourself. We need you."

I returned her hug and tried not to contemplate losing them. They were more than friends to me. They were family. "I'll see you soon."

They gave me one last worried look before hustling after the Templar Arcanes.

I turned around and saw Kanaan walk out of the barn across the yard from us. His eyes seemed to assess me as he strode our way. "It is good to see you again," the Magitsu master said when he neared us. "I assume you are here to fend off the assault."

"That would be correct," Phoebe said. "Are the Blue Cloaks here to help as well?"

He nodded. "Our plan is to slow them and perhaps inflict a few casualties before a retreat."

"Shouldn't you be with the other Blue Cloaks?" I asked.

"I am to hang back and take out any targets of opportunity." He touched the wand at his side. "Considering the Seraphim battle tactics, I do not expect to find many who separate from their main force, but it is worth a try."

"Three minutes to assault," a voice rang out from a loudspeaker somewhere. "Ready positions."

I handed the tablet back to the Templar coordinator. "Go see to your duties."

"Thank you, sir." He saluted. "Good luck."

"I think I will accompany you two," Kanaan said. "Perhaps we *will* get lucky."

Phoebe looked him up and down. "I remember seeing you before the Blue Cloaks joined us at Kobol. You're impressive with a wand."

"You are as impressive with a blade." Kanaan offered her a curt bow.

I clapped my hands. "Great pep talk, people. Let's all go be impressive together."

Phoebe bared her teeth. "Sounds like a plan to me."

We each grabbed a flying carpet from a stack where the coordinator had been standing and flew toward what would soon be ground zero. Flying above the trees, I spotted the glimmer of Seraphim armor shining in the dark.

The enemy was here.

Chapter 29

Glowballs shot high into the night air, casting a bright white light across the surroundings. Some Seraphim soldiers looked up at the hovering spheres but didn't seem the least bit concerned by the sudden illumination.

Arrogant bastards.

The enemy reached the tall fence surrounding the perimeter and cleaved through it as if it were paper. I watched their glowing forms as they tore down a patch of trees in their path and threaded through the utility poles the noms used for electrical cable. They crossed into the pasture. A few yards into the field, the first row of soldiers slowed considerably as they sank up to their knees in the muddy mess created by the soggers.

I heard someone shout orders. Eyes wary, the Seraphim took a step back to solid ground and seemed to assess the area. Soldiers at either end walked along the marshy ground, testing it with their feet. They soon realized the ground was thoroughly saturated in either direction.

"Forward!" Daelissa's voice boomed from somewhere. I looked and spotted her hovering beyond the trees on a carpet.

Qualan floated next to her on a carpet of his own. He added his commands to Daelissa's. "Push through!"

Hatred boiled in my heart at the sight of the two people I hated the most. I sensed my inner demon awaken. It strained against its cage. *Not yet. We'll have our blood soon enough.*

The front row of soldiers formed back up and pressed on. Despite the thick mud, they still moved forward at a steady pace.

"Behind us," Kanaan said in a calm voice.

I turned and saw Templars pushing catapults on levitating platforms into a line. Scores of our soldiers quietly formed ranks and moved toward the edge of the field. A fleet of Templar Arcanes and Blue Cloaks rose on carpets.

The Seraphim soldiers tightened their ranks, presumably so their armor could distribute any damage once they came under fire. I saw smug smiles on their faces. They knew we'd thrown everything we had at them at the nexus and it had hardly fazed them. They obviously didn't expect the results to be different this time.

The field was about a hundred yards across. Already, the first ranks of Seraphim had cut the distance in half. Looking down, I could barely make out where the ground wasn't boggy a few yards in front of the Templars.

When the Seraphim were about three-quarters of the way across the pasture, a trumpet rang out. The catapults unleashed a volley of crucibles at the enemy. Each glass sphere glowed with destructive energy. Just before the crucibles hit, Templar Arcanes and Blue Cloaks cast hundreds of spells at the enemy front line. The result was a blinding light show.

I squinted until my eyes adjusted to the light. The Catapults launched more crucibles. I timed a burst of destruction at the front line to coincide with the next attack. The racket of explosions filled my ears. Afterimages of each attack danced in my eyes. I saw flaming meteors fall into the Seraphim. Pulsating nova spells exploded. Spears of light every color of the rainbow rained down on the enemy advance.

A trumpet sounded and our attacks died away.

When the smoke cleared and my eyes adjusted, I saw the Seraphim formation was even tighter than before. A dozen or so soldiers lay in the mud, either dead or incapacitated during the attack.

"Impossible," Phoebe said. "We only killed twenty-three." One of the fallen soldiers staggered upright.

"Twenty-two," Kanaan corrected.

"That should have annihilated most enemies." She peered at them with uncertainty.

I looked down our lines and saw looks of disbelief on the faces of Arcanes. Shelton was looking at his staff as if something might be wrong with it.

Laughter rang out from behind the enemy lines. Daelissa and Qualan flanked by Brightlings I recognized from our assault on Thunder Rock flew their carpets over the bog and stopped a quarter of the way.

"That was pathetic," Daelissa said, her voice amplified by magic. "You've tried everything in your power to stop us, and it has failed."

Qualan sneered. "You cannot stop destiny. Surrender your little lives to us and we may take mercy."

Daelissa preened her hair and regarded us as if we were ants. Her eyes lit on me and flashed. "I see you have already replaced your dead woman with her sister."

Phoebe's hand gripped my bicep and tightened as my face heated with anger.

Qualan's haughty gaze found us. "It was I who burned her heart from her chest, boy." He leered. "I hope you feel the pain I felt when you killed Qualas, you worthless pile of dung. Perhaps I'll let you grow attached to this creature and kill her as well."

My hands shook with rage. An inferno seemed to boil in my chest and it was all I could do not to fly at him.

"Notice the enemy armor," Kanaan said in a quiet voice.

I managed to break my furious gaze from Qualan and looked down at the Seraphim soldiers. Raw energy crackled and pulsed within the translucent armor. The mass of our destructive spells had accumulated into something resembling malaether. Some soldiers were pressing their swords to the armor, possibly transferring the energy so they could use it offensively.

Daelissa and Qualan continued to speak. Some of their words were directed to me, but all I could think of was what would happen when the Seraphim redirected our spent energy back at us.

Qualan's voice penetrated my thoughts. "Slade's head on a platter would be a fitting gift for your new rulers."

Phoebe tugged on my arm. "The Seraphim armor acts like a magical conductor."

"I think we established that."

Her violet eyes grew fierce. "Shut up and listen."

I looked at her expectantly.

"Water is also conductor." She pointed to one of the crates on the ground beneath us. "If we use those EMP grenades, we might cause an electrical current that could destabilize all that contained energy."

"Perhaps we could utilize something even more powerful," Kanaan said. He looked toward an electrical utility pole fifty yards to our right. A thick cable ran from it to the poles along the road. Reaching it would require flying over part of the Seraphim army while avoiding Daelissa, Qualan, and the other Seraphim on flying carpets.

"Give us his head!" Qualan roared.

I stared at the creature who'd nearly killed Elyssa and let the hatred ignite my blood. "When I divert their attention, go do what you need to do."

"Justin, no." Phoebe gripped my arm. "You'll get yourself killed."

I shook my head. "No, I'm saving lives." I jerked my arm free. "Get ready." With that, I rose higher on my carpet and directed it toward the edge of the bog. I aimed a sliver of Brilliance at Qualan's butt. Across this distance, I couldn't do much damage, but with a jackass like him, I didn't need to.

Smoke rose from the seat of his fancy blue tunic. He yelped and almost jumped off his carpet.

I grinned. "You want my head, coward? Come and get it." I flew my carpet further to the left to draw everyone's attention away from Phoebe and Kanaan as they glided away.

Qualan cupped both his hands and released a wide blast of Brilliance. I shielded myself and stuck out my tongue.

"That's weaksauce, brah." I tsked. "No wonder you can't face me in a fair fight."

"I would destroy you in any fight!" Qualan bellowed.

Daelissa gripped his arm. She said something to him I couldn't hear.

The rage faded from Qualan's face and was soon replaced by a sneer. "I will be sure to save your death for last, boy. Until then, I plan to amuse myself by killing everyone you love."

I looked toward the opposite end of the pasture. The light of the glowballs was weaker there, but I could make out faint silhouettes approaching the electrical pole from behind the edges of the Seraphim

245

army. The pole stood only a short distance from the enemy. If any of them looked up and to their left, they'd see Phoebe and Kanaan.

That just wouldn't do.

"You'll never kill the ones I love, you sick bastard!" I cupped my hands and channeled twin spheres of Brilliance. "I'll kill you like I killed your sister." I flung the pulsars at Qualan. They splashed harmlessly against a shield he threw up.

Qualan gave me a contemptuous look. "Is that truly all you can muster? You are the weak sauced one."

"Enough of this nonsense," Daelissa cried. "Forward march! Kill them all!"

The Seraphim soldiers moved forward. I didn't know what was taking Phoebe and Kanaan so long. I fired a lance of destruction into the front ranks of the enemy. The armor on one soldier shattered in a brilliant burst of light, but the others kept coming. They closed to within striking distance of land.

The Templar front line braced to greet the enemy. I knew from the fight at the nexus, our people would be slaughtered.

Something crackled like fireworks going off. A blue arc of electricity traced across the ground from a thick black cable. As if guided by an invisible hand, the cable floated a few feet and then dropped into the water.

A loud hum filled the air. The Seraphim closest to the cable began to shudder. Blue arcs raced across their armor, jumping from one to the next like an angry snake. The street lamps in the vicinity dimmed or exploded in a cloud of sparks. Cylindrical transformers exploded one by one, sounding like cannon shots as they went up.

Like a string of light bulbs caught in a power surge, the crystal armor worn by the Seraphim nearest the power cable exploded. The chain reaction spread across their ranks. The portion of the Seraphim army that hadn't entered the boggy pasture retreated while those still caught in the mud panicked and made for the closest shore.

Screams and shouts of pain echoed with every new explosion.

A trumpet sounded and our troops backed away from the carnage to avoid being caught in one of the explosions.

I heard Shelton's voice ring out. "It's like freaking New Year's Eve!"

A trumpet sounded two quick tones. The catapults renewed their assault while our Arcane troops unleashed everything they had at fleeing Seraphim.

The enemy ranks descended into pure chaos.

I saw Qualan's stunned face through the smoke and haze as he flew his carpet higher to avoid the destruction. As much as I wanted to end his miserable life, he wasn't the one I was interested in. A moment later, I sighted Daelissa, her face red with fury as she screamed at her fleeing troops.

It was terribly risky, but this was a chance I couldn't pass up. I turned my carpet toward Daelissa and shot toward her.

I might die tonight, but I'd take her down with me.

Chapter 30

I zipped high and came at Daelissa from overhead. Her carpet was a nice, large, area rug woven with ornate designs as befitting someone with Daelissa's narcissism. It presented a nice, big target. Clenching my teeth to restrain a battle cry, I leapt from my carpet and landed on hers. She spun. I blurred to her. My hand locked around her throat and squeezed.

Her eyes flared with shock. I channeled Brilliance into my hand and saw her fair flesh smoke from the heat.

Daelissa screamed. Her body glowed and I felt my hand being pushed away from her skin as she channeled a shield. I blasted a wave of Murk into her shield to balance the Brilliance. If I could turn it to gray stasis, I might be able to punch through. My attack merely splashed across the shield instead of mingling with the energy powering it.

She burst into laughter. "Weakling. You think you can harm me?"

With a primal roar, I manifested. My armor grew to accommodate thick muscles. I felt the weight of horns sprout from my forehead and a tail stretch against the seat of my armor.

I spread my lips in a gruesome smile and said, "I think I can harm you a lot, bitch." I threaded Murk and Brilliance into a thick cloud of stasis and surrounded her. Her shield froze, cracked, and shattered.

Pain pierced my shoulder blades. From the corners of my eyes, I saw a brilliant white wing unfold on the right, and an ultraviolet one on the left.

What the hell?

My hand renewed its grip around her neck. Abandoning all magic, I did something I'd wanted to do for a very long time. I punched Daelissa in the nose. The blow made a satisfying crack. Her head reeled back and blood spattered her face. I punched her again. Heat exploded against my stomach. My armor absorbed her attack, but the force of the blow nearly bowled me off the carpet. I released my grip on her, sidestepped, and karate-chopped her arm.

Her bone made a satisfying crack.

"You are an abomination!" Daelissa screamed with rage. Her knee flashed for my groin. I barely twisted to the side in time to stop the blow from emasculating me. I heard a roar an instant before someone slammed into me from behind and drove me to my knees. Daelissa leapt from the carpet and landed on one flown by another Seraphim. An arm locked around my throat.

"You're mine now, Slade." Qualan's breath warmed my ear.

I struggled against his grip. "Get your elderberry stank-ass breath out of my face."

His grip tightened. "I will breathe wherever I want!"

More Seraphim on flying carpets surrounded us, their eyes glowing white. Daelissa, her face a bloody mess, bared her crimson-stained teeth. "How fitting you will die as Moses did."

One by one, the Brightlings channeled Brilliance in the palms of their hands while Qualan held me immobile. I had one chance at surviving this mess I'd gotten myself into.

I used the tactic I'd used with Aerianas's stone grip. Drawing upon Murk, I imagined it flowing from every inch of my body. I even thought of it flowing from every centimeter in case magic preferred the metric system. My skin tingled. Qualan's grip receded from my neck.

"Kill him now!" Qualan shouted.

Daelissa's eyes blazed white as she thrust her hands forward. In a gloating voice, she said, "Goodbye, boy."

A flying carpet rammed into the female Brightling on the far left. A figure in a tight Blue Cloak slammed her in the face with a roundhouse and sent her plummeting into the bog below. Before the male Seraphim next to her could react, the Blue Cloak leapt to his carpet. Jammed a wand into his nose. Green light exploded within the Brightling's head, lighting it up like a jack-o'-lantern.

A beam of ultraviolet slammed into the next Brightling, while a blade of Brilliance cut through the flying carpet beneath him.

"We're here to save you, Justin!" Nightliss yelled as a flying carpet bearing her and Lanaeia swept past me.

I took advantage of the confusion and pushed my shield of Murk with everything I had. Qualan bellowed with anger as it knocked him away from me. Daelissa unleashed a sizzling attack. It splashed against my shield but superheated the thin layer of air between it and my skin.

Nightliss wrapped her sister in tendrils of Murk. She spun once and threw Daelissa screaming into the tree line. I turned and saw Qualan pulling himself back up over the edge of the carpet, murder in his eyes. The heated air within my protective shell burned my lungs so I dropped it and sucked in a cool breath.

Qualan rushed me, arms swinging.

I ducked under his clumsy attack and punched him hard in the stomach. A loud *oof* burst from his mouth. Using skills Elyssa had taught me, I aimed my fist, pushed straight up with my legs, and nailed him with an uppercut. I heard his teeth clack together. His body sailed up several feet and then slammed back onto the carpet. Blood poured from his mouth.

He staggered to his feet and screamed, "Nyuh nubb glug ooo!"

"Gee, you must've bitten your tongue really hard." I flashed him a smug grin. "Because I sure as hell don't understand that Cyrinthian dialect."

Qualan unleashed an incoherent roar of rage and thrust his arms forward. A blistering beam erupted toward me. I bent over so far backwards I had to catch myself with my demon tail to keep from falling. Even so, a heatwave washed over my chest. I dropped and rolled up to one knee. He redirected his fiery blast. I met his attack with a mirrored shield of Murk. The death beam reflected and incinerated an enemy Brightling unlucky enough to fly his carpet into it.

Dazzling beams of Brilliance and Murk lanced through the air around us. I saw Mom flying a carpet with Joss and Otaleon on the back. Nightliss and Lanaeia were playing tag-team against a group of Brightlings who looked like teenagers. In the mud below, surviving

Seraphim soldiers fought Templars. Without their fancy crystal armor or swords, the enemy was being pushed back.

Qualan balled his fists and bellowed at the sky in frustration.

"Having a hard time?" I said. "No matter how powerful you think you are, you're a one-trick pony just like your mistress."

He shouted something incoherent at me again. His eyes widened as if a good idea had finally occurred to him once in his miserable life. A thin, white beam fired from his index finger. I shielded myself, but his strike hit the carpet in front of me. The material smoldered, smoked, and caught fire. I put it out with Murk, but Qualan struck several other places on the carpet and it burst into flames at one end.

Before I could smother the flames, he rushed me. The carpet abruptly took off at top speed. I barely managed to keep my feet as the bonding spells that functioned to keep riders from falling off began to fail.

Qualan punched me in the instant I windmilled my arms for balance. One foot remained bonded to the carpet and the blow sent me pivoting on one foot. I felt my ankle trying to break. My tail acted as a third arm and caught me, but pain jolted up my leg from the awkward angle. The enraged Seraphim leapt on me and punched me in the side of the head. I shifted my head so his fist slammed into one of my thick horns while I desperately tried to free my stuck foot.

I heard his bones crack. He screamed like a little girl.

The carpet refused to let go of my foot. Qualan resumed punching like a schoolyard bully. He had no technique. Once he'd come to Eden, he'd probably never seen the use in learning hand-to-hand techniques since he was so powerful with magic. My girlfriend had not only kicked my ass multiple times during sparring, she'd also shown me how to get out of sticky situations like this.

I thrust my elbow up to block another punch and slammed my huge fist into the sensitive nerves in Qualan's solar plexus. His eyes bulged. His face turned crimson and he gasped. I pressed my palm to the carpet and channeled a burst of Murk. It thrust me upright and sent Qualan sprawling. My foot ripped out the section of carpet holding it, leaving a hole. The shred of carpet released its grip and fluttered away in the wind.

The starry night sky surrounded us. I saw flashes of light from the battle far below. Our malfunctioning carpet had carried us hundreds of feet into the air. The circular pattern on the carpet where the driver usually stood was in flames. I smothered the blaze with Murk and stood on the charred spot, hoping I could control the carpet, but it was too badly damaged.

"Kill you," Qualan said, his voice thick. Blood matted dark hair to his face and one of his eyes was swollen with a purple bruise. "Just like your woman."

Even though his words were difficult to understand thanks to his swollen tongue, I understood him just fine. I didn't say a thing. I shielded myself as he predictably tried to hit me with every ounce of destruction he could muster. The energy flowed around my barrier. He was obviously weakening, but deep in my bones, I felt exhaustion creeping in too. Qualan pressed his attack with a roar. I reinforced my shield and felt it wavering.

Sweat beaded on my forehead and trickled into my eyes. I dropped to one knee. Qualan staggered. His aim flew wide. With a pathetic fizzle, his death beam sputtered and faded.

I forced myself to my feet and walked toward him. The feat grew more difficult since, at that moment, the carpet decided to spin out of control. I grabbed Qualan by the throat. He snarled and managed a weak grasp on the collar of my armor. The stars blurred around us like a kaleidoscope.

"Who do you think you are to kill a god?" Qualan croaked.

My black talons drew blood from his neck. I tried to squeeze the life out of him, but my hands hardly responded. His head lolled and recovered. Summoning all my hate, anger, and rage at this murderer, I pressed a finger to his chest. "Who do I think I am?" I bared my teeth. "My name is Justin Slade."

I shot a thin beam of Brilliance into his chest. "You tried to kill the woman I love."

He tried to slap my hand away but I blocked with my elbow. His blue tunic smoked. I smelled burning flesh.

"Prepare to die." I pushed with a final burst of will. Qualan howled in pain. His howl turned to a gurgle as the white ray burst from his back. He slumped forward against me.

My inner demon surged against its restraints. I was almost too tired to care.

I stepped back and let Qualan face-plant on the rug. A wisp of smoke rose from the hole in his back. "That's for Elyssa, you son of a bitch." I kicked his body over the side of the carpet and watched it fall. It made a nice splash in the mud hundreds of feet below.

My stomach rose in my throat as the carpet abruptly went into a steep dive, hitting terminal velocity in seconds. I held on with all my remaining strength and watched the battle grow larger. I'd soon be splatting into the bog right next to Qualan. From this height, the mud might as well be concrete. The carpet went completely limp and folded up around me until I couldn't see a thing.

This is a really embarrassing way to die.

I clawed through the carpet. Without the enchantment protecting it from damage, it quickly fell away in tatters. I was about to be a demonic pancake. Only one desperate chance presented itself. I unfurled my wings and drew upon all the aether in the sky around me. With a burst of will, I channeled everything into my wings. They caught the air. My descent slowed ever so slightly.

Gritting my pointy teeth, I leashed more power to my wings and willed myself to levitate. I slowed almost to a stop a hundred feet or so off the ground.

I would have shouted something celebratory, but all my strength abruptly abandoned me. My wings puffed into sparkling mist. My head lolled. I fell.

Ultraviolet webs wrapped around my torso. Nightliss and Lanaeia swooped in on their carpet and arrested my fall. I subdued my inner demon and shrank back to normal size as they gently lowered me to solid ground. My knees gave way and I slumped on the grass.

Phoebe and Kanaan stood over me.

"That was beyond impressive." Phoebe looked at me in open astonishment. "A demon with angel wings?"

Kanaan gave me a look of respect. "I have never seen its like."

"Can you help me?" My voice sounded weak. "I've fallen and I can't get up."

They each gripped one of my hands and pulled me to my feet. Before I slumped again, they hoisted my arms over their shoulders.

My gaze rested on the lake of mud that had once been a pasture. Grass and dirt mixed with dark blood. Hundreds of bodies lay in the bog. Many were Seraphim, but I counted plenty of Templars as well. I saw Qualan's legs sticking up from the mud. His blue tunic and white leggings made the sight even more ridiculous. I imagined his head must have speared into the ground. If I'd had the strength, I would've waded out and taken a selfie with him behind me and posted it on the Overnet for all to see.

The Seraphim army lay in ruins, but there was one important person missing.

"Where is Daelissa?" I asked.

"She retreated with the rest of her army," Kanaan said. "Our forces were unable to pursue."

"We'll get her," Phoebe said. "I wish I could say we won this battle, but the truth is, both sides lost."

Shelton's worried face filled my view. "Holy barf muffins, man. You look even worse than before."

"Thanks, bro." It was all I could do to keep my head upright.

"You have an awful bedside manner, Harry," Bella said in a chiding tone. She pressed a hand to my face. "Healers are on the way, Justin."

"I just need a bath and some sleep." I said.

Shelton sniffed the air and waved a hand in front of his nose. "Whew. You got that right."

Nightliss and Lanaeia joined the others. Nightliss pressed a hand to my chest. Her green eyes widened with worry. "Justin, you're far past your limit. You must rest this instant."

I was about to make a smart remark when my head grew so heavy I could hardly hold it upright. I heard Nightliss commanding someone to put me on a cot and then the world blissfully faded away.

Chapter 31

Daelissa

How did this happen? How did he beat me?

Daelissa led a weary and defeated army back to Thunder Rock. Despite the number of human houses and businesses in the area, the way back seemed as devoid of life now as it had during their march to the Borathen compound. She suspected the Custodians had something to do with it. No doubt Templar scouts had discovered her plans to feed the army on humans while traversing the city the humans called Atlanta.

Qualan was gone. The last she'd seen, he was battling the Slade boy on her flying carpet. Over a hundred Seraphim soldiers had perished. Many who'd survived the ferocious attack in the bog had lost their armor and swords. Fifty or so still had theirs, but she would have to send back to Seraphina for replacement equipment.

Daelissa looked at Skazaeleus, with whom she shared the carpet she now rode on. "I need more soldiers."

"You will have them, Divinity." He bowed. "As I told you, the mass of my troops were stationed in the far reaches of the empire to protect against the Darklings."

She gripped his chin and jerked his gaze to meet hers. "If we'd had them, we would have crushed the resistance tonight."

"My apologies, Divinity." He dropped to a knee. "They will be here soon. Even now, those stationed near the ruined city of Azhka will be coming through the Alabaster Arch there. Its location coincides with Thunder Rock in this realm."

Daelissa pushed his face away and looked forward. "I need more than troops. I need someone who can lead them effectively."

"The troops stationed in Zbura have grown soft over the years." Skazaleus's voice took on a whining tone. "Primarion Coifious was assigned as a political favor and has little battle knowledge. I promise you that Primarion Arturo has far more experience. He will not let you down."

"He had best not," Daelissa said in her coldest tone.

Tovaard flew over on his carpet and bowed. "Divinity, our controllers are opening omniarch portals to take us back to Thunder Rock." As he spoke, gateways shimmered open in front of the troops. "Halt!" Tovaard cried out. The soldiers below stopped. Tovaard bowed again. "Almighty Divinity, the gateway to Thunder Rock awaits you."

"At least one of my servants is not worthless." Daelissa kicked Skazaeleus off the carpet. He yelped and fell onto the soldiers below. Daelissa looked at him over the edge. "I saw how you cowered away from the fight." She would have channeled a sphere of Brilliance to accompany her words, but the fight with Nightliss and Slade had left her sorely drained. "If you hold back like that again when your Divinity is in peril, I will kill you myself."

Skazaeleus pushed himself up, but kept his head bowed low. "My apologies, Divinity. I would have joined the battle, but—"

"Shut your mouth, you craven fool." Daelissa guided her carpet into the gateway and back to Thunder Rock. She flew from the control room and out into the main way station. The place was filled with non-Seraphim troops. Red Cell vampires camped in one corner. Her remaining battle mages had erected temporary dwellings on the opposite side. There were few Synod Templars here as they now reinforced the most important Obsidian Arch way stations she needed to control in order to keep the cancerous resistance from spreading.

Very few Nazdal remained. Before the battle at the Grand Nexus, Serena had attuned the nexus to Sturg and summoned several hundred of them. Most had been killed during the battle. "How does the boy keep winning?" she asked herself as she took the carpet down a long corridor where enslaved Darklings used their abilities to carve more space for Daelissa's troops.

The creatures bowed their heads as she passed. If she'd possessed any remaining strength, she would have struck one of them down just to sate the anger boiling in her veins.

Daelissa went to her private chambers, a grand room rivalling even that of Skazaeleus's chambers in his palace. Only a few hundred paces down the corridor from this room, an underground river flowed. The Darklings had carved a trench into the rock, creating a large pool in the room. Daelissa snapped her fingers. A young human woman appeared from the adjoining servants' room and bowed.

"Warm the water," Daelissa commanded.

The woman obeyed without a word. She powered on an aether generator, which sent heated currents into the water. When the water began to steam, Daelissa threw off her filthy rags and stepped into the water. The woman approached with soap and rags.

"Shall I wash you, Divinity?" she asked.

"Of course, you fool." She halted the woman with a look. "But first, ring the bell and have them bring me sustenance."

The woman looked at the floor. "Yes, Divinity." She walked to a rope, tugged it. A bell chimed. Seconds later, two men dragged another man into the chamber. He squirmed and squealed like a pig. Apparently, he already knew what was going to happen to him. From her comfortable position in the steaming bath, she raised her hand toward him. In order to replenish her energy, he would only be the first of many.

Kjoeriss appeared in Daelissa's doorway as she finished eating a meal the human woman prepared for her. "Divinity, Primarion Arturo has arrived." The minister spoke in heavily accented English. "Shall I have him report to you?"

Daelissa flexed her aching hand and rose. "How many soldiers does he have with him?"

"A hundred archangels and three hundred soldiers."

"Archangels?" Skazaeleus had never mentioned them to her.

Minister Kjoeriss dropped to a knee. "At the risk of angering you, Divinity, I must admit that the soldiers Skazaeleus mustered were little more than city guards. The true army consists of archangels and infantry. Most of those units were stationed near the borders with the Darkling nation and took time to recall."

Daelissa felt her rage simmer. That fool who pretended to be emperor had lied to her. It was no wonder he'd been able to gather his troops so quickly. *The city guard?* She would make certain

Skazaeleus saw action at the front lines during the next encounter. "I would see this army."

"As you wish." Kjoeriss led her to a waiting carpet.

They boarded it and flew back to the main way station. Before Daelissa had come to Eden, the Brightlings had little in the way of an army. The Seraphim Empire had spanned the known world and had no true enemies since the Darklings were kept firmly in their place. After Daelissa had overthrown the Trivectus and taken over as the Divinity, the Brightling army had tried to forcibly remove her in an ill-conceived coup. She, Qualan, Qualas, and others in her inner circle had handily destroyed the army and cemented Daelissa's rule.

After that, it seemed unnecessary to form another Brightling army, especially since she and her comrades had their own armies of human playthings. Daelissa was quite curious to discover what the Brightling military had evolved into during her long absence.

Now that she was somewhat rested, they had best not disappoint.

When at first she saw the neat rows of Seraphim infantry soldiers, they seemed not unlike the city guard. True, they stood a bit taller, and their weaponry varied, some consisting of long spears with slender black hafts and crystal blades at the end. Their swords were slightly shorter than those used by the guard. Rather than translucent armor, they wore what looked like black leather overlaid with thick padding on the shoulders and abdomen.

"Why do they not have the crystal armor?" Daelissa asked.

"The Darklings were able to counter the way our crystal armor absorbs magic attacks," Kjoeriss said. "Though it looks like normal clothing, it repels magic and physical attacks, much like the Templar Nightingale armor."

The archangels were easily discernible from the infantry. They wore massive swords slung diagonally across their backs and red armor embroidered with symbols that reminded her of seals used by feudal lords to indicate their house affiliation. Such markings of nobility had died out on Seraphina long before Daelissa had been born. They had apparently seen a revival during her long absence.

Kjoeriss landed the carpet before a towering seraph in blue armor embroidered with the Sphere of Brilliance, the symbol Daelissa had adopted as her own when she'd established her rule. She felt a sense of satisfaction that it had survived the millennia.

The seraph knelt. "Primarion Arturo at your service, Divinity." His voice was deep and commanding, and his Cyrinthian was exceptionally crisp.

She could not help but smile at this magnificent being before her. "Stand, Arturo," she said in Cyrinthian.

He stood. "The First Battalion awaits your command."

Daelissa looked them over appraisingly. "Besides their large swords and decorated armor, what makes archangels different from the foot soldiers?"

Arturo straightened. "By your leave, I will demonstrate myself."

She waved her hand. "By all means."

The tall Primarion's eyes glowed white. Ethereal wings blazed into existence at his back. They unfolded until they were twice his height from tip to tip. Arturo leapt into the air with a thrust of his mighty wings. He soared high into the cavern and unsheathed his sword. Jagged bolts of white lightning danced around the blade. He swooped low and slashed at empty air, as if attacking an enemy. In one fluid move, he sheathed his sword, wings spread wide, and gracefully landed in front of her.

Daelissa felt a wide smile spread her lips. "I am impressed, Primarion." She could hardly wait to try her new toys against the enemy.

Arturo returned the smile. "From what I have been told of our opponents, we should defeat them handily."

"Indeed you shall." Eager though she was to destroy the rebels, she would not rush to battle this time. Instead, she would give her troops time to feed on human essence.

Serena appeared at her side. "Divinity, might I have a word?"

Daelissa tore her gaze from Arturo and looked down at the small woman. "What is it?"

"We have captured a large number of humans to feed the army." Serena looked at Arturo for a long moment. "I request that they not drain them to death. If we rotate the humans and give them time to recover, it should be possible to reuse them many times and give our troops the essence they need."

"Do not tell me you pity them," Daelissa said.

Serena shook her head. "It is nothing like that, Divinity." She shrugged. "With so many Seraphim to feed, this will optimize our operations."

"I think her reasoning is sound," Arturo said. "By your leave, Divinity, I will have my people ration the humans."

Such a grand specimen this seraph is. She nodded. "You have my leave, Primarion."

He bowed. "As you command."

Daelissa felt her cheeks warm. It had been too long since someone worthy had gained her attention. She would have to invite him to dinner in her quarters at some point in the very near future. "Let us inspect the troops."

Arturo offered her his arm. Daelissa took it and let the handsome seraph guide her. The enemy had proven more resilient than she'd expected. Today marked a new beginning. This war was all but won.

Chapter 32

Nightliss held my hand as I stared at the casket with Elyssa's body. Tears blurred my vision. *I thought she could be healed!* "Why couldn't you save her?"

"I'm sorry, Justin." Nightliss sobbed and buried her face on my shoulder. "I failed you."

Thomas and Leia stood on the opposite side of the casket. They looked at me accusingly.

"You let her die," Thomas said in a cold voice. "You let her take the shot that was meant for you."

"You let her die." Leia's voice was harsh.

Michael came to stand behind them. "She died because of you."

"It's my fault," I said in a harsh whisper. I reached for Elyssa's fair cheek. Her eyes sprang open.

"You let me die!" she screamed.

I jerked awake with a shout. My body was drenched with sweat. Looking around, I realized I was on a cot next to other injured Templars. *It was just a dream.* But it might soon be a reality if Nightliss didn't do something. I threw off the covers and climbed to my feet. My body felt numb and the room seemed to sway. I found clothes at the foot of the cot and put them on.

One unsteady step after another, I made my way outside of the room. Leviathan dragons slumbered in the middle of a huge cavern. *I'm in El Dorado.*

Next to the dragons, the aether pods glowed as they worked to revive more Darklings. Nightliss stood with Mom and Fjoeruss. My legs ached as I walked across the cavern toward them.

Cinder walked from between the dragons and saw me coming. "Justin, should you be out of bed?"

Mom and the others turned toward me. Before I knew it, Nightliss and Mom stood on each side of me.

"You're in no condition to be up and about," Nightliss said.

Mom pressed a hand to my forehead. "I think you have a mild fever." She pulled her hand away. "You overextended yourself at Thunder Rock and then did it again at the Ranch, without resting."

"I'm fine," I said just as my legs tried to make me do the limbo.

Nightliss caught me. "Obviously, you are in prime condition." Her eyes grew sad. "Elyssa's condition is very grave. While I am somewhat skilled at healing injures, I do not think I could repair her heart quickly enough to keep her alive."

Fear gripped my heart. "What do you mean you can't?"

"If her heart does not start beating several seconds after I release her from the preservation spell, she will suffer irreversible brain damage." Nightliss looked away. "I am not that fast."

"What about Joss or Otaleon?" I asked.

"I asked them, but neither of them expressed confidence in their healing abilities." She turned her pleading eyes back on me. "I promise I will find a way."

I hardly dared ask the next question. "How long will that preservation spell keep Elyssa alive?"

"Perhaps two or three weeks." She swung her gaze toward the aether pods. "If only we had more time, I'm sure there are many skilled Darkling healers awaiting rebirth."

My stomach knotted. "I can't rely on that sort of hope." There was only one place I could find a Darkling with the healing abilities I required. "I'm going to Seraphina."

Mom's eyes flared with alarm. "You have no idea what kind of reception you'll get there, Justin."

"I was planning to go as an emissary," Nightliss said. "It would be safer if you remain."

I shook my head. "No. As soon as I eat and recover, I'm going."

"Well if it ain't the next best thing to battery-operated underwear," Shelton said from behind me.

I turned unsteadily and saw Shelton and Bella walking from the direction of the control room, big grins on their faces.

"Are you guys staying here?" I asked.

Shelton shook his head. "We came from the new base of operations in Queens Gate."

I blinked at him. "Queens Gate? I thought Thomas said the new location would be secret. Why in the world would we go back there?"

"It's the last place they'd think to look for us," Bella said.

"Exactly." Shelton poked me in the chest. "We actually came by to see if you were up to taking a little trip."

"He's in no condition for travelling," Mom said.

Shelton widened and blinked his eyes at her as if trying to convey a secret message via brain waves. "This is the one trip that would do him some good."

Nightliss touched Mom's arm. "Alysea, I think Shelton is right."

"Fine, but I'm going along to make sure he doesn't get overexcited." Mom took my hand as if I were a little kid who needed guiding.

"Overexcited?" I couldn't hide the disdain in my voice. "It's not like I'm going to wet my pants."

"Justin, I think you should come over here," Cinder said before Mom could reply.

I turned and saw the aether pods springing open. Fjoeruss and Cinder were staring at one in particular. "On my way." I released Mom's hand and hobbled over with the others close on my heels.

The sound of wailing babies filled the air. A group of human volunteers emerged from between the dragons and comforted the newly revived cupids.

Fjoeruss reached into the first pod and removed an infant. When he held up the cupid, the gender was obviously female.

His sister.

With everything else going on, I'd completely forgotten about that part of our deal. I was about to ask if he was certain the baby was his sibling when she began to cry. Her mouth stretched opened inhumanly wide and the fuzzy hair on her head seemed to writhe. Her crying sounded more like singing than the wailing of a baby.

Ice cold shock knifed into my chest. "That's no Seraphim child."

Fjoeruss calmly took a blanket offered by one of the human volunteers and swaddled her. "Indeed. She is of the race that I believe built the arches."

263

"A siren." Cinder stared at her with open fascination. "She is not your sister."

"Not by blood. I did, however, adopt her as my own." Fjoeruss looked at me and raised an eyebrow. "Is something the matter, Mr. Slade?"

I tried to keep my voice calm. "You lied."

"Actually, I was quite truthful." He ran a finger through the baby's writhing peach fuzz. "I adopted her as my sister. The contract did not specify how she was related to me."

"Is she really the one who caused the desecration?" My voice was a hoarse whisper.

He nodded. "She said the way the Seraphim used the arches was an abomination. Everything happened as I said."

Mom hissed out a breath. "Now I know why I couldn't remember you having a sister."

Fjoeruss simply offered her a smug smile.

"Do sirens feed on Murk and Brilliance?" I asked.

"I don't know." Fjoeruss handed the baby to the human volunteer. "I do know she requires food." He watched as the volunteer walked away with her.

I felt my forehead wrinkle. "You're just leaving her here?"

Fjoeruss turned to me. "A deal is a deal, Mr. Slade. I do not believe you will try to keep me from her or you will be in violation of the contract."

A part of me felt tricked by him. Another part of me didn't really give a damn. The sirens were an enigma. I'd seen them building arches with my own two eyes, but that didn't mean they were the masters of the universe. For all I knew, they might just be the hired help. If I played nice with Fjoeruss, maybe we could get some information out of this deal. "How is it you adopted this siren, but you don't know if she requires soul essence? How is it she registered as gray with the affinity sphere?"

"I have no idea." He smiled. "It's exciting, is it not?" Fjoeruss watched as the volunteer with his adopted sister vanished between the dragons. "So much we don't know. So many mysteries to uncover."

"So many ways to trick people," Mom said.

Shelton entered the group. "I know you ladies love babies, but can we get outta here? All this crying is giving me a headache."

I narrowed my eyes at Fjoeruss and wondered if he had any more tricks up his sleeve.

He seemed to sense what I was thinking. "The contract holds, Mr. Slade."

I nodded. "Good." We'd beaten Daelissa soundly today, but the war wasn't over yet. I wondered if adding a siren to our alliance would help, or if she'd try to pull another Desecration on us.

"Until next time." Fjoeruss turned and began talking to Cinder about the care his sister would receive.

I rotated back to Shelton. "All right, let's go." I gave him a suspicious look. "Where are we going?"

"You'll see when we get there." He grinned. "I think you'll like it."

"Definitely," Bella said.

"Lead the way." I motioned with my hand and started walking while Mom and Nightliss helped me. "I'm not an old man."

"Sure are walking like one," Shelton said. "Looks like you're clenching a marble between your butt cheeks."

"Ha, ha." The more I walked, the more it felt like my butt was on fire. We went into the control room and through a portal, ending up in a room that looked vaguely familiar. I spotted a stove against one wall. "Are we in a kitchen?"

"Sharp as a tack." Shelton took out a blindfold.

I raised both eyebrows. "What's that for?"

"Just let me put it on."

I crossed my arms. "This isn't something kinky is it?"

Shelton gave me a blank stare. "Don't make me knock you out."

I laughed, took the blindfold, and slipped it over my eyes. "Lead the way."

I heard a nervous giggle from one of the females as they guided me across what sounded like a wooden floor. I heard a thudding noise and smelled fresh wood and mortar. Someone turned me around. The blindfold lifted.

My next breath caught in my throat at the sight before me. Cheers erupted. I almost fell over backwards with surprise and the inability of my legs to keep up with my reflexes. Templars, Daemos, Lycans, Felycans, Blue Cloaks, and a host of others stood around me. Thomas and the other Templar commanders stood with Captain Takei, Colin

McCloud, and the other leaders in front of a huge house under construction.

It was far more than a house. It was a reproduction of the mansion. The only out-of-place part was the surroundings. We were in a large perfectly rectangular chamber carved into the rock. Large construction golems lumbered about doing stonework and fitting huge beams into the structure. An Arcane motioned with his wand and the golems stopped where they were.

I felt my eyes mist. My heart leapt with joy, though sadness still tugged at it. I wished with all my heart Elyssa could be here to see this.

Shelton slapped my back. Bella kissed one cheek and Nightliss the other.

I walked over to the faction leaders, fighting back tears with every step. When I reached them, Thomas motioned me to stand by him and held up a large, golden, skeleton key. "I present you with this ceremonial key to the house, Justin."

I took it. "Thank you." I was so overwhelmed with emotion I didn't know what else to say.

Commander Taylor grinned. "I loved the look on Daelissa's face when you punched her bloody."

"Amen to that," Takei said.

Smiles broke out all around.

My smile faded. "I wish Elyssa could be here."

Thomas put a hand on my shoulder. "We will find a way to make that happen." He wiped at his eye and cleared his throat. "Would you like to address the troops?"

I was afraid I might break into tears, but knew I should say something. I nodded.

Captain Takei waved his wand at me. "They should be able to hear you now."

It took me a moment to compose my words, but something finally came to me. "Today, we bloodied Daelissa's troops and sent her packing."

A roar burst forth from the assembly.

I waited for it to die down and continued. "Though this war isn't over, we have weakened her. Now all that remains is to finish the job." I pointed to the partially constructed mansion behind me. "This structure behind me is more than a house. One just like it was once my home. I fought for it and lost it to Daelissa. But what was once destroyed can be rebuilt." I pounded a fist into my palm. "Eden is our home. We will fight Daelissa to the bitter end, and we will reclaim our homeland. We will rebuild what she has so cruelly destroyed and it will be even better than before."

A resounding cheer went up from the troops. It was so loud I almost had to clap my hands over my ears. Instead, I raised a fist high into the air. "For Eden, for victory!"

"For Eden! For Eden!" the assembly chanted.

I pumped my fist one more time and let hope wash over me.

I saw Mom with tears in her eyes. Ivy clapped and jumped by her side. I saw Dad with a huge grin on his face as he wrapped an arm around Mom and whispered something in her ear.

Thoughts of Elyssa filled my mind. *I will save you, my love.*

The final battle loomed.

We would fight the good fight.

We would win.

###

I hope you enjoyed reading this book. Reviews are very important in helping other readers decide what to read next. Would you please take a few seconds to rate this book?

Section A
MEET THE AUTHOR

John Corwin is the bestselling author of the Overworld Chronicles. He enjoys long walks on the beach and is a firm believer in puppies and kittens.

After years of getting into trouble thanks to his overactive imagination, John abandoned his male modeling career to write books.

He resides in Atlanta.

Connect with John Corwin online:
Facebook: http://www.facebook.com/johnhcorwinauthor
Website: http://www.johncorwin.net
Twitter: http://twitter.com/#!/John_Corwin